KALANON'S RISING

DARIAN SMITH

ACKNOWLEDGEMENTS

I'd like to say thank you to my wife, Adrienne, for her support, advice, and patience while I rambled about what was to happen in this book.

I'd also like to thank my editor, Linda Kimpton, and my proofreaders, AJ, Kamla, Leif, Luana, and Ruth. Your help is greatly appreciated.

A huge thank you also to SpecFicNZ, who chose this story as the winner of their novel manuscript competition and then awarded me a funding grant to publish it.

And most of all, thank you to the readers who buy, enjoy, and review this book. Your support means the world to me and enables me to produce more.

Enjoy!

PROLOGUE

The gas lamps on the street corners of Alapra cast deep shadows. Keldan Sandilar skulked in their darkness with a woman of dubious repute. He felt a kind of thrill across his skin as he moved through the back streets, that had little to do with the coolness of the night air. The son of a duke, mere steps from the Kalan throne, rarely had occasion to skulk. Here, in the capital, he had a lifestyle that could be publicly enjoyed. His name was a skeleton key for the highest echelons of society and there wasn't a craftsman or trader who wouldn't throw open their doors, day or night, for his convenience.

But tonight was for activities best kept in darkness.

"We really should have done this somewhere else," he muttered, as they neared their destination. "They know me at the Rose."

The floral fragrance from walled, scented gardens mixed with that of horse manure and lantern smoke. The sound of laughter and music spilled from up ahead and the full moon slipped from behind a cloud. Keldan's footsteps sounded very loud on the familiar cobblestones. He was grateful, at least, that he had left the carriage some distance away.

His companion shrugged. "It was your choice, Your Highness. And a wise general fights on familiar ground, they say. Don't worry, my employer is very discreet." Her voice lowered to a throaty purr as she added, "And so am I."

Keldan noticed the front of her cloak had parted and the cut of her bodice offered an inviting glimpse of bosom. He chuckled. "Thus far I have enjoyed our dealings very much. I'm sure that will continue."

The Blue Rose came into sight ahead and Keldan's steps quickened. The sooner they were in a private room, the better. The Rose was an elegant, stone and plaster, converted manor house built well before the war. A mosaic path led up to the wide double doors, through an outdoor dining area ringed by balustrades and climbing, steel-hued roses. The area was strung with colored lanterns, giving it a joyful air. There were few patrons outside this time of night, however. The main action was inside, where some of the best singers and dancers the city had to offer were regularly seen on the ballroom's stage.

He had almost reached the door when a tall, broad-shouldered figure stepped out into the light. Keldan recognized the man's easy movement well before the familiar scar came into view. He gestured for his companion to move and tried to step aside before the King's Champion saw him but, exposed as he was in the center of the mosaic path, there was nowhere to go.

"Prince Keldan." The man known as Bloodhawk nodded in Keldan's direction. "Good to see you. How's your father?"

Keldan forced a smile and walked forward. Of all the timing! "Very well, Sir Brannon. You know Father—he's a prize stallion. I can pass on your regards when I next see him."

Brannon nodded. "I'd appreciate it. I don't get to see him as often as I'd like these days. Nor you, in fact. Would you care to join me for a drink?"

Keldan wondered, as he often did seeing Sir Brannon's simple clothes and military style haircut, how he managed to stay so well connected at court. The reality and the legend were strange bedfellows in this man. "Another time. I'm afraid I have business to attend to right now."

The girl giggled at that, giving the perfect vapid impression. She'd arranged her cowled cloak so that the comely shape of her body was unmistakable beneath the fabric, but the details of her face were lost.

Brannon's expression barely flickered. "Of course." He inclined his head slightly to them both. "Enjoy the rest of your evening."

"That could've been a disaster," Keldan murmured as he guided the girl through the back corridors of the Blue Rose to the VIP area and then into the private room he'd booked. "The last thing I need tonight is for a war hero friend of my father to discover me making a deal with Nilarians."

She pushed back her hood and flashed him a pretty smile as he closed the door behind them. "It's just a meeting. To be honest, I think you'll have to be an even

3

shrewder businessman than your father to get a deal with my employer."

Keldan felt his jaw tighten. He turned his focus to the room, allowing the tension in his body to ease.

It was a room he'd used many times before, decorated in his favorite sky-blue and deep mahogany. The fresco cherubs always made him smile to think of all they'd witnessed in that spacious, four-post bed. Today, there was a box on the scroll-worked writing desk in the corner.

"Yours?" he said as the girl stripped off her cloak and laid it across the bed. The gown underneath clung to her curves.

"My employer's. I had it sent over earlier to make things easier for us."

Keldan smiled. "Easy is good."

Her full lips twitched upward. "It has its advantages. Shall I set up?"

He nodded, moving to the liquor cabinet. A decanter of his favorite wine had been set out and he poured himself a glass while the girl opened the box and laid its contents on the desk. A selection of fabric swatches, pots of pigment, a knife, and some brushes.

Keldan wondered if his father had ever seen the secrets of Nilarian silk. He doubted it. The old man was too bound up in the old enmity to have gotten so close. He was a shrewd businessman, all right, but Keldan's own skills were nothing to be sniffed at and this extra, personal touch of showing interest in the details would secure the deal. He was certain of it.

He lifted the wine to his lips and savored the taste of successfully out-dealing his father. Delicious.

"I should go and fetch my employer now," the girl said, turning away from the carefully arranged desk. She lowered her head a little and looked up at him, slyly. "Perhaps I could come back after the business is completed?"

Keldan chuckled softly. "You do that. I'll be here all night."

As the door closed behind her, Keldan wondered which outcome he was looking forward to more—the closing of the business deal or the return of the girl. Already he could feel his body reacting to the excitement of both. His stomach fluttered and his skin felt more sensitive, like a cool breeze was brushing through the room. His lips, especially, tingled as though from a phantom kiss.

He took a breath and shook it off. He wasn't some nervous virgin at his first ball. He tugged at his sleeve, straightened his back, and considered how he would greet the Nilarian.

The tingling in his lips intensified.

Keldan frowned. He took a few steps toward the bed before the tingling began in his legs as well. His toe caught on the thick carpet and he fell, sprawled, face down on the bed.

The sensation spread up his thighs, and crippled his hands and forearms. His tongue felt like a handful of needles in his mouth. Then the tingling was replaced by a terrible numbness, swallowing his body's ability to move, like a mouse down a cold, reptilian throat. He struggled against it and almost managed to pull himself up before his muscles gave out completely and he fell back on his face.

The world huddled close around him, pressing in with his fear. A shout for help produced only a weak sound, muffled by bedding. After that, it was an effort to draw in enough air just to stay conscious. Time was lost. There was nothing in existence but his own fast-beating heart and loud, rasping breaths.

A rivulet of sweat ran across the skin of his forehead, grazed the side of his temple, and slipped into his wide open eye with the sting of salt. The sensation penetrated his panicked mind: the numbness was wearing off. Perhaps the paralysis would too.

Relief almost deafened him to the sound of the opening door. Footsteps approached the bed.

"Ah," said a voice. "I believe you're almost ready."

Keldan tried to respond but the paralysis had now completely taken his voice.

The footsteps moved over to the desk. "Here we are." The scrape of the knife blade on the wood as the intruder picked it up was unmistakable. "Now, let's have some fun."

CHAPTER ONE

Brannon was trying to not kill a man. It wasn't easy. The hot sun pricked at his skin and he blinked salt from his eyes. The air smelled of dust and sweat and the tang of blood. Not a lot. Not like it once was. But there, nonetheless. This tiny battleground, circled with stone and law, was enough to remind him of things he'd rather forget.

The court building was one of the older structures in Alapra, grand with carved masonry and walls painted with historical murals. The magistrate and witnesses needed a clear outcome and, technically, that meant death. They huddled around the edges of the arena in their formal robes, waiting for the moment they could go back into the courtroom and approve the blood result in ink.

Brannon watched his opponent approach again, nose bloody, and pitched his voice so the magistrate wouldn't hear it. "You can still back out of this, you know, Darnec. Plead guilty."

The younger son of the Earl of Raldene had been caught stealing to pay for gambling debts and had chosen trial by combat rather than magistrate. He had the pride of his family name and the confidence of his youth egging him on. He almost had the skill to back it up, but not the experience.

"You'd like that, wouldn't you?" young Raldene sneered.

Brannon sighed. "Yeah, I would. But, hey, it's your trial." Over the younger man's shoulder, Brannon could see Master Jordell and a small team of physicians. And an undertaker.

Darnec swung his sword and Brannon quickly moved to block it with his own. The clang echoed loudly in the arena. Brannon pushed his opponent's sword aside with his blade, then twisted it to strike at Darnec's shoulder. The young man was too quick, and slipped away before he could be cut.

"You've been taught well." Another swing and block, followed by a lunge.

"I may not have fought in your war, Bloodhawk, but I know my way around a blade." This time Darnec faked a move to the left, then swung for the jugular.

Brannon dodged, and his own sword snaked across the younger man's thigh, sharp and fast. Red licked out from the blade's bite. Brannon stepped back. "Imagine if you applied that discipline to the rest of your life."

Darnec's eyes stayed on Brannon. He shifted his weight, testing his wounded leg. "It's a bit late for that now," he said.

Brannon shrugged. "Perhaps."

Darnec took a slow breath and the point of his sword

drifted slightly downward. Then he took another. Brannon began to hope. The Earl of Raldene would be embarrassed to have a son sent to the mines for thievery, but when the sentence was done, he would still have his son.

"Perhaps not." With those words, Darnec launched himself as if from a catapult, his sword aimed at Brannon's heart.

Brannon turned his body and rammed forward his arm, blade vertical, pushing the thrust aside but it sliced his left arm, just below the shoulder. Blood and Tears! The boy was quick.

Or, he thought, I've gotten slow.

The fight was on in earnest now. Darnec was a demonic fury, intent on Brannon's death. His sword thrust and swung again and again. Each time was intended a killing blow. Each time, it was blocked.

Years of battle experience gave Brannon a kind of detached calm when fighting. He could see where the blade was intended to go almost before it began to move. His muscles remembered even when he would rather not. He saw an opportunity in the younger man's style and lashed out. His sword spiked Darnec's thigh and pulled back. The muscle was damaged, but he had stayed clear of the artery.

Darnec screamed, but kept fighting.

The opportunity rose again. This time Brannon slashed across his opponent's stomach, tearing through leather and cloth. Flesh and muscle parted, but not enough to expose entrails.

Darnec clutched at the wound with his left hand, his voice an animalistic sob as it came away covered in blood. He gripped the hilt of his sword with both hands and swung hard.

Brannon double-handed his own sword, bringing it up to meet head on. The arena rang with an awful crack and the younger man's blade shattered against the Bloodhawk's.

Darnec's eyes widened. He stared at the stump of his sword and then at Brannon, his mouth open and wordless.

"Nilarian steel," Brannon said, hefting his own blade. "I got this in that war you mentioned." He turned to the magistrate. "I believe that satisfies the requirements of defeat."

The robed figure shook his head. "Not yet, Champion."

The sound of boots scuffing the dirt provided a warning. Brannon turned in time to see Darnec lurch toward him, the remnant of his sword outstretched.

"Oh, for Blood's sake!" Brannon grabbed the boy's wrist with his left hand and twisted his arm up and away, bringing his own sword up to skewer Darnec's shoulder. Darnec screamed and his knees buckled. Brannon let go of his wrist and pulled his sword free, giving him a nudge so that he fell forward onto the ground. "Now?"

The magistrate nodded. "Now."

Brannon turned and strode from the arena. He brushed past Master Jordell and into the medical annex. The old physician followed him in, green robes billowing at the shoulders.

"You're angry."

Brannon scowled. "I'm fine."

Master Jordell chuckled, his face becoming even

more wrinkled than usual beneath his mop of white hair. "Then I'd hate to see you irritated." He gestured and a servant hurried forward. "Here, let this lad clean up your sword and you sit down with me a while."

Blood dripped down the blade and onto Brannon's fingers. "How can you expect me to mentor an apprentice physician when I can be called up to do this at any time?" he asked, handing over the sword.

The medical annex of the courthouse was set up to deal with the results of trial by combat. It was a requirement that both parties be assessed here after the fight. The room was divided by a long bench covered in bandages, needles and thread, scalpels and bone-saws. To either side of this was a mirror image of bed and hot bath.

Brannon walked across to one of the beds and sat down.

"The reason I expect it," Master Jordell said, "is because it is part of what you have dedicated your last six years to." He hooked a stool from the center bench and sat facing Brannon. "You're a physician now, no matter what else you are, and physicians at your level are required to take an apprentice."

Brannon snorted. "You don't see the hypocrisy in my teaching anyone healing?"

Master Jordell's eyes grew flinty. "No, I do not. Your role as King's Champion did not stop you seeking physician training. Nor did your history as a war hero. I don't see why they should become an impediment to you now."

"But . . ."

"No buts. Part of your training is to mentor others as

I have mentored you. Just do your duty, Brannon, and stop behaving like a child!"

Brannon sat up sharply. "A *child*?"

Jordell's face was impassive. "Clearly. You've only recently come to your new career. Thus, this is your second childhood. Some wait for senility, but you were always an overachiever."

Brannon shook his head slowly, a chuckle low in his throat. "Now I see why you had that boy take my sword. Don't you have something better to do than pester me? Seeing to the Pride of Raldene, perhaps?"

"He's in good hands. Get out of that shirt and I'll stitch your arm."

As if summoned by their words, the other physicians entered the room, Darnec Raldene carried on a stretcher between them. The young man was pale and sweaty, but conscious.

"He's losing a lot of blood," Brannon muttered as they placed Darnec on the other bed. Two of them pressed wadded bandages over the leg and shoulder wounds while a young woman with a blond ponytail peered at the abdominal slash.

Master Jordell pushed him back with surprisingly strong hands when he tried to get up to take a closer look. "He'll be fine." The old man picked up a pair of scissors and Brannon knew better than to resist as his shirt was cut away from his still bleeding shoulder.

"You're sure?"

Jordell pursed his lips and reached for a wet cloth and bowl to wash the cut. Across the room the blond woman was doing the same with the abdominal wound. "Yes, Sir Brannon, I'm sure. You were very precise.

Nothing vital was hit and you know it. You sterilized your sword beforehand?"

Brannon felt his face flush. "Yes."

Jordell shrugged. "There you go then—not even much chance of infection. You did all you could for the fool. Now, for goodness' sake, lay back and try not to be one yourself!"

Brannon did as he was told and held still as his mentor pulled needle and thread through the cut on his shoulder, tugging the flesh gently back into place. He separated himself from the pain and let the detached part of his mind simply observe. He'd experienced Jordell's stitching many times in the war. On so light a wound, he probably wouldn't even be left with a scar.

Unlike his opponent. The blond haired girl was about to work on the stomach cut and, at her age, it was unlikely she was as deft as the Master.

"Jordell, why don't you stitch the Raldene boy? That girl doesn't look too experienced."

The old physician didn't even look up. "Jessamine? She's perfectly adequate to the task. Better than most at her level." He pulled the thread tight on the last stitch and cut the thread. "Actually, she's even been requested by of some of the nobility—your friend, Duke Roydan, for example."

Brannon sat up and flexed his arm a little, testing the stitches. "Really? Roydan?" He looked across and watched as the girl continued to work. She looked very young. "I'm surprised she's high enough level for that."

Jordell shrugged. "She's not. But she's very talented and he's asked for her specifically."

"Ah." Brannon grinned. "He always did like a pretty

face. She should be careful there."

"Well then, it's lucky she'll have you to guide her." Master Jordell beamed. "She's your new apprentice."

Brannon's grin vanished. "What? No! It's still a bad idea for me to have an apprentice."

"Second childhood!" Jordell teased. Then his voice grew serious. "It's not optional."

Brannon sighed, the energy that had sustained him through the fight draining away in a rush. He covered his face with his hands and rubbed at his eyes. When he pulled them away, nothing had changed. "Fine."

Master Jordell turned and called across the room. "Jessamine, let one of the others finish up, would you? I want to introduce you to your mentor."

"Yes, Master Jordell." The girl waited until one of her colleagues had taken the needle, then fairly bounced across the room. Up close, she looked even younger than Brannon had thought. Blue eyes peered at him from beneath a slightly too-long fringe of blond hair that had escaped the ponytail. Her small nose was kept company by a scattering of freckles to either side. Her pale lips were parted slightly in an open smile. "Sir Brannon," she said, bobbing into an almost curtsey. "I'm so pleased to meet you."

Brannon stifled another sigh. She was going to be difficult to keep track of. Roydan wasn't the only man in court to like a pretty face. "I'm pleased to meet you too, Jessamine," he said. "I'm told you're ready to apprentice. How old are you?"

"I'm twenty-two, sir."

Brannon turned to Jordell, an eyebrow raised. "Really? A twenty-two-year-old? My raw recruit days

14

are well behind me."

"It'll do you good," Master Jordell said. "Anyway, the girl can't help her age. You went to war younger than that."

"True. I'm not sure when it started looking so young though."

Jordell snorted. "Wait until you're my age!"

"No thanks." He turned back to the girl, who had watched the exchange with her head tilted to one side. "My apologies, Jessamine. I'm a little out of sorts today. Apparently you're very skilled already, so I'm sure you'll do fine. Even if I'm not sure what you'll learn from me at court."

She straightened up with a smile. "No problem, sir. I hope you don't mind that I asked to be matched with you. When I heard the famous Bloodhawk needed a physician's apprentice—"

Brannon held up a hand to stop her. "Do you want to be a physician or a soldier?"

"A physician, of course."

"Then don't talk to me about Bloodhawk. And stop calling me 'sir.' Brannon is fine." He stood up and pulled what was left of his shirt around him. The top of her head barely reached his chin. "Now, tell me about your patient."

"Well, he'll need some time to heal and we'll have to work his arm to get full movement back to his shoulder, but, for the losing side of a trial by combat, he's in remarkably good shape," Jessamine said, leading the way back to where Darnec Raldene lay, now sleeping thanks to an application of fumes. "Although he must be very skilled because he managed to cut the

King's Champion and people say that's only happened once before."

Brannon studied Darnec's wounds. The thigh damage was minimal. The skewered shoulder had two physicians working on it still. The abdominal cut was stitched surprisingly well, a red belt across his middle with black notches all the way across. "Good work. Put the stitches a little closer together next time, but good." He looked up at her and pointed to the scar on his own cheek. "And if you really believe I got through the entire war with only one scratch, you're an idiot."

Jessamine grinned. "No. But I have to admit, the legend of it is appealing."

Brannon rolled his eyes. "Appealing to idiots. But there may be hope for you yet."

She gave her little curtsey-bob again. "I hope so."

"Sir Brannon Kesh!" A voice sounded loudly from the doorway where a messenger in full court livery waited for an answer.

"Yes?"

"The king has sent for you. Something's happened to his cousin."

CHAPTER TWO

B rannon forced himself not to run as he hurried through the corridors of the royal palace. His footsteps sounded like hoof beats on the marble tiles, echoed by the lighter, more rapid taps of Jessamine trying to keep up. His suggestion to Master Jordell that she begin her apprenticeship another day had fallen on deaf ears so she would simply have to follow him as best she could.

The corridor leading to the king's private audience chamber ran along the east side of the palace and was lined with open windows showing all of Alapra spread below. Anyone approaching was reminded of the huge domain ruled by the monarch they were about to speak with. Raised up as the palace was, it was possible to see not just the older stonework buildings like the courthouse and town palaces of the Kalan elite, but beyond to the lesser neighborhoods and even to the edges of the city, where new wooden buildings had been hastily constructed during the war to house those driven from their homes as the Nilarian invaders cut their way ever closer to the river Tilal. Here and there, blue and gold banners heralding the upcoming fiftieth birthday celebrations for the king draped buildings and crossed streets, giving the city an air of festival it hadn't had for as long as Brannon could remember.

With the messenger's words replaying in his mind, Brannon felt as though it had taken hours to quickly change and travel the short distance to see his friend the king. When the gilt door handles of the audience chamber finally came into view, a small bubble of relief swelled in him, and he slowed his steps, took deep, calming breaths, and allowed the guards to let them inside.

The chamber was richly and comfortably appointed. There was no throne, but then Aldan had never needed the trappings of royalty to command respect. The walls held heroic frescos of kings and queens of old in colors that competed with the sunlight.

King Aldan and two others sat at a small table near the window. One of them was Duke Roydan, the king's cousin. The other was a stylish young man in his early twenties. They looked up as Brannon led Jessamine forward. Roydan's eyes were red and tears gleamed wetly on his grizzled face.

Brannon faltered. "What's happened?" He'd known the older two since the beginning of the war and the seven years since and he'd never seen Roydan weep.

"Take a seat, Brannon," the king said. His eyes flickered over Jessamine. "Who is this with you?"

"My apprentice."

Aldan frowned a moment, then nodded. "Right. The

physician thing." He fixed Jessamine with a stern look. "You may stay, but you are to repeat nothing of what you hear, understood?"

"Yes, Your Majesty."

Brannon ignored the exchange, trying instead to catch Roydan's eye. The man turned away, his body shaking in silent sobs. "Aldan, what's going on? What's happened?"

The king sighed. "Keldan was killed last night. They found his body in a room at the Blue Rose this morning. Apparently he was tortured."

Brannon felt his eyes widen and his stomach dropped away. "But . . . why?"

"That's what I want you to find out."

Brannon stared at his king for a long time, trying to process what was being said. Keldan, the son of his longtime friend, had been murdered. "You want me to investigate. I . . . Ahpra's Tears, I saw him last night. At the Blue Rose. It must have been just a little while before . . . " He couldn't finish the sentence. The pain in both men was too clear. This was not a loss in battle—they had experienced plenty of those. This had been a personal attack—a family member slaughtered in a place he believed to be safe.

Brannon might not be of royal blood, but these men were family to him just the same. They'd protected each other since long before Aldan inherited the crown. Their lives and responsibilities since the war might have molded them differently, but at heart they were still three young men fighting back to back against the Nilarian horde. He saw the same feeling in Aldan's eyes and the king gave a small nod. One of their number had been wounded. They would hunt down those responsible and pay it back in kind.

Brannon reached out to squeeze his friend's shoulder. "We'll get whoever did it, Roydan. I'll find them."

Roydan turned to meet his eyes with a fierce hardness in his face. "They killed my heir, Brannon. My first son! I've not even been allowed to see his body. You bring his murderer to me and I'll take my revenge with a sword!"

King Aldan leaned forward and the sunlight caught the silver in his golden beard. "It's best you don't see him yet, Roydan. I don't want you remembering him like that."

The duke's face darkened with fury. "He's my son. Do you think this memory could get any worse?"

Aldan sighed.

"My Lord Roydan." Jessamine's voice was soft and gentle. "Perhaps you and I could take a break. I brew an excellent comforting tea."

Roydan was still and for a moment Brannon wasn't sure if he had heard, but then he shook himself and nodded. "Yes." He stood up and followed Jessamine. "A cup of your tea would be good."

"She's good, that apprentice of yours," Aldan said as the door closed behind them.

"So it seems," Brannon said.

"I suppose you can brew medicinal teas as well, now?"

"I can." Brannon nodded, then offered a weak smile. "But I doubt Roydan would drink it."

The king chuckled softly. "You're probably right.

You never were much of a cook."

The young man at the table leaned forward. Brannon had almost forgotten he was there. "Even I remember that," he said. "Your attempt at a campfire stew was possibly the worst thing I've ever put in my mouth. And that's saying something."

He had brilliant blue eyes that were quite striking beneath dark, stylishly cut hair. His clothes were flattering and modern enough to be fashionable while being individual enough to catch attention. Brannon frowned. "Do I know you?"

The pretty young man smiled. "Maybe if you think really hard, you'll remember."

"I hardly think this is the time to play games," Brannon began, but then trailed off as the man turned his head and stretched his neck. Curled between the edge of his jaw and his earlobe was a tattoo of a sleeping dragon. Brannon blinked and looked again. "That's not possible."

"That's what I said when he first showed up like that," King Aldan said.

Brannon looked between the two men, his mind fumbling for understanding. "Magus Draeson? But . . . but . . . you're old!"

"Ever the wordsmith, I see," Draeson drawled. "Aldan, do you really think this murder could be a political attack?"

The king shrugged. "I don't know. That's why I need people I can trust to investigate it." He looked from one to the other. "Both of you."

Brannon held up his hands. "Whoa. Before we go any further I'm going to need more of an explanation as to why the oldest man I've ever met now looks twenty-three."

"I've been keeping out of the sun," Draeson said.

"At the Battle of Tilal, you looked decrepit."

The mage shrugged. "Yes, well, I've had time to study since then. I've learned some new tricks. Why shouldn't I do something nice for myself after chasing you lot around for more than three hundred years?" He turned to the king. "Speaking of which, you haven't forgotten the deal, I trust. That'll need to be settled."

Aldan waved them both to be quiet. "Yes, yes. We can all talk when the current issues are dealt with. In the meantime, I need you to work together and find out what happened to Keldan and why. Brannon, you're my representative in this. Take what resources you need. I'll send you what help I can, but I trust my champion and my mage have the skills between them to solve this. Soon."

"Of course."

"Now go. I've ordered the room where Keldan was found guarded until you arrive."

They rose to their feet and bowed. As he turned to leave the room, Brannon hesitated. "My apprentice, Jessamine . . . "

The king nodded. "Yes, take her with you, definitely. It will be good for you to have a young pair of eyes on the team."

Brannon nodded, his lips pressed together. There was no getting rid of the girl now. He'd just have to make the best of it. "Thank you."

He followed Draeson from the audience chamber, watching the magus for any sign of the age that had crippled his body a decade ago. There was none. The man walked with the energized stride of the youth he now appeared to be.

"Draeson, this deal you mentioned. Is it something to do with your . . . " He waved his hand to indicate the mage's new body.

"Why? You think the king pisses the Fountain of Youth and forgot to mention it? My magic is my own, Brannon. Nothing to worry your soldier boy head about."

"Then what is the deal?"

Draeson smiled, the expression turning his attractive face into a sculpture of handsome innocence. "None of your business."

CHAPTER THREE

The Blue Rose in daylight was a more somber affair than at night. Music came from a quiet string quartet and the staff served light lunches and scones with tea. On a sunny day like this one, most of the patrons were in the outdoor area. On a day when a murder had taken place on the premises, there weren't many patrons at all.

The day manager, a short, rounded woman in a mauve dress and gray hair, met them at the door. "Sir Brannon," she said, her eyes roving over Jessamine and Draeson before settling back to him. "You and your friends are here regarding the incident?"

Brannon nodded. "I'm afraid so, Mala. Can you tell us what happened?"

She swallowed and glanced at the customers. "Of course, dear. Why don't we go inside?"

The bar was deserted at this time of day. Mala hoisted herself up onto one of the stools, increasing her height almost to that of Jessamine. "Nasty business," she said. "Horrid."

"I saw Prince Keldan arrive last night, just before ten o'clock. Did any of the staff see him?"

Mala's head bobbed like a cork in a bathtub. "That's right. He'd booked one of the private rooms early yesterday but didn't come to use it until late, just as you say. He's a good friend to the Blue Rose. The staff all like him 'cause he tips well. And the lads say his lady friends are always worth looking at twice." She reached out and patted his hand. "You know how boys are."

Brannon gave her the expected chuckle and she jiggled with mirth.

"Did he have a lady friend with him last night?" Jessamine asked. "Or his wife, perhaps?"

"Oooh, asks the right questions this one," Mala cooed. "Or the wrong ones! The likes of Prince Keldan don't bring a wife here, my dear. But, yes, he did have a lady friend with him last night."

"So I recall," said Brannon, remembering the giggling cloaked figure. Exactly the sort of girl Keldan liked to play with. His father too, for that matter. "And is she still here?"

Mala looked horrified. "Is she dead in the room too, you mean? No, thank Valdan. One of them like that is more than enough. No, I don't know what happened to her, but she's gone."

"I take it once they checked in, they weren't disturbed," Draeson said. "So when did you realize something was wrong?"

"Not until I went up to get the breakfast orders." Mala shuddered. "I'll not forget that shock in a hurry. And I don't envy you the job of looking at it now."

Brannon shrugged. "Best we get it over with then."

Mala led them to a back corridor and upstairs to a closed door with an armed royal guard on either side. The guards snapped to attention when the saw Brannon. "At ease," he told them. "Unlock the door and wait here while we're inside. We won't want to be disturbed."

"Good luck with that," Mala muttered while one of the guards reached for the key she held out. "I'll leave you to it then." She made the sign against evil and hurried back downstairs.

The guard stepped back, seemingly reluctant to open the now unlocked door.

Brannon glanced at his companions. Draeson, for all his newfound youth, had seen plenty of horror in his centuries of life. Jessamine, however, seemed a little pale.

"You don't have to go in, you know. You can wait for us here."

She pressed her lips firmly and shook her head. "If I'm going to be a physician I have to get used to dead bodies. It's funny, I can handle sewing up live ones, but . . ."

Brannon closed his mind to the images of gored and hacked flesh on the battlefield. "It's not something you need to rush," he said.

"It's not something we need to stand here talking about all day either," Draeson said.

Brannon shot the mage a sharp look.

Jessamine shrugged. "I'm fine," she said.

Brannon nodded. "Okay then. By the way, you did a good job with Duke Roydan earlier. Well done."

Jessamine beamed at him.

"Oh good," muttered Draeson. "Daddy issues."

"Dry up and get your own apprentice," Brannon told him.

The door opened onto death.

The bed had been pushed out into the center of the room and stripped of curtains, sheets, and mattress. Keldan Sandilar was positioned on the base, spread-eagled and nude, his arms and legs tied to the four posts. His genitals were a mass of gore, as was the hole in the center of his chest. His stomach, legs, arms, and even neck and face had been covered with rune-like symbols that twisted like vines over his skin. On the walls, the same symbols were smeared in black, brown, and red, standing out harshly against sky blue. His eyes were open wide and glassy.

"Blood and Tears." Brannon could barely recognize the man he knew. He heard a retching sound behind him as Jessamine fought her stomach. "Thank the gods Roydan hasn't seen this."

As he stepped into the room, the stench of blood and meat filled his nose. The smell of death was still familiar after almost a decade of peace. It'd accompanied the loss of too many friends and comrades. Sometimes he would even smell it in his dreams and he would wake with sweat-soaked sheets believing, for a moment, that he was still covered with enemy blood.

Keldan's white face stared up at the ceiling where a fresco cherub gazed down, splatters of red ruining its innocent expression. Another friend fallen. The son of a friend.

Brannon took a deep breath. "Try not to touch anything until we've looked at it closely. You never know what might be a clue."

The others followed him carefully. Jessamine had her arms folded around herself.

Draeson whistled softly. "He pissed somebody off."

Brannon scowled. "He was a friend, Draeson. Have some respect."

"I knew him too," the mage said, pointing to the dead man's mutilated crotch. "But that looks personal. Maybe the woman he was with? Or her husband?"

Brannon turned away, concentrating on Keldan's arms. The bindings were tight but there was no evidence of rope burn on the wrists. "He didn't struggle against the rope so he was probably already dead when they tied him up."

"He wasn't dead when they stabbed him though," Jessamine said. "There's too much blood for that. Right?"

Brannon nodded. "They must have held him down. He's a big man and he would've fought. It wouldn't have been easy. Definitely not something a woman could do on her own. Or a woman and a man for that matter. I'd say at least one man for each limb and one to wield the knife."

Draeson shook his head. "I find it hard to believe a group of five men got in and out of here without being seen or heard. What if it was a surprise attack that incapacitated him right from the start?"

"That might work if he was hit in the head," Brannon said. He ran his fingers over Keldan's scalp, checking for bumps, cuts, or soft-spots. There was no sign of head injury. The chest wound was filled with semi-congealed blood. Brannon probed it gently with his fingers. "This doesn't hit his heart either, so he probably didn't die quickly."

He fell silent, trying not to think about how Keldan must have felt as he died. The physician-trained part of his mind kicked in and began identifying how the patient could have been treated if he'd been found in time. Staunch the blood flow, sew up the damage, bathe the wounds in antiseptic to try to prevent infection, give a tonic to help replace the blood.

Brannon looked away. With the amount of damage that had been done, there was no way Keldan could have been saved.

"Either way, if he was dead or incapacitated, why tie him up at all? Why position him like this? And what about the markings?" Brannon waved his arm to take in the entire room. Now that he could see past the corpse and the lurid symbols, he noticed other small items that were out of place: candles on the floor, ash on the discarded bedspread, dirt in small piles around the room. "This is more than just a murder. This was a ritual. Draeson, is there magic in this?"

The mage frowned. "Nothing local." His mouth twisted as he studied the symbols closer. "It could be Djin. They use runes and earth in their Raisings."

Jessamine gasped. "Djin? You mean the dead armies?"

Brannon shot her a look and she went quiet. "Jessamine, could you see what else you can find that might provide clues?"

She pressed her lips together and nodded. "Of course, Sir . . . um, Brannon. Sorry."

"Djinan has been neutral as long as anyone can

remember," Brannon said, turning back to the mage. "Do you really think they'd do something like this?"

Draeson shrugged. "Attack a member of our royal house on our own soil? No, that doesn't sound like them. But from what I know of their ways, this ritual does."

Brannon chewed his lip. "Kalanon isn't ready for another war, and we certainly wouldn't survive one with Djinan, so let's not jump to any conclusions just yet. It could be that someone is setting this out as a red herring. Or that it's a rogue Djin. Either way, no one's been Raised, so I don't think we need to panic. Maybe it was done as a scare tactic."

Draeson shrugged again. "To be honest, I've had very little to do with the Djin. They're all about dirt and death and elementals. I can't say for sure if this is their kind of thing but it's enough like it that we should ask them to send us an expert to take a look."

"Agreed," Brannon said. "Jessamine, can you take a message to the palace bird master, please?" He turned to find the apprentice studying the writing desk in the corner of the room.

"I'm not sure," she said, "but is this *silk*?" She held up a square of fabric.

Brannon ran his fingers over it, feeling the smoothness. "Yes," he said, amazed. "Where did you find that?"

Jessamine pointed to the desk. "There's a selection of them, just laying here."

"Well, well," Draeson muttered, coming closer. "Djin rituals, Nilarian silk, and a dead Kalan prince all in one room."

The three investigators crowded in close around the

desk. The squares were spread in a patchwork of vibrant colors. Some had patterns picked out in the thread, others birds or horses, and still more were a single hue. All were obscenely out of place in a Kalan room.

"How does silk end up in Prince Keldan's room?" Jessamine said. "I didn't think there was any in the whole country."

"There's some," Draeson said darkly. "In the Nilarian ambassador's wardrobe."

"That's not what this is, though," Brannon pointed out. "These are samples. Why would Keldan have samples of Nilarian silk in his room?" He turned away from the desk and froze. They were no longer alone in the room.

A young man in clerical robes bent over Prince Keldan's corpse. He was slim, average in looks, with light brown hair, and a slightly pointed nose. As Brannon watched, the young priest put out his tongue and licked the dead man's lips.

"What in all Hooded hells are you doing?" Brannon bellowed, pulling his sword from its scabbard.

The priest jumped. "Oh," he said, his eyes wide. He took in Brannon, with Draeson and Jessamine crowding behind, then looked around the room as if surprised to find himself there. "Oh," he said again, looking back down at the body. "Oh! You mean . . . No! Nothing like that! I'm not doing anything!"

Brannon raised an eyebrow. "Really?"

"Well, yes, something, obviously," the young man admitted. "I'm checking for poison. Well, not one that would kill him, obviously, but a paralytic drug. It leaves a very particular taste on the lips. Do you want to see?"

He gestured at the bed.

Brannon stared, incredulous. "Who are you?"

The man stepped forward with a piece of paper in his outstretched hand. "Brother Taran of the Third Alapran Monastery. King Aldan sent me to help out. I'm something of a chemist, you see. Drugs and poisons are sort of a hobby."

Brannon carefully took the paper. It verified that the bearer was Brother Taran, allocated to work with the King's Champion on the murder of Prince Keldan. At the bottom was the royal seal.

"Typical of Kalan kings to send people blundering into things," said Draeson. "Although Aldan did mention he'd be sending us help."

Brannon called one of the guards at the door and handed him the paper. "Take this to the palace, verify it, then report back. While you're there, tell the bird master to prepare for a message to be sent to Djinan. I'll send it along later."

"Wow," said Brother Taran. "Not very trusting."

"I'll trust you well enough until I know otherwise," Brannon said. "Tell me about this poison you think Keldan was given."

"Oh, I'll need to do some tests to be sure, but I think it's loredin. It puts the muscles to sleep." Taran waved his hand over Keldan's body. "It made it so he couldn't fight back."

Brannon chewed his lip. "That would explain why there's no sign of him struggling against the ropes."

"It also means the whole thing could have been done by one person after all," Draeson pointed out.

"Hooded Blood and crap," Brannon swore. "We're

back to square one."

"Sorry." Taran shrugged and bent over the body again. "Hey, what's with the bite marks? Does he have a kitten or something?"

"What?"

"There." Brother Taran pointed to the inside of Keldan's wrist, where two small teeth marks were almost healed.

"Is that likely to be how he was poisoned?"

"Oh, um, no, he'd have eaten or drunk the poison."

Brannon sighed and covered his face in his hands, rubbing at his eyes. "Then I don't really care about an old cat bite. Let's try to focus on what's relevant, shall we?"

Draeson stepped forward. "I think we should preserve this room and the body exactly as they are until the expert arrives from Djinan to tell us if it matches their ritual."

Brannon pulled his hands away. "You can do that?"

"Of course."

"Good. And in the meantime, we look into how Keldan came to have samples of silk, any enemies he may have personally, and what happened to the woman he was with. The gods only know if this is personal, political, or something else entirely. We need to follow up on all the possibilities."

"That sounds very sensible," Brother Taran said.

Brannon glared at him. "Do you need anything more for your tests?"

The priest held up a ball of cloth. "I swabbed his mouth already."

"Then I suggest we let Magus Draeson seal the room."

They watched from the hallway as Draeson reached his arm back through the door and placed his hand on the wall inside the room. His sleeve fell back, revealing the dragon tattoo on his bicep. For several breaths, nothing happened. Then there was an eerie crackling noise and what looked like green chunks of glass spilled out from the walls and began piling up on the floor. They settled softly over the desk, the bed, and Keldan's body. The chunks were flexible and light, melding to the shapes of the things they came into contact with, not shifting or pushing them, but oozing over and around them. When the chunks had finally reached the ceiling, they shimmered and their edges blurred into one another, becoming seamless so that the entire room was trapped in a transparent magical resin. A wave of cold flowed out from the doorway as Draeson pulled back his arm.

"That should do it," the mage said.

Brannon pushed the door shut, hiding the scene from view. "Good work."

As the others headed for the stairs, Brannon felt Jessamine's hand on his arm and she pulled him aside, her brow furrowed.

"Haven't you seen magic before?" he asked.

She shook her head. "Yes. Well, no, but that's not it." She paused. "I just saw Magus Draeson's dragon tattoo on his arm."

"Yes." Brannon said, knowing what was coming next.

She looked up at him, her head tilted to one side. "But, earlier . . . wasn't it on his neck?"

Brannon sighed. If only that were the biggest puzzle facing them. "Yes," he said. "Yes it was."

CHAPTER FOUR

S unlight shone warm and bright over the Djinan Isles, the perfect complement to the gentle breeze that brought with it the smell of drying grasses and salty sea air. On such a clear day, Ula could see, if she chose to look, all the way across to Uldhal, the furthest island of the archipelago visible from Gradinath Keep. For now, however, her focus was on the gentle hum of bees, and the decayed figure shambling toward their hive.

"Open it gently," she called, raising her voice even though she still held enough connection for it to feel her command without words. "I don't want it damaged more than necessary."

The Risen turned back for a moment and looked at her with empty eyes. The kaluki within was still strong for such an old corpse. It had repaired much of the body it inhabited, but, of course, could not resist the bindings of that body's limits. It nodded to Ula and proceeded to the hive.

The bees, sensing the danger of an intruder, buzzed about in fury, some impotently stinging the exposed flesh, their poison meaningless to one already dead. The Risen ignored them and pulled open the top of the box hive to inspect the wax combs inside.

Ula already knew what it would be seeing. The hive population had grown too large for the space that housed it. If something was not done soon, the bees would swarm.

"Take a third of the brood combs to the new hive," she said. "Make sure you get enough worker bees with them, but be sure to leave the queen."

As the Risen began pulling apart the hive, Ula dug her toes into the dirt and grass, enjoying the connection to the earth spirits. She closed her eyes and felt the strength and peace flow into the soles of her feet and up to the rest of her body. She swayed in a gentle communion dance as the breeze brushed over her skin. The spirits were happy today.

When she opened her eyes, she saw she was no longer alone. One of the apprentice shamans sat cross-legged on the grass nearby, her head bowed, awaiting acknowledgement. Her rough leather tunic bore only a few coral beads stitched on as decoration and the freshly tattooed rune on her shoulder was red and inflamed.

"What is it?"

The girl looked up and Ula could see the mixed adoration and fear with which so many of the apprentices regarded her, in the girl's eyes. "Prioress, a message came from the Kalan king. There's been an incident and they're calling the Council of Priors to discuss it."

Ula glanced across at the hive. The Risen was packing the last few combs into a box for transport. The remaining bees would now have space to expand the hive with their existing queen. Those that were transferred would quickly create a new queen from the larvae in the transported combs and begin a new hive of their own.

They were managed. Contained. There would be no uncontrollable swarm.

"You will need to keep watch on this Risen for me," she told the apprentice. "When it has finished the task, bring it to the Keep and have someone put it back in the earth." She crouched to dig a half-handful of dirt from the ground beneath her feet, spat into it to make it mud, and inscribed a symbol on the girl's forehead, binding the kaluki tether to her.

The girl's face was full of pride. "I can give it back to the earth spirits myself, prioress. I've been learning."

"Perhaps you can," Ula said. She poked the infected tattoo on the apprentice's shoulder, making her draw a sharp breath. "But not until this has healed, at least. You're not a shaman yet. Don't take foolish risks."

The path from the hives to Gradinath Keep was short in distance but rich with tactile sensation. The grass beneath Ula's feet rose up to tickle her ankles before giving way to the worn, dusty road, pocked here and there with gravel-filled potholes.

The Keep itself was the largest building in the Djinan archipelago, rising as high as a beached whale was long. It was constructed from the usual mud bricks and plastered over with clay so that the entire thing grew out of the ground like an organic entity—a kind of man-made termite mound.

As Ula stepped inside, she felt the coolness of the lower levels, not yet warmed by the sun. Later, in the evening, the baked clay would release the stored heat of the day to keep the inhabitants warm through the night, but for now the cool shade was a welcome relief after her brisk walk.

The Council of Priors met in the central chamber, a room designed to be the impregnable seat of Djin decision-making. Every brick of that chamber was a spirit-brick, bound and blessed by earth spirits to keep kaluki away. No Risen had been used to build Gradinath Keep. It had been done entirely by Djin shaman hands.

"The safest place in the world," Ula's old master had told her once. She'd never thought of anywhere to contradict him.

The others were already there, sitting cross-legged on the dirt floor. Ula quickly took her place and looked around. There were seven other priors in attendance at the moment. The rest were visiting tribes on other islands and would not return for this discussion. Those that were here were a mix of men and women, most with gray in their dreadlocks or beards and the ink of their tattoos faded with age. Their leather and flax clothes were beaded and painted as befit their status and a candle flickered on the floor in front of each prior.

Ula let her breath gently move the flame of her candle, then spat on her fingers and rubbed it into the dirt at its base. The familiarity of the ritual calmed her, strengthening her connection to the elements and earth spirits. She placed her hands palms down on the ground and waited.

Prior Caal broke the silence after only the briefest of communions. He held a scrap of paper out like a token. "King Aldan of Kalanon sends word and a request. He wishes one of us to break isolation and journey to Alapra."

A murmur passed through the council and a snort from Prioress Lule. "The Djin do not answer to foreign kings. We are not his to summon."

Ula waited for quiet before speaking. "Why does he make the request, Caal? Does he give his reasons?"

Prior Caal peered at the paper in his hand and read it aloud. "His Royal Majesty greets the Priory of Gradinath Keep and wishes prosperity, blah blah blah . . . " His free hand traced circles in the air beside him. "Ah, here it is, 'requests assistance with a matter of urgency. A heinous crime has been committed, the trappings of which appear Djin in nature. A prince of the royal house has been murdered. Kalanon requests an expert in the matters of the Risen to establish how this was done and for what purpose. Let the expert make haste to Alapra . . . ' and it closes with the usual salutations." Caal lifted his gaze to take in the silent group. "So you see, it seems quite serious."

Ula stared at the candle flame, thinking. The murder of a royal prince was serious indeed, but that alone would not cause a foreign king to approach the ruling body of Djinan. They had been neutral throughout history—and never more so than in the war between Kalanon and Nilar. Their isolation had been a carefully guarded treasure, keeping them pure of distractions and blood.

"Not a lot of detail to go on," a voice murmured.

"Foreigners kill each other all the time," said another. "What's it to do with us?"

Ula looked up sharply. "Don't you see? He thinks a Risen did it. Or a shaman trying to turn the prince into a Risen. Why else would he request an expert on such things?"

Lule looked shocked. "You can't be serious. Why would any of us want to do such a thing?"

"I don't know. But he must have some evidence to make him think it."

"Then he's a fool," growled Prior Glaak. The lids of his eyes sagged with age but fire sparked beneath them. "When have we ever had an interest in foreign politics? To accuse us of assassination is an insult."

Caal lifted a placating hand. "There is no accusation. Merely a request for help."

"The accusation is implied," Lule argued. "Ula is right about that."

Glaak shook his head, the beads in his dreadlocks clacking together. "Either way, we should ignore it. Perhaps they're bored with peace. If they want to pick a fight, let them come to us and meet the Risen on our shores. We've no need to send a sacrifice to their bloodthirsty gods."

"I didn't mean to say the Kalan king accuses us," Ula said quickly. Her heart felt dark when she thought of actually having to use Risen to defend Djinan. "Just that he seems to think there's something similar to our ways in what was done."

"That's right," said Caal, brandishing the paper yet again. "The request is for someone with knowledge to give him clarification on the matter. It's very likely nothing at all."

"That's true enough," Lule said. "Kalans know nothing about being a shaman. Write him back and tell him he's mistaken."

"Ah," said Caal, just as Ula opened her mouth to speak. "But what if he's not?"

Ula nodded. "I think we need to be sure. Kaluki are very sneaky. What if they've found an unguarded door to this world? Worse, what if there is a rogue shaman bringing Risen to Alapra?"

"What if there's not?" Lule frowned. "I, for one, do not relish the thought of travelling to Kalanon only to find the king imagined a movement in this prince's corpse and thinks it's a Risen."

Ula took a deep breath. She hated contradicting Lule. The woman always held a grudge. "If he didn't imagine it, though, Lule, think of the disaster it would mean. Our sacred responsibility is to keep the kaluki contained and siphon their power so that they can never be a threat for our world. If we ignore even the hint that they could be getting past us somehow, then we give up our purpose and it will be only a matter of time before the breakthrough. We must remain vigilant."

The candles burned in silence for a moment before Glaak spoke again. "We have always been vigilant, Ula. We always shall be." He sighed and shifted his weight, moving one of his legs out from under him. "Perhaps we must now take our vigilance to Kalanon."

Ula nodded. "I believe we must."

To her relief, the mood in the room seemed to agree. For a moment, she had worried that they would ignore the risk leaving such a report uninvestigated would pose.

Now, however, she concentrated on grounding herself again. She dug her fingers into the dirt floor beneath her, and let her vision linger on the candle flame as the remaining priors signaled their agreement that a shaman should be sent to Alapra to speak with the Kalan king.

"And I believe we know who this representative should be," Prior Glaak said.

Startled, Ula looked up to see who he meant. The eyes of all the other priors were on her.

"Oh no." The words came with such force that her candle blew out.

CHAPTER FIVE

L ady Latricia of Sandilar, Keldan's wife, was a strikingly angular woman. The sharpness of her was accentuated by widow-black. Brannon had seen her at court enough to know that she was a handsome woman who normally embraced the latest trends in color. Seeing her now, perched on the edge of a lawn chair opposite him, mouth tight beneath a net mourning veil, one hand clutching her young son close, he couldn't help think of her as a dark-hued mantis, ready to rear up and defend her territory against intruders.

The territory—the reflection garden of the townhouse the Sandilars used when in Alapra—was outstandingly beautiful. Positioned to catch the afternoon sun, the garden was discretely screened from the house and the surrounding neighborhood by hidden fences and cleverly positioned flowering shrubs and vines. A small grassy area provided space to sit and drink tea with friends or spend time alone. To one side was a pond, stocked with a variety of fish to provide easy sport for those who enjoyed fishing. In the center of the pond was an artificial island of stone, inlaid with a shiny mosaic of the Sandilar crest. A broken path of stepping stones across the water led to and from the island. On the other side of the lawn was a rose-covered arch, framing a love seat nestled in the fragrant shadows.

The boy wriggled in his mother's grasp. "Mom, can I go look at the fish?"

Lady Latricia's hand tightened convulsively. "No, Tommy. Sir Brannon and Magus Draeson have come to pay their respects. You wouldn't want them to think you're rude, would you?"

He shook his young head gravely and turned to his guests. "Thank you for your," he paused for a breath before carefully pronouncing the next word, "con-dol-enc-es."

"You're welcome, Tomidan." Brannon smiled at the boy. He couldn't be more than six years old. The last time he recalled seeing him he'd seemed much smaller. Blood and Tears, last time the child had barely been able to speak at all! He glanced up at the boy's mother. "How do they grow up so fast?"

Latricia's mouth softened a little. "I honestly don't know."

Brannon turned back to the boy. "Tommy, I wonder if you could do me a favor. Could you go and count how many fish are in the pond for me? Maybe you could feed them too."

Tomidan's face lit up, but Latricia stiffened. "I'd rather he stayed here with me."

"We need to talk about Keldan and what happened,"

Brannon said softly. "It's probably best if he's not here for that."

Latricia hesitated, her fingers twitching on her son's shoulder.

"It's just over there," Draeson said, gesturing to the pond. "It's not like we're sending him to Nilar. He'll be in sight the whole time."

She nodded slowly. "Off you go then, Tommy. Make sure you stay where I can see you."

"Yes, Mom." The boy raced off before the permission could be withdrawn, skipping across the stepping stones with speed and ease before flinging himself onto his belly at the edge of the mosaic island and peering into the water. "There's lots of orange ones!" he called back.

"Okay," Latricia replied. "Play quietly."

"He's a good boy," Brannon said. "It must be hard on him to have lost his father like this. Hard on you both."

"He's only six. I don't think he really understands it yet," she said, her voice becoming hard. "After all, we haven't been able to have a funeral yet because of what you've done to Keldan's body. Did you know the staff at the Blue Rose are charging a dollar to view my husband's corpse through your enchanted ice, Magus Draeson? Strangers can see him for a dollar but his family cannot see him at all, let alone give him a decent burial. Now, does that seem right to you? You knew my husband quite well. Do you think he would approve?"

Draeson remained impassive, his hands spread in the slightest of gestures.

Brannon felt his face burn. No matter how often

he'd seen death in his new role as a physician, it was as a soldier that he was most familiar with it. In battle, dignity for a dead man was rare and his family got the news late and the body often not at all. Master Jordell always insisted that when a patient died, the physician's role was to help the family heal. He had forgotten that lesson for Keldan. But with good reason. "We need to find out who killed him, Latricia. Keeping the scene as it is will help us do that. There are other experts that we want to see what was done."

She snorted in disbelief. "Yes, the king told Roydan all about your plan to get some Djin hedge-witch to investigate. Apparently a war-hero physician and immortal mage aren't enough. And what is it that the two of you are doing while we wait for this person to arrive?"

"Questioning you," Draeson said.

Brannon shot him a sharp look. "We're following other leads and gathering as much information as possible. We'll get Keldan's body back to his family as soon as we can, Latricia. And I'll make sure to set guards I know will keep the sightseers away."

Her body collapsed in on itself, making her seem smaller now that she was alone. "I suppose that's something," she said. Her eyes followed Tomidan as the boy got up and started making little twig boats to throw in the pond. Finally, she sighed. "Ask whatever it is you came to ask. I'll tell you what I can."

"Thank you," Brannon said. "Do you know of anyone who might have a reason to hurt your husband?"

Latricia straightened her back and shook her head. "No. I don't think so. Keldan was a good many things but he was pleasant enough to everyone and he didn't really make enemies the way others do at court. The only thing remarkable about him worth killing for was his inheritance." Her glance flicked quickly to her son.

"I suppose it's Tommy's inheritance now," Brannon said.

"Yes, it is. When he gets old enough to claim it."

Brannon caught Draeson's eye and the mage raised a brow. "What about business associates? Any deals that went bad or things like that?"

"Not that I can think of. Keldan was always a bit more ambitious than he was smart, but he never would have cheated anyone, if that's what you mean. He wanted to impress his father but Roydan is a hard man to compete with when it comes to business."

"Could he owe someone money, perhaps? Someone he wouldn't want you to know about?"

Latricia bent the net of her veil up over her hair, leaving her face unobstructed. "Have you been to Sandilar, Sir Brannon?"

"Not recently."

"When Keldan and I were first married, he took me to the back reaches of the province where the gold mines are. He showed me a cave where the walls shone like starlight. I thought he'd used paint to play a practical joke on me, but it was gold." She raised her bare wrists. "Most of the women at court wear gold bracelets to show off the wealth of their husbands. I don't bother because the stuff is so common. So, no, Keldan did not have any money problems. And if he did, whomever he owed would know that Duke Roydan would cover it."

Brannon couldn't help but agree. It was no secret

that Sandilar was a huge source of wealth. "What about business difficulties of a different kind? You mentioned his ambition. Could he have overreached in some other way?"

"Dealing with Nilarians, for example," prompted Draeson.

Latricia's eyes went very wide. She shifted uncomfortably in her seat. "Actually, yes. He was negotiating with the Nilarian ambassador for a silk deal. There's been no trade between Nilar and Kalanon since before the war and Roydan wanted to establish exclusive trade rights for silk. He thought there would be a demand for it now that the war is seven years past. Keldan heard about it and thought he could get a better deal for himself. He . . . he wanted to impress his father." She looked from one to the other of them. "Surely he wouldn't have been killed over that?"

Brannon shrugged. "I don't know. Maybe if there were other competitors trying to get the same deal?"

"Or the Nilarians took a disliking to him," Draeson muttered. "This confirms why there were silk samples in the room, at least."

"It does," Brannon agreed. "What it doesn't confirm is whether it has anything to do with why he was killed. Latricia, what did Keldan tell you about the deal?"

She shook her head. "Nothing. Just that negotiations were going ahead. Other than the fact that it was with Nilarians, there was nothing unusual about it at all, as far as I know." She reached for the tea service on a small table between them and poured a cup. "I'm afraid I need something to settle my nerves. I hope you'll join me."

She handed the cup to Draeson, then a second cup to

Brannon, who took it carefully, feeling as though his large hands could crush the delicate china with only a moment's inattention.

"Did you know Keldan was unfaithful?" Draeson said. "Witnesses say he was with a woman in the room where he was killed."

Brannon slopped tea over the edge of his cup.

Latricia, however, seemed unsurprised by the bluntness. She set down her own teacup, as yet unfilled, and looked at her hands. "Keldan has had many mistresses over the years."

Brannon felt his eyebrows go up. "So you knew? Weren't you angry?"

Latricia sighed. "Only when he wasn't discreet. But usually he was very good about not embarrassing me."

"So you didn't mind your husband sleeping with other women?"

She gave a wry, tight smile. "My, how very black and white of you. Things aren't always so clear in a marriage. I suppose, never having been married yourself, it might look strange."

Brannon frowned. "What do you mean?"

Latricia shrugged. "I mean, Sir Brannon, that marriage is about a range of things and some of them are more important than fidelity. My mother always told me that to understand a man, you must look to his father. Duke Roydan is a powerful and respected man, but he's also a notorious philanderer who has scattered bastards throughout the kingdom. I knew what I was getting into when I married his son."

Brannon took a gulp of tea. There didn't seem much to say to that. He knew Roydan's reputation well enough—he'd been there as a young man when it was being established. His friend had always had an eye for the ladies and it seemed he'd passed the tendency along to his son. Perhaps Latricia had made peace with it the way Roydan's wife eventually had.

"Sounds like a motive for murder to me," Draeson said.

To Brannon's astonishment, Lady Latricia laughed. At first it was an involuntary chuckle, then an uncontrollable giggle, then at last she gave in to it and howled with laughter, hugging her stomach as she did.

Brannon found himself leaning forward, watching her intently for a sign of whether this was an act or genuine mirth.

"Mama?" Tomidan, distracted at last from the fish, came and took his mother's hand. "What are you laughing at?"

"A good question," Draeson growled.

Latricia quieted to a few gasping breaths. "Oh dear. Nothing you'd think was funny, Tommy. Why don't you go and pick me some roses from the arch over there."

When her son was once more out of earshot, Brannon spoke up. "You think being suspected of murder is funny?"

Latricia gave a bitter snort. "I think the suggestion that I would murder Keldan over some floozy is funny, yes. If you had any idea how worried I've been since I heard about his death, you'd think it funny as well. Look around you, gentlemen. Where are we? Who do you think pays for all this? Where do I live? What do I spend? Why do I mix with the people I do?"

Brannon began to understand. "This is the Sandilar

townhouse. You rely on Sandilar money."

Her lips made a sneering smile beneath angry eyes. "Oh well done! I have nothing of my own. My family was a good one, you understand. Very well pedigreed, but our lands were on the wrong side of the river and when the Nilarians came we lost everything. I'm the only one left and my entire Hooded life relies on Sandilar money. So why, by all that is holy, would I kill my husband?"

"Perhaps," Brannon said slowly, "so that your son could inherit that money."

"At six years old?" This time the sneer was a snarl. "What kind of fool would do that? With Keldan alive, the line of inheritance was clear. If Roydan dies now, no one will accept a six-year-old duke. We'll have older, illegitimate children fighting for the title at every turn. Ahpra's Tears, Roydan may even make one of them heir while he's alive just to secure everything. Better a bastard grown son than a child grandson to run things. If that happens, Tommy and I can both kiss our lifestyle— if not our lives—goodbye."

Brannon opened his mouth to protest that Roydan wouldn't do such a thing, but a part of him knew it could be a lie. It would be a much more practical thing to have an heir who was grown and capable of running such an important province as Sandilar. The king himself might even suggest it.

"And even if Roydan keeps Tommy as heir," Latricia continued, "there's no guarantee he'll continue to support me. As Keldan's wife, I was guaranteed a place and standing as the next Duchess of Sandilar. As his widow, I exist entirely on Roydan's charity. He could put me out in the street at a moment's notice with nothing but the clothes on my back." Her dark eyes were chips of rock. "You may think I had a motive for wanting my husband dead. I had many more motives for keeping him alive."

"I'm sorry to upset you," Brannon said, choosing his words carefully, "but we have to explore all possibilities. If it wasn't a business partner and it wasn't you . . . what about Keldan's mistress? What do you know about the woman he was seen with?"

"Nothing at all. It wasn't something we discussed." She reached for the tea service again and filled her cup at last. She cradled it in both hands, lifting it slowly to her lips.

Brannon leaned forward. "Anything you can remember would be a help. Even if she didn't do it, she may have seen something that will help us find out who did."

Latricia looked at him over the teacup, and Brannon was struck with how red-rimmed her eyes were. The energy seemed to have drained from her, leaving her hollow and weary. "I think I've been as much help as I can be," she said. "If I find anything among my husband's things that might be useful, I'll let you know. But for now, I think you should leave."

Brannon couldn't help thinking she was probably right. He set down his cup and began to stand. "Of course. I hope we haven't offended you."

Latricia shook her head, rising to her feet as well. "Not at all. It's a painful situation is all. Please, finish your tea while I find my son so he can bid you farewell. If he's going to be Duke of Sandilar sooner than expected, he'd best remember his manners." With a sad little smile she walked across the lawn in the direction of the rose-covered arch.

Brannon watched her go, unable to decide between pity and suspicion. Was she a grieving, defensive widow or a clever manipulative murderer? The black of her gown slipped into the shadows without a trace as she stepped beyond the arch.

"You don't think she did it?" Draeson said.

He sighed. "I don't know."

"In my three hundred years of experience," said the mage, "when there's a murder, it's usually the spouse. Especially when one of them was cheating."

Brannon turned to look at him, still unnerved by Draeson's new, young face. "That makes sense, but why do it in such an elaborate way? Not to mention that Keldan's death puts her at risk of losing everything. If infidelity was enough of a reason, she'd have killed him years ago." He traced the edge of the scar on his cheek. "We're still missing too much information."

Draeson frowned. "I expected you to be much more slash-and-bash about this. Somehow it's affecting you personally."

"Of course it is." Brannon felt a flash of annoyance. "Keldan was the son of one of my oldest friends. Roydan, Aldan, and I fought together for years. You might not remember—I suppose it's not much out of three hundred years—but, for us, most of our lives were spent together, bathed in blood. That's not a bond that breaks in peacetime."

"I suppose not." Draeson's eyes grew distant. "I do remember, you know. The three of you were practically inseparable, always riding off into the thickest part of the battle. Madness when he was the heir at the time! But how everyone cheered when you came back. Thousands of people calling for Bloodhawk and the prince. Him for his royalty and you for your violence. I've never known anyone to be quite so bloodthirsty."

Brannon looked away and swallowed. "Not anymore."

The garden was uncomfortably quiet, despite the muffled sounds of the city beyond its gates. The water in the pond gently rippling in response to the movements of the fish just beneath its surface. The movement of the leaves on the surrounding plants. Beyond the garden boundary, a horse and carriage clattered along the cobblestoned street. A dog at one of the neighboring townhouses barked.

A child's voice called out, "Mama!"

Brannon jerked alert. "Something's not right."

Draeson opened his mouth but, before he could speak, a woman screamed.

Brannon ran for the rose-covered arch. Beyond the love seat it sheltered was an ivy-covered stone wall that edged the Sandilar property. A shadowy path ran parallel to the wall in either direction, hidden from the rest of the garden by the shrubbery.

"Latricia? Where are you?"

Her voice came from the right. "Help!"

Brannon could hear Draeson's crunching footsteps following his own on the pebbled path as they ran toward Latricia's voice. He drew his sword, keeping the point low as he rounded the corner.

Latricia stood to the side of the path, almost in the

bushes, her widow veil completely torn off and her hair wild. She held Tomidan to her chest with one arm. Her other hand pointed urgently toward the wall. "There!"

Brannon looked, just in time to see a figure disappear over the wall. He turned back to Latricia. "Are you all right? Are either of you hurt?"

She shook her head. "No, we're fine. He was in the garden. *Watching us*."

Draeson had caught up now. He stood with his feet shoulder width apart and held out his hands toward Brannon, fingers wide. The dragon tattoo circled his wrist now. "Hold still."

It felt as if the air around him had somehow thickened to take hold of his body. For a moment, Brannon worried it might crush him, but it remained soft and then he was lifted up and over the wall. His feet touched down on the cobbles as gently as if he had taken a step.

The street was deserted. The intruder was gone.

CHAPTER SIX

Master Jordell tied off the end of the bandage he was wrapping around a young man's forearm almost without looking at it as he watched Brannon and Jessamine approach. Brannon felt sure the old man could perform all but the most complex of surgeries blindfolded. Brannon's own skill was wasn't nearly as good— although he was fairly certain he could have found his way around the hospital wing of the College of Physicians without sight. In the latter part of his training, he'd spent more time here than in his own rooms in the palace.

The hospital was divided into wards, each with five or more beds lining the walls and space in the middle for the physicians to move back and forth. Trolleys of equipment waited at either end of the ward, their soft bandages and hard knives a startling contrast. The whole place smelled of sickness and bedpans and antiseptic. Volunteers brought flowers to try to lighten the scent, but the smell of the hospital was stronger.

"No," the old physician called, tucking his patient's arm under the bedcovers. "You cannot return your apprentice."

Brannon chuckled. "Don't worry, I'm not. She's turned out to be very useful—although she's not really learning anything from me. I did warn you both that it wasn't a good idea."

Master Jordell straightened up, frowning at them both. "That right, girl?"

Jessamine shook her head. "Actually, I'm learning lots of things. We're investigating a murder."

"We've done nothing medical at all," Brannon protested.

Jessamine shrugged. "No learning is ever wasted. Plus, there were medically based clues at the scene—like the lack of rope burns and amount of blood being an indicator of when he died. And anyway, I still put in my hours here at the hospital."

Brannon tried to remember if he'd intentionally taken the time to teach those things.

"So you're both happy with the situation," Jordell said.

"Um," said Brannon.

"Excellent. Follow me."

He led the way out into the corridor. Brannon and Jessamine hurried to keep up.

"Actually, Master Jordell, we're here for your assistance with the investigation. Has anyone strange shown up seeking medical attention?"

Jordell stopped at the doorway of one of the small, private rooms. "After this."

Inside, there was only one bed. The walls painted light green but unadorned. Around the bed stood a man in magistrates' robes, and two armed guards. Darnec Raldene lay on the bed, bandaged and in chains. When he saw Brannon, he groaned and pushed himself backward on the bed, only to be stopped by the manacles on his wrists which held him down.

Brannon felt his stomach go hot. "What's this?"

Master Jordell spoke up first. "Sir Brannon, as a physician, I'd like you to assess this patient and make recommendations as to his care."

The shackles pulled both shoulders down and out of alignment, and Brannon could see fresh blood seepage through the dressing over the wounded one. The young man's skin was damp with sweat and the bandages on his stomach and thigh were grubby around the edges and black with dried blood in the middle. Clearly they hadn't been changed since he'd arrived. The skin around the thigh bandage was puffy and pink.

Brannon felt his anger and disgust rise. "Well, for starters, I'd suggest removing the heavy restraints that are pulling on his shoulder wound. If he's kept like this the muscles won't have a chance to heal properly. All the wound dressings need changing and he should be bathed with antiseptic. Why hasn't that been done already?"

The magistrate, a sharp-faced whip of a man, looked embarrassed. "The prisoner is a convict, Sir Brannon. You, of all people, should know that he was found guilty in trial by combat. We're not yet certain of his sentence or whether we should allow him to be treated. He may yet go to the mines."

Brannon fixed him with his best dressing-down-subordinates glare. "I thought losing a trial by combat was its own sentence."

"Well, yes, but that's because losing usually means death. That's the problem. Should we allow a prisoner who technically should be dead, medical attention? We're waiting for a ruling."

Brannon felt the pressure of his clenched teeth as an ache low in his jaw. "And in the meantime, you're preventing the physicians here from fulfilling their oath to care for anyone who needs it? That oath is sworn to the king so his is the only ruling that could overturn it. Is it King Aldan you're waiting on? Because I will go and talk to him right now if it is."

The magistrate's eyes widened in horror. "No, Sir Brannon. The High Magistrate is listening to arguments from the boy's father and those he stole from. We didn't think . . . "

Darnec looked from Brannon to the magistrate and back again, his breath shallow and fast.

"Apparently not," Brannon growled. "In the king's absence, I think I can safely say that the physician's oath takes precedence and that Darnec's defeat was sentence enough. Justice in trial by combat is handed out by the King's Champion. If anyone has an issue with that, they should challenge me directly. Is that clear?"

The scrawny magister nodded several times. "Yes, yes, of course. I'll carry the message back to the court. Thank you for the clarification." He gestured to the guards, who unlocked the shackles and carried them away.

As they left, Darnec rubbed at his wrist, made as if

to get up, then fell back down to the mattress.

Brannon sat on the edge of the bed. "I just stuck my neck out for you, Darnec Raldene. I'd like to see you make it worthwhile. Will you?"

Darnec's eyes were bright. His face was flushed, as if slightly feverish, but his expression was determined. "Yes, sir."

Brannon laid a hand on his uninjured shoulder. "Good. I'll put a word in for you with the palace guard. Let's put those skills with the sword to good use. When your shoulder heals up, you'll be an asset to your country." Military discipline would do the boy a great deal of good.

"Thank you, sir. Would you . . . " He looked away. "Would you speak to my father as well? Let him know how I'm doing?"

"If you do well, I'll make sure that he knows it." Brannon said. "Now rest and let the physicians here do their work."

The boy nodded and his eyelids slid shut. In a few moments his breaths evened out into sleep.

If only my own worries could be sorted so easily, Brannon thought. He stood and indicated to Jessamine and Master Jordell to follow him out into the hallway.

"I assume that's all the consultation you needed from me for this patient?"

Master Jordell lips curved very gently upward. "I'm sure we can take it from here. Now, what was it you were so keen to ask me about?"

"You've heard about the Prince Keldan murder?"

"Of course."

"We have two people we need to find in connection

to it. A tall, slim man with light brown hair, and an attractive woman."

Jordell snorted. "Pretty thin descriptions to go on."

Brannon sighed. "Yeah. But they're all we have. It's possible one or both of them may have sought help from a physician in the last three days. The woman was with Keldan the night he died. She could be his attacker or she could be an innocent bystander. Either way, it's possible she was injured in the process. The man was caught spying on Lady Latricia. She thinks she scratched his face, and he might have picked up some other injuries getting away over a wall. Have any patients come through here that might fit?"

Master Jordell shook his head slowly. "Not that I can think of. But not everyone comes here. There are plenty of physicians operating independently of the college. Once their training is complete, they go where they're needed."

"What about unexplained bodies?" Jessamine spoke up. "They might have turned up in the morgue."

"What a delightful notion. No, there hasn't been anything like that, I'm glad to say. Although we do get unidentified bodies from time to time, but usually someone comes along with a claim and an explanation."

Brannon rubbed at his scar. "Well, it was a long shot," he said. "If something does show up . . . "

"I'll send word at once," Jordell finished. "Of course. And I'll spread the word around the other physicians in the city. If they've treated anyone that fits what you're looking for, I'll hear about it eventually."

"Thanks," said Brannon. "It seems the majority of our clues require waiting. Wait to hear from Djinan, wait to speak to the Nilarian ambassador, wait for Brother Taran's test results. It was never something I was very good at."

Master Jordell gave a little shrug. "Wisdom comes with age, they say. Not patience."

"I'm not even sure about wisdom." Brannon started to say more, then stopped himself.

"Spit it out," Master Jordell said.

Brannon hesitated, touching his scar again, then spoke. "Do you know Brother Taran, at all? He claims to know about drugs and poisons."

The older man crinkled his face. "From the Third Alapran Monastery? I know of him. He makes some of our medicines. Very young and reclusive, I understand, but quite brilliant. I don't know of anyone else who can brew the kinds of things he does. Why?"

Brannon sighed. "Because I don't know him at all and it seems I'll have to trust him anyway. So much for wisdom."

CHAPTER SEVEN

Brother Taran had once heard his laboratory called "a collection of abominations that behave in a most peculiar and inappropriate manner." The phrase had been delivered with venom from the tongue of a visiting bishop. Taran couldn't help but smile whenever he thought of it. Though he'd meant to insult, the bishop couldn't have come up with a better description for Taran's lab, as viewed by an ordinary man.

The large, stone walled chamber in the basement of the monastery was indeed filled with oddities. Glass jars of powders, herbs, and minerals filled the shelves, each carefully labeled and kept in its place, the more toxic of them kept near the chimney so that their vapors could be expelled quickly when unstoppered. Larger jars and tanks contained exotic and usually poisonous animals—spiders, snakes, scorpions, and the like—which had mostly been imported from the desert at great expense.

There were several workbenches throughout the

laboratory, each with its own set of equipment, much of it in motion. There were beakers of liquid that appeared to boil with no flame near them, metal wheels that rotated without being touched, Bunsen burners and steam valves sending jets of mist high into the air, and pipettes that measured careful dosages of one chemical into another—often with dramatic and colorful results.

To a scientific mind like Taran's, however, everything behaved exactly as it should. It was in his laboratory that he was able to forget the life he had come from, forget the limited existence of his exile to the church, and enjoy the wonderful secrets the gods had hidden in the world.

He was so wrapped up in his enjoyment, in fact, that he almost failed to hear the footsteps on the stairs until they were right outside the door. As the handle turned, he continued writing his notes with his right hand, but slid his left beneath the workbench to grip the handle of the dagger strapped to the underside.

The door opened and a pretty blond girl stepped inside. "Brother Taran?"

"Oh." He let go of the knife. "Oh, Jessamine. Hello. I didn't realize you were coming. Is everything all right?"

"Yes, everything's fine." She looked around the room, eyes darting from object to object with every step. "Brannon said you were expecting to have the results of your tests today and I said I'd come and see while he interviews the Nilarian ambassador. To be honest, I've been curious to see where you do your work." She squinted into one of the larger tanks. "Are they locusts?"

Taran nodded. "The creagor spiders like to eat them."

She looked at him to see if he was joking, then burst out laughing. "Amazing! You have such interesting things here."

"You should see what eats the creagor spiders," Taran told her and was gratified when she laughed some more.

"Is it true that the Assassin House likes to put creagor spiders in people's beds?"

He shrugged. "That's the rumor. I guess it'd be effective as long as the thing stayed put until the person went to bed. Usually they move around a lot though. There are probably more efficient ways to kill someone."

"Speaking of which . . . " She looked at him expectantly and for a moment Taran's mind went blank.

"Oh, the test results! Yes, we should be able to do the final confirmation right now." He led the way to the central workbench and checked the beaker in which the swab had been soaking. The leaching fluid was a gentle shade of pink. That fit loredin, but also a range of other poisons and drugs. They needed to be more specific.

"He was definitely given something," he said, reaching for the tongs and using them to lift a boiling beaker away from a flame. "But three drops of this solution and a piece of gael stone will let us know if it's loredin or not."

He used a pipette to suck some of the steaming solution away from the beaker, then carefully added the three drops to the leaching fluid.

"Nothing happened," Jessamine said, her voice barely above a whisper.

"Not yet." Taran took a jar of purple pebbles from a shelf and held it out to her. "Would you like to do the honors? Drop it in gently and stand back."

She took a gael stone between her thumb and forefinger and gingerly dropped it into the mix.

Immediately, the fluid turned a brilliant green, like new leaves, and froth bubbled up over the rim.

Jessamine looked from the beaker to Taran with wide eyes. "Is that it? Was it loredin?"

"Yep, that's it."

She punched the air. "Yes! You're a genius! That was brilliant!"

Taran felt himself beaming foolishly under her regard and searched for something else interesting to say. "How has the rest of the investigation been going?"

She tilted her head to one side. "Well, I think. It's hard to say. So far it's been a lot of asking questions of a lot of people. I think I've interviewed everyone who ever worked at the Blue Rose. Brannon and Draeson are interviewing the more interesting people themselves."

Taran gave her a sly look. "I'm not interesting?"

She laughed again, delighted. "You're not being interviewed! You're one of the team, not a suspect."

"Oh. I'm glad to hear it!"

"Ooh, there was something promising this morning actually," she said, touching his arm. "Just before Brannon and Draeson went to meet with the Nilarian ambassador, Master Jordell sent word that they found the body of an unidentified woman in a rubbish heap. We think it might be Prince Keldan's mistress."

"Really?" Taran was very conscious that she hadn't yet moved her hand away. "How can you be sure?"

Jessamine spread both hands in a shrug. Taran felt the cool air rush in where her warmth had left. "I don't know," she said. "We just have to hope that things match up. Maybe she'll have something on her from the crime scene. We're going to the morgue to look when Brannon and Draeson get back." She paused and looked at him thoughtfully. "Actually, you should come with us. Maybe whoever killed Keldan used loredin on his mistress as well. You're the only one who could tell."

Taran swallowed. "I'm not really the only one. Anyone could check to see if . . . " He trailed off. Somehow he couldn't let himself tell Jessamine to taste the dead woman's lips. "Ah, I suppose I could come though. That's probably best."

She beamed. "Good. We can wait for the others in Brannon's apartment and tell them about the loredin test results together."

"Okay." As he followed her to the door, Taran touched his chest where the "king's pass" rested under his clothes. He rarely left the monastery, but when he did, he liked the comfort of knowing the amulet was with him. He'd never had to use it yet. In fact, the closest he'd been was when he'd first met Jessamine and Sir Brannon at the Blue Rose. A good example of how he could let his enthusiasm make him sloppy. He took a deep breath and followed her through the labyrinthine corridors of the monastery and out into the city.

"You know," Jessamine said cheerfully, "when I first arrived in Alapra I would get hopelessly lost. Now, though, it's just like home."

Taran nodded, careful to keep his face neutral. Home wasn't quite the comforting concept to him that others expected it to be. He supposed that was why he liked the monastery. It didn't fit the traditional idea of home, but it was quiet and safe—aside from the occasional visiting bishop.

"It's amazing how quickly the mind picks up new information," he said. "You find your way from one place to another just a couple of times and suddenly you know it."

It sounded stupid to him when he said it out loud, but Jessamine didn't seem to think so. "Exactly," she said. "I suppose it's like you with all your animals and potions. Most people wouldn't know what a creagor spider eats or what loredin is, but you've learned it and now . . . well, now you're a very valuable man to have around!"

Taran shrugged. "I guess."

She went on as if she hadn't heard him. "That's why I wanted to become a physician. Well, part of it anyway. There's so much to learn in the world. I want to take as much of it in as I can."

They were now within the grounds of the royal palace but not within the palace itself. The royal household was supported and surrounded by a number of important buildings—official offices like the courthouse and taxation department, but also barracks and training areas for the palace guard and key members of the army, and housing for important dignitaries and support staff. Many members of the nobility chose to maintain their own town houses in the better neighborhoods of Alapra, but the King's Champion had always remained in one of the basic apartments provided for specialist army officers. It was one of the things Taran had always admired about the man's reputation.

Jessamine led the way to a modest stone and plaster

building, not unlike Taran's monastery in design, although the monks preferred to leave the stone exposed. Inside, a simple woven rug followed the path from the door to the stairs and, one flight up, continued down the hallway.

Jessamine stopped at the third door and knocked. "Brannon said if they're not back, to just wait inside. I have a key."

The lock was a fairly simple one. With or without a key, Taran knew it wouldn't take much to open it. Brannon didn't seem the type to keep a lot of valuables around. There was a second flight of stairs at the other end of the hall. Two exits. Sensible.

Jessamine knocked again, each bang sounding very loud, and when there was still no answer she began searching her pockets for a key.

There was an odd silence to the place. Taran felt some instinct prickle the back of his neck. He gently nudged between Jessamine and the door, pressing his ear against the wood. "Sir Brannon? Are you in there?"

No response.

He tried the handle and the door swung ajar on silent hinges.

Jessamine stopped looking for the key. "That's weird."

Taran nodded. "Maybe he forgot to lock it."

The rooms inside were simply laid out and empty of life. The entrance led into a sitting room area with three straight-backed chairs, a small, low table and wide windows, opened to the fresh air. The kitchen was spotlessly clean and tidy, almost as if it hadn't been used, although the wood piled beside the burner indicated otherwise. In the bedroom area the bed was perfectly made, covers tight. Around it, each against a separate wall, were a wardrobe, a desk stacked with medical textbooks, and a rack for armor and weapons. There was little else in the way of decoration. Sketches of the human body, with muscles and bones labeled, were tacked to the wall above the desk. One end of the armor rack had a spike, on which hung a number of medals and commendations. Taran wondered if Brannon ever wore them.

"Bloodhawk and the physician, side by side." Taran had been taught that a man's home told a lot about his personality.

Jessamine shrugged. "Plenty of men still have that army way of doing things. But the war's over so they need something else to do. Why not make it something positive for the world?"

Taran nodded. "I didn't mean it as a bad thing." He paced the apartment slowly, still a little unnerved by the unlocked door. Still, there was no sign of anything awry.

"I know." Jessamine paced with him in slow, graceful steps.

Taran caught himself watching her and pulled his eyes away. "How long do you think they'll be?" he asked, drifting over to the weapons rack. There were some fine things here.

"I don't know." Jessamine headed toward the desk with its treasure load of books. "I guess it depends how much the ambassador has to say."

The creak of movement pulled Taran's attention away from the weapons and medals and he turned to see the door of the wardrobe slowly open. Jessamine shrieked as the figure of a woman slumped forward out of the wardrobe and fell, with a sickening crack, onto the floor.

"Blood of the Wolf," he swore.

Jessamine screamed again, and backed up against the far wall. "Ahpra's Tears!"

Taran could feel his heart thumping as he crept toward the dead woman, his breathing fast. Her body was twisted and broken. Her skin was gray and her face was hacked like butcher's meat. Her clothes had once been fine but were now torn and filthy. Taran could see maggots where her eyes should be.

His shocked mind was alert for any twitch. The wardrobe was empty of other surprises—a few shirts and pants hung innocently in their places.

Taran bent down to check under the bed—nothing there.

The dead woman lay like a grotesque doll.

"What in the name of the Hooded is a corpse doing here?" Jessamine was trembling, but her composure was returning fast.

Taran frowned. "You said you'd been asking questions about Prince Keldan's mistress. Apparently someone is making sure you get answers."

CHAPTER EIGHT

Obtaining an appointment with the Nilarian ambassador was a tricky business. Even now, having arrived at the scheduled time, Brannon and Draeson were left to wait.

The suite provided for the ambassador's home was a luxurious one in the palace proper. Efforts had been made to smooth difficulties and clasp the representative of the now peaceful neighbor close to the royal heart. It also allowed for better protection from those who still held a grudge in the general populace and a better ability to be watched by those who still held a grudge in the royal court.

The room in which they waited was barely recognizable as Kalan. Charcoal-gray silk panels were draped across the ceiling and walls, giving the impression of being inside a large, expensive tent. Each panel was edged in a thin border pattern in a different color. At eye level, each had a word in fluid Nilarian script as large as Brannon's hand.

Brannon stared at them, slowly summoning what he had learned of the enemy language when trying to decipher messages from intercepted spies. "Courage," one of them said. Others were "honor" and "wisdom" and "patience." At the last one, Brannon rolled his eyes and stopped reading.

Draeson was dressed in very tight pants and a peacock-blue shirt in the style of very young men at court. He lounged in the soft embrace of an armchair as though it were his bedroom.

"You're dressing to match your new age, I see," Brannon commented.

Draeson grinned, his teeth very white. The dragon was nowhere to be seen today. Somewhere under his clothes, no doubt. "I'm embracing it. It takes an old man to fully appreciate youth."

Brannon sighed. "That's true enough." He'd certainly not appreciated the extra energy he'd had as a youngster at the time. Nor, of course, had he had things like wisdom or patience. It would be nice to have the mind he had now in the body he'd had then.

"Speaking of youth," Draeson said. "That apprentice of yours is an attractive lass."

"Nobody says 'lass' anymore. Your vocabulary's still old."

"Fine. The girl who checks with you if the sun will rise—are you and she an item?"

"What?" Brannon felt his mouth fall open. The room felt very warm. "No, we are not! Blood and Tears, even if she wasn't my apprentice, she's half my age!"

The mage shrugged. "When you're as old as I am, age doesn't really matter anymore. And as for the

73

apprentice thing, well, more than one of my masters didn't let that bother them." He chuckled softly. "Well, if you're not interested yourself, do you mind if I . . . "

Brannon leaned forward, surprised by the sudden protective fury he felt. "Magus Draeson, if you lay a hand on that girl, I will cut you three times for every wrinkle you used to have. Are we clear?"

Draeson held up his hands in a pacifying gesture. "All right, all right. I was just asking. A young body has young needs, is all."

"Well, see to them elsewhere," Brannon growled. "Not among the people I work with."

He was saved the necessity of hearing the mage's response, by the return of the servant who had asked them to wait. He bowed deeply, the tassel on the top of his hat making a sweeping motion from side to side. "Gentlemen, I present the honorable Ambassador Ylani Shaylar."

He stepped aside and the ambassador glided into the room, her every movement smooth and graceful. She was tall for a woman, and slender. Her hair was delicately curled and hung down past her shoulders in dark waves. A miniature red top hat perched on her head at an angle and trailed crystals on three long wires, like glittering feathers. Smaller crystals lined the cuffs of her gown, which was pale silk trimmed with red to match the hat. It was long and sleek with a hem that brushed the polished wood floor with yet more of the sparkling crystals. Her skin was smooth with just a hint of color, making her lips and long-lashed, deep brown eyes stand out like jewels.

She nodded slightly to each of them and took a seat,

gesturing to them to do the same. As she brushed past, Brannon noticed she smelled of spice and vanilla.

"Welcome to you both. Sorry for the delay," she said, with barely a trace of accent. Her lips formed a little half-smile. "Sir Brannon Kesh, I never expected to have the Bloodhawk in my parlor. Am I to be skewered on your stolen sword?"

Brannon blinked. "Ah, no, nothing like that. I'm not sure if we've been introduced at court, ambassador. I hope you'll forgive us for intruding. We're only here to ask a few questions."

Ylani waved her hand. "Of course. You must forgive me as well. I know who you are from your reputation. Back home, we use you to scare our children into behaving. And in Government House, we use you to scare the adults!"

Brannon felt his stomach burn. He forced himself to put on his court smile. "I'm only scary in defense of Kalanon, ambassador. So I'm sure you have nothing to fear."

Ylani nodded graciously. "Thank you. Does the magus show the same restraint?"

Brannon saw startlement cross Draeson's face before he could hide it. His head tilted to one side. "You recognize me?"

The little half-smile returned to the ambassador's face. "I like to know who it is I let into my parlor, magus. Surprises can be messy."

Draeson's eyes narrowed. "Indeed."

Brannon cleared his throat. "Draeson and I were both in the army, ambassador, but the war is over. Your role here wouldn't exist if it wasn't. We're not interested in making you uncomfortable but we need your help with our investigation. If you're not involved in Prince Keldan's death, then we'll leave you alone."

Ylani watched him for a long moment, then visibly relaxed. "Very well," she said. She gestured and the servant who announced her turned and left the room. It was then that Brannon saw he'd been carrying a small crossbow behind his back. "Please understand, I must be careful. Not all of your countrymen are happy to have a Nilarian in the palace."

"I can't say I'm happy about it either," Draeson muttered, barely loud enough for Brannon to hear.

"I was waiting to meet with your king last week," Ylani said, "and one of the courtiers told a joke. 'What do you call half the Nilarian army drowned at the bottom of the Tilal?'"

"A good start," Brannon said softly. It was an old joke that hardly seemed funny. Bloated and waterlogged bodies had clogged the shoreline for weeks. Even now, fishermen sometimes pulled up bones or pieces of rusted armor. "I'm sorry."

She shrugged. "I don't mean to be maudlin. As you say, the war is over. You said I can help you solve the death of your prince. How?"

Brannon pulled out the samples of silk cloth and held them out to her. "Do you recognize these?"

"Yes, of course."

"Can you tell us about them?"

Ylani chewed her lip a moment. "There are delicate trade issues involved."

"There's the murder of a Kalan prince involved!" Draeson snapped.

Brannon shot him a look. "We'll make sure to keep things confidential, if we can."

"Thank you," Ylani said. She stared across at one of the word-panels for a long moment before speaking again. "Your Prince Keldan was one of several Kalan nobles interested in establishing a trade agreement. His father was the first."

"Duke Roydan?" Brannon was still surprised that Roydan would have anything to do with the Nilarians, let alone be first in line. But then, he wasn't one to pass over a good business opportunity either.

"Yes. Duke Roydan approached me shortly after I arrived to suggest that the time was right to introduce Nilarian silk back into the Kalan market. Since the war, trade has been . . . limited. And silk is such a distinctly Nilarian commodity that it wasn't welcomed—nor did we want to share it."

"But that's changed?"

"Roydan believed so. He wanted to establish exclusive rights to import silk from Nilar. He thinks a monopoly will ensure the exclusivity of the product and help it retain its value. Supply and demand."

Brannon nodded slowly. "If he's the only one Nilar will allow to trade for silk, he controls the supply and can charge whatever he likes for it. People will pay more for something that's difficult to have and you both get rich."

Ylani shrugged. "That's the point of trade."

"So if it's supposed to be a monopoly, how did the others get involved?"

"Word leaked. Prince Keldan approached me wanting to get the deal for himself and to outbid his father. One or two others have also made enquiries."

"Who?"

Ylani shook her head. "Negotiations are still underway and it's important that the competitors don't know who each other are. I'll not tell you their names and risk messing up the best deal for my country."

"You told us Roydan's name," Draeson pointed out.

"Roydan is Keldan's father. I'm sure he would have told you himself, had you asked. The names of the other competitors are not relevant to your investigation."

"They are if one of them killed Keldan so he wouldn't get the deal," Brannon pointed out.

"If Keldan were the mostly likely to have his bid succeed, then I would agree," Ylani said. "But he wasn't. If you were trying to eliminate the competition, surely you'd start with the one who was the biggest threat?"

"And who is that?" Draeson asked.

Ylani remained silent, the little half-smile on her lips.

"You realize that refusing to help us makes you look suspicious."

She shrugged. "I have already told you that I would not reveal the names. Once the negotiations are complete, you may ask me again. Or, if it appears that they may be involved after all, I will tell you. But not now."

Brannon took a deep breath and let it out slowly. "There's no way for you to know if they're involved or not if you won't let us investigate them."

Ylani chewed her lip again. "Well, none of the other potential traders have come to harm. If they do, we'll know one of them is behind it."

"That's cold," Draeson said. "Even for a Nilarian."

The ambassador spread her hands helplessly. Her voice was soft. "Your investigation is your priority. Mine is to negotiate on behalf of my country. I'm helping you as best I can, but I have to protect the trade negotiations. Nilar needs the funds this deal will bring in to help in the recovery. We spent too much in the war and silk is one of the few things we have that can help us back on our feet."

"Perhaps," said Draeson, just as softly. "Or perhaps the opportunity to get revenge on a Kalan prince was just too tempting. Your precious trade deal lured him in and perhaps you killed him yourself. Is that it? You're here to finish by subterfuge and murder what you started with war?"

Brannon watched the ambassador's face closely as a complex array of emotions flickered across her features.

"Contrary to popular Kalan opinion," she said, "we are not all murderers."

"Tell that to the hundreds of families killed by your invading army." Draeson's voice could have cut stone.

Ylani's eyes flickered to one of the wall panels. Brannon followed her gaze. The word "peace" was an emerald-green.

When she spoke, there was a rawness to her voice. "Tell me, wizard, how do you feel about the part you played in the deaths of so many of my people? When you held back the waters of your river Tilal and waited for us to cross, did that feel like murder? It certainly wasn't the clean death of battle. The wave you released rushed over everything and everyone in its path. They drowned without ever having a chance to surrender or escape. If you want to call someone a murderer for what was done in the war, start with yourself!"

Draeson's face was red with fury. "I'll not apologize for defending my country against attack!"

"Nor should you," Brannon soothed. He reached a calming hand toward each of them, struggling to keep his own emotions in check. He could feel the battle rage burning at the edge of his mind, ready to blaze the way it used to. Even this many years later, the anger that another country would invade his Kalanon and kill his countrymen was a force that could fuel him for days. He forced it away and concentrated on the current issue. "We're not here to talk about the past."

Draeson and Ylani stared at each other for a long moment, then the ambassador shook her head. "Of course. I'm sorry. Emotions get the best of all of us sometimes."

Brannon felt his breath release. He hadn't realized he'd been holding it. "That's okay. Draeson has that effect on people."

She laughed and the sound instantly lightened the mood in the room. "I can't imagine it!"

The mage turned away, scowling at the door.

"We have to investigate all the possibilities though," Brannon continued. He shrugged, palms up. "Given the history, and that you've a connection to the victim, we have to wonder if you're involved."

Ylani's laugh faded. She licked her lips, then gave a little nod. "Fair enough. But I didn't do it. I assume you have not found any connection between me and the *other* murders, however, and if they are all linked, then there's no reason to suspect me at all."

Draeson's head snapped back around to face them.

"What?" Brannon felt as though he'd been kicked in the chest. "What other murders?"

Ylani's eyebrows raised. "Ah. You didn't know. How awkward."

"Know what? What have you heard?"

The ambassador gave a delicate shrug. "I only know that there have been other killings that looked the same. I assumed you would have known by now." Brannon opened his mouth to ask questions but she held up a hand to forestall him. "I truly don't know anything more than that. I'm sorry. If I did, I would tell you."

"Where did you hear about it?"

She shook her head. "I can't say."

Brannon frowned. If this was true, then the Nilarian ambassador had better sources of information than the royal court. Or, at least, than he and Draeson did. It was possible King Aldan had kept them in the dark to keep them focused on Keldan's death specifically. If the murders were connected, however, Ambassador Ylani was right—it would change the suspects.

If, in fact, there were any other murders. The woman was a politician and a Nilarian. For all he knew, the entire story was made up as part of some manipulative game.

"It seems there's a lot you can't tell us. Or won't."

Ylani sighed. "Yes, I suppose there is."

As the door closed behind them on their way out, Brannon turned to his companion. "What do you think? Do you believe her?"

The mage shook his head. "Not at all. There's something about her that isn't right. I just can't put my finger on exactly what."

Brannon covered his face with his hands and leaned back against the door. "Blood, Tears, and Wolf-shit. Why couldn't this be easy?"

Draeson shrugged. "It never is."

Brannon lowered his hands and pressed them against the wood of the door to push off. The wood was warm.

He pulled away, looking up and down the corridor. There was no one but Draeson.

"What is it?" the mage asked.

"Feel that."

The mage ran his hand over the door. "Body heat? Someone was pressed up against it while we were inside."

Brannon nodded. "Listening to everything we said."

CHAPTER NINE

Latricia Sandilar entered her late husband's office in her nightgown. Her bare feet made no sound on the carpet. The light from the single candle she carried pushed back the darkness just enough to see her way into the familiar room. It was a warm night and the soft glow made the world seem gentler and safer than the harsh sun had allowed in the last few days.

Daytime was given to the business of mourning— the black clothes, the receiving of visitors, the organizing of the rituals as best she could when Keldan's body had not been released to her. She was familiar with mourning—she'd buried her father and brothers and many more during the war—but it was a surprise how deeply this loss cut. She had become soft in the seven years of peace. And, she had to admit, in those other times of grief, she'd had Keldan to lean on. Now she had only her father-in-law and her young son. She knew Keldan would have teased her if he'd seen how clingy she'd been around Tommy of late, but she couldn't help herself. Her son was all she had left. Everything she did was for him.

At night, however, there was no one to see when she slipped into her empty bed. No husband to discuss the day's events with or plan for the future. For all his faults, Keldan had been a good husband. The thought that she'd never see him again, nor hear his careful assessment of some political intrigue or business deal, kept her from finding rest. She found she couldn't bear to stay in the room where Keldan spent most of his nights. Instead, she came to the room where he spent much of his days.

The room was filled with Keldan's trophies. The mounted wolf's head he had killed himself as a boy, the marble bust of himself commissioned from a sculptor he'd found and introduced to court. Even the portrait of Latricia herself. Keldan had always striven to prove himself and he liked to be reminded of what he had achieved.

He'd liked *others* to be reminded of it more, Latricia supposed, a smile on her lips at the memory. But why not? She'd always been prouder of him than he was of himself. Oh, certainly he'd had his flaws—great men always did. But he was a good man just the same and it cut her to know he wouldn't get the chance to see how great he could become.

She made her way to the wide mahogany desk and set the candle down. She settled into the comfy suede chair and curled her legs up under her as she had done as a younger woman, visiting Alapra for the first time as a wife. Things had changed a lot since then. The country girl she'd been had learned a lot of city politics and intrigue.

She ran her fingers along the smooth wood of the desk. How would Keldan react if he could see her now, at the mercy of his father's whim? Roydan had never particularly warmed to her. It was frustrating that he now had her future in his hands.

She pulled open the middle drawer and took out the leather-bound journal inside. She'd never really understood Keldan's desire to record his thoughts and plans on paper. He was always careful to keep his journals locked away in a hidden panel cavity, but she'd considered them a security risk to his plans. He claimed they helped him order his thoughts better and she couldn't argue with that. Now, they were the only part of him that remained.

She had taken this one from the hiding space two nights ago. It was an early journal, of the time when they had first been in love. Reading it made her feel like Keldan was courting her all over again. She pulled back the covers and read a random entry in the dim candlelight.

"I heard Latricia singing tonight," read Keldan's slanted handwriting. "She really does have the most beautiful voice. Algaly Harwood tried to steal everyone's attention at her parents' ball by singing with the band. Then my Latricia got up and put the poor girl to shame! It was brilliant!"

Latricia smiled. Keldan had hated the Harwoods in those days. He'd been in competition with Algaly's brother for a lot of the same activities. She couldn't remember that young man's name—he'd since died in the war. She did remember Keldan complimenting her on a masterful move that had "put that shrew in her place." She hadn't known it at the time, but Algaly Harwood had been suggested as a possible wife for Keldan.

She hugged the journal to her chest and breathed in the memories. In the dark, it was easy to pretend they weren't a lifetime ago. She could feel the warmth of his hand on her back as they danced and he told her he was proud of her singing. And his breath on her ear as he whispered other suggestions for the evening. They swooped across the dance floor, young and happy and in love. The country was at war, but they didn't care. Their life together was just beginning.

She felt the hard edges of the journal cover bite into her palm and the memory faded. It was time for another.

"The king gave me a special assignment today. I am to be given special treatment and, in return, I am to fulfill a deal that was made with the Magus Draeson."

Latricia leaned forward, thrusting the journal closer to the candle as she read. This was something she didn't know about. Draeson had been a regular visitor to Keldan throughout their marriage, but Keldan had never mentioned being part of a deal with the mage. He'd simply explained it as an old and powerful family friend.

As she read the entry, Latricia's eyes widened. At last, she closed its pages and set it down on the desk, pushing it as far away from her as she could. She stared at the candle flame.

"Information is power," she whispered to herself. She could still hear Keldan telling her that. Whether it be business deals or politics, it was a truth he'd firmly believed.

A noise outside caught her attention. Someone was

in the garden.

Curious, Latricia blew out the candle and moved to the window, shifting the heavy drapes just enough to peer through a crack. A dark figure moved, just inches away from the glass. She let out a gasp and froze, but the figure didn't seem to hear her and moved on. With a trembling hand, she pulled the drape aside a little more and watched as the dark shape followed the line of the house, then paused at another window. Roydan's office.

The figure knocked on the glass and, after a moment, the window opened and light spilled out, silhouetting the figure as he passed a slim crate, the length of a man's arm, through to whoever had opened the window, then climbed inside.

Latricia frowned. Who would be climbing into Roydan's office in the middle of the night? If it had been his bedroom, the answer would be obvious, but not the office.

She moved back from the window, fumbled in the dark for the journal and slipped it back into the drawer. Keldan would have wanted to know who was visiting his father as well. She could almost hear his voice coming from the journal, encouraging her to find out.

"What's the old goat up to now?" he'd have said. "Middle of the night means something sneaky."

Her lips moved silently to the rest of it. "And something sneaky means something we can use."

She slipped out of Keldan's office and pushed the door closed behind her with the barest of clicks. The hallway was black, but her eyes had adjusted to pick up the faintest trace of light and her feet knew every twist and turn. The crack beneath the door to Roydan's office was like a strip peeled off the sun and left lying on the floor. She crept up to it and pressed her ear against the wood.

"Are you happy with it?" a strange man's voice said.

"Yes." That was Roydan. "That will do nicely. You think they'll be able to deliver to Sandilar, as promised?"

"I do. They're very eager for you to succeed."

"Good." There was a scraping sound like a chair being shifted on the floor. "What about Brannon and his lot? Are they getting anywhere close to this? I don't want everything messed up because Keldan was in the wrong place at the wrong time."

Latricia felt a shock run through her. Was Roydan interfering with the investigation? What could he possibly be doing that he would value over finding his son's murderer?

"I don't think so," the stranger's voice said. "He spoke to the Nilarian ambassador today but I don't think there's any harm in that."

"Good. Keep an eye on him and make sure he doesn't get in our way." Roydan paused for a moment. "Bring anything he finds out about who killed my boy to me as quickly as you can. Whatever Aldan has planned for him, I'd like to get there first."

"Of course, My Lord."

"Hooded Blood and Tears, I hate that he's gone." Roydan's voice was thick with emotion and Latricia sagged in relief. For all their differences and competitive ways, Roydan had loved his son. Somehow that helped. "Do you think . . . Is it possible that our arrangement is somehow responsible for what happened?"

Whoever the stranger was remained silent for a

moment, considering. Latricia felt as though her insides had been hollowed out with a giant scoop. If Roydan had somehow caused her husband's death . . . her mind struggled to comprehend the betrayal. It must have been possible or Roydan wouldn't ask. What had he been doing? Almost without thinking, her hand reached for the door handle, but she held it still when the stranger spoke again.

"I don't think so. There was silk in the room, but that doesn't mean anything. It's a very strange case. It doesn't seem like business to me. It seems personal."

Roydan sighed. "But personal to whom?" The chair scraped again as he got up. "I'll fetch your payment."

Latricia scurried away from the door, her heart thudding painfully until the moment she was inside her bedchamber and alone. She took several deep breaths to calm herself enough to think.

Information was power, Keldan had always told her. Well, she'd found information aplenty tonight. The question was, how was she to use it?

CHAPTER TEN

It was a warm day with just a light haze of cloud obscuring the sun as Brannon waited on the docks with Draeson and Jessamine for the expert on Djin rituals to arrive. The smell of freshly caught fish, wet wood, and boat tar mingled with the screech of gulls fighting for scraps and the shouts of fishermen and sailors going about their daily business.

A message had come early that morning from Valda that the boat from Djinan had turned into the Alapra Canal and was moving fast. They should expect the arrival of their expert in just a few hours. Brannon could see it approaching now, a kind of multihulled canoe on a large scale, travelling at least three times as fast as the boats around it.

"Jessamine, could you go and see if the harbor master has a scope we could borrow? I'm curious to get a look at this boat."

"I'd rather not," Jessamine said, scrunching her face apologetically. "If it's okay, I'd rather stay here with you." Since coming across the body in the cupboard, she had become almost clingy, as though the fright had regressed her to a girl much younger.

"You'll have to get used to being alone again soon," Brannon told her gently.

"I know. But . . . " She shrugged. "I never had anyone murdered and stuffed in a cupboard back home in Trallene."

"Don't worry," Draeson said, putting a protective arm around the girl's shoulders. "I'll make sure you're safe." He made as if to walk with her on the errand.

"Ah, no, Draeson." Brannon held up three fingers. "Three cuts."

The mage looked puzzled. "What?"

Brannon gestured to his face. "For every wrinkle. Three cuts." He gave him a stern look.

Draeson pulled his arm away from Jessamine with a huff. "Fine. But this is boring."

"You should have made yourself look like a teenager," Brannon told him.

A familiar figure was moving toward them through the crowd. Sailors and fishermen alike moved aside for Master Jordell as the old man passed by. Brannon felt a warmth in his chest. It was good to see the kind of respect the master physician engendered in regular people. Respect based on having been a force for good and healing when they needed it. Brannon had always been given respect for his battle prowess and his position close to the king, but the natural, easy grace Jordell commanded was something different.

Jordell's craggy face broke into a smile as he came closer. "There you are. I hear you have a Djin arriving this morning to help with the investigation."

Brannon nodded.

"I'm impressed. They usually keep to themselves. Meanwhile, you might like to know that we still haven't had anyone come to claim the body that was put in your closet. I'm fairly certain it was the one taken from our morgue that morning though—despite the extra facial mutilation. The poor girl was the one I sent you the message about. I guess whoever it was couldn't wait for you to come and see her at the morgue."

"Perhaps they didn't know if I'd be told about her. Which rules out someone working at the physician college. Were there any strangers seen in the morgue that morning?"

Jordell shook his head. "If only it were that simple."

"Where was she originally found?" Jessamine asked quietly.

"Not far from here, actually. I would have pegged her for a dock whore, but that doesn't fit if she was with Keldan Sandilar."

"No, Keldan's definitely not the type to go slumming with his women," Draeson said. "She must have been dumped here by the killers."

"But why?" Brannon said. "Why not leave her at the Blue Rose? And why move her body again later?"

"Taran thinks it was a message," Jessamine said. "That the killer wants us to leave him alone now that he's given us what we were looking for."

"If he wanted to be left alone, he wouldn't have murdered a member of the royal family," Brannon said. "There's something bigger going on here but I'll be a Hooded Wolf if I know what it is."

The Djin boat was closer now, and Brannon could see that the deck built across the canoe hulls like a raft had small cabins on it and rails around the side. It had a single mast with a wide, square sail but little effort seemed to have been made to make the most of the wind. The water beneath and around the boat churned as though boiling as the craft approached the docks at high speed. There was no sign of any oars or propellers.

"How are they doing that?" Brannon wondered aloud.

"They have elementals pushing the boat," Draeson said. "I wonder what they're paying them."

"Paying them?" Brannon turned to look at the mage as the boat began to slow and approach the dock. "What would elementals want?"

"Exactly. And if you get it wrong, they'll run amok."

"Great." Brannon watched the water closely. It roiled and thrashed. "How many elementals do you think are in there?"

Draeson's voice was low. "To get here this quickly? A lot."

The boat pulled up and dusky-skinned sailors scurried to secure it. Brannon and the group moved forward, but kept a healthy distance from the water itself.

As the sailors worked, Brannon sidled up to Master Jordell. "Were you able to find out anything about the other thing I asked you? Have there been any similar murders?"

"Nothing in Alapra," Jordell murmured, not taking his eyes from the water. "But there have been rumors of it elsewhere. Details are scarce and no one seems to have a clear idea of where. It could just be that people are speculating. Keldan's death was strange enough to spawn all sorts of rumors."

Brannon sighed. "True. I guess I should just ask Aldan directly."

Jordell clapped him on the shoulder. "You were always fairly successful with the direct approach."

At his words, a plank was lowered from the boat and a single figure walked across to the dock. Brannon hurried forward to meet her.

The Djin woman was barefoot. She wore a leather smock decorated with colorful stitching, coral beads, and painted marks. It was low cut at the top, clung to her curves, and finished mid-thigh, leaving her legs bare. Her skin was the dusky purple of all Djin, and she was covered in black tattoos similar to the marks painted on Keldan when he had been found. The symbols twined up her calves and thighs, spilled down her arms from her shoulders, and trailed across the space above her cleavage like ink necklaces. Her hair was dark and dreadlocked, with threads of gray, and hung down past her shoulders. Beads were threaded through the dreadlocks, some polished or painted wood, others coral or shell. Her face was kind, and her age hard to judge with only a few crow's feet wrinkles in the corners of her eyes.

Brannon approached, his hands raised and open. "Welcome to Alapra. On behalf of King Aldan of Kalanon, I offer you welcome and our thanks for coming. I am Sir Brannon Kesh, King's Champion."

The woman held up a hand to pause him and tilted

her head to one side as though listening intently. "Please to talk not fast," she said, her thick accent sounding as though she spoke through a mouthful of her hair beads. "I am Ula. Am good to meet but first to thank the spirits."

"She means the elementals," Draeson said as the others moved up beside him. "Introductions won't mean much if she doesn't keep them happy."

Brannon watched as the Djin woman knelt on the dock and spoke to the water elementals beneath. The language was a mix of guttural sounds, clicks and trills, a rough, earthy sound. He found himself wondering if the Hooded One, with his connection to animals, sounded something like this.

After speaking for a while, Ula cupped her hand under her chin and spat big gobs of saliva into it.

"What is she doing?" Jessamine said, her eyes pinned to the strange woman.

"I don't know." Brannon looked at Draeson but the mage only shrugged. "Just hope it works."

Careful not to spill the captured saliva, Ula lay on the edge of the dock, heedless of her smock riding even further up her legs, and reached her cupped hand down toward the canal.

The water churned even more violently than before, slopping and sloshing about, boats rolled and strained against their moorings. Then a huge wave spurted up and washed over Ula's hand, washing the saliva she'd offered into the water. Instantly the disturbance ceased, and the canal went back to normal.

Draeson swore. "What the Blood and Tears was that? They should have torn her apart!"

Ula rolled back to face them, smiling. "Done now," she said. "Show me dead person."

Brannon was pleased they had a carriage to take them to the Blue Rose. Somehow he couldn't imagine walking or even riding through the streets with the Djin woman. Already a small crowd had gathered outside the Rose when they arrived.

"You might want to dress differently while you're here," he suggested to her. "I can arrange for some Kalan clothes, if you like."

Ula looked down at herself then met his eye directly. "No," she said.

Jessamine smothered a snort of laughter.

"Er, that's fine too," Brannon stuttered.

The Djin woman was the only one of her people to remain in Alapra. As soon as her belongings—two leather bags painted like her clothes—had been unloaded, the multihulled boat had pushed off, this time sliding down the canal at a more usual pace. It seemed the elemental assistance had been for Ula's benefit only.

Brannon helped Ula and Jessamine down from the carriage then stood aside for Draeson before leading the way up the stairs of the Blue Rose. Mala met them at the doorway.

"You're back at last. Does this mean I'll have my room back? Who's going to pay for having blocked it up all this time?"

"You'll be paid, Mala. Don't worry." Brannon said. "Besides, I thought it was good for business having something so exciting on site."

"It was, until you told your soldiers not to even let anyone take a peek. Now we just get disappointed sightseers taking up space from my regular customers."

Brannon gestured to Ula. "Well, this is the expert we've been waiting for, so we should have things back to normal soon."

Her eyes widened as she took in the Djin woman. "Well, good." She huffed and waved them toward the stairs. "Go on up then. The sooner the better."

The temperature dropped at the top of the stairs, and was markedly cooler when they reached the door to Keldan's room. The guards stepped aside and Brannon opened the door to reveal the clear, green-tinged resin encasing the room.

"Better let me deal to that," Draeson said, stepping forward. He placed his hand on the substance and closed his eyes. His lips moved silently and then there was a hissing noise and the crystal dissolved into mist.

White fog rolled out from the doorway. It swallowed Draeson, then rapidly filled the hall until Brannon could see nothing. A chill that had nothing to do with the temperature ran over his skin. "Draeson? Everything okay?"

Somewhere behind him a foot scuffed the ground. A cough came from somewhere else nearby. "Draeson?"

Something touched his hand and he grabbed it roughly, reaching for his sword before he recognized Jessamine's fingers. "Sorry," she said. "Just a bit spooked."

Draeson's voice emanated eerily from somewhere inside the room. "Probably should have opened a window first. Hang on a minute."

Moments later a breeze swept through and the fog broke into tatters that drifted apart and dissolved entirely.

Brannon stepped into the cleared room. "Some warning would be good next time."

Draeson shrugged.

Ula and Jessamine followed them in. Ula murmured something in her odd language as her eyes swept the room.

Nothing had changed since Brannon had seen it last. There was an odd sort of shock in seeing it all the same. Keldan's corpse lay exposed with the same level of indignity, without even natural decay to offer release. The only difference was the smell. It was a moment before Brannon realized that Draeson's magical fog had taken the smell of death out of the room.

"This be just as you find him?" Ula asked.

Brannon nodded. "Yes. The symbols on his skin and on the wall made us think . . . Well, they're like yours." He gestured to her tattoos. "Do you think someone could be trying to work Djin magic? Or could it have been a Djin?"

Ula shrugged. "If there be Djin in Alapra, you know it. Look like me—look different to you. Maybe someone copy."

"Maybe." Brannon had to admit, there was little chance of someone like Ula going unnoticed in Alapra. Kalanon was still a nation nervous of foreigners and the dusky purple skin and dreadlocked hair of a Djin would certainly stand out.

He watched as Ula leaned over the body, showing no sign of discomfort at the proximity of a corpse. She peered at the symbols, her fingers tracing them on the gray skin. Her mouth worked and she muttered angrily to herself. She lifted her finger to her nose and sniffed, then shook her head.

"What is it?" Jessamine asked, curiosity propelling her a step forward

"Was done by person that knows too much and not enough." The Djin woman straightened up. "These symbols are ours. They are powerful and only known by shamans. No Kalan would know them."

Brannon rubbed at the scar on his face. It couldn't be a Djin because they'd be too noticeable and it couldn't be a Kalan because they wouldn't know the symbols. At this rate Ula would eliminate the entire world of suspects. Perhaps the Hooded One had snuck in and drawn the symbols for a laugh. "What are they used for?"

"They part of magic to make Risen, but not work here because done wrong. Not shaman trained," Ula said. She flapped her hand at the markings on the wall and laughed. "Foolish to mark on wall. Want Risen building? Ha!"

"But they are true Djin symbols?" Brannon said.

Ula's laughter died. Her jaw tightened. "Yes. This be very bad. Someone try to make Risen. Or maybe try to make it look like Djin are here making Risen. You say there other murders like this?"

"Not here in Alapra, but yes, we think so."

"Then you must take me to see this also. Maybe person want something else too." She paused, one hand circling in the air as she searched for words. "Maybe a thing bigger than . . . " Her hand jerked toward the body of Prince Keldan.

Brannon sighed. "Maybe. Either way, it's time we had a talk with the king."

CHAPTER ELEVEN

The lock on Duke Roydan's office door gave way with a satisfying click. Latricia slipped the key into her pocket, stepped inside, and closed the door behind her. The room had a musky, incense sort of smell, mixed with that of leather and old books. It was a little bigger than the office Keldan had used, but shaped much the same way. The desk was the same rich mahogany, but the chairs were high-backed, polished brown leather. The ceiling was a fresco of the battle between Valdan and the Hooded One, their violence spilling gold blood into the mountains of Sandilar. The walls were lined with bookshelves and cabinets with elegant mother-of-pearl inlay designs on the wood.

Latricia crept forward, her eyes scouting for the box she'd seen the mysterious figure bring with him the night before. Whatever Roydan was up to, it had to do with whatever was inside. When her maid had mentioned that Roydan had been summoned by the king for an update on Sir Brannon's investigation, Latricia had been angry that he'd not thought to invite her as well. How could he not realize she wanted to find out what happened to her husband? But she'd quickly recognized it as an opportunity to find out more about her father-in-law's plans.

Keldan had often snooped in his father's office—sometimes even with Latricia standing guard at the door—but Latricia herself had spent very little time in the room. Everything was very orderly. The papers on the desk were in careful stacks, the books were carefully in place. There was no sign of anything resembling a crate.

"Well, of course it wouldn't be easy," she murmured to herself.

The cabinets yielded nothing, even after a search of the desk drawers turned up keys for the ones that were locked. She'd hardly thought Roydan would have kept something important and secret in so obvious a place anyway. Certainly, Keldan never had. So she started searching for hidden compartments, levers and latches that were cleverly disguised.

A wall panel popped open with a nudge, to reveal a cavity holding nothing but gold ingots. It was the same panel in the same place as one of the secret spots in Keldan's office, so hadn't been hard to find. Latricia pushed it closed again. All these years she'd learned to be unimpressed with gold. Now, without her husband's connections, she wished she had some of her own.

Her gaze passed over the desk again. It was longer than the drawers had been, she realized. There could easily be a hidden space in the desk, behind the drawers.

She circled it, trying to spot any break or crack in the wood that would indicate a hinge or door. She pressed and pulled at the corners and edges, trying to find a switch to open it. Nothing.

Moving behind the desk, she pulled the heavy chair to one side, its feet silent on the rug, then got on her hands and knees to crawl into the leg-space. Her skirt tangled around her legs and she struggled a bit, trying to keep quiet as she did so.

She was about to try tapping the inside of the desk when realization struck her that the chair had moved silently. Last night, she'd heard it scrape on the floor. Last night, there had been no rug on the floor.

She crawled back out and looked at the rug. Lightweight, maroon and gold, and, she discovered when she pulled it up, tacked in place along one side only. It flipped up easily to expose the floorboards beneath. Floorboards which, with a little exploration, slid aside to reveal a cavity below the floor. Inside was the crate she'd seen the night before.

The outside of the crate was unmarked. Her fingers trembled a bit as she pried open the lid.

The contents were instantly recognizable. Latricia sat back on her heels. A bolt of silk. All this over the trade deal with the Nilarian ambassador? Why? The entire household and some of Roydan's competitors already knew the negotiations were underway. That's how Keldan had become involved. Why keep another delivery of samples hidden? And why receive them in the middle of the night?

She thought about the conversation she'd overheard between Roydan and the mysterious stranger. They'd mentioned the Nilarian ambassador, but hadn't thought she could reveal anything of danger to their plans. But if their plans were to do with the silk, surely she had to be involved?

Latricia turned the lid of the crate over in her hands. No ambassadorial seal. When Keldan had begun talking to Ambassador Ylani, he'd mentioned to Latricia that everything from Nilar had to go through the ambassador and be marked with the seal before it could be released to any Kalan. Could it be that this crate of silk had bypassed Ylani entirely?

Latricia tugged at the crate, tipping it this way and that so that she could see the sides. It was heavier than she'd expected. There was no sign of the seal anywhere.

A noise out in the corridor made her jump. She lost balance and put out her hand to catch herself. It pushed into the silk and struck something else hidden in the fabric—something hard.

A deep voice said something just outside the door. Latricia fumbled the lid back onto the crate and pulled the floorboards back into place. She stood just in time to see the door handle turn and Duke Roydan stepped into his office. He saw her and stopped. "Latricia?"

Her breath seemed to be squeezed out of her by the tightness in her chest, but she forced herself to speak. "Roydan! You surprised me. Ella said you'd gone to see the king."

His eyes narrowed. "Not yet. I'm about to leave."

"Oh. I . . . I thought you'd already left." She could feel her face flushing and prayed there was enough powder on her cheeks to cover it. She nudged the rug back into place with her foot, speaking very fast. "Do you think he will release Keldan's body to us at last?"

He moved toward her. "I don't know. Latricia, what are you doing in here? I usually keep this door locked."

"I'm sorry. I didn't mean to intrude." Her heart was racing as she stepped out from behind the desk. "I was playing hide-and-seek with Tommy and I forgot to tell him your office was off limits. I thought I'd better check to see if he's in here."

Roydan looked her over, his face stern. "Hide-and-seek?"

Latricia nodded, her mouth suddenly dry. "Yes. Given that he's lost his father so recently, I wanted to spend some time with him—let him have a little fun. You understand."

"Hmm. Well, mind you don't spoil the boy with too much attention. We don't want him crying for his mama all the time when he gets back to Sandilar, do we?"

His words were like a cold shard in her stomach. "Why would that be an issue? Surely I'll be there as well?"

"Will you?" Roydan's voice was painted with consideration, but Latricia could hear the gray, flat words underneath. "I thought you'd like to stay here, in Alapra. You've friends here, after all."

So it was beginning already, Latricia thought. She was being edged out of her son's life so she could be abandoned without a fuss. Or was this merely a threat to let her know how things could go for her if she made her presence difficult?

"I think I'd rather stay with my son," she said. "It would be hard on us both to split what's left of our family."

Roydan shrugged. "Well, there's no need to decide right now, is there?" He reached out a hand to her shoulder and gently guided her toward the door. "Why don't you go check in the drawing room? I suspect Tommy could still fit in the cupboard there if he was keen to hide."

She forced a smile. "Good idea."

When the door closed behind her, it was all Latricia could do not to pick up her skirts and run. She forced herself to walk at a proper pace, but her head was swirling with thoughts.

She now knew the silk was just a cover. Whatever Roydan was really up to had to do with whatever was hidden beneath the silk in that crate. Though she tried to deny it, Latricia felt the heavy sensation in her gut that told her she'd already figured out what had been hidden there. Thin and hard, she was almost certain that her hand had pressed against a sword. The crate was long enough for one.

Nilarian silk and Nilarian swords hidden in a Kalan nobleman's office. It sounded like treachery. What possible legitimate reason could Duke Roydan have?

She could imagine Keldan's response. "Go to the king," he'd say. "Expose him for what he is!" Impatience had always been his flaw.

No, she thought, reaching the parlor at last. This would have to be thought through carefully. If she made an accusation without clear proof, the king would not believe her. He would listen to his cousin and, even if a search was conducted, Roydan would likely have time to move the evidence.

Worse, if there *was* a legitimate reason for what was

going on, she would have made herself Roydan's enemy for nothing.

"Ahpra's Tears." She sank into a chair and covered her face with her hands. She could not afford to make Roydan an enemy. Her position was tenuous enough as it was. If she gave him any excuse to cut her off, she would be out on the streets and never see her son again.

She needed someone else to work with her. Someone who could find the evidence. Someone she could trust to keep her involvement secret and that the king would have to listen to. Someone Roydan had no hold over.

But who?

CHAPTER TWELVE

Brannon expected that they would be shown to the throne room for a formal presentation of Ula Lanok to the king. He was surprised when, instead, the steward led the way along the east corridor to the private audience chamber. The king sat alone at the window table and gestured for them to join him. Extra chairs were quickly brought for Taran and Jessamine, who sat just behind Brannon, Draeson, and Ula.

"Welcome," King Aldan said after Brannon introduced Ula. "Our thanks to you for your journey and your expertise. We are very grateful."

Ula bowed her head. "You be right to send message. It be our duty to monitor the kaluki."

"Kaluki?" Aldan looked to Brannon, who shrugged.

Ula's nose wrinkled and her hands moved as she tried to find the words to explain. "Kaluki make Risen. Djin be to limit power of kaluki in this world."

The king leaned forward in his chair. "And you

think one of these kaluki is here in Alapra?"

Ula shrugged. "Probably no. Maybe."

Brannon couldn't help a chuckle at Aldan's expression. It was so like the way he'd looked as a young man when Brannon had tried to explain to him a particularly complicated battle plan.

The king caught his eye. "Perhaps you could give me the summary of what you've discovered so far. I've asked Roydan to join us shortly, but I'd rather know what there is to tell before bringing him in. Some things are too upsetting for a father to hear."

Delivering mission reports was something very familiar to Brannon, but this one was unusual. As he described the various facets of the case, he watched his old friend's expression. Aldan listened intently, occasionally asking questions of Brannon or one of the others—he queried Taran about the drug used and whether he could be absolutely certain of the type. Taran assured him that he was. When Brannon mentioned the rumors of other killings of a similar nature, Aldan looked sheepish.

"Ah," he said. "I should have known you'd learn about that on your own."

"So it's true." Brannon leaned back in his chair and spread his hands wide. "Why didn't you mention it?"

Aldan tightened his lips and looked around at the group. "I suppose there's no harm in it now. You're my eyes and hands in this matter. But keep what I tell you to yourselves. I don't want any of what I'm about to say to be repeated to anyone else. Do I have your oaths?"

They all swore except Ula. "I must report to the Council of Priors," she said. "But will not tell for any other if your wish it."

"Fair enough," the king said. "I couldn't expect more than that. The priors never interfere with the politics of other countries anyway."

Ula nodded. "Is correct policy."

Brannon frowned. "So you think this is political?"

Aldan sighed. "I don't know what to think, but I'm worried. The day after Keldan was killed, a report came from Sandilar describing two murders there with painted symbols on the body and surroundings. It's hard to believe they're not connected."

Brannon swore. "Was there a connection between the victims? What did Roydan say?"

"He doesn't know."

"What?" Brannon sat forward. "It's his territory. How can he not know?"

"When the report came in, he was in the first day of mourning and would see no one. The messenger brought it to me instead. I decided it was best to keep it quiet because I don't want people panicking and I didn't want to upset Roydan further. Grieving his son is burden enough for now."

"He'll hear about it eventually," Draeson pointed out.

"Eventually," Aldan agreed. "In the meantime, it seems that investigating all three murders is the best way for you to figure out what's going on."

"Agreed," Brannon said. "Someone is playing a bigger game here. I just wish we could see what it is. The obvious notion is that someone is trying to start a war between us and the Djin. Deaths set up to look like Djin rituals would do the trick. But it's a sloppy attempt at the ritual and the whole thing would be out of character for the Djin."

"We wouldn't have known how sloppy it was if Ula hadn't come," Jessamine pointed out. "Magus Draeson only knew enough to identify the symbols as being from Djinan. Perhaps that's all they expected us to know." She fell silent under their collected gazes.

"Good point," Brannon said. "So who would benefit from a war with Djinan?"

"No one," said Ula.

"Nilar," said Draeson.

King Aldan sighed. "I'm afraid the magus is right. Our current peace with Nilar has lasted so well in part because our resources are balanced. We were both weakened by the war and both rebuilding. If Kalanon were to go to war with Djinan, our forces would soon be weakened enough for Nilar to invade again and win. I doubt they want our gold mines any less now than they did seven years ago."

Brannon stroked his scar. "As plans go, it's a bit of a long shot."

"Maybe," said Draeson, "but they don't lose anything if it fails. Worst case scenario for them is they've killed a few Kalans. They probably think that's a good day's work."

"They haven't been afraid to play dirty in the past," Aldan said.

Brannon let his hand slide up to rub his eyes. He suddenly felt very tired. "Let's not let that idea get out to the public either. So far, it's just speculation."

A knock on the door preceded a page announcing the arrival of Duke Roydan. Brannon watched his old friend closely, trying to gauge how he was coping with the loss of his son. Roydan held himself tall and moved with a kind of challenging stiffness. He bowed to the king, then took his place beside him. "What can you tell me about who killed my boy?"

Brannon stayed quiet as Aldan spoke. The king relayed most of what he had just been told, but left out some of the conclusions and speculations. "Obviously there is more investigation to be done," he finished. "Brannon and his team will keep digging until they find out who did this and why."

"Thank you," Roydan said. "I've been thinking about that myself. You know about the negotiations for a silk trade deal with the Nilarian ambassador. I suspect that whoever killed Keldan was one of my rivals for the deal. You say Keldan was after it as well, so that means they were able to remove him and throw me off my game in one move."

"Someone would kill over that?" Jessamine asked.

"People have killed for less," Draeson said.

Roydan nodded. "The deal will be worth a lot of money. I can't think of any other reason someone would want to kill Keldan."

Brannon met the king's eye and tilted his head.

Aldan sighed, and nodded. "It's not just Keldan, I'm afraid. There have been other murders that look similar. People who aren't connected to the silk deal."

Roydan frowned. "There have? Who?"

The king moved across to his desk, pulled a sheet of paper from one of the drawers and handed it to his cousin. "This came from Sandilar."

Roydan looked over the report then closed his eyes.

"You knew them?" Brannon asked.

The duke nodded, then opened his eyes and shrugged. "Not well. It's nobody important."

Brannon scratched at the corner of his scar where it met his earlobe. "Well, just the same, we'll go to Sandilar and see what we can find out. There has to be a link between them."

Roydan shook his head. His voice was dull and flat. "No, stay here. Keldan is what's important. I guarantee this was a trade rival. I'll give you a list of names to investigate."

Brannon opened his mouth to protest, but then thought better of it. "That'd be good. Thanks. In the meantime, you'll be pleased to know you can have Keldan back for burying. Ula Lanok has seen him today and given us her insight."

The tension visibly left Roydan's shoulders. "Thank you. You said they were trying to perform some kind of ceremony?"

"A raising."

Roydan went very still. "Raising?" He turned to Ula, a terrible intensity in his face. "You can raise him from the dead? You can bring back my son?"

Brannon felt a chill run through him. How had he not thought to ask that?

Ula tilted her head and the beads in her hair clacked together. "I can make him Risen. You want?"

"Yes!" Roydan leaped out of his chair. "Bring him back! Where's his body now?"

"I had him moved to the crypt here in the palace," Aldan said. "Are we sure this will work? Draeson?"

The mage shrugged. "I think . . . I don't know."

112

"Ula," Brannon spoke carefully, wanting to be sure the Djin woman understood what he was asking. "If you make Keldan a Risen, will he still remember his life? Will he know his friends and family? I always thought the Risen were a mindless army."

She shook her head vehemently. "They have mind. Big mind or little mind, depending. Have memory too and body will work. But will be . . . not like before."

"Not like before—what does that mean?" Roydan asked.

"Oh," Brannon grimaced. "There was a lot of damage done to parts of the body, Roydan. I don't know if that will heal."

"Kaluki heal some," Ula said. "Not all."

"I don't care!" Roydan said. "Do it!"

Ula bent in a shallow bow, shadow falling across her face. "As you wish."

CHAPTER THIRTEEN

The palace crypt was one of the oldest parts of Alapra. Built of granite and marble and lit with smoky torches, it had a stifling, claustrophobic feel, heavy with the lives of the dead. Carved wolf heads adorned the walls, watching over the fallen. Some were interred in the walls, with plaques to mark their places. Others were in freestanding sarcophagi with painted representations of themselves on the lids. Kings and queens slept peacefully in faded pigment as preparations began to raise one of their fellows back to life.

Keldan's body had not yet been interred, but he had been cleaned and dressed and lain on a stone slab ready for his family to say their goodbyes. The inked marks had been scrubbed from his skin and the blood washed away. There was no sign of the mutilation that had been done by his killer. He wore a white linen shirt, and a teal coat embroidered with gold thread. Brannon thought he looked peaceful and very young.

Roydan stood and held his son's cold hand, his face a curious mix of emotion. Brannon couldn't help being glad his old friend had not seen Keldan the way he had been found. If Ula's magic failed, then at least Roydan would remember his son like this: clean, calm, and with dignity.

The others stayed back to give the duke a moment. Brannon and Aldan stood together beside the sarcophagus of Aldan's father. Brannon was still surprised to see how well the painter had represented the old king on the lid. Somehow it was always startling to see him there and remember he was gone.

Jessamine had stayed near the door, with Taran and Draeson on either side of her. Ula stood between the two groups, her bag at her feet and open curiosity on her face as she looked around the crypt. Brannon supposed Kalan ways of dealing with death must be as strange to her as the Risen were to them.

At last, Roydan stepped back from Keldan's body and looked up. "Okay," he said. "Do it."

Ula carried her bag to the slab and began removing several small clay pots and setting them next to Keldan's body.

Jessamine followed her. "Can I help?" she said quietly.

Ula handed her two of the clay pots. "One in every corner," she said, gesturing around the crypt.

Roydan hovered, seemingly unwilling to be more than a few steps from his son. Brannon took a step forward, thinking to go and comfort his friend, but Aldan caught his elbow. "Let him be," the king said. "He'll be okay."

"I hope so."

They watched as Ula now took a bundle of chaff from her bag, separated it, and tucked the larger portion back in.

Aldan leaned closer to Brannon, and lowered his voice. "Did you know Ula was a shaman or kaluki or whatever it is that can do this?"

Brannon shook his head. "Like a prize idiot, I never thought to ask."

Aldan chuckled. "I wouldn't worry about that. It's not a natural thing to think about. To be honest, it gives me the creeps."

"Death magic," muttered Draeson, joining them with an expressive shudder. "It gives anyone with sense the creeps."

"I expected Brother Taran to object," Brannon said as the young man helped Jessamine place clay pots around the crypt. "But he just seems fascinated by it all."

"He has a very inquiring mind," Aldan said.

Jessamine and Taran returned to the stone slab just as Ula opened another of the clay pots, this time dipping her fingers inside and bringing out a gob of reddish-brown which she used to trace symbols onto Keldan's skin.

"What's that?" Jessamine asked.

"Is earth from homeland," Ula said. "Help guide kaluki to this body."

Behind her, Roydan's clasped hands were trembling.

Brannon looked to his king. "Do you think this will work?"

Aldan sighed. "No. But Roydan needs us to try it." He met Brannon's eyes and for the first time Brannon

116

noticed his friend had aged. There was a fear in his eyes that hadn't been there even in the depths of battle. "I hope I'm wrong though. If it does work, it will solve a lot of problems. A living Keldan could tell us who attacked him and we'll have all our answers to what's going on today. Better yet, we'll be able to put a stop to whatever it is they're planning before it affects the birthday celebrations."

"You're really worried about this, aren't you?"

The king tilted his head. "This is a critical time for us as a nation. We've finally rebuilt to a point where we can throw a festival and celebrate." He gave a wry smile. "I'm not just throwing a party for my own sake, you know. It's a statement about our country's morale. If the people think we can't stop some lunatic committing multiple murders throughout Kalanon at a time of celebration, how do you think that will affect them?"

"They'll survive it," Brannon said. "They always have."

"But they shouldn't have to. And if it looks like Nilar is responsible for it, then sooner or later they'll get angry again and demand war." His face grew very serious. "You better hope we can clear this up quickly, Brannon. You won't get to play physician anymore if we go to war again. I'll need you back on the front line."

Brannon let his hand trail over the painted form of Aldan's father. "I know," he said. His sword felt very heavy at his side. How much more blood would it soak up before he could no longer lift it? "I know."

Over at Keldan's body, Ula was waving the others back. "The living must not be too close or might confuse kaluki."

Jessamine and Taran moved away and, after a brief hesitation, Roydan followed them.

Ula began to chant in her own tongue as she took the bundle of chaff and held it up to a torch flame. It burned easily and she moved it slowly across Keldan's body, just a finger-length above his skin. Ash drifted onto him like dark snowflakes, melting blackly into smudged marks. As the last of it burned, Ula crushed the flame between her hands, rubbing the remaining ash into her palms. Then she dipped a finger into the pot of dirt once more and drew a line from the top of her forehead down to the tip of her nose.

She fell silent and the crypt seemed to swallow up all other sound.

Brannon's skin prickled with sensation as the room filled with energy, lifting the hairs on his arms. He looked across at Draeson and the mage's face was tight. The dragon tattoo was stretched across his neck, tail reaching his collarbone and the head on his cheek. As the feeling of energy in the crypt intensified, the little dragon turned its head and hissed.

Brannon took a step back. When he looked again, the tattoo was still.

Ula began making a long, low hum in the back of her throat that seemed to vibrate the energy in the air. She leaned over the body and a string of drool oozed from her lips, glistening in the torchlight, onto Keldan's face.

Roydan scowled and started forward but Jessamine caught his arm and held him back. "Let her finish."

Ula spread her feet wide and squatted, bringing her face level with Keldan's. She stopped humming and took a deep breath. As she did so, the tingling left Brannon's skin, rushing toward the Djin woman as though drawn in with her breath. Then she blew. The sound of it echoed in the crypt like the north wind howling in the mountains. Her breath hovered at the edge of vision, as though it shimmered with something more than air. The shimmer spread across Keldan's face and seeped over the rest of his body, absorbing like ink into blotting paper then vanishing entirely.

For a moment, all the torches in the crypt dimmed, almost going out. Then the flames rose again.

Keldan sat up.

Brannon felt himself twitch in shock. He was not the only one. Jessamine gave a little yelp and King Aldan swore. "Blood and Tears!"

"Hooded Wolf, more like," Draeson said.

Roydan shook off the restraining hands and moved forward, his eyes wide. Brannon held his breath as his old friend called out. "Keldan? My son? Are you awake?"

Keldan ignored his father and turned to Ula. He worked his jaw as though stretching the muscles in it, then spoke. "So, shaman, you have brought me from my place to this one. It is not yours."

Ula stood and Brannon noticed suddenly that she was quite a small woman. She spoke with authority beyond her stature and appearance. "Kaluki, you are bound and must obey. Agreed?"

Keldan growled at her. "Agreed."

Duke Roydan paused in the process of reaching out to touch his son's shoulder. "Bound? Obey? What does that mean?"

Keldan's hand reached out and grasped his father's shirt. He lifted Roydan bodily into the air. His toes kicked above the floor and his hands grasped Keldan's arm.

"Blood and Tears!" Brannon was halfway across the distance between them, sword in hand, when Ula spoke again.

"Kaluki! Put down! No harm do! No touch!"

Keldan set his father down gently and sat still.

Brannon watched him and Ula warily, his sword up. "Back away, Roydan," he said. Let's keep everyone out of reach."

Roydan ignored him, his eyes on Ula. "What have you done to my son, witch? What have you done?"

Ula tucked the pot of dirt from her homeland back into her bag. "I do what you ask. Make Risen. Fresh body mean kaluki have much power. Very strong. Do much work."

Brannon felt as though something horrible was uncoiling in his stomach. "What do you mean when you say you made him Risen? Why would Keldan do that to his father?"

She gestured to where Keldan sat, impassive. "I put kaluki in body so can work. Is not Keldan. Is kaluki." She looked from Brannon, to Roydan, to Aldan and back. "Keldan dead," she said, as though explaining to a child. "He die."

"Ahpra save us," Aldan said. "What is a kaluki?"

Ula's mouth twisted and her hand traced circles as she searched for the right words. "Kaluki like spirits but not. They bad spirits. Want come from bad spirit place to here. Put in dead body so they use power to make it live

120

and not build up too much power in bad spirit place."

"Demons!" Brother Taran exclaimed. "You mean they're demons?"

Roydan began to tremble, his breathing fast and shallow. Brannon, not wanting to put up his sword, gestured to Jessamine who hurried to take the duke's elbow and ease him back to sit down on a bench. Aldan joined her, and took his cousin's hand.

"You put a demon in my son?"

"Let's not get too caught up in definitions," Draeson said. "Demon is a scary word. What you're saying though, is that something from another dimension is in Prince Keldan's body right now, is that correct?"

Ula nodded. "Yes. That is what it is to be Risen."

Brannon held out his left hand. "But wait. Before, you said you could bring Keldan back. You said he would remember his old life and everything."

She shook her head and the dreadlock beads clacked in chorus. "Not say can bring Keldan back. Say can make Risen." She pointed to Roydan, who sat with his face in his hands, shoulders shuddering. "He say he want it! Risen can use memory of life from body they have. It remember from Keldan memories, like you say."

Brannon finally lowered his sword as the full impact of the misunderstanding sank in. "By the Wolf."

Ula's voice took on an almost pleading quality. "No one can bring back dead person! Foolish to think!"

Brannon sighed and rubbed at his scar. "Yes, I suppose it was." He looked across at the animated body of his friend's son. This was worse than seeing him bloody and abused. At least then he had been himself. "What do we do now?"

"We question him," Aldan said. "If this kaluki has access to Keldan's memories, he can still tell us who killed him and why."

The thing that was Keldan began to laugh, a high-pitched, nerve-scraping sound. Brannon raised his sword again, half expecting the thing to lunge at one of them. It let the body shake with mirth for a few moments, then leaned forward to speak. "I can access memories of life, not of death. The closer the memory is to when the body died, the more likely it is lost." It pulled Keldan's lips back from his teeth in a malevolent smile and gave a mocking bow. "I cannot help you, Your Majesty."

"Ula?" Brannon turned to the Djin woman for confirmation.

She shook her head, unable to meet his eye. "I sorry. I did not understand what you asked. I cannot give you Keldan and cannot give you answers from his memory. I can only make him Risen or put him back."

Duke Roydan stood up, his hands clenched into trembling fists at his sides. "Then what good are you?" he said fiercely. "What good are any of you?" He strode from the crypt, and Jessamine, after a quick glance at Brannon, followed, with Taran on her heels.

Keldan began to laugh again and Brannon couldn't stand it. He pointed the tip of his sword at the thing's chest. "Shut up."

It obediently fell silent, lips twisted in a smirk. This was definitely not the Keldan Brannon knew. No matter what memories the kaluki inside had access to, it would not be kind to the dead man's family to allow them to see him like this. Brannon couldn't help feeling responsible for the pain this had caused Roydan. If only he'd known the right questions to ask before they'd started.

"Put it back, Ula," he said, sheathing his sword. "For Ahpra's sake, undo what you've done."

The Djin woman held out her hand and Keldan lay back down on the slab. Brannon turned and walked away. As he reached the door of the crypt, he felt a hand on his shoulder.

"Take the team to Sandilar," Aldan said. "Find out whatever you can about the other murders and get back here with some answers before the festival."

"What about Roydan's trade rival idea?"

The king shook his head. "Give him some space. After this, he's not going to be in a hurry to see you again soon."

CHAPTER FOURTEEN

Brannon had never really enjoyed travelling by boat. He could adjust to the gentle rocking motion easily enough, but there was a detached boredom involved in watching the world slide by on the banks of the river and not being part of it, that he found intolerable. In his younger days, he'd tried learning tasks to be useful but quickly discovered he had no aptitude for sailing. Now he knew to just keep out of the sailors' way and spent much of the time at the rail, watching the river and the various other boats as they passed.

The River Queen was a mid-level passenger and small cargo ship with big square sails and a crew mostly consisting of the captain's family. It wasn't the best boat available but it was the one willing to leave quickly and make a direct run to Trallene without stopping.

They had rounded Valda, the port sister city to Alapra, two days ago, entering the Tilal river from the canal and heading north. Little villages and farming communities lined the riverbanks on either side, houses, people, and animals like toys in the distance. Watching them made him feel alone.

On the river, there was nowhere to hide from your own thoughts and memories. Lately, too many of his had been about death and failure. He'd hoped that some space away from the happenings of Alapra would allow his mind to provide some clue or solution he had missed, but so far it had been unsuccessful.

When Ula joined him, he was glad. The Djin woman had spent much of the trip trying to improve her use of the Kalan language. It was one of the few distracting things on the boat and he suspected they both felt some lingering guilt about the misunderstanding at the palace crypt.

She still wore the same leather tunic-dress she'd arrived in and had refused offers for anything else. She had a musky, earthy aroma that was unmistakable. "Is peaceful," she said, then corrected herself. "*It* is peaceful here, no?"

Brannon nodded. "It is."

"Hard to think it be place where many died. It is near here that Nilarian army try to cross?"

"They crossed between here and Valda, yes." Behind his eyes he could see the soldiers spread out wide, as far as anyone could see. All of Eastern Kalanon was lost, and the Tilal, down to just a trickle, had been all that stood between the invaders and the cities and goldmines of the West. "They didn't know the Tilal and they figured the low water level was because of dry summer weather and that it was safe to ford."

"But it was not."

"No. We knew we didn't have the army to stop them. The river was all we had. It took all of our engineers and mages but we managed to dam the Tilal. Then we waited for them to cross. When the first quarter of their soldiers reached the other side, the water was released." He held his forefingers out, using them to divvy up the section of railing. "The middle half of their army drowned. The first quarter was stranded without support and the last quarter eventually ran for home. And that is how we won the war."

He looked up at Ula's face. Her dark eyes were somber. "A sound strategy," she said.

He gave a sigh. "Yes. Very."

In the distance, the riverbank on either side showed no sign of the carnage he remembered. But then, life was different in peacetime. As Aldan had pointed out, he was free to train and work as a physician much of the time now. As King's Champion, he still had duties at court and in the justice system but they were limited. Rather than plotting ways to kill more and more soldiers, he could spend time healing people who needed help. Going back to war meant being responsible for the kind of strategies that had drowned thousands. He wasn't sure he could face that.

He shook off the melancholy mood before it could overwhelm him.

Ula was quietly staring down at the water flowing past the hull.

Brannon followed her gaze. "Are you talking to the water elementals? The spirits, I mean?"

Ula shook her head. "I not know this river. The spirits here do not choose to speak."

"So, no chance of them speeding up the boat for us, then, huh?"

She gave him a rueful shrug. "Sorry."

"No problem." He scratched at his scar. "So what's the difference between the spirits and the kaluki? Are they the same sort of creature?"

Ula wrinkled her nose. "Same but not same." She spoke slowly, clearly trying to ensure she was understood. "In my language we call the earth spirits *kaluk* and the ones who inhabit the Risen *kaluki*. Earth spirits are good. They belong in this world and make it grow. Kaluki are evil. They want to destroy and control. They build power in their world so we bring them here and put them in Risen so they must use up power and not build too much."

The wind started to pick up, blowing a chill over them both. "So you make the Risen as a way to siphon off power from the kaluki in their realm? For you, managing demons is like draining a boil before it bursts or pruning a hedge so it doesn't grow too big?"

"Yes."

"And using a dead body, what? Contains them? Makes them use up their power? The one you put in Keldan was very strong."

"No," Ula disagreed. "It was a weak kaluki. Only strong because the fresh body let it bring most of its power. An old body uses up the power for repairs and making it work."

"And if you gave it a live body? Or no body at all?"

Ula's eyes opened wide and she muttered something in her own language before shaking her head in short, staccato bursts. "No, no, no. Must never! Kaluki in live body too powerful to control! Unbound kaluki in this world be bad. Very bad!"

Brannon thought about Keldan picking his father up off the ground with one hand. And that was a weak and bound kaluki. "Yes, I suppose it would be."

"It is the reason I come to your country. We cannot allow such a thing here."

"I suppose we're lucky the murderer doesn't seem to know what he's doing then or we'd have Risen or worse running around Kalanon causing problems."

Clouds were rolling in from the mountains and the afternoon turned dark. "Lucky, yes," said Ula. "Unless they try again."

The first heavy drops of rain splattered onto the deck and they turned and made their way inside. Passenger cabins ran along both sides of the ship, directly under the deck, with the cargo hold below that. A large hatch behind the main mast allowed access via winch to both levels but remained tightly closed when not in port. On the passenger level, this area beneath the hatch had floor boards put in place so it could be used as a shared living area where passengers could play cards, chat, or read a book in comfort without having to be restricted to their cabins.

Brannon and Ula moved toward the communal living area, passing Draeson and one of the sailors heading in the other direction. Draeson opened the door to his cabin and guided his companion inside with a hand on the small of the blond sailor's back.

"That's not the same one he was with last night, is it?" Brannon asked as the door clicked shut behind the pair. The Malon family, who ran the ship, were all deeply tanned with white-blond hair.

Ula smiled. "No, that be a different one. Lucky we have private cabins, no?"

"Indeed!" Brannon shook his head. Draeson seemed intent on sleeping his way through the entire family, male and female. He supposed he should be grateful the mage had turned his attentions to someone other than Jessamine. He much preferred him satisfying his "young body's needs" with someone Brannon wasn't responsible for.

Jessamine and Taran were in the living area playing cards. She looked up with a smile when they entered. "Just in time. We can deal you in, if you like."

Brannon shook his head, taking a seat nearby. "Thanks, but I'll just watch for now."

"I not know the game," Ula said.

"I think Jessamine's winning anyway," Brother Taran said. He had traded his full monk's robe for a shortened tunic version over pants and had left the cowl pushed back.

"Well, you can entertain us with stories instead," Jessamine said. "We were talking about scars and tattoos before you came in." She held out her arm and pointed to a pale patch of skin. "This is from getting too close to a forge when I was younger. Turns out I wasn't cut out to be a blacksmith! Brannon, I know you have a few scars from the war. Any good ones?"

Brannon snorted. "Good scars, or good stories of how I got them?"

Jessamine started dealing cards to herself and Taran. "Both."

He ran a finger along the scar that ran from his

earlobe across his cheek. "Well, this is the most obvious one and you probably know the story behind that."

"People say you got it fighting a Nilarian commander after infiltrating his command tent in the middle of their camp. That you killed him and kept the sword that cut you, as a souvenir."

Brannon shrugged. "That's pretty much it. I have a few others but they're just from being in a battle. Everybody gets a few cuts on a battlefield. Some of them scar."

"What about tattoos? Got any of those?"

"No." Brannon raised his eyebrow at her. "Did you ask Draeson about his dragon tattoo?"

She stuck her lip out in a mock pout. "Yes, and he told me to mind my own business."

Brannon laughed. "Yeah, that sounds like Draeson."

"He put it more, uh, colorfully than that, though," Taran said, causing Brannon to laugh even more.

Jessamine set down the deck of cards and picked up the hand she'd dealt herself. "What about your tattoos, Ula? Do they have a special meaning?"

Ula shifted in her seat and held out her arm to show the symbols inked into her skin. "They be rune magic taught us by the earth spirits. They keep this body from being home to kaluki." She tapped her temple. "Knowledge of shamans too dangerous to give kaluki. All shaman have runes to keep kaluki out even after death."

The tattoos twined extensively over her limbs and Brannon was willing to bet there were more that where hidden by her clothes. It must have hurt to get them done. That showed real commitment to learning to become a shaman. Would he have become a physician if Master Jordell had required tattooing before he could be taught?

"Fascinating," Brother Taran said. "I wonder how it works."

Ula shrugged with a little half-smile. "If you want to know, you must first get tattoos."

The sound of raindrops pelting down on the deck above grew loud and the conversation stopped while they waited for the summer squall to pass. Jessamine and Taran concentrated on their game, but with the sound of the rain and the boat's gentle rocking, Brannon found himself drifting into a doze. He woke when one of the sailors walked through the room. The rain had stopped and Ula was gone. The other two were still playing cards.

"Sorry to disturb you," the sailor said. He was tall and thin, with dark hair and pale skin. "Don't mind me. Just passing through. Do you need anything?"

Brannon shook his head and the sailor left by the other door, toward the ladder that lead down into the cargo hold. As he closed it behind him, Brannon noticed a couple of almost healed scrape marks on his neck.

"Glad you could join us again," Jessamine said as he wiped the sleep from his eyes.

Brannon stretched. He still had the soldier's trick of snatching sleep anywhere he could, but it no longer meant a comfortable body when he woke. "How long was I asleep?"

"Oh, not long," said Taran, collecting the cards from the table. "We just finished the game."

"Good timing then." He stood up and dragged the

chair he'd been sleeping in closer to the table. "Jessamine, with everything that's been happening, I've been failing you as a teacher. I'm supposed to be expanding your medical knowledge and helping you treat patients." He turned the chair backward and dropped onto it, folding his hands over the back. "So . . . let's make use of the time we have. What questions do you have?"

Jessamine sat back and fiddled with the end of her ponytail. "Actually, there is something I've been wanting to ask you. But it's not really medical. At Physician College, they say no one can progress beyond apprentice level without taking the oath. But you have, haven't you? How come?"

Brannon let his chin rest on his hands. "I'm something of an anomaly. I'm still King's Champion but I wanted to be a physician. They agreed that I couldn't take the oath under those circumstances because it refers to doing no harm. A physician's knowledge is a lethal weapon and part of my role as King's Champion is doing harm—either in trial by combat or, gods forbid, if we go to war again. That wouldn't apply in your case, for instance. If there's a war, you'll be a physician only. No one will expect you to fight."

"I know," she said, looking at her hands. "It's more the part about treating anyone who needs it. Mostly that's okay, but what if there's someone I can't bring myself to save?"

"You mean like the murderer?"

Her head gave a little shake. "A murderer I could treat and then the justice system would deal with him. It's just . . . " She swallowed and took a deep breath, her fingers knotting and unknotting together. "My mother died when I was young. She worked for a man in Trallene but she was very poor. When she got sick, I begged him for help. There weren't any physicians in Trallene, but Duke Roydan had one in Sandilar who could have been sent for. My mother had no money to pay for it and her employer refused and she died." Jessamine glanced up and there were tears in her eyes. "I don't think I could treat that man if he came to me dying himself."

"Nor would I," Taran said, gripping the deck of cards very tight. "Let the bastard die."

Brannon shot him a frown. Not a very helpful attitude from a priest! He tried to keep his voice soft. "I'm sorry about your mother. That was horrible. Especially when you were so young. I think every physician has someone in their past that they feel that way about. It's not supposed to be an easy oath to take. But being a physician is special. It's not like other jobs. We're a gift to everyone and we help keep life alive. It's not ethical to pick and choose who we'll deal with and who we won't. It's not as if we were sailors or . . . Blood and Tears!" He felt as though a chill had blown right through his clothes to bite into his skin.

Jessamine half stood as if to steady him. "What is it?"

Brannon stood and stared toward the door that lead to the cargo hold, finally seeing what his sleep-fuddled brain had missed. Dark hair. No tan. He wasn't one of the white-blond Malon family and he hadn't been working outdoors. Scratches on his neck. Lady Latricia had said she'd scratched the man in her garden.

The boat made a horrible groaning sound as if something was scraping its bones.

"That sailor isn't a sailor," Brannon said. "And we need to find him. Now."

CHAPTER FIFTEEN

Ylani felt the eyes of the mourners digging at her like hot needles. They didn't think she should be there, that much was clear. Hated her, in some cases, despite never having met her before. She made certain not to let any emotion register on her face. She'd had plenty of practice. Kalans were never shy about their dislike of her kind.

She kept her head lowered in respect. She'd been careful to research Kalan funeral customs. Her mere presence at the funeral of a murdered nobleman was challenging enough. She couldn't afford to stir up more trouble.

The ceremony was much as she'd expected for a church funeral service. The bishop led from the old stone altar at the front and offered comfort to the family as well as acknowledging the gods for their contributions: Ahpra for her gifts, Valdan for protection, and the Hooded One for mystery and the afterlife. The king spoke of the role Keldan held, as a member of the royal family and in Kalan society. Then family and friends were offered a chance to speak about their feelings and memories of Keldan.

Ylani, who had only known Keldan Sandilar briefly as a potential business partner, felt very out of place. Back home, she might have attended the funeral of a business associate as a mark of respect and an opportunity to network. Here, she thought she was probably doing her reputation more harm than good.

She tried to make herself seem as unobtrusive as possible. Her slim frame took up little space in the crowded pew and she'd chosen somber colors to reflect the occasion. Her hat was a small brown box with a fabric swirl on one side and one long feather. She'd considered it appropriately formal without being flashy. Nevertheless, she felt like a black mark on white silk and was still no closer to understanding why she was here. It seemed like a very long time before the ceremony came to a close.

The bishop urged everyone to stand as the family escorted Prince Keldan's remains from the church. Surprisingly, Duke Roydan had bucked family tradition and insisted that his son be cremated. King Aldan picked up the ornate box of ashes and led the way down the aisle to where priests waited at the door to take the remains to either a graveyard or family crypt. Ylani hoped she wouldn't need to push her way into that part of proceedings. She couldn't see it being well-received.

She fingered the note in her pocket as the box of ashes went past. It had arrived yesterday morning. The elegant script on thick paper made it look like a formal invitation, but the words were simple; a personal plea.

"Please attend the funeral of Keldan Sandilar. I need to speak with you in private."

The sense of importance that she got from touching it was still strong. Importance and sincerity. As soon as it had arrived yesterday morning, she'd known she was going to ignore good sense and do as it asked.

She let her breath rise and fall in a slow, deep rhythm, trying to find a place of calm where the instinct could speak to her. Somewhere in this church was the person who had sent this note.

"You've caused quite a stir being here today." She turned and saw Lady Latricia Sandilar had made her way back down the aisle. Her face was hazed by a thin veil of charcoal-gray. "In Kalan tradition, only the widow or mother wears a hat at a funeral."

Ylani licked her lips and nodded. She'd known that. "I don't mean to give offense. In my culture, we must always wear something on our heads."

"So I heard," Latricia said. "People say it's so you can try to hide from the gods when they look down on our world."

Ylani could tell there was no malice in the words. "Not at all. Actually, it's out of respect for them. We give them something pretty to look at."

There was a pause, as if Latricia was weighing up her answer. "Follow me," she said, and walked away.

Ylani moved swiftly after her. The widow was stopped several times by those who wanted to express their condolences, and Ylani kept her distance, not wanting to intrude. Each time, Latricia moved on, moving toward the back of the church until she slipped through a stone arch doorway.

"We won't be able to stay here for long," Latricia said, "but I need to ask you something important."

Ylani pushed the door closed. "Okay."

"Did you have any silk samples delivered to Duke Roydan in the last week?"

Ylani watched her face, trying to see a hint of the expression behind the veil. In the dim light of the small side room, it was impossible. Good sense insisted she could not tell a stranger, the widow of one potential business partner and the daughter-in-law of another, any information about trade negotiations at all. But she could feel the urgency coming off this woman in waves.

The last time she got a sense this strong was when she'd opened her mouth about additional murders to Sir Brannon Kesh. That'd been a mistake. The man hadn't known about them at all and now wondered how she did. This had the feel of digging herself into a similar hole. But a hole that needed to be dug.

"No," she said, truthfully. "Why?"

"Because some were delivered without your seal."

Ylani's head jerked up. "Silk? Nilarian silk?"

"Yes."

She chewed her lip for a moment. Someone back home was bypassing her. Someone on her staff was probably helping them. The knowledge clicked in her mind: True. She took a deep breath and forced herself not to swear aloud. "And?"

This time it was Latricia who took a deep breath. "And I think there were weapons hidden in it. And more are set to be delivered to Duke Roydan's manor."

"Blessed goddess!" Ylani covered her mouth with her hand and stared at the woman before her. If this were true and came to light before she could do anything about it . . . any hope of building on the fragile relationship she'd built between Nilar and Kalanon would be shattered. There was only one reason a Kalan noble would receive Nilarian weapons. "Do you know what you're saying?"

"That my father-in-law is planning to depose the king. Or, I think so, anyway." Latricia shook her head. "Do you understand why I came to you?"

"If you accuse him in public he will disown you and everyone will think you were trying to discredit him so that you could control Sandilar for your son. You want me to unmask the conspiracy in your place."

"Yes." The widow pushed the veil up from her face, her eyes boring into Ylani. "I don't think you knew. Your seal wasn't on the box. But that just means you have as much to lose as I do. Your people are betraying you and if King Aldan finds out about this he won't believe you weren't involved. You won't get out of Alapra alive."

The door opened suddenly and a balding priest blinked in the candlelight. "I'm sorry," he said. "Lady Latricia, Duke Roydan is looking for you."

"No problem. I'll come now." The widow pulled the veil back into place. She brushed past Ylani, clasping her hand for the briefest of moments. "Do we have an understanding?"

Ylani nodded, her chest tight. "Yes, I believe we do."

DARIAN SMITH

CHAPTER SIXTEEN

B rannon thumped on the locked cabin door
again. Muffled giggles could be heard on
the other side.

"Draeson, get out here!"

This time the mage called back. "Kinda busy right
now. Come back later."

The ship shuddered and groaned, the sound coming
from deep below Brannon's feet. "Hooded Blood,
Draeson, this is urgent!"

"Then you deal with it!"

Brannon took a deep breath, his jaw clenched hard.
He couldn't waste any more time on this. "Jessamine, go
and tell the captain that there's a stowaway on board
who may try to sabotage the ship. Taran, stay here and
try to get through to Draeson. Maybe he'll listen to a
priest."

Jessamine blinked once, then turned and ran for the
steps leading up to the deck.

Taran's mouth moved silently for a moment before

he found voice. "I, um, I'm not sure I want to interrupt him while they're doing . . . um . . . you know."

Brannon was already walking away. "Get him out of that cabin!"

He reached the other end of the ship quickly, found the ladder down to the cargo hold and took it two rungs at a time. He drew his long knife and held it in a loose, easy grip. It was dark and he let his eyes adjust for a moment, then felt his way forward carefully. The sound of rushing water was loud here, with the river directly beyond the straining timber of the hull.

In the dim light that spilled down from the hatch above, he could make out the hook where a lantern should have been. It was empty. Brannon felt around beside it for the matches that were kept there. He took one and struck it. The flare of light showed crates stacked and webbed in place. Nothing seemed amiss.

"I know you're down here," he called. "Why don't you show yourself and we can talk this out."

The match burned down to his thumb and went out. He got the next one ready but didn't strike it. Instead, he took a few steps forward, listening intently for any hint of where the sailor-spy could be hiding.

Something shifted to his left and he turned, knife ready. The shadowy shape of crates gave no hint of what might be hiding there. He moved closer and his feet made a little splash when he stepped, suddenly wet and cold.

"What are you doing here? You might as well tell me. You've been following us around. Who do you work for?" The noise came again and he struck the match in time to see several large rats scamper away, squealing.

Brannon carefully controlled his breathing and held the match out as he looked at his feet. They were submerged almost to the ankles in water. He looked behind him—there was water there now too.

"Ahpra's Tears!" He dropped the match and lit another, pushing past the crates and heading further into the hold as the water deepened. As he reached the hull, he realized that what he had first taken to be the sound of the river rushing by was in fact the sound of water pouring in through a hole the size of a man's head, in the side of the boat below the waterline.

The sound of splashing came from the other side of the hold as a dark figure dashed toward the exit. Brannon dropped his match and raced after him.

The figure was halfway up the ladder when he caught up to him. Brannon grabbed at the fake sailor's ankle, missed, and lunged at the man's leg with his knife. The foot lashed out and connected with his knuckles, hard. Brannon swore as the knife flew from his fingers.

The foot vanished to the deck above and Brannon followed after drawing his sword in case of ambush. His quarry hadn't waited. Brannon heard the door slam as he disappeared down the hall.

Cursing, Brannon started after him, then stumbled as the ship shuddered. The water pouring into the hold was already having an effect. He wondered how long it would take for a boat this size to sink at the rate it was filling. He hoped the captain could get them to shore before that happened. The only bright side was that this stowaway saboteur—and there seemed no doubt that he was the spy they'd seen in Alapra—was trapped on the sinking boat with them.

He ran through the empty common room and past Draeson's (still closed) cabin door, following the spy up the stairs to the open deck. "There's nowhere for you to go," he called. "You might as well give up."

The spy turned to face him and Brannon was vaguely surprised at how ordinary he looked. Even with the scratch marks on his neck, had it not been for the blondness of the family of sailors that ran this boat, he would never have stood out. His face was round and bland, lips just a fraction thin. His hands both held knives. "Don't you have a hole to plug or something?"

Brannon crept forward. "Who are you? Why have you been following us?"

The man shrugged. "You think I've been following you?"

"I know you have." Brannon watched for signs of an attack. Behind the spy, he saw Taran make his way toward them from the bow of the boat, then slow as he took in the situation. Brannon kept his eyes fixed on the intruder so as not to give the priest away. "What I don't know yet is whether you're the one who killed Keldan Sandilar, or if you want us to find the killer. I mean, why put the dead mistress in my apartment?"

The man gave a mocking little smile. "My, what an interesting life you lead."

"Tell us what you know and help me be boring."

"Why would I do that?"

Behind him, Taran dropped into a surprisingly good combat stance. "Um, peace of mind?" he said. "Unburdened conscience?"

The spy glanced around, trying to keep both of them

in view as best he could. "Huh," he said. "An unexpected surprise. Where'd you come from?"

Taran blinked but stayed silent.

"How about you focus on me," Brannon said quietly. "Put down your weapons and we'll talk about what's going on here."

The spy shrugged. "Not sure there's time for a chat, what with the boat sinking and all."

"We'll make time," Brannon said.

Jessamine's voice pulled his attention to the side. "Brannon, the captain says she can't control the ship. The rudder's not responding."

"Stay back, Jessamine!" he yelled, but it was too late. She'd stepped too close and the dark-haired spy seized her, one of his knives at her throat before she could scream.

Her eyes were wide and Brannon could see she was trembling. "What's going on?"

"What's going on," the spy said, "is that you gentlemen are going to back away and let me go or I'll kill your pretty friend."

Brannon felt his teeth clench. He put his sword on the deck. "Yeah, that's what's happening. Taran, back away."

"But . . . "

"Let him go."

The spy was already moving away, pulling Jessamine with him as he went. "Keep your distance, gentlemen. These knives are very sharp and I'd hate to get startled."

Despite his words, Brannon and Taran trailed after him as though tethered by rope. Brannon felt the rage like a tensed muscle inside him, ready to strike. His voice was low but it carried. "Jessamine is my apprentice. If you hurt her, I'll make sure you regret it."

Sailors gathered around, watching the strange procession as they made their way to the middle of the boat. The spy's grip on Jessamine remained tight and the knife tickling her throat kept everyone at a safe distance. He pressed his back against the main mast. Jessamine's lips were moving as though in prayer. She whimpered when one of the sailors got too close and he backed off.

"Don't do anything stupid," Brannon called softly.

"I have a question," the spy shouted, looking around at the sailors. "Do you think the captain can get a ship with no rudder to the riverbank before it sinks?"

"Don't you worry, sir," one of the sailors said. "As long as there's a sail to angle, the captain will get us safe."

Brannon thought he saw something shift in the spy's eyes.

"That's what I thought," he said. Before anyone could react, he slashed the knife across Jessamine's throat and pushed her away. She fell onto the deck, her fingers grappling at her neck as it turned red with blood. He stuck the knife through the hook in his belt, gripped the mast ropes, and began to climb.

Brannon lunged forward, as did several others, his stomach twisted sharply, warrior and physician fighting within him. He slid to his knees at her side and rolled her over to assess the damage. Jessamine was shaking, her hands pressed tight to her wound. Blood was welling up around them, but not as much as Brannon had feared.

"Let me see, Jessamine. It's okay. Let me see it." He

gently pried her fingers away. The slash was shallow and across the front of her neck. It had missed the arteries. "Thank the gods."

Taran hovered at his shoulder. "Will she be okay?"

"Yeah." Brannon's attention had already shifted to the man in the rigging. "Yeah, she'll be fine. Help her keep pressure on it. And see if you can sort out a bandage. She can tell you what to do, can't you Jessamine?"

She nodded shakily.

"Good girl."

The mast had rope loops tied around it and tacked into place as footholds. Brannon found they made scaling it easier than he'd expected. Ahead of him, the dark-haired spy had moved out onto the crossbeam and was sawing through one of the sail ropes with his knife. As Brannon got closer, the rope gave way and a small corner of the sail flapped loose. The man moved further along, stopped, and began cutting through the next rope.

"Why are you doing this?" Brannon called as he climbed.

The man didn't look up. "I don't like to leave a job half-done."

"What job?"

There was no answer. The next rope sliced free and he shifted again.

The boat shuddered and Brannon gripped the mast tightly. He looked down. Already the people below seemed like dolls. Crowded, worried dolls. The boat was listing obviously to one side as the pressure of the water flooding into the hold took its toll. He wondered how much longer they could stay afloat.

He reached the crossbar and wrapped his legs around it, using one hand to steady himself while he drew a dagger with the other. He slid along the bar, closing the gap between them quickly. "I warned you not to hurt my apprentice."

The spy shifted his weight then scissored his legs, twisting around so that he was facing Brannon. Then he shuffled backward to the next rope and began cutting. "How much of this do you think I need to cut to keep this Tear-stained boat from shore?"

Brannon moved into range. "I think you've done enough."

His first strike was lightning fast, but the dark-haired spy was faster. He blocked and lashed out with his other hand—and a second knife of his own. Brannon leaned back to avoid it and the tip tore the fabric of his jacket. His balance took a moment to recover and the spy jabbed down at him with the first knife in a rough, stabbing motion.

Brannon grabbed his wrist, stopping the blade before it reached his torso, and twisted. His assailant gave a satisfying yelp and pulled back. Brannon kept hold of the arm and yanked it to one side, hoping to throw him off the beam. The spy threw his weight in the other direction and they both gripped hard with their legs to stop the momentum.

Shouting from the sailors below distracted him for a moment and he glanced down to see them pulling a lifeboat from its cover. Ula was already with them, helping. The ship was clearly going down now, the back end of it very low in the water. Taran was still with Jessamine. Draeson had finally left his room and was looking around as though uncertain where he could be the most use.

"Help with the lifeboats!" Brannon yelled.

He felt, rather than saw, the shift in his assailant's body that meant a swing at him with the knife, and parried it quickly. Almost as quickly, the man jabbed again. Brannon scooted back on the beam, not letting go of the man's arm, and stabbed his own knife at his thigh. It was blocked.

The return strike aimed at the arm holding the man's wrist. Brannon let go to dodge, then thrust his other arm up and hooked him around the elbow, pulling him back and trapping the other arm instead—and his own knife hand with it.

There was barely a breath and the spy lashed out with his newly freed hand. Brannon jerked him to one side, pulling the aim away from its target. He felt the trapped hand twist, and the tip of the knife it held gouged into his side. This was no ordinary thug. This man had excellent training.

Brannon loosened his grip enough for the trapped arm to pull away, then dropped his own dagger and grabbed the wrist when it came close.

He drove his fist into the spy's stomach and when he grunted, followed it up with another punch to his throat. The second knife was ready though and scored a long slash across Brannon's forearm. He ignored the sting of the blade and rolled his hand around the other man's wrist. Now he had both wrists and they grappled, the fight quickly turning into a test of strength.

Keeping one arm out and high, Brannon concentrated on bringing the other one down and bashing the man's knuckles against the crossbeam. The man fought it, sweat dripping from his face, but Brannon was stronger. Blood covered his fingers before they loosened and the dagger fell to the deck below.

Brannon tightened his grip around both wrists. "Let go of the other one too," he growled. "Or it'll get the same."

The spy winced. "Okay, okay. You win."

There was a loud scraping noise and a splash from below, followed by loud swearing. Brannon risked a glance downward. The lifeboat had been launched and was rapidly filling with water. It slipped beneath the river, leaving sailors clinging to ropes to be pulled back up.

"Oops," said the spy, and laughed.

"What did you do?"

The man shifted his weight and swung his leg into Brannon's side, knocking them both off balance. Brannon gripped hard with his legs, refusing to let go of the other man as they both slipped off the beam. They hung there, Brannon upside down, ankles locked around the beam, the spy dangling from his grip. Below them, the ship shifted again and Brannon felt gravity trying to slide him along the beam toward the sail ropes. He squeezed his legs tighter.

"Hang on!" His fingers felt slick with sweat. If he lost his grip, the spy would be lucky to survive the drop. He needed to keep him alive if he was going to get answers. The sail flapped against his ear, one corner cut free, the rest still held in place. If he could grab it, perhaps he could use it to pull them back to safety.

"You are determined," the spy said. "I'll give you that." He pulled one hand free of Brannon's grasp, swung himself closer to the sail and grasped it. The other hand twisted and Brannon felt the edge of the knife it still held against his forearm. He swore and let go.

The spy slid down the sail, cutting the canvas as he went, leaving Brannon watching helplessly.

"Stop him!" he yelled as the dark-haired figure reached the end of the strip of sail and began to swing at the end of it like a trapeze.

No one was listening. Those on deck had abandoned the lifeboats—no doubt they'd all been punctured like the first. Some were gathered around the captain, others made their way to the bow of the ship, the highest point out of the water.

Draeson stood at the rail, his arm outstretched over the river. Even from this distance, Brannon could see the darker patch around his wrist that was the dragon tattoo. Mist jetted from his palm, down into the water. Where it touched, the river turned to ice. The mist spilled onward, circling the boat and freezing it in place.

Brannon swung himself back up to the crossbeam and scurried back toward the mast. He knew he would be too late. He slid down the mast, barely touching the rope footholds as he raced toward the deck. He barely felt the friction burn or the splinters.

The wooden deck hit his feet like a hammer. "Hey!" he yelled, pointing up at the saboteur who was swinging in wider and wider arcs on his strip of canvas. "Stop that guy!"

Even as they turned to look, the spy's swing took him out over the water and he let go, disappearing into the river with a splash. A moment later, Draeson's mist iced over the spot and he was gone.

CHAPTER SEVENTEEN

Ylani gave the page a moment to announce her before stepping through the door to King Aldan's private audience chamber. She wore her hair up, pinned under a small trilby with flowers on the side, with just a few loose ringlets to soften her face. Her dress was maroon silk with panels of burnished silver in the skirt and a flattering, low-cut bodice. The Kalan king was a man, after all.

Aldan sat alone with a checkered board and what looked like a chess set in front of him. As she approached, she noticed that only the white pieces were on the board. Aldan carefully moved a knight forward, then gestured to the seat opposite.

"Welcome, ambassador. I didn't think I'd be seeing you for a while."

Ylani settled in to the chair. "Why's that, Your Majesty?"

He shrugged as the page came forward and handed her a goblet of wine, then refilled his. "With everything that's going on recently, I thought perhaps you'd be laying low."

"There's no reason to," she said, taking a sip. "I've done nothing wrong."

The king pressed his lips together. "Of course." There was an odd silence for a moment and he gestured to the page and the game board. "Check with Ralvin." The page nodded, stared at the board for a moment, then left the room.

"That's not chess, is it?" Ylani said, intrigued.

Aldan shook his head. "It's similar, but the players are in different rooms with only their own pieces. You only get to know small amounts of what your opponent has done via a go-between. You have to try to think about what the other player will do, and respond accordingly. Then you hope you're right and that your pieces survive. Much like politics." He gave her a very direct look.

"It sounds like a difficult game. Easy to make a mistake."

"It is. But I find that it's often best to assume the worst scenario based on the information available at the time." He lifted his goblet to his mouth.

Ylani bit the inside of her lip as she searched for the right words. This wasn't going to be easy. How could she tell a king who was already suspicious of her to be suspicious of his cousin instead? "You're worried that I had something to do with Keldan Sandilar's death. I've heard the talk. But there's no reason for me to have done something like that."

Aldan shrugged. "Perhaps it would benefit your government."

She met his eyes and tried to put as much sincerity as she could into her words. "I can assure you, there is no official Nilarian plan at work here. My government would never sanction something like this."

"I find that hard to believe," he said coldly. "Given that the Nilarian government paid for an assassination attempt on my life only a few years ago."

Ylani sighed. "There are always elements within any government that are . . . unpredictable." She wished she could like Aldan. He was a likeable man, but his walls were high when it came to her people. "I'm sure you know what it's like. Politics isn't really like a game. You don't always know what your own pieces will do, let alone your opponent's."

"You're accusing one of my people, are you?" There was an edge to his tone.

"I'm saying that I'm willing to entertain the idea that a Nilarian might do something foolish without official sanction," she said carefully. "And I'm asking if you're willing to consider that the same might be true of the people close to you. What if the real threat is somebody you trust?"

The king set his goblet down abruptly and stood up. "Thank you for your concern, ambassador, but it's unnecessary. No Kalan would do something like what you're suggesting. We have never been the aggressors in a war. You can rest assured that I will keep control of my people as long as you are able to do the same with yours."

Ylani felt her hands clench and forced them to relax. The sad truth was that they had both already lost control of their people. What Lady Latricia had uncovered was clear evidence of a plot, but, just as clearly, King Aldan was not going to listen. Instead, she smiled politely, nodded graciously, and stood to leave. "Of course, Your Majesty. I can only hope this unpleasantness is resolved soon and doesn't do any further harm to the new relationship between our two countries."

In one of the gardens outside the palace, she found Latricia waiting. She had set aside her mourning gown and veil in favor of a day dress, and sat with a lace parasol next to a fountain in the shape of a dancing fish.

"Well?" the widow asked as Ylani approached.

Ylani shook her head. "There's no way he will hear it from me right now. Anything I said against Roydan would just make him dig his toes in more. He needs proof and he won't look for it on my say-so. We need to go to plan B."

Latricia snapped the parasol shut. "And what is that?"

Ylani perched on the edge of the fountain and let her fingers trail in the cool water. "We're going to pick up where your husband left off. You and I are going into business together."

CHAPTER EIGHTEEN

It was hilly, grassy terrain, speckled with large rocks and broken away cliff sides, but despite all that, what stood out most as being different to Alapra was the lack of water birds. This far from the river the familiar gulls and ducks were replaced by sheep and occasional cattle.

The journey from the wreck site had taken longer than Brannon would have liked. Draeson's magic had iced a path across the river for them to get to shore, but there was no town or pier for at least several days' walk in either direction and no hope of catching another ship without one. The sailors had split into three groups and sent one in either direction, with the third setting up camp where they were to keep an eye on the boat. Draeson had assured them it would stay partially afloat but couldn't say for how long.

Faced with the prospect of walking up river to Trallene, then inland as planned, or simply cutting across on the diagonal, headed straight for Sandilar, Brannon's group had decided on the latter. It was rough going, but a shorter distance to travel overall.

"I grew up in Trallene," Jessamine pointed out. She still had a bandage around her neck, but the cut was healing up nicely. Whoever he had been, their attacker had not intended to kill her. "Other than the port, we're not missing much."

"How far to Duke Sandilar's territory?" Taran asked as they trailed along a row of boulders.

"Already in it," she replied. "From about a day's walk south of Trallene, up to Fargrate, and then inland all the way to the mountains, is all Sandilar land. But Sandilar village and the manor are over that ridge ahead."

Behind him, Draeson tripped on a rock and swore. Brannon quickened his step to bring himself closer to Jessamine and Taran. "How long has it been since you were here last?"

She shrugged. "I spent a little time in Sandilar village before I came to Alapra to join the Physician's College. I haven't been back since."

"I still don't see why we couldn't have at least tried to get to a village and buy some horses," Draeson complained loudly.

Brannon ignored him.

"A horse would really be useful about now."

"Oh for Blood's sake, Draeson, shut up about the horses! You know why we're avoiding major settlements. There are likely others like the man on the boat, waiting for us. Do you want to get attacked again? You weren't much Hooded use the last time!"

The others stopped walking. Brannon felt his face

flush. He'd been furious about how things had gone on the boat for days.

"Sounds like you have something to say," Draeson said. He lifted his chin. "Spit it out."

Brannon looked around. The others were staring. This wasn't the time to do this. And yet, when would there be time? "You know what? Fine. You put us all at risk with your behavior on the boat. I don't understand how you can be four hundred years old and behave like a child!"

Draeson blinked at him. "I saved us on the boat!"

"No, you got us off the boat once it was already too damaged to continue. If you'd helped when I asked you to, instead of shagging random sailors like a teenager in heat, we could have saved the boat and be in Sandilar by now. You've let your new appearance go to your head. Grow up and stop acting like this is your second childhood!"

Draeson's jaw tightened. He stared into the distance for a long time, his breath loud and forceful through his nostrils. "Do you know why there are so few mages?" he said at last.

"Because they were all as annoying as you and killed each other?" Brannon said, before he could stop himself.

"It's because it takes at least a hundred years to master magical energies. How many people do you think live long enough for that, Brannon?"

Brannon frowned. "But, Ula . . . "

"Ula dabbles in freaks and elementals! What she does is nothing compared to true magic!" Draeson's eyes narrowed fiercely. "I spent my entire natural lifetime studying hard and searching for a way to live long enough to achieve my dream and serve my country. I had no childhood. No youth. I sacrificed them to become what I am. And what I am keeps this country safe. You and your army boys spending their wages on whores would be overrun by Nilarians now if it wasn't for me."

"You're not the only one who fought for Kalanon," Brannon said darkly.

"I'm the only one who has done it for almost four hundred years! Most of which was in a very old body—decrepit, I believe you described it as. So forgive me if, when I finally get a chance to return my body to a youthful state, I'd like to enjoy it!"

Brannon's anger drained away. "You still have to think about your responsibilities, though, Draeson. You can't put the rest of us at risk. Have your fun, but do it in your own time."

"Blood and Tears, Brannon. I'm well aware of my responsibilities, thank you very much. Nobody died. Leave it alone!"

Brannon opened his mouth to press the point, but Ula laid her hand on his arm.

"Draeson give up much to be powerful wizard," she said. "Is to be understood."

"I'm not a wizard," Draeson snapped. "I'm a mage. Wizards are fools with parlor tricks. What I do takes a bit more than that. You wouldn't understand."

"Ah. Is my mistake of words. Kalan not my language and I only dabble in freaks and elementals. Sorry, Mr. Wizard Draeson." Ula's face remained deadpan.

He huffed loudly and stalked off, shaking his head.

Brannon rubbed at the scar on his face and sighed. "He was never this much trouble during the war."

"Really?" Taran raised an eyebrow. "Maybe you just didn't notice because he was older."

Brannon thought about it. Actually, he did remember Draeson being a cranky old man. "Huh. He was older and I was younger. You might be right. Funny how things change."

"We've got company," Draeson called from up ahead.

Brannon looked to see two riders coming toward them over the hilltop. He dropped his pack to the ground and drew his sword. "Stay behind me until we know it's safe."

As the riders came closer, he saw they were a woman in her forties and a younger man. Both had dark hair and freckled features.

Jessamine suddenly lurched forward and waved. "Hey! Hello!" She turned to Brannon. "It's okay. I know them. They're from Sandilar."

Brannon put his sword away but kept his hand on the hilt as the couple approached.

"Jessamine?" the woman called. "Is that you? Don't tell me you're a physician already and come back to our town?"

Jessamine shook her head. "Almost. I've reached apprentice level. This is my teacher, Sir Brannon Kesh. Brannon, this is Shillia Vere and her son Morgin. When I was last in Sandilar, Shillia was the mayor."

"I'm still the mayor," Shillia Vere said, swinging down from her horse. "No one's fool enough to take that job off my hands, as yet. We were headed out to check for good grazing but . . . " She looked over Brannon and the rest of the group. "The King's Champion. Does that mean you're here to sort out these murders?"

"We are," said Brannon.

"Well, Ahpra's Tears, it's about time. It's been difficult keeping people from freaking out about the whole thing. We think we've found the culprit though. And I see from who you have in your group that your thoughts have been along the same lines." She gestured to Ula.

Brannon felt his eyes widen. "You caught someone in the act?"

Mayor Shillia shook her head. "Not in the act, no. Unfortunately we don't have any proof, which is why he's not already locked up. But we're pretty sure and, with you here, we can hold him for questioning again at least."

"What makes you think it's him?"

"Whoever it is has been using some kind of dirty Djin magic. And there's only one dirty Djin in all of Sandilar. Until now, of course."

"Ula Lanok is a guest of the king," Brannon began.

Jessamine spoke over him. "You mean Kholi? You think Kholi Gruul the blacksmith did it? I can't believe it!"

"There's no one else it could be."

Brannon held up his hand. "Let's not get carried away just yet. We'll need a bit more evidence first. We've had a similar murder in Alapra so, unless this Kholi has been out of town recently, he couldn't be responsible for both."

"An accomplice, then." The mayor shrugged.

"Possibly. But I'd like to do a thorough investigation before passing judgement."

She shrugged again. "Fine. Morgin here has been helping keep track of things. He can let you know everything that's happened. Let's get you settled into rooms at the inn first though. While you do that, I'll have Kholi Gruul picked up."

"Ah, let's hold off on that too." She frowned at him and Brannon gave his best conspiratorial smile. "We don't want to tip our hand too soon. Let me and my team snoop around a bit first, bring us up to speed, and hopefully we'll find something to confront him with. Better that than hold him overnight, find nothing, and look incompetent."

The mayor nodded. "Good plan."

The town of Sandilar lay in a shallow valley just east of the manor itself. The majority of buildings were made of the stone which was so prevalent in the surrounding countryside, and roofed with thatch. The roads were cobbled and well maintained. The homes had picturesque little gardens, and the main square and many of the side streets were lined with shops almost as well stocked as some of those in Alapra.

"We get a lot of traders through here," Mayor Shillia said. "They like Sandilar gold." She and her son were leading their horses and walking to keep pace with the group. They'd let Jessamine and Ula ride to rest their legs. Draeson stalked a few paces away from the rest of the group.

Brannon nodded, admiring the town. "I'm surprised you can keep it so tidy with so many miners around."

"Miners don't come here." Morgin's voice was

surprisingly low. "Not the live ones anyway."

His mother, perhaps sensing the group's discomfort, hurried to explain. "Morgin is our undertaker. He can have something of a dark sense of humor."

"Ah." Brannon remembered black humor as a staple of army diet. "I take it mining is a dangerous job?"

"It can be. The mines are further back in the mountains and they have their own accommodation there. We send provisions as required, but there's really no need for them to come to town. Many of the workers are criminals so they're kept under guard."

"Are you certain none of them could be responsible for the murders?"

"There have been no escapes and it's much too far for them to come and go without notice." She shook her head. "No, it's someone local, I'm afraid. Someone in town or one of the nearby farms."

Brother Taran chewed his thumbnail as he walked. "So, ah, who was actually killed?"

"Well, first it was Molly, who does all the tailoring for them at the manor. Then one of the stable boys. Then Garrath, who was apparently a distant cousin of the duke himself. A bit too distant, I'd say, judging by the name, but close enough that he got his home and a small allowance from His Grace."

"Did they have anything in common?"

"Not that I could see. They're all locals, is all. And, of course, how they were found." She gave a delicate shudder. "Morgin can tell you about that, if you must know. It's not something I care to remember."

Her son nodded, his head bobbing like a sunflower in a strong wind. "I've kept good records. Wrote everything down. Even copied out the symbols we found on their bodies and all around them."

Brannon tried not to let disappointment register on his face. "I suppose that means the original symbols aren't still there?"

Shillia Vere looked horrified. Morgin simply shook his head. "We cleaned everything up nice and proper. People were getting upset seeing that sort of thing."

"Yes, I suppose they would." Brannon glanced up at Ula, who clung to the horse's mane as though it were the only part of the beast she could be sure was solid. He wondered how much use Morgin's copied symbols were going to be with no undisturbed evidence to check. He wondered how useful any of it would be. "Well, I'd like to see the sites anyway. It'd help to get an idea of where it was done."

"I can take you now, if you want," Morgin said.

"We should look at the bodies too," Taran put in.

"But they've been buried," said Morgin.

"Oh."

Mayor Shillia gave Taran a sideways look. "It's a strange group you've brought us, Sir Champion. I hope they can help you find some answers." She gestured to the building up ahead. "This is the inn. Dargin Knox and his family will take good care of you while you stay."

The inn was one of the larger buildings in town, three stories high with painted wooden shutters. A stable to one side cornered off a courtyard, and a wide, colorful sign proclaimed it to be the Knox Inn & Tavern.

"Blood and Tears," said Jessamine as she swung down off the horse and unstrapped her pack. "I'm so glad to be having a proper bed and decent food tonight.

You've no idea!"

"Um, if you feel anything like how I feel right now," said Taran, "then I have a very good idea."

A young woman greeted them at the door. She had auburn hair and warm eyes. She spoke with the mayor for a few moments, then invited them all inside. The main tavern room had a stone floor, long wooden tables, and a roaring fire over which a huge pot simmered, wafting a delicious aroma throughout the room. On the walls were pieces of mining equipment, hung like art. Broken pickaxes, blunt chisels, toothless cogs, and hole-poked buckets, reminding patrons where the wealth of the region came from.

"Leave your things here if you like," the woman said. "We'll bring them up to your rooms later. I can draw baths for you to relax in and we can see to food and drink before you settle in."

Morgin took a few steps forward and raised a hand as though to catch her attention. "Hi Karia. This is the King's Champion, Sir Brannon Kesh. I'm helping him with the murder investigation."

She spared him a half-glance. "Good for you, Morgin. If you see Caidin around, can you let him know I'll be a bit later than expected? I'll need to see to supper for these fine folks." Her smile increased several notches when she turned back to the guests. "Now, if you'll follow me, I'll show you to your rooms."

"Actually, I think maybe we should do a little investigating before we get too settled," Brannon said. He was thinking of the mayor's attitude. She was ready to convict her suspect on circumstantial evidence at best. If that was the view of the woman in charge, chances were that the general populace were even less patient. "I'd like people to know that we're here and we're doing something."

Draeson shrugged. "Do what you like. I need a drink."

Brannon felt his jaw clench. "Fine. Morgin, if you're still available to show me the murder sites, I'd appreciate it. The rest of you can come or not as you please."

Ula came with him, but Jessamine and Taran both pled exhaustion and stayed at the inn with Draeson. "Young people not always know when to put important things ahead of their own needs," the Djin woman said as they made their way out of the inn.

"What's Draeson's excuse?" Brannon muttered.

Morgin led them just a short way from the inn, then down a side street to the door of what was essentially a cottage with a shopfront built onto it. His mother had made her apologies and gone about her business. Morgin seemed to stand a little taller as he pulled out the key to the cottage.

"This is Molly's place. Mother and I have kept it locked up since."

Inside, bolts of cloth were stacked on benches up against the walls. A handful of dressmaker's models were scattered around, some with half-made clothes attached. When he looked closely, Brannon realized that many of the fabrics were stained with blood.

"This is where you found her?"

Morgin nodded. "In the middle of the floor, there. Like she'd been laid out specially. She had the symbols on her and they were all over the floor and walls too." He pulled out a small notebook and opened it to show them. "These ones."

Brannon glanced at the page and tried to picture the symbols in the room. Probably in blood or paint as they had been with Keldan. He passed the book to Ula. "Are they the same?"

She nodded, her lips pressed together.

"She was pregnant," Morgin said. "I don't think anyone knew about it, but you find stuff out as an undertaker. Her husband's been dead for years so . . . " He reminded Brannon a little of Jessamine in his eagerness.

"Any idea who the father was?"

He shook his head.

Brannon sighed. At this rate, the Djin connection really was the only lead. "So, what's the story with this blacksmith?"

Morgin shrugged. "He met Alena when she was a soldier in the war. Apparently he was one of the scary ones that would wander around with dead servants and stuff, spying on us. A total freak." He blinked as though realizing Ula was in the room. "Sorry."

She shook her head. "Is true we send some shamans out to watch. More when countries fight. We like to know what happens in the world."

Morgin took a half step back. "Anyway, he gave up all that stuff to marry Alena. He came back here and set up the smithy. We haven't had any trouble from him until now. I guess he just couldn't leave the dead alone and decided to make some."

Brannon looked around the abandoned shop. "Well, somebody did. And they haven't stopped yet."

CHAPTER NINETEEN

D raeson swirled the last of his drink around the bottom of the glass as he watched the normals in the tavern. There weren't many of them. It seemed the local murders had put people off their drinks. For midweek at least. Soon they'd be back, he had no doubt of it.

He threw back the last of his drink and swallowed.

"Shall I get you another?" Karia Knox was running a cloth over the wooden tabletop.

Draeson looked her over. "Perhaps something different," he said, laying his hand over hers. "What would you suggest?"

Karia pulled away but softened the gesture with a smile and a wink. "I'd suggest finding someone else to flirt with. You're definitely a looker, but I'm an engaged woman. If you like, though, I can take a drink to the target of your choice."

He sighed. "Never mind. It's probably time I went and unpacked anyway."

Taran and Jessamine had gone up to their rooms already. Brannon and Ula had yet to return. No doubt he would be in for a lecture on his absence when they did.

Everything was always a drama for regular people. They were always so shocked when the obvious happened. He found it irritating and moronic, but also, just a little bit, he was envious. For them, the developments of life were new and exciting. Very little seemed that way to him these days.

He pushed the empty glass toward Karia and stood up.

"I'm sure your friends will be back soon," she said.

"No doubt. Time flies and all that."

"Every year goes by faster than the last, they say."

Draeson watched her walk away. "That it does," he said to no one in particular. "That it certainly does."

He made his way upstairs, letting the sounds and smells of the tavern room fall away behind him. The upper levels of the inn were surprisingly well-furnished for an establishment in a town this size—another sign of the wealth of the area. Draeson remembered when the gold mines were first discovered here. It had been the work of decades to get them running and providing a profit for the Crown. And it had taken much longer to hammer into the psyche of the kings of Kalanon that only the most trusted of allies should be allowed to ever see what was in Sandilar, let alone have any control over it.

The kings and queens of Kalanon could be a thickheaded bunch. This latest one was no exception. Draeson had no objection to being part of the investigative team for these murders, but he had berated himself since leaving Alapra for not having insisted that their deal be taken care of first.

As he reached the landing, he heard a scuffle up ahead. Then a scream. He ran into the hallway, listening intently to try to identify the room the sounds had come from. "Jessamine? Is that you?"

"Help!"

He shot toward the sound of her voice and almost collided with her as she stepped out from one of the rooms.

Jessamine was disheveled, some of her hair had pulled loose from her ponytail, but she seemed unharmed. "Did you see him? Where did he go?"

"Who?" Draeson peered past her. The room was a mess. The contents of Jessamine's pack and Ula's bag were strewn across the floor. "What happened?"

"I found someone going through our stuff. I think he took something."

Draeson swore. "Yet another drama. Well, he can't have gone far. Come on."

A few steps down the hallway, a door was open on another room. Inside, the window was open.

"Ahpra's Tears," Jessamine said. "Do you think he jumped?"

Draeson stuck his head out the window. There was a garden below with soft, springy ground cover. It would have made a gentle landing. "If he did, he's long gone now. Did you recognize him?"

"No." She hung her head. "It happened so fast, I barely saw his face."

Draeson sighed. "No matter. Go back and see what was taken. I'll ward the rooms so it doesn't happen again."

Jessamine went back to the room she was sharing

with Ula, and Draeson stepped back into the hallway. He pulled up his shirt to check the dragon tattoo. It was curled into a sleeping ball, just above his right hip. He knew it was his imagination, but he could almost have sworn the colors were a little lighter.

He let the shirt drop and focused on each of their room doors one by one. Slowly, he pushed power into them, shaping it into an image and a warning. The wood groaned at the impact, but held strong, and eventually he was able to tie off the flow of magic.

"Wow." Jessamine looked at his work with wide eyes. The lower half of each door was now painted with the image of a large dog. Each one appeared slightly different to the others in color or breed. They all turned toward Jessamine and sniffed. Seemingly satisfied, they sat still. "What are those?"

"Wards." Draeson said, suddenly tired. "They'll let us know if anyone they don't recognize tries to get into our rooms."

"Impressive." Her eyes flicked from the shifting images of the dogs to Draeson and back again. "Is that what your dragon tattoo is, then? A ward of some sort, like these?"

Draeson couldn't help a bark of laughter and the dogs looked at him, startled. "No. No, my dragon tattoo is nothing like my ward-dogs."

"Then what—?"

He cut her off. "Did you figure out what was taken?"

"Not really. He must have been after money but there wasn't any in my bag. I think maybe he got some of Ula's stuff. We'll have to wait for her to get back and check to know for sure. What do you think we should do now?"

He shrugged and opened the door to his own room. "I'm going to get some sleep and then solve some murders in the morning. You might want to run along and ask Brannon first, though, since you're his apprentice."

And, he added silently to himself as he closed the door behind him, when we get back to Alapra I'm going to pin that brat king to the wall and make sure he personally satisfies the terms of the deal.

CHAPTER TWENTY

Moonlight made sleeping sheep almost indistinguishable from the rocks that dotted most of the pasture around Sandilar. In the distance, the larger shapes of buildings huddled together in the dark. The wind blew cool and sharp, shifting the small grove of trees so their branches seemed to be reaching out, ready to grasp passersby. The creaking sound of their movement carried in the otherwise silent night.

They stood, two figures between the trees and the flock of sheep, unnoticed by the town.

"Are you sure this will work?" he asked, shifting his feet.

"I think so," a female voice answered. She held up a small leather bag. "We have what we need now. The missing ingredients that Kholi Gruul never revealed."

"And you're sure we don't need a fresh dead body for this?" He gestured back toward town. "I can do it, you know. I'm getting good at it. I have just the man in mind."

172

She smiled, her teeth gleaming in the moonlight. "I'm sure you do, but no, we need to stick to the plan. If you start deviating from our intended targets you'll mess everything up."

"That's easy for you to say. Everybody loves you."

"Not everybody." She reached out and stroked his cheek. "Don't worry. After this, nobody will be able to ignore you. Not even your father. You'll be the most important person in this town."

The smile bubbled up from within him to burst across his face. "You really think so?"

She pulled a small clay pot out of the bag and dipped her fingers into the contents. "I know so. Now hold still. We want to do this right."

The paste felt cold and wet as she traced the symbols onto his skin. When she was done, she took four new pots and placed them around them like corners of a square. Then she took what looked like straw out of the bag and set it on fire. The light flared like a warning beacon and one of the sheep gave a sleepy bleat, then it burned out and she rubbed the ash onto his skin.

"You're sure about this?" he said, hating how quiet and unstable his voice was.

She spat into her hand and rubbed that onto the ash. "I'm sure. Now hold on."

The wind felt suddenly stronger, and warmer. It was like a thousand mouths blowing hot breath over his entire body. "Blood and Tears and Hooded Wolf. What is that?"

She laughed and he could barely hear it over the rushing in his ears. "Here it comes!"

His skin burned and rippled, sensation burrowing

into his body from every pore. There was a howling in his ears and in his mind, driving away all thoughts.

The entire flock of sheep awoke, bleating in terror, and scattered like leaves in the wind.

Deep inside him thrummed the beat of an enormous drum. For a moment, he thought perhaps they had miscalculated. Perhaps he had died. Then breath rushed into his lungs again and his eyes opened for the first time. Light poured over the landscape like magnificent golden oil. He could see everything. The veins on the leaves in the trees, the fibers of wool on the fleeing sheep, the flecks of darker blue in his companion's eyes and the eagerness in her face.

"It worked, didn't it?" she whispered. "How do you feel?"

He smiled. It was not a pleasant smile.

"I feel strong."

CHAPTER TWENTY-ONE

"I seriously doubt there's a wolf." Caidin gripped the pitchfork tightly and quickened his steps across the grass. The moon had clouded over and the night was cooling fast, but thoughts of his ultimate destination that evening kept him warm. Karia would be waiting for him back at the inn. By now the latest guests would be well-settled into their beds and he could join her in hers.

"Well, something spooked the sheep," Malvon said. He held the lantern high. "I lost five to wolves last year. They're getting bolder."

"That was in winter. Why would they risk coming close to town this time of year? There's plenty for them to hunt closer to the mountain."

"I don't know." Malvon hugged himself nervously. "But what else would terrify the whole flock in the middle of the night? Unless it's that murdering lunatic."

Caidin snorted. "Yeah right, he gave up on stabbing people and decided to take up sheep buggery instead."

"You sure you can handle the competition?"

"Shut up."

Malvon laughed.

Caidin grabbed his arm, bringing them to a sudden stop. "Seriously. Be quiet. I think there's something out there."

Malvon's laugh vanished like a snuffed candle flame. Both men scanned the darkness. "What is it?"

The wind picked up, carrying with it the sounds of restless sheep huddled together in the corner of the paddock. Caidin turned slowly, straining his ears. There, in the distance, a faint squeal.

"Over there."

As they moved closer, the sound came again, and this time there was a scuffling noise.

Malvon unshielded a little more of the lantern and the light revealed a single ewe on the ground. Its eyes were wild and its front feet scrabbled on the ground, trying to get away. Its wool was dark with blood and its back legs were gone entirely, ripped away like the heel of a loaf of bread.

"Hooded Blood!" Malvon dropped to his knees beside the animal, which pulled back from him even as he did so. "Bloody wolves didn't even finish the job, let alone eat."

Caidin laid his pitchfork down and took the knife from his belt. "It's your sheep. Want me to finish it?"

His friend nodded. "You're the butcher. Do it quick."

When the animal's suffering was finished, Caidin sat back on his heels. "That's definitely not a wolf," he said. He pointed to the wounds. "The flesh is torn, but not bitten. There are no bite marks anywhere."

"Then what?"

Caidin shrugged. The night felt darker, ominous. "Let's go back. We can look for tracks in the morning when it's light."

Malvon looked around. "Yeah, that'd be best."

The trip back felt painfully slow, despite their long-strided pace being just shy of a jog. Caidin felt the eyes of the mutilated sheep watching him. He'd butchered many animals and none had been so afraid. His stomach was knotted with the same fear now. Something had been strong enough to pull the legs off a sheep like a vindictive child with an insect.

"What could do that?" Malvon's voice was slightly breathless.

Caidin hesitated. "I . . . maybe we were wrong. Maybe it was a wolf after all. It's hard to see in the dark."

"No, you were right. There were no teeth marks."

"Yeah."

Malvon's home was on the edge of town. "You want to stay here tonight? Get an early start tracking in the morning?"

The stone walls looked very inviting, but the clustered buildings of the town beyond held more appeal. Caidin shook his head. "No. Karia's expecting me."

Malvon chuckled. "Fair enough."

Caidin felt the tension drain from his body as he walked deeper into town. The streets were always so peaceful at night. Despite the recent murders, he felt secure here. The familiar buildings were like guardians against the night. No wild animal—wolf or otherwise—would risk venturing so far into human territory.

He used his pitchfork like a walking staff as he rounded the corner leading to the inn. As he approached, he frowned. The large swinging sign saying "Knox Inn and Tavern" was gone. The post and crossbar from which it usually hung was there, but the sign itself lay on the ground.

He moved closer. The metal rings that attached the sign to the crossbar were buckled and broken. The night felt suddenly colder. Something had pulled the sign down with impossible brute force. His breath caught in his chest and he backed away.

A figure stepped out of the shadows.

Caidin felt as if fire surged through him, then flowed away as light caught the familiar face. "Blood and Tears." Relief bubbled up as laughter. "You gave me such a fright. Do you know what happened to the sign?"

"Yes." The man stepped closer and reached out toward him. "Me."

The hand closed around Caidin's throat.

CHAPTER TWENTY-TWO

Brannon awoke from disturbing dreams to an insistent pounding on the door of his room. A moment later the sound of dogs barking dragged him out of bed.

"Who is it?" He thrust his feet into the legs of his pants.

"Shillia Vere," a voice said. "Meet me downstairs. I want you to see what your delaying has done."

The barking stopped.

Brannon sat on the bed and swore. Last night's exploration of the crime scenes had turned up very little in the way of useful evidence. The mayor's well-intentioned cleanup had destroyed any subtle clues. He'd stayed up late pouring over Morgin's notebook, trying to glean what he could, but despite the young man's faithful sketches and careful notes, all he'd succeeded in doing was feeding his nightmares and imagination. Morgin could only record what he'd thought relevant of what he could see. It was no substitute for seeing the scene firsthand.

Downstairs, the dining room of the inn felt hollow without any customers. The innkeeper and his family huddled together around a table in the far corner and did not look up. Karia, the girl who'd served them last night, was crying. Shillia Vere stood in the middle of the room with her hands on her hips.

"Now we have another crime scene to show you," she said.

Brannon's stomach felt as though he'd swallowed lead pellets. "Someone else was attacked last night?"

"Follow me."

Dawn had barely broken and the cobbles of the courtyard were still damp with early dew. The town was yet to fully wake to the new day. In Alapra, the smell of new-baked bread and last night's chamber pots would be roiling out from every corner. Here, there was just the crispness of a country morning and the faint scent of the stables.

The fleeting peace of it was quickly burned away as the mayor gestured to the signpost at the front of the tavern. For a moment, his mind would not register what he was seeing. It was part of the signpost. It was a shadow. It was an effigy. Then it clicked into sharp focus: It was a man.

Limp feet dangled two or three handspans above the ground, a pool of blood beneath them, staining the cobblestones. The back of his skull was impaled on the crossbar and the blood made his blond hair red. His eyes were wide in shock.

"Blood and Tears." Brannon felt himself flood with sadness. After all they'd gone through in the war, how could people do this to each other? "Who was he?"

Mayor Shillia's voice was clipped. "Caidin Ray. The fiancé of Karia, the innkeeper's daughter crying inside."

Brannon nodded. "I remember her."

Shillia's eyes narrowed. "This wouldn't have happened if we'd had Kholi Gruul in custody last night, like I wanted."

He sighed. "We don't know that for sure."

"You wanna tell that to Karia?"

Brannon met her eyes. "Please bring the rest of my team here. We need to get to work."

While he waited, Brannon examined the scene. The sign had been torn down to make way for the victim. Caidin Ray had been hung very deliberately in its place. This was a message of some kind. Like enemy troops putting the heads of fallen soldiers on their walls. This was personal.

He stepped back and looked at the Knox family inn. There seemed nothing out of the ordinary about them so far. Was the message for someone in the family? Or, and his chest felt heavy at the thought, was it a message for the investigators who had just arrived in town?

The door opened and the rest of the team followed Shillia out into the courtyard.

"That's different," Draeson said.

Jessamine paled and her lips were tight. "It's horrible."

"There's bruising on his throat," Draeson said, peering closer. "It looks like finger marks. None of the Djin symbols though."

"Exactly," Brannon said.

"Maybe it wasn't done by the same person as the

181

other murders?" Taran said.

Brannon shot a glance at Ula. "It takes a lot of strength to drive a skull onto a spike like that. Especially a living, strong man lifted up off the ground."

Ula looked away.

"We all saw how strong Keldan was when he attacked his father in the crypt. He picked him up one-handed." Brannon nodded toward the body of Caidin Ray. "This man was picked up with one hand around his throat and rammed onto the spike. Could a Risen have done this?"

Ula stared at the ground.

"Ula?"

She looked up, her eyes dark. "Risen very strong. If the body is fresh, then, yes, very strong."

"Ahpra's Tears," Jessamine breathed. "They've done it. Whoever it is, they've been trying to raise a dead slave and they've finally succeeded."

Brannon reached out and squeezed her shoulder for support. His own chest felt very tight. "It looks that way," he said. "Which means there's likely evidence somewhere else in town of the actual raising ceremony itself. There's also the question of what they did with the Risen once they had it. Why use it to kill Caidin? They could have killed him at any time before—they've killed plenty of others. Why him now?"

Mayor Shillia turned so that her back was to the corpse. "Why does this lunatic do anything? He's mad and evil."

Brannon shook his head. "No, there's a reason. No one goes to this much trouble without a reason. This has been a lot of effort for someone. If we could figure out why, we'd have a better chance of finding who. Did Caidin have any enemies? Anyone he didn't get along with?"

She shook her head. "Not that I know of. Nor did the other victims. They were just innocent people."

"They may have been practice runs for Caidin."

"Or whoever it is lost control of the Risen and Caidin was just in the wrong place at the wrong time," Jessamine said.

Brannon frowned at her. "Let's not make that kind of assumption, just yet. Whoever this is has been very clever and controlled up to now. There's no need to frighten people more than necessary."

She blushed and nodded.

The mayor looked between them, then obviously set aside the more frightening suggestion. "You should talk to Karia about whether Caidin had any enemies. She would know best of anyone. But give her time to recover first. The poor girl was the one to find him." She looked past Brannon and scowled. "What in the name of the Hooded are you doing?"

Brannon turned to see that Brother Taran had crept forward and was kneeling beneath the body with a small sponge, which he dipped into the blood before dropping it into a vial.

"Oh," he said, looking up and around in small jerky movements. "I thought I should get a sample of the blood for testing. I mean, in case he was drugged like Prince Keldan was." He pointed upward. "I can't reach to taste his lips right now."

Shillia's eyes bulged. "You can't what?"

Brannon held up his hands in a pacifying gesture.

"Trust us, mayor. Our methods may seem strange, but we know what we're doing." He put as much conviction into the statement as he could, willing Taran to hurry up and finish his collection.

Even as Taran stepped back, Draeson's eyes narrowed and he held out his hand toward the body, fingers spread and his lips moving.

"Draeson," Brannon said, stepping back from the mage. "A little warning would be nice."

The magus ignored him. A moment later he dropped his arm. The pooled blood on the cobblestones began to glow with a golden light. As Brannon watched, the glow became brighter and seemed to seep through the corpse's skin as well, as though the blood left in his body was afire. Then, just as suddenly as it had started, the light went out.

Brannon raised his eyebrow. "Draeson? What does that mean?"

The mage pursed his lips. "It means I need to see the rest of the bodies. Or at least something with their blood on it."

"For?"

"For testing."

Brannon sighed. Getting information out of the man was like pulling teeth. "Remember what I said about behaving like a teenager?"

Draeson said nothing.

"Fine. Taran, you go with him and collect more samples. It'd be good to know if drugs were used on any of the other victims here, not just Caidin."

A ruckus sounded from the street and Mayor Shillia smiled. "I sent Morgin to bring in the blacksmith. People need to see some action being taken over this."

Townsfolk spilled into the courtyard in a wave, like the flash flood waters of Tilal all those years ago, and potentially almost as dangerous. At the head was Morgin, leading another man with muscles nearly three times the size of his own by a rope tied around the man's wrists. The prisoner's purple skin proclaimed him to be Djin, but he had long since cut off his dreadlocks in favor of a Kalan style.

The crowd scowled and muttered when they saw Caidin's body. Brannon straightened up and let his hand rest on his sword hilt. He may need to be the rock this wave broke against.

Draeson, however, seemed oblivious to the danger the angry crowd represented. He bustled forward with Taran following him like a puppy. "Ah, Morgin, perfect. Do you have anything with the other victims' blood on it? If not, we'll need to exhume their bodies."

Morgin looked to his mother for guidance and she nodded. "Take them. We'll deal with the blacksmith."

Morgin jerked the rope, pulling the Djin man forward, then pushed him to his knees. The townsfolk cheered. Brannon stepped forward quickly to take charge of the prisoner. The last thing he wanted was mob justice to take hold before he could question him. He'd seen prisoners of war beaten to death by angry soldiers in the past. Peacetime deserved better.

Taran paused before following Morgin and Draeson out of the courtyard. "You know how to check for loredin when they get the body down, right?"

"Really?" There was no way Brannon was going to lick a dead man's lips, let alone in front of a crowd of angry townspeople. "No. You can do it when you get back."

Taran nodded, apparently satisfied. "Okay."

Brannon touched the blacksmith on the shoulder, noting he had the same tattooed markings as Ula did. "You can stand up," he said. "You haven't been convicted yet and you'll get a fair trial. But we do need to talk."

The Djin man ignored him, staring instead at Ula, who had kept quiet until now. "Prioress Lanok. What are you doing here? *Ga shool na feil ra ga.*"

Ula's hand jerked in a sharp cutting motion and her voice cracked like a whip. "Ssh. *Ngo ga, Kholi Grul. La gru yol.*"

The crowd grumbled loudly.

"Speak Kalan or not at all," Mayor Shillia snapped. "This isn't some Djinan backwater island. I'll not have you colluding with him behind our backs."

"Thank you, mayor," Brannon said, putting iron in his tone. "Ula is part of my investigation team. She will do what is necessary to get answers."

Shillia scowled but Ula was quick to soothe her. "You're right, of course. We will speak only Kalan in your presence."

Shillia settled, but it was clear that emotions were running high among those gathered. Brannon took Kholi Gruul by the scruff of the neck and addressed the crowd. "King Aldan has sent me and my team to investigate the murders that have been committed here. Including what was done last night to Caidin Ray. You have brought me this suspect and I will question him now, but this investigation is not yet over. When it is, the king's justice will be obvious and severe. For now, however, I ask that you let us do our job and, for the sake of Caidin's dignity, go back to your homes while we have him brought down and examined. Thank you."

Thankfully, his words seemed to stir the mayor's sense of civic duty. "All right, people, you heard Sir Brannon. Move on back about your business. We'll let you know when there's any word."

Brannon guided the prisoner toward the inn, passing Ula as they went. "You never told me you were one of the Council of Priors," he hissed.

"I not tell all of my life to you," she said with a shrug. "I think this is same as you with me."

Brannon's jaw tightened. "Next time, try not to surprise me when we're trying to prevent a mob lynching."

As they pushed inside the main tavern room, the Knox family rose to their feet.

"Is that him?" Karia's voice rang out. "Is that who killed Caidin?"

Jessamine hurried forward. "We don't know yet. I'm so sorry to do this, but we need somewhere safe to question him."

"Do it here," Dargin Knox said quietly. "We'll wait in the kitchen."

Brannon guided the blacksmith to the table by the door and pushed him into a chair. Ula, Shillia, and a hard-eyed blond woman with a lattice of scars across the back of her right hand, followed them in, and Jessamine joined them a moment later when the Knox family were gone. As he sat down, Brannon met the blacksmith's eyes. "Kholi Gruul, correct? I am Brannon Kesh, the

King's Champion."

The blacksmith tilted his head toward the blond woman. "This is my wife, Alena."

"A wife who is sick of her husband being unfairly targeted by the racist pricks in this town," she said, her hands curled into fists. "I was born here and I came back after serving my country in the war, with the man I fell in love with. We've been hard-working members of this community for seven years and as soon as something starts going wrong, Kholi is the one everyone wants to blame it on. It's Hooded horseshit."

"If that's the case," Brannon said, "we'll figure it out. But we have to do this the right way and ask the questions. It will go a lot easier for everyone if you both try to help us, okay?"

The husband and wife looked at each other, then nodded. "Okay."

Brannon smiled at them both. "Good. Now, first up, what are these tattoos?" He pointed to the markings down Kholi's shoulders.

The blacksmith immediately tensed and looked across at Ula.

Ula nodded. "It is all right. You may tell him."

Kholi licked his lips. "They are shaman marks. To protect me from kaluki."

Brannon nodded. "They stop you from being brought back as a Risen when you die, right? Because the knowledge you have would be dangerous for them."

Kholi stared at the table. "Yes."

"Because you know how to make a Risen."

"Yes."

Mayor Shillia gave a sharp intake of breath but

stayed silent at Brannon's glance.

"Did you raise the one that killed Caidin Ray last night?"

Kholi's head jerked upward. "No! I haven't made any Risen since I left my home to marry Alena seven years ago. I would never do that!" He turned to Ula, his eyes pleading. "You must know that I wouldn't use the kaluki for such a thing. I know the price of leaving the isles. I left my powers behind."

"And yet," Ula pointed out, "someone did."

Alena's fist twitched on the tabletop. "It wasn't Kholi. I was with him last night. He couldn't have done it.'"

Brannon fingered the point where his scar met his earlobe. "Were you awake the whole night, Alena?"

Her eyes narrowed. "No, we slept. But believe me, I know when my husband leaves our bed at night. I'm very aware of that. Last night, he was at home the entire time."

Brannon raised his eyebrow, then dropped it again. "Okay. What about the times of the other murders?"

Kholi opened his mouth but it was Alena who spoke again. "There's no way of knowing exactly when the murders took place so the question is meaningless. And besides, if my husband already had the ability to raise these demons, as you've just pointed out, why would he have failed to do so in those previous attempts? This whole thing is ridiculous."

Brannon shrugged. "Perhaps he was rusty and forgot how to do it. Perhaps he's innocent. The fact remains he's the only one in the region with knowledge of how to do what was done. Unless . . . " He turned to look at

Kholi. "Did you tell anyone else the secrets?"

The blacksmith refused to meet his eye. "That is forbidden."

"So are a lot of things, Kholi," Brannon said. "It doesn't stop us doing them. I reckon knowing something special like that would impress a lot of people."

Kholi's head was moving side to side in slow denial. His gaze scraped over each of them, seeking reassurance. "I would never tell the sacred information. I . . . I wouldn't give away enough for someone to make a Risen. I haven't ever said that much, have I?"

Jessamine, who happened to be the one his gaze rested on for those last few words, shrugged helplessly. "I'm sure you haven't," she said.

Brannon's suspicions took a stronger hold. "Jessamine, would you and Alena fetch drinks for everyone? You don't mind, do you Alena? I think we all need to take a moment."

Alena's knuckles grew white. "I'd rather stay with my husband."

"Of course. It's just that certain drugs have been used in some of these crimes and, with the way people have been reacting today, I think it would be best for Kholi if someone he trusts can oversee his drink. You understand?"

Her eyes widened but she nodded curtly and followed Jessamine to the bar.

Brannon waited until they were out of earshot before addressing the blacksmith again. "Kholi, you've been unfaithful to your wife, haven't you? That's who you told forbidden information to. No one at this table will tell Alena if that's the case."

To his surprise, Mayor Shillia supported him. "Everyone knows I'm not one to cast judgements on such things."

"I . . . " The blacksmith's gaze slid toward his wife. He hung his head. "It was a long time ago. We've gotten past it."

"Who was she?"

"It doesn't matter. I told her harmless details to impress her. There's no way she could have raised anyone with what she knew."

"Tell me anyway."

Jessamine and Alena were making their way back, mugs of drink in hand.

Kholi covered his face. "I'm sorry. I can't have you digging up the past. I won't put Alena through all that again."

Brannon sighed. "Well, I'm sorry, Kholi, but if you don't, I'm going to have to lock you up until we find more evidence or take you back to Alapra for a hearing. At the moment, you're the best suspect we've got."

Kholi stood and held out his hands. "Fine. Then lock me up."

Jessamine and Alena reached the table. The blacksmith's wife looked around, her eyes narrowed. "What's going on here?" She put down the mugs she carried with a thump.

Kholi lifted his chin. "They've run out of questions for me."

Alena frowned. "Really?"

Brannon pursed his lips. His promise to keep the man's secret notwithstanding, there was no point pressing the matter now. Perhaps some time in a cell would change his mind. "For now. But your husband has agreed to stay in protective custody and I'm sure we'll need to talk to him again."

Mayor Shillia stood as well. "I'll have my men escort him."

Alena blinked and looked from one to the next.

"One final question though," Brannon said. "Have either of you been to Alapra recently?"

Kholi frowned and shook his head. "We haven't left Sandilar in seven years."

"What could Alapra possibly have to do with the murders here?" Alena demanded.

Brannon shrugged. "That's what I'd like to know."

CHAPTER TWENTY-THREE

"This is my little collection," Morgin said, pulling out boxes of blood-crusted clothes. "The families didn't want them anyway and nobody wants to bury people in the clothes they were killed in, so I kept them."

"Morbid," Draeson said. "But useful. Lay them out according to who they belonged to."

The morgue seemed to be a kind of sanctuary for Morgin Vere. He came alive here, among the things that had belonged to the dead. Draeson looked around as the eager boy laid out the bloodstained clothing on a long bench for inspection.

Like most of the buildings in town, this one was made of stone. Although the thatched ceiling clearly leaked, the lower levels were still sound, if mostly abandoned. Some rooms contained coffins ready for use, others were laid out with comforting furnishings as viewing rooms. The biggest room was Morgin's workspace, with wide benches, wicked-looking tools, and pots of color and rouge. Beneath it all, unlike most buildings in town, was the cellar vault for storing corpses.

"This is one of the oldest buildings in town. There are all sorts of tunnels and secret rooms down there," Morgin said, gesturing toward the bolted door. "I don't know what it was originally built for but it has the coolest temperatures in town so it makes a perfect morgue."

"It was where the first Duke of Sandilar lived," Draeson said. "Before the main manor was built. It was a dangerous time back then and he needed escape routes and places to hide the treasure extracted from the mine. Not that it did him any good. Building this place was about the only thing he ever took advice on."

"How in the Hooded's name do you know that?" Taran asked.

Draeson gave him a flat look. "It was mostly my advice."

Morgin finished laying out the clothes on the benches. The torn and bloody garments told the frightening story of their owners' last moments. The young man's leather pants and jerkin, still stuck with horse dung and straw. The pregnant woman's oversized dress, designed for comfortable wearing in her own home at night. The blue velvet with embroidered cuffs of a nobleman. All punctured with holes. Outerwear, underwear, accessories—Morgin had kept them all and painstakingly laid them according to group.

"I'm glad they can help your investigation," the young undertaker said. "What are you hoping to learn from their clothes?"

Draeson said nothing. Instead, he pulled up his sleeves and passed his bare arms over each item, trying to feel for the tingle that had alerted him to the truth of Caidin's blood.

Eventually Taran filled the awkward silence. "Ah, for me, at least, I'm hoping I can test the blood and maybe see if any drugs were used on the victims."

Draeson dropped his arms. "Ahpra's Tears, you're not going to be tasting them, are you?"

Taran looked startled. "No. No, of course not." He held up a small pair of scissors. "I'll just take a snippet of each and test it back in my room with my, uh, chemicals and things."

Draeson shook his head. "Well, that's a blessing at least." He looked closer at the clothes. The blood was so old. So dead and dry. He paused over the woman's loose dress. "Look here. There are two areas of stab wounds. One in the chest and one in the stomach. The others aren't like that."

For both sets of men's clothing, the puncture marks were concentrated in the chest. He could imagine the bloody mess the knife had made of the heart and lungs.

"With Keldan the genitals were mutilated," Brother Taran said. "Perhaps this is like that?"

"No." Draeson shook his head and pointed to the men's trousers. "If genital mutilation were part of it, then why leave these men alone? Assuming these were done by the same person as in Alapra. Besides, these marks are too high to be aimed at the genitals of a pregnant woman." He lifted the middle of the dress to simulate the swell of a pregnant belly.

"Oh," Taran's voice was barely above a breath.

"These were meant for the baby."

Draeson let the dress fall. "Yes. So what do they all have in common?" He held out his hand, fingers wide, and chanted the identifying spell in his mind. When he released the power, his chest tightened as his worst fear was confirmed.

Each set of clothing began to glow with soft golden light. The blood that had soaked into the fabric responded to Draeson's magic and let itself be known. Light spilled from the blood of Roydan's distant cousin and the stable boy. But on the dress of the seamstress, there was no glow from the killing blows to her chest, only from the blood of her unborn child, spilled from the stab-wounds in her belly.

Taran let out a long, low sound of wonder. "Something in common indeed."

"Yes." Draeson felt his fingernails cutting into his palms. Someone was working to a very deliberate hit list.

Behind him, Morgin Vere cleared his throat. "Excuse me, but, whatever it is . . . does this mean I have it too?"

Draeson turned to see the undertaker standing, trembling, with his arms spread wide. Clearly traced beneath every visible part of his skin were the lines of veins and arteries, beaming with golden light.

CHAPTER TWENTY-FOUR

B rannon watched through the window as they carried the body of Caidin Ray, wrapped in a sheet, to the cart that would take him to the morgue. The undertaker had been told to keep him, untouched, until further notice. In a case like this, Brannon couldn't be sure they'd seen every piece of evidence the body had to offer. He couldn't face it if some vital clue was washed away or buried before he thought to search for it.

As Mayor Shillia directed the men on securing the body and driving slowly, he couldn't help wondering if what she'd said that morning was true. If he'd locked up the blacksmith last night, would the young man in the cart still be alive?

He shook his head. It didn't add up. Shillia herself had confirmed that neither of the Gruuls had been to Alapra in years, nor received any visitors from there that she knew of. So how could they be connected to the murder of Keldan? He was sure the murders were done by the same person or, he shuddered to think, group of people. It was clear there had to be a purpose uniting them all; he just couldn't be certain what that purpose was. But the look of fear in Kholi Gruul's face when he thought Ula might believe he'd given away too many secrets of Djin magic, made Brannon think that, whatever that purpose was, the blacksmith would not have wanted any part of it.

He turned away from the window. The tavern had started to fill with regular customers again, but the atmosphere was dim. Ula sat at a table with several large bowls containing dirt, ash, chaff, and clay. She'd also laid out several large pieces of leather, a bottle of ink, and a sharp knife. She claimed she could do something to protect the village.

Brannon moved closer and laid his hand on the back of the chair next to hers. "Do you think Kholi Gruul is the murderer?"

Ula looked up at him as if studying his face. She gave a tight shake of the head, setting the beads in her dreadlocks clacking together. "No. I not believe. Kholi is shaman. Will always have love for life. More interesting to me is that *you* do not think him murderer. Why?"

Brannon shrugged. "Honestly, I'm not sure about him. I don't think he's a killer but he's definitely involved. I just don't know how much. I wish he'd told us who he shared the pillow talk with and exactly what he told them."

Ula put down the piece of leather she was working. "I know what he told."

Brannon's grip on the chair tightened. "You do?"

"Yes. It be the runes. The ones painted on all the

bodies but this last one. They be the runes of Kholi's tribe. They could only come from him."

Brannon pulled out the chair and sat down. "So he is involved. He gave them the key to creating a Risen. He must have known what it would be used for."

Ula shook her head again. "No. Those runes be nothing. Every tribe shaman have different runes because they not important. He give away something that be nothing. Distraction only. Yet somehow they find out the true knowledge."

"And what is that?"

She patted his hand. "Not for you. No shaman tattoo on your shoulder." There was a finality in her tone that did not brook challenge.

Brannon stroked his scar while he thought. "So the runes on Keldan's body were the same? They're all from Kholi's tribe?"

"Yes."

"Is there any chance that someone else from his tribe is in Kalanon?"

Ula snorted. "Kholi only Djin of his generation to leave our home. Only shaman too."

"Blood and Tears." Brannon stared around the tavern room, his mind mulling it over. This, if nothing else, linked the murders here in Sandilar with that of Keldan back in Alapra. But with no clear evidence of anyone who had been back and forth between the two. The bigger question was, had the blacksmith finally given up the true secrets or had the culprit figured it out some other way?

The few townsfolk inside stared back at him with blank eyes. Karia Knox and her father were still nowhere to be seen. The kitchen was being run by other staff, turning out simple, late breakfasts of scrambled eggs and porridge and bread.

"You should have told me about this before, you know. Even if you thought he was innocent. You're the only other Djin around here. If you start holding back information, people are going to wonder why."

Ula nodded to the items on her table. "That is why I make these. Kalan buildings have no protection from kaluki. No spirit bricks in their walls. Most of my things were stolen last night, but from these local ingredients I can still make totems to ask the earth spirits to protect the buildings and keep Risen out."

"So you think there really is a rogue Risen out there."

Ula shrugged. "I do not know, but I would rather be safe if there is."

Brannon nodded thoughtfully. "So would I. I wish there was a way to know for sure."

She shrugged again and went back to spooning dirt into a leather pouch.

The door opened and Jessamine, who had supervised the wrapping of the body, came into the room. Brannon caught her eye and she hurried over to join them. She raised an eyebrow at the contents of the bowls on the table.

"I'd have gone with the porridge, myself."

Brannon gave her a weak smile. "Have you eaten yet?"

She shook her head. "I don't think I could stomach anything just yet." She sat down at the table and started fiddling with a piece of straw that had fallen from one of the bowls. "I've been trying to wrap my head around this whole thing. It's a long way from training at the College."

Brannon thought about it for a moment. "Actually, it's not. This is just like figuring out a difficult diagnosis. You look at all the symptoms and try to find what fits. And if you can't, then you try to learn more about the patient's history and symptoms and possible diseases until you have enough information to make the call. Solving this is the same."

Jessamine dropped the straw and tugged her ponytail tighter, her expression thoughtful. "Okay, so currently we're not sure what fits the 'symptoms' we have so . . . the next step is to find out more. You'll be talking to Karia about the latest victim. Maybe I could ask around town and see if anyone saw anything suspicious last night."

"Excellent," Brannon agreed.

"Do you think Kholi will tell you anything else?"

Brannon shrugged. "I hope so. He's given information to someone. Chances are good that it's someone who's involved." A burst of inspiration struck him. "Check the graveyard. If someone really did successfully perform the raising ritual last night, there has to be a body missing somewhere. If they didn't kill a fresh one, that means they got one that was already dead."

Jessamine grimaced. "Thanks. I was happier not thinking about that."

Brannon chuckled. "Yeah, sorry. Will you be okay? I don't need to tell you to run away if you actually do see a Risen, do I?"

She shuddered. "No, after bodies in cupboards and assassins on boats, I am starting to learn to be careful."

"Not quite what a physician's apprentice should be learning, but it's something! Take someone with you, just in case."

She smiled. "Will do." She started to get up, then sank down again, her head tilted to one side. "What if that's what the murderer is doing?"

"What do you mean?"

"Learning. First he tries to do a raising, then he succeeds. Maybe he's someone's apprentice. Like me. Learning the ropes?" Her eyes flickered to Ula, who appeared absorbed in her work and now had several little pouches lined up on the wooden table. "But then, who would be the teacher?"

The door opened again and the noise in the tavern fell silent.

A tall, slender woman with dark hair glided into the room. "I'd like a room please," she said. Her dress was deep russet silk with black trim, over black lace-up boots that showed the dust of the road. A small black hat with silk flowers in the same color as the dress sat daintily at an angle on her head. Men made way for her as she moved gracefully past. Brannon knew those closest would smell the hint of spice and vanilla.

"Who is that?" Jessamine breathed.

Brannon sat up straight. "That is Ambassador Ylani Shaylar of Nilar."

CHAPTER TWENTY-FIVE

"What, in the name of the Hooded, is she doing here?" Brannon muttered as he watched Ylani speaking to the woman behind the bar. He found himself rising to his feet and crossing the room. When she passed a few coins across the counter and turned to point toward her luggage, he was right there.

"You're a long way from Alapra," he said.

A little smile graced her lips. "As are you, Sir Brannon. Are you following me?"

To his surprise, he felt himself blushing like an idiot. "Actually, I was here first. Maybe you're following me."

The corner of her mouth twitched. "Maybe."

Brannon felt his calm face slip. Between the murder and the difficulties with the mayor, not knowing who to trust or how to make sense of the clues, his brain was already swirling. Now this? He forced himself to stand straighter, pushed his shoulders back, and raised his chin. He was not some raw recruit to be flustered by a pretty face.

"You realize there have been several murders here connected to the one I questioned you about in Alapra?" he said. "It seems awfully coincidental that you should show up here as well."

Her smile vanished. "No, I didn't realize that."

Brannon shook his head. She was baffling. "You were the one who first told me about the other murders. You must have known where they took place."

She bit her lower lip. "I did, didn't I? My information was . . . incomplete."

"So, then why are you here?"

She shrugged. "Business. Lady Latricia and I are negotiating import rights for Nilarian silk."

Brannon blinked. "The deal Keldan was after? And his father?"

"Many people have shown an interest in this deal, Sir Brannon. But I find Lady Latricia to be uniquely persuasive. More so than her husband."

"And why is that?"

Ylani laid a finger over her lips. "Business secrets. You understand. We'll be going up to the Manor shortly, but I like to have my own base so I suggested we stop here and get a room. It's nice to have a bit of independence, don't you think?"

The door opened and a gust of fresh air stirred the smell of beer, porridge, and people. Draeson and Taran entered the tavern along with Lady Latricia, her son Tomidan, and some servants.

"Look who we found," Draeson commented, leading the way to where Brannon and Ylani were standing. "I see you found one too. So many suspects all in one place."

"Magus Draeson," Ylani said. "A delight, as always. Will you be sticking with just the wild accusations today, or adding a dash of hypocrisy as well?"

Brannon bit down hard on the chuckle that threatened.

Draeson's eyes darkened. The dragon tattoo that lay across his throat like a necklace shifted like a restless sleeper. "There's no good reason for you to be here, Nilarian. Yet, wherever there's a threat to Kalanon or the royal house, there I find Nilar. If we prove you have something to do with what's going on here, it'll take more than clever words and pretty dresses to save you."

Brannon felt the hairs on the back of his arm lift. The urge to chuckle was gone.

"Believe me," Ylani said, her voice soft but framed by the sudden quiet. "I want matters resolved as much as you do. I have no interest in reigniting old quarrels. Both our countries need peace."

Brannon did believe her. There was something in the tone of her voice and her expression that seemed genuine. Jaded as he was from seven years with court politicians, he thought this foreign ambassador had just spoken the truth as she knew it. Or perhaps it was the truth as he, himself, knew it. He knew what he would become in wartime. The murderer they hunted hadn't even scratched the surface of the deaths Brannon had caused as the famed Bloodhawk. A few short years as a physician had yet to redress the balance.

Draeson, however, seemed unconvinced. He leaned forward, his finger raised, when Ula joined them, her hands full of the little pouches she'd been making.

"The wizard returns," she said, beaming at Draeson.

"Did you learn a useful thing?"

Draeson gritted his teeth. "I'm not a wizard. I'm a mage. Try learning that useful thing." And with that, he pushed past and made his way up the stairs.

"Nicely done," Brannon murmured under his breath.

Ula blinked at him with exaggerated innocence. "I not know Kalan very well. Get words mixed up sometimes."

"Indeed." He turned back to Ylani. "If you're serious about wanting to keep the peace, maybe try not to irritate the four-hundred-year-old magus."

Her lips twitched upward. "That's much more difficult than it sounds."

"You're not wrong." Brannon gave a wry grin, then caught Brother Taran's eye. "Taran, I'm interviewing Karia shortly to see what she knows about her fiancé's death. Would you like to join me? She might find it comforting to have a priest present."

The young man's face paled. "Um, I'm more of a solitary monk. A very private order. I don't know if I'd be much help with that sort of thing." He held up a satchel. "Also, I have these samples to test."

Brannon nodded. "No problem. Do the tests. I can handle it."

Ylani raised a hand and her silk sleeve slid back to reveal a wide silver bracelet. "I wonder if perhaps I could help? I know I'm a foreigner here, but I'm good at reading people. I might be able to pick up something a Kalan would miss."

Brannon hesitated. The idea of one suspect being part of the interview for another was inherently flawed. And yet she had a point. "Perhaps you could help. When you get back from your business at the manor, of course. I'll be talking to the Djin blacksmith. Ula has spoken with him already but perhaps you would have better luck—as one outsider living in Kalanon to another."

She nodded graciously. "Of course. As one outsider to another."

CHAPTER TWENTY-SIX

Taran made it almost to the door of his room when he heard Jessamine's voice behind him. The ward-dog sniffed at him, then settled back down as if going to sleep. He turned the handle and dropped the satchel of blood samples inside before turning to see what she wanted.

She smiled at him as she strode along the corridor. Her blond ponytail bobbed gently in time with her steps. "Hey, Taran. I was wondering, when you do the testing, could I help? Maybe you could teach me? I find all your chemicals and things really fascinating."

Taran gave a kind of half shrug. "I guess, if you want to. I mean, most of what I know is poisons. The rest are chemicals for making them or treating them or testing for them. It might not fit with a physician's beliefs."

She frowned. "I don't see why not. Who better to know about treatments and tests for poison than a physician? What if someone came to me looking for help? Besides, lots of medicines are poisonous in the wrong dose so I know a lot of that sort of thing already. Maybe it could be my specialty or something."

"I guess so." Taran nodded and gestured into his room. "Come on in, then. I was just about to start."

She grimaced. "I can't right now. I have to go check out the graveyard. Brannon's worried that maybe one of the bodies was used to make a Risen so he wants me to take a look. You could come with me?"

Taran hovered in the doorway, uncertain. "Um."

Jessamine's nose wrinkled. "I'd rather not go alone."

"Oh, right. Of course." He glanced into the room, then pulled the door shut. The tests could wait. "I'll come with you."

The graveyard was on the edge of town and even in daylight had a somber, eerie feel to it. A line of crypts ran through the middle with a well-manicured path linking them to the gate. Each tomb was intricately carved and decorated with paint, flowering plants, and, in some cases, gold. Surrounding the crypts were the graves of common people, those without noble blood or enough wealth to afford a crypt. The graves varied greatly in age and care. Some were indicated only by wooden markers, others by elaborate stone statues or simple plaques with writing etched deeply or worn away by time.

"There are a lot of graves here," Taran said. They strolled between them, checking each for signs of disturbance. So far, it seemed every blade of grass was in place. "Any ideas for narrowing it down?"

Jessamine shook her head as she prodded at the

ground covering one grave with her toe. "Not really. I think Ula said newer bodies make for a stronger Risen, but I don't know. Maybe the crypts? Disturbing as it sounds, they might be easier to access than digging someone up."

Taran grimaced. "You might be right."

The first crypt door was painted with an image of Ahpra's weeping form on one side, reaching across to her husband, Valdan, on the other. Between them was the Hooded One in the form of a huge mountain wolf, guarding the underworld. The wolf's baleful eyes stared out in challenge to anyone approaching to disturb those inside. The latch clicked open easily and the well-oiled hinges made no sound.

Sunlight spilled into the musty darkness, illuminating several stone sarcophagi and a wall of square, painted panels, each representing the life of the person entombed behind them. A large space in the center of the burial slots was filled with a family tree, a tiny wolf head beside each name of a deceased.

Taran inspected the wall first. "These are plastered over after they're occupied, then painted. You'd have to smash your way through the panel to get inside."

Jessamine traced the edges of one with her fingertips. I guess that means these are safe then." She pointed to the sarcophagi. "What about those?"

"The lids are heavy, but they could be moved."

Jessamine braced herself with both hands against one of them and pushed. Nothing happened. "Not by me," she said, falling back at last, her chest heaving.

Taran took her place, feeling a little self-conscious as he pushed his muscles to their limit against the stone.

His arms protested and he couldn't hold back the grunt of effort that escaped his throat, but the lid of the sarcophagus moved.

"Oh, brilliant!" Jessamine exclaimed, clapping her hands excitedly. "Well done."

Taran smiled. He'd only shifted it by a few finger spans but it felt like he'd moved the whole world.

Jessamine edged closer. "Can you see inside? Is there, you know, someone home?"

Taran's smile faded. "I'll check." The smell coming from the opening was like fungus and old meat and sewerage. Taran felt his throat spasm and the sharp taste of acid on his tongue. He'd seen the freshly dead many times before—often creative forms of death—but never the effects of decay.

"The body is still in there." He pulled away and quickly moved around to push the sarcophagus closed. "Hooded Blood. We're going to have to open them all."

She wrinkled her nose. "That'll take forever. Let's split up. You do the crypts since I'm not strong enough anyway and I'll check the graves."

"You sure? I thought you didn't want to do this alone?"

"Well, I won't really be alone. How about we call out to each other between each one and make sure we're okay?"

"Okay."

He watched her leave, her slender figure silhouetted in the doorway for a moment before she slipped out into the sun. He shook himself. "Focus on the job at hand. Distractions get you killed." The words made him smile. Distractions of any sort—and particularly pretty girls—

were in short supply at the Third Alapran Monastery and the worst such a thing was likely to bring was the rage of a bishop. It was nice to be out in the world again, even if it required more care.

He pushed open the second sarcophagus. This one, thankfully, did not have the stench of the first one. The corpse inside had withered away to something resembling dry sticks. He pushed the lid closed again and walked to the door. Jessamine was walking between gravestones a short distance away.

"Everything okay?" he called.

"Yeah, I'm fine."

Feeling a little foolish, he went back inside the crypt and opened the next sarcophagus. This one also contained an ancient skeleton. The remnants of long hair clung like loose tapestry threads to her skull and a golden bracelet circled the bones of her left wrist. He wondered who she might have been as he covered up her resting place once more.

He went back to the door again, and called out for Jessamine.

Her head appeared over the top of a statue of a kneeling mourner. "Are you starting to feel silly yelling back and forth so often? Because I am."

Taran grinned. "Yeah, a bit."

"Let's just call out if we find something or if we get scared."

"Agreed."

The rest of the sarcophagi in the first crypt proved uneventful and he moved to the next, noting Jessamine had moved a little further away as he did so. She seemed to have worked out a system and was moving through the graves with purpose. The door on this crypt stuck a little and there were a lot of cobwebs inside. Once his eyes adjusted to the gloom, however, he found it was a very similar layout to the first. It had the same kind of wall of undisturbed plaster panels and a few carved or painted sarcophagi for special family members.

The smell, for the most part, was bearable now. He found he was able to block it out and even made a sort of game out of guessing which sarcophagus would have the oldest bones and which the most disturbing corpse. One had been buried with its head removed, the skull tucked down beside its knees. Another had been buried with many pieces of colored glass, like tiny stained glass windows for him to look at through eternity.

Taran moved through the next three crypts, faithfully checking and searching each one. None appeared to have bodies missing. Nor was there any sign of disturbance.

He began to relax. This search was really just a formality anyway. If there was a Risen out there—and having seen what had happened to Caidin Ray, he had to admit it was likely—chances were it wasn't with an older body. Up until now, whoever was responsible had always killed someone new every time they tried their ritual. The mayor was checking the populace to see if anyone was unaccounted for in case the same was true again. This job, he thought, pushing open yet another stone tomb, was about crossing every disgusting t and dotting every smelly i.

As he pushed the door closed on another crypt and, squinting in the strong sunlight, made his way to the next, Taran wondered what the next move would be. Up until now, the investigation team had been following along behind, picking up clues like breadcrumbs trailing from a baker's cart. They needed to think about where that cart was headed so they could reach the market ahead of it.

He took a deep breath and enjoyed the freshness of the air as he climbed the steps to yet another crypt door. Jessamine was somewhere out of sight and he envied her the chance to be out in the sunlight instead of the darkness of the tombs. His muscles ached and he knew he would feel pain in them tomorrow.

He paused, trying to put himself into the mindset of the person behind it all. They were clearly intent on creating a Risen, but why? What was the next step in all this?

As he faced yet another heavy stone sarcophagus lid, he had a realization. Using a Risen gave someone extra strength. The physical strength to do heavy tasks, but also psychological strength in terms of generating fear in others. This was about accumulating power. Whoever was behind this wanted control.

"So," he murmured to himself. "If I've just had my first real success and am on my way to building an army or taking over or whatever it is . . . what's the next step?"

Another of his old master's sayings came to mind: see the problems before they are problems and remove them. So what might the perpetrator of all this perceive to be potential problems for his grand scheme? Whatever that grand scheme might be?

Taran felt the chill of the crypt cut through his cowled, woolen tunic as if it was made of paper. The biggest potential problem for the perpetrator was the team of king's agents investigating his crimes and trying to stop him. The next logical step would be to remove them.

"Blood of the Wolf!" He pulled a knife from the sheath in his sleeve and ran out into the sun. "Jessamine! Jessamine, are you all right?"

The graveyard was quiet but for the sound of summer crickets. Taran turned full circle, his eyes scanning the gray stones, flowering shrubs, and occasional weeping willow for any sign of movement. "Jessamine?"

The hilt of the knife pressed hard into his palm, a sharp spot of cold in the searing sun on his chilled skin. Jessamine had asked him to come so that she would be safe and he had left her alone. If something had happened to her because he had left her vulnerable, he didn't know how he would face Sir Brannon.

He started walking, his steps increasing with his heart rate. She had to be here somewhere. Surely he couldn't already be too late?

He called out again, and this time there was an answering yelp.

"Jess?"

She squealed and there was a thud. Taran ran toward it. He rounded a huge stone representation of the gates to the Hooded One's realm, to see a figure on the ground.

Jessamine was sprawled, half on the grass and half across a moss-covered gravestone. She moaned and rolled over and Taran could see blood on her sleeves.

He quickly knelt at her side, checking her for any major wounds. "Are you all right? What happened?"

She waved him away and sat up, brushing her hands on her skirt. "Yeah, I'm fine. I'm a clumsy idiot, is all. I tripped and scraped my arms on that." She pointed to the offending stone.

Taran felt the tightness in his chest loosen a little. "Really? You're sure you're okay? That's all it is?"

She nodded, her expression sheepish. "Yeah. Sorry, I didn't mean to scare you."

"Oh, that's okay." Taran flushed. His gaze traced the ground. "What was it that tripped you?"

"It was . . . " She frowned as she stood up, eyes searching for the offending object, but there was none. "I don't know. That's weird. I guess I really am just clumsy today."

"Or not." Taran eyed their surroundings. "Let's stick together now, okay?"

He slipped his knife back into the sheath in his sleeve and they walked slowly back toward the crypts.

"Did you find anything?" he asked.

She shook her head. "I've been right around the whole place and I can't see anything that looks freshly dug up. What about you?"

"Not yet. But I haven't finished checking."

"Well, let's get it over with."

Taran sighed and looked back toward the crypts that huddled together like gossips. He could almost hear them cackling at him as he led the way back to the next one in the row. Now that he'd found Jessamine unharmed, his fear had left, taking his enthusiasm for the task with it. But at least he would have her with him for these last few. Then they could go back to the inn and work on testing the blood samples.

He froze with this foot on the first step and Jessamine collided gently with his shoulder.

"What is it?"

"The door's open."

"So?"

"So I haven't been in this one yet. Someone else has been here."

Her mouth formed a startled circle and Taran edged forward, straining his eyes to try to see into the gloom of the crypt.

Something rattled inside.

Taran felt Jessamine's fingers close tightly around his arm.

"Who's in there?" he called.

There was a thud and a creak as the door opened wider. A boy of maybe six or seven stepped out into the light, his hair a mop of dark-honey and his face grave.

Jessamine's fingers loosened. "Tommy? Tomidan Sandilar?"

Taran felt a burst of relief and confusion. "You're the boy that was at the inn earlier. The one with Lady Latricia and Ambassador Ylani."

The child nodded. "Lady Latricia is my mother."

"What are you doing here? Where's your nanny?"

"I wanted to tell Grandma about Daddy. She might wonder where he is. Nanny thinks I'm sleeping. She's boring." The boy squinted at Taran's cowled tunic. "You're a priest."

Taran nodded and the boy took his hand, tugging him toward the crypt.

"Come and see."

Taran shot a look at Jessamine, who shrugged. There

didn't seem any harm in it, so he let Tommy lead him inside.

This crypt was at least twice the size of the others he'd been in. The sarcophagi were all carved in intricate likenesses of the deceased and then painted with gold leaf. Some even had canopies over them like four-poster beds to give the illusion of sleep. The walls were painted elaborately with images from the history of the Dukes of Sandilar. A lantern and matches were on a shelf just inside the door. Taran quickly lit it so they could see more clearly.

"Here." Tomidan pulled Taran forward and pointed to the family tree. "Somebody ruined it."

The light from the lantern spilled across the large, scroll-worked representation of the Sandilar family, past and present. Deep scratches had been gouged across it, scraping the paint from the stone in harsh lines. Names had been crossed out and a huge X carved through the entire thing.

Tommy tugged on his sleeve. "Why'd they do that?"

Taran stared from the vandalized image to the upturned face of the boy beside him. His shoulders raised in a helpless shrug. "I . . . I have no idea."

CHAPTER TWENTY-SEVEN

V ery few guests ever saw the kitchen of the Knox Inn and Tavern. The wide doors swung in both directions and opened into a broad space with long preparation tables and three wood-burning ovens. Stacked baskets held bushels of vegetables and fruit, waiting for chopping. Ready-to-pluck geese hung from the ceiling over a basin, and a sheep carcass slow-roasted on a spit over a low fire in preparation for the evening meal.

As Brannon walked in, Dargin Knox looked up from kneading a knob of dough larger than his head. "We're behind with the cooking and don't need any more distractions."

Brannon opened his mouth to say that people wouldn't complain if the meals were late after a murder had taken place on the premises, but then changed his mind. Perhaps they would. People had short memories and little tolerance when problems started affecting them personally. "Karia?"

"She's not here."

"Do you know where she is?"

The man's fist punched into the dough. "She wanted time alone."

Morgin, who had squeezed through the door behind Brannon, touched his shoulder. "I know where she'll be," he said.

Brannon followed him back through the tavern room where Ula was creating more of her spirit pouches, spitting into each one in turn and murmuring incantations. Draeson joined them as Morgin headed outside, then turned away from the courtyard, where stable boys were scrubbing at the blood on the cobblestones, and led the way around the back of the building. A thin path was fenced on one side with a hedge and sported weeds pushing their heads through every crack. It opened into a wider space some distance round and several large wooden doors punctured the side of the inn like holes in a belt.

"Before they expanded the stables, they used to keep the horses around here. Nobody comes back here now." Morgin pushed open one of the doors. The hinges shrieked a protest.

Brannon and Draeson followed Morgin inside.

The space was clearly designed as a stable but had not been used as such in some time. The floor was packed hard dirt and the feed trough was empty. There were pegs on the wall for hanging tack and the like, but while a dim lantern hung from one, the rest held nothing but cobwebs.

Karia Knox sat on the floor, her body turned into the corner, her face hidden from sight. Her shoulders trembled. "Go away, Morgin. I can't deal with you right now. Just leave me alone."

"Miss Knox," Brannon said, making his voice as gentle as possible. "We need to talk to you about your fiancé. We need you to help us catch the person who killed him."

Karia turned to face him, her eyes were red and puffy even in the dim lamp light. "Do you think you will catch who did this, Sir Brannon?"

He nodded. "We'll do our best."

"And we are the best." Draeson added, with an expansive wave of his arm. Brannon turned to shoot him a glare, thinking the mage was about to put the moves on the grieving girl, but Draeson's face held a distracted kind of intensity that was at odds with his playboy mannerisms.

Karia had already shifted around to face them square on. She hugged her knees to her chest. "What do you need to know?"

Brannon lowered himself down to eye level and sat with his back against the wall. After a moment, Draeson and Morgin did the same. "Well, how well liked was Caidin? Did he have any enemies?"

She shook her head, her hair falling forward until she reached up and tucked it behind her ear. "No, not at all. Everybody liked Caidin. I mean, I know I'm supposed to say that because I loved him, but it's true. He was a truly wonderful man."

"The town golden boy," added Morgin.

Brannon raised an eyebrow. "How so?"

Morgin shrugged.

"He'd always help out anyone who asked him,"

Karia said. "He was really good that way. That's how we met."

"Any idea why someone would want to kill him?"

"No." Her voice was thick with emotion. "I don't know why they would want to kill anyone in our town. This whole thing has been horrible."

Draeson leaned forward. "Karia, who are Caidin's parents?"

"Good question," Morgin murmured, just loud enough to be heard.

Karia glared. "Rogan and Melly Ray are good people. Honest farmers and upstanding members of this community. There's nothing wrong with having them as parents. We can't all be the bastard son of a duke."

"Of course there's nothing wrong with having them as parents," Brannon said, puzzling over her words.

Draeson leaned forward even more. "Are you sure they *are* his parents?"

She blinked at him. "Why wouldn't they be?"

The mage said nothing, but leaned back with a thoughtful expression. Silence held for a moment as Brannon wondered what Draeson was getting at and if he should intervene with a new question. Eventually Morgin spoke again.

"If he was some sort of changeling, then maybe it's for the best." He put his hand on Karia's shoulder. "He was never really good enough for you."

The girl shoved the intruding hand away. "For Ahpra's sake, Morgin, would you leave it alone? Take a Hooded hint: I'm not interested in you and no amount of bad-mouthing my dead fiancé will change that! Get lost!"

The young man jerked back as if her words had burned him. He stood and raised his fist and, for a moment, Brannon thought he might have to restrain him. Then he turned and slammed it into the wall beside him. The wooden beam cracked and split beneath the force of the blow. "I don't understand you," he wailed.

Karia sighed. "And you never will. Go away, Morgin."

Red-faced, Morgin fled.

Brannon looked between the empty doorway and the girl on the floor. "Do you think one of us should follow him?"

Draeson shrugged. "Why? He has to learn about rejection sometime."

"He'll be okay," Karia said. "I've been harsh with him before. He always comes back like a little puppy, telling me how his daddy is Duke Roydan and that makes him better than the rest of us."

Brannon felt his eyebrows raise. "His father is Duke Roydan?"

"The mayor was the duke's mistress for a while. I thought everyone knew that."

Brannon tried to keep his expression neutral. He shouldn't have been surprised. His old friend had enjoyed many a mistress over the years, he just hadn't realized how openly some of them had been acknowledged. He wondered which had come first for Mayor Shillia: the position of mayor or the acknowledgement of her son as a bastard. It seemed likely that one had caused the other.

"Are there any other things about Caidin you think it would be good for us to know? Anything strange that he was involved with or doing lately?"

"No. Things have been normal."

"What about in town generally? Any strange happenings? Other than the murders, I mean. Anything out of the ordinary?"

She rubbed her hands over her eyes. "No, nothing. This isn't that exciting a town. We get a few traders and sometimes people making deliveries up to the manor, and of course the law carts taking criminals to the mine, but that's it. And Caidin doesn't have anything to do with any of that."

"What about other crimes? Do you know if there has been an increase? You must hear a lot from people in the tavern."

"Yeah, people talk but I don't think there's been anything like that."

Brannon caught her gaze. "One of my team was robbed in your inn the night we arrived. Somehow someone got into her room while it was locked and went through her bags."

"I . . . I don't know how they could have done that. We keep the spare keys locked up. My family are the only ones who have access to them."

"What happens when a guest loses a key?" Draeson asked.

"We get the lock replaced."

"And who makes the new lock?" Brannon thought he knew the answer already but he had to ask.

"The blacksmith," Karia said, her eyes wide. "Kholi Gruul."

Brannon sat back, letting it sink in. "I think we need to talk to Mr. Gruul again. Now."

CHAPTER TWENTY-EIGHT

S andilar Manor rose above Ambassador Ylani and Lady Latricia, like one of the mountains that formed its backdrop. A huge stone edifice set in expansive gardens, it somehow melded the stern strength of generations of mining families with the softer opulence of wealth. The architecture included sweeping curves carved into the outer walls, balustraded balconies trailing flowering wisteria, and intricate finials decorating each peak or corner of the tiled roof.

Ylani felt very small as she trudged the long, straight road between topiary animals to the huge, brass-worked double front doors. The tiny hat she wore made her feel naked but she knew anything larger would only make her more noticeable as a Nilarian. She already drew enough attention as a foreigner.

In fact, the one bag she carried with her had been pressed into her hands precisely because she was foreign. Ula, the Djin witch Sir Brannon had summoned from the isles, had given her a selection of small pouches and insisted that they be distributed throughout the manor as a protection spell against whatever had been murdering townsfolk. "You and I both not trusted here," she had said. "You give them help, they like you more." Looking at the manor house, she didn't think offering leather pouches of mud and herbs would engender any goodwill here.

She made a conscious effort to hold herself tall and straight. One thing she had learned in politics was that confidence, or the appearance of it, got one much further than anything else.

Latricia fidgeted. Not a good sign from the woman who was Ylani's passport inside.

"Are you still nervous about having left Tommy back at the inn with his nanny?"

"That boy can get himself into all kinds of trouble." The widow clenched her hands in the folds of her skirt. "I haven't been this far away from him since his father died."

"You can do this, right?" She felt a shift in the other woman.

"Yes. Tommy will be fine in town. Everyone loves him there. It's his future I need to worry about. And mine."

"Good. Now hold onto that."

Ylani turned her attention to their destination once more. The gravel driveway was worn with wheel tracks and sorely in need of raking back into place. As they got closer to the house, she saw that the main tracks followed the path around to the left toward the stables and carriage shed. But another track turned right and had churned up the manicured lawn, disappearing behind the house. It was from this right hand track that a number of armed men appeared and stopped, watching the two women approach.

"Is there a barracks or something on that side of the house?" Ylani asked.

"No."

"Then this might be about to get interesting. Just smile and keep walking."

The doors of the main house swung open and a thin man with dark hair stepped out to greet them. He was quickly flanked by two larger men in house livery but carrying truncheons.

"Lady Latricia," the thin man called out. "This is an unexpected delight. Welcome home."

Ylani felt Latricia pause, then determinedly lead the way up the wide stone steps to the atrium. "Thank you. Where's Steward Herolt?"

The man smiled. "Duke Roydan sent for him to come to Alapra. He asked me to take care of things here."

"And you are?"

"The new steward. Fressin."

"Well, thank you, Fressin. This is Ambassador Ylani of Nilar. She will be joining us for a few days."

Ylani felt Fressin's gaze travel up and down, a burning, swift assessment. "I'm afraid that's impossible," he said.

"What?"

Ylani stepped forward, unable to stop herself. "Is this not Lady Latricia's house?" she demanded.

Fressin spread his hands expansively. "Of course. Hers and young Lord Tomidan. Where is he?"

"Back in town with our luggage. We thought to send for them when we were settled," Ylani told him.

"If I'm still the lady of the house, Steward Fressin, then I am entitled to have as a guest anyone I choose. Ambassador Ylani is a business partner and I intend to show her Sandilar hospitality." Latricia's lips pressed into a thin line.

The steward shook his head. "I'm afraid Duke Roydan left specific instructions. With these troubled times, we've had to take extra security measures here at Sandilar Manor. I'm sure you understand, Lady Latricia, that it's not appropriate to have a Nilarian in the house of one of the royal family."

Ylani saw Latricia's face flush.

"This is my guest. If she is not welcome then I will not stay either."

Fressin shrugged. "That is your prerogative."

"You forget yourself, Steward Fressin!"

The instinct blazed in Ylani, hot and fast. She felt sharp edges around the steward like arrowheads bursting through her skin. She swayed and grasped Latricia's arm as the widow stepped forward angrily. Her fingers squeezed tight.

"It's okay, Latricia. He's only following the duke's orders. I'm sure I shall be perfectly comfortable at the inn. Would you walk back with me?"

Latricia hovered for a moment, and Ylani was terrified that she would press the point, but then she felt the arm beneath her hand relax. "All right. But I insist on showing you around the garden first."

The armed men to the right of the house took a few steps closer.

Ylani gave her most graceful smile. "Actually, dear, I'm a bit tired after walking up from town. Perhaps another time?"

"Of course." Latricia shot a venomous look at the new steward. "When things are back to normal."

Ylani kept her grip on Latricia's arm and pulled her back down the stairs. The instinct's warning was still strong. She felt the crunch of gravel beneath her feet when she realized she was still carrying Ula's bag. Turning, she tossed it up the stairs to land at Fressin's feet.

"Sir Brannon Kesh is in town investigating the murders," she said. "His team asked that we deliver that. Put a pouch in each corner of the house and it will offer protection."

Fressin left the bag where it fell. "Tell him thank you."

Ylani forced herself to stick to a measured pace as they walked away. It would not do to have the enemy see them running. A topiary lion seemed to mock her with green claws.

"That," she murmured to Latricia as they crossed the threshold of the gates and gravel gave way to cobbled road, "is a very dangerous man."

Latricia nodded, her voice sounding high and short of breath. "There's definitely something not right going on. That is not how Herolt would have behaved. If Keldan were still alive, he'd have all their heads." Her boots clacked angrily on the stones. "I'm so glad we thought to leave Tommy behind. That man would have snatched him up and left us out in the cold."

"Yes, I believe he would." Ylani felt a surge of relief

that they had at least avoided that level of unpleasantness. She'd have had no chance of extricating Latricia if Fressin had taken her son. "I'd wager whatever they're up to has to do with those tracks leading around the right side of the house. If we're right about Duke Roydan dealing for Nilarian weapons, then I think delivery has already been made."

"What do we do about it, though?"

Ylani caught her bottom lip between her teeth but her smile soon pulled it free. "We do what we set out to do. We make sure someone more trusted than we are gets the evidence and brings it to the king. I'd say the King's Champion would be a suitable choice, wouldn't you? We have Sir Brannon Kesh packaged and waiting for us here in Sandilar."

"Of course!" Latricia clapped her hands. "He'll hate it, of course. Roydan and Brannon go way back. But he'll report it, I think. He's too honorable not to. I'll talk to him when we get back."

Ylani's steps faltered. "Will it hurt him very much, do you think? To betray his friend?"

"Not as much as finding out what kind of man his friend really is." Latricia shrugged. "Rather him than us. We need to find a way to bring that bastard Roydan down."

Ylani chewed her lip again. There was no arguing with that. If she could reveal Roydan as a traitor, she could likely get the name of the Nilarian he was dealing with. That would enable her to take action back home and try to put a stop to this inter-country needling and warmongering. That was worth a little heartache to any man.

Latricia continued to growl as they walked. "I can't believe he put that horrible man in charge. Where did he even find . . . " She trailed off, her eyes wide. "Ahpra's Tears! I've seen him before. He was the man in my garden. The one who was spying on Tommy and me after Keldan died."

Ylani stopped walking. "Are you sure?" She turned slowly, watching the countryside. Sheep, rocks, grass.

"I can't believe I missed it. He's in different clothes but . . . I'm sure it's him. Roydan wouldn't have really put him in charge, surely. What if he's an imposter? We need to do something."

The sharp, invisible arrowheads pressed hard against her skin. "Latricia . . . we need to run. Now!"

They had barely moved three steps before he struck.

The instinct gave Ylani just enough warning to fling herself to the side as a thrown dagger spun past. She fell hard, hitting her knee on the cobblestones, then rolled onto the grass beside the road. She looked up to see a slim, masked figure punch Lady Latricia hard in the face. The Kalan noblewoman went down like a dropped sack of potatoes. The dark-clad figure pulled out another knife.

"No!" Ylani hurled herself at his back as he drove the blade down toward her friend's neck. She grabbed his descending wrist with one hand, wrapped her other arm around his neck and leaned backward with all her might. "Latricia, run!"

Blood poured from Latricia's nose, vividly red against her stark white face. She was frozen in place, her wide eyes the only part of her that seemed able to move as they darted from the knife to Ylani and back again.

Ylani felt her breath driven from her body as their attacker simply reversed the movement of the arm she was restraining, jabbing his elbow into her ribs. She tightened her grip around his throat but, a moment later, felt his body shift and twist as he threw her over his shoulder. Her back slammed into the ground, hard.

Ylani realized she'd shifted their attacker's primary focus onto herself, but Latricia still wasn't moving. Her entire body ached and she didn't have the breath to speak. She flicked her hand at Latricia, trying to indicate for her to go. The widow pushed out with her heels, sliding herself back along the ground maybe half a body-length before coming to a stop again, whimpering. No help there.

The attacker straddled Ylani, his knife raised. "You should have minded your own business," he said.

The knife swung down and Ylani reached up with both hands to try to halt its decent. For a moment she thought she could hold him off. Then he reached out with his other hand and slowly, deliberately, twined his fingers into her hair. As she struggled against the hand with the knife, he pulled her head up and bashed it against the cobbles.

Pain exploded sparks through her brain and into her vision. She felt her fingers slip on the warm skin of his arm and then light flashed on the dagger blade as it slid toward her throat.

Ylani screamed.

CHAPTER TWENTY-NINE

The streets bustled with people. Carts laden with produce headed for market, vendors called out from shop doorways and, at one point, a small flock of sheep were herded along an alleyway. The little town seemed to have forgotten the murder of the morning and was going about its daily business in a protective haze of denial.

Brannon paused at a crossroads. It wouldn't take long to get to the manor and back. Whatever Lady Latricia and Ambassador Ylani were doing up there, they were likely to be finished soon. Latricia wouldn't leave her son for long.

"I think I'm going to get Ylani to help with this."

Draeson pouted. "The Nilarian? Why?"

"I think he'll relate to her as a fellow outsider. We might get more from him that way."

The mage shrugged. "Whatever. You can go beg her for help if you want. I'll meet you there." He wandered off into the crowd.

Brannon scowled after him. As an old man, Draeson's temperamental attitude had seemed fitting, a good-natured crotchetiness from a respected elder. From his current, youthful form, it was the behavior of a spoilt brat.

The King's Champion turned his feet toward the manor, a road he'd travelled several times in younger years, when Roydan was new to his title. Back then, going to war was a bright and exciting thing, shining like a new coin in the sun. Brannon, Roydan, and Aldan, the inseparable trio, had trained together and come to spend their last break at Sandilar Manor before heading to the front. He remembered the crowd from the town—women, children, and old men mostly. They had lined the streets, throwing flowers and cheering for the young men. It was his first experience of being treated like a hero, despite not yet having done anything heroic. Certainly no one in Alapra had treated raw recruits that way! But these had been Roydan's people and they were proud of their young duke. Not long after that, Brannon earned the name Bloodhawk, and cheering crowds became commonplace for him and Aldan both, but he fondly remembered that first time, when Roydan had been the center of attention.

A lot had changed on the road since then. The cobblestones had been updated and lain in decorative patterns—something he'd never seen in wartime. There were even little gardens of wildflowers planted alongside the road as it led away from the town. But the biggest change he could think of was the fact that he was walking this road in search of a Nilarian. The first one to get this far into Kalanon in a decade.

Brannon wondered if Draeson was right to mistrust the ambassador. Away from the mage's irritating presence, he had to admit that the man's passionate hatred of Nilarians was almost enough to push him toward accepting Ylani's word in and of itself, just for spite. He wasn't foolish enough to take her at absolute face value, of course. She was a politician and a Nilarian, and she was definitely up to something . . . but he felt that she was honest in her offer to help, and that, if nothing else, made him think perhaps she was innocent of involvement in the murders. Despite the connection Keldan's silk trade deal seemed to make.

"Or," he muttered to himself, "she's playing me like a reed pipe and only offered so she could get close to the investigation and make sure we're not onto her." The woman was ridiculously confusing to be around. He hadn't been affected this much by a pretty face in quite some time. If a new recruit had reacted like this, he'd have given him a good talking to. Or, more likely, a good pounding in the training arena to smack some sense into him. Maybe both.

He shook his head in exasperation. "The Nilarian Ambassador, no less."

Still, the woman had a gift with words and a good sense of people. She would be an asset in the interrogation of Kholi Gruul.

And this time, it would be an interrogation. The revelation that he'd made the locks at the Knox Inn was one piece of evidence too many. Someone with a key had stolen Ula's supplies. Those supplies had likely been used to create the Risen that had killed Caidin Ray. Added to what they already knew about the man, it made a substantial stack of questions requiring answers. Brannon would use every tool he could to get those answers from the blacksmith.

He peered ahead, hoping to catch a glimpse of Ambassador Ylani and Lady Latricia on the road. Sure enough, two figures appeared from where the road bent around a rocky outcrop. He waved to get their attention, but it was clear they had not seen him. He quickened his pace.

A moment later, as he watched, a third figure appeared, knocking both women to the ground.

Brannon swore. His feet broke into a run, seeming to barely touch the pavement as he hurled himself forward as fast as he could. Ahead of him, the attacking figure was being held off by one of the women. As he came closer, he could make out that it was Ambassador Ylani, pulling the attacker away from Latricia. Within moments, the man had her pinned to the ground and she wrestled with him for control of a knife.

Brannon didn't slow down at all, and he barreled into the would-be assassin at full speed. Both of them were flung free of Ylani and tumbled over each other. The knife skittered across the stone road. Brannon felt the sting of grazed skin on his legs and arms, but ignored it. The assailant scrabbled toward the knife. Brannon reached for him, his fingers closing on the fabric of his shirt. He tugged hard, pulling him off balance.

The man's entire head was covered in a mask of thin black fabric. Only slight curves and indentations marked his features. Brannon plucked at the mask, but the man jerked back out of reach, breaking Brannon's grip on his shirt. He held out a finger and wagged it back and forth.

"Really?" Brannon said. "You're happy to attack innocent women on a public road but not to show your face. What a surprise."

He could see Ylani lying very still on the road. Latricia was to the side, frozen in fear.

The attacker got to his feet and Brannon did the same, keeping his knees bent and his hands wide, ready to act. The man's head turned slightly toward the place where the knife lay.

"Go on then," Brannon said.

With a guttural growl, the assailant left the knife and fled.

For a moment, Brannon warred with himself as to whether or not to follow. The physician in him won out and he knelt beside Ambassador Ylani.

There was no sign of a stab wound, but she appeared unconscious. Brannon felt around the back of her head gingerly. The brim of her hat was crushed. His fingers came away with a little blood.

Her eyes fluttered open. "Ouch," she said, and tried to sit up.

"Don't move," Brannon told her. He let his hand rest on her shoulder, holding her down. "You may have a concussion."

"Oh." She frowned, but didn't fight him, only twisted her head slightly. "Is he gone?"

"Yes."

"My hero." Her eyes fixed on Brannon's and her smile was a little crooked. He couldn't tell if she was mocking him or thanking him.

"You're welcome. Now just lie still while I check on Latricia."

The widow waved him away but her hands were trembling. "I'm fine. A grazed knee is all. Ylani saved my life."

The ambassador chuckled, a rich, delicious sound. "You're practically my only friend in Kalanon, Latricia. I could hardly let anything happen to you, could I?"

"Do either of you know who that was?" Brannon asked.

"I don't suppose you'd believe 'bandits,' would you?" Ylani suggested.

Brannon gave her a look.

"No, I suppose not."

Latricia scrambled forward and clutched his arm in a grip that could crush armor. "You remember the man who was going to attack us in the garden, back in Alapra?"

Brannon nodded. "Of course."

Her eyes were very wide. "It was him! Somehow he's here. He's the steward up at the manor."

Brannon blinked. She was distraught, terrified and in shock. He laid his hand over hers gently. "That's impossible, Lady Latricia. That man was a spy on the boat we came in. I caught him myself and he went overboard just as Magus Draeson froze the river. There's no way he survived."

She stared at him, her mouth moving silently for a long time. "But . . . I saw him."

Ylani sat up slowly. "The mind does strange things when you're stressed. We can figure it all out back at the inn, where it's safer. Sir Brannon, would you mind acting as our escort?"

"Sure. I was actually coming to look for you. I

wanted to take you up on your offer to help interview Kholi Gruul. But if you're not feeling up to it, that's okay. It doesn't look like you'll need stitches but you might still have a nasty headache."

"I'll be fine. I think my hat took most of the impact." She fingered the high crown, now somewhat crushed.

"Great."

In the end, Latricia came with them. Brannon didn't want to leave Draeson waiting any longer than necessary and the widow quickly made it clear that she did not feel safe, even in town, without someone nearby for protection.

"What about Tomidan?" she asked. "What if they come for him too?"

"He'll be fine at the inn," Brannon assured her. "I saw him coming in with Brother Taran and my apprentice as I was leaving. They'll keep him safe."

She took a deep, quivering breath and nodded.

The mayor's office was in the side of the town hall. It was in the basement of this hall that the cells for keeping prisoners were built. There was only one way in or out. Like so many of the buildings here in Sandilar, this was made of the stone carved out of the mountains by gold miners. Here and there, a teasing flicker of light sparkled in the rock, giving the illusion that, perhaps, there was still wealth in the walls of the building itself. Mayor Shillia assured them there was not.

"Just a fool's gold glimmer," she said. "Not much real gold gets past our people." She gestured to the stairs leading down to the basement. "Head on down. Magus Draeson went down a few minutes ago. He's an interesting chap, isn't he?"

"You could say that."

Brannon led the way down the shallow steps. At the bottom, a corridor looped back beneath the hall. Iron banded oak doors ran down both sides of the corridor, each leading to an individual cell.

Halfway down the corridor, Draeson sat on the floor, his back propped against a cell door. He looked up as they approached.

"You're not going to like this," he said. "Gruul's dead."

CHAPTER THIRTY

L atricia stared at the corpse of the Djin blacksmith. His eyes were empty, like glass orbs pushed into his face. He'd been stripped of all but his underwear, his clothes piled in the corner of the room as though waiting to be taken to the laundry. His skin was covered in lacerations, all but his tattoos.

Blood covered the floor, far more than the shallow cuts on his skin would allow. Latricia watched as Sir Brannon crouched beside the body, touching it ever so gently on the shoulder. The movement was enough to send the head rolling back and pulled open the wide gash below the man's chin. Kholi Gruul's throat had been cut. The weight of his skull tugged at the edges of the torn flesh. Latricia turned away and covered her eyes. She'd not seen wounds like that since the early days of the war and had hoped to never again.

"Correct me if I'm wrong," Sir Brannon's voice said softly, "but aren't these cuts in the same shape as Ula's tattoos?"

There was a pause as Draeson moved closer. Latricia's fear warred with necessity. She had to look. Information is power, as Keldan used to say. Her own safety and that of her son depended on her knowing what was going on now. Depended on her finding them protection.

"You're right," the mage said. "He already had some tattoos himself. It looks like someone wanted him to have the rest."

"Which means they didn't want him being Risen."

"Is that what they do?"

Latricia could see what they were talking about. What she'd taken as random cruel lacerations where actually carefully drawn runes, like those on the Djin woman in Sir Brannon's party. "Were . . . were those the symbols they drew on my husband?"

Sir Brannon turned to look at her, his eyes sad. "The same language. Different runes. But Keldan wasn't cut like this, Latricia. His were painted on." He rubbed his scar. "You don't have to be here, you know. You could wait in the hall if you like. I'll take you back to the inn shortly."

Latricia shook her head. "I'd rather stay with you."

He nodded. "Okay." Then turned back to his investigation. "The mayor says no one has been allowed down here since he came in. But she wasn't in her office all day, so she can't know for certain."

Something touched Latricia's fingers and she jumped.

"Sorry." Ambassador Ylani gave her hand a squeeze and pulled her gently into a corner of the cell that seemed relatively untouched. "How about you come over here with me. I don't think either of us are any use now. The best we can do is stay out of the way."

Latricia felt as though her body was heavy. As though her skin had forgotten how to feel. Her eyes, however, did not forget and the image of the dead man was burned into her brain. But somehow, in her mind, she saw her husband's face instead of the blacksmith's. "Why would somebody do this?"

She left the bigger questions unsaid: What if they did it again? To herself? Or to Tommy?

Ylani squeezed her hand again. "I don't know. I wish I did."

Latricia watched as Sir Brannon went through the victim's clothes, no doubt looking for clues. He'd dismissed her assertions about the attacker out of hand. There was no way she'd get him to believe anything about his boyhood friend, Duke Roydan. Their whole expedition had been a wasted trip and she'd done nothing but put herself in harm's way. In trying to keep her position safe, she'd somehow blundered into a game she wasn't ready for.

Magus Draeson stood over the body, his arms bent at the elbows, palms up. He muttered softly to himself and suddenly light bloomed in both his hands. The seemingly young man looked down at the corpse at his feet, swore, then closed his hands, extinguishing the light.

Sir Brannon looked across at him. "Not what you hoped?"

"Apparently not."

Latricia felt her mind go still. She'd only ever seen a mage's magic in person once before, when Draeson had levitated Sir Brannon in her garden. There was power there. Real power. If she could tap into it, she'd never need to feel unsafe again. Draeson was the perfect ally to keep her safe in this dangerous time and Roydan would never turn her out if she had a mage on her side.

She could almost feel Keldan's spirit chuckling as she turned the memory of his journal over in her mind. It seemed she had a card to play in this game after all.

She cleared her throat. "Magus Draeson," she called softly. "When you're done here, I'd like a word with you." He looked over at her, his incredibly handsome face made interesting by the dragon tattoo curving over his left cheekbone. She pitched her next words low so only he could hear them, and felt a thrill of warmth when they made his blue eyes widen. "I'd like to talk about your deal with the royal family."

CHAPTER THIRTY-ONE

"It's getting so that there isn't anyone in this town I can trust." Brannon sighed and lowered himself into a chair beside his apprentice. They were back at the Knox Inn and Tavern. The evening crowd was thin in the dining room. It seemed the coming of darkness at the end of a day that had contained two more murders, and tales of a rampaging Risen, had sent the townsfolk of Sandilar hurrying to their homes and locking the doors. Brannon hoped it would be enough. After all, there had been a lock on the cell where Kholi Gruul had died.

He brushed at his fresh shirt, grateful to the innkeeper for the bath and laundry service. He never liked to stay in bloodstained garments for long. Ever since the war, one of his chief, private luxuries was clean clothes—something hard to come by on the front. Or travelling after a shipwreck, for that matter. And, of course, when he'd come to physician training, Master Jordell had drilled the habit into him. Dirty clothes helped breed infection. It was one of the simple things a physician could do to remove risk for his patients.

If only removing all risks were as easy.

"Here for a day and our best suspect is murdered in custody. Brilliant."

"You really think there's no one here we can trust?" Jessamine asked. Her fork hovered absently above her plate.

Brannon sighed. His eyes tracked Shillia Vere and her son Morgin as they stood at the bar, chatting to Draeson. "I don't know."

Jessamine set down her fork. "I still can't believe what happened to Kholi. But then, I found it hard to believe he was involved at all."

"Oh, he was involved," Brannon said. "I just don't know how much."

"So weird," Jessamine said. "He always seemed so nice."

Brannon turned to her. She had inside knowledge of Sandilar but no vested interest in the case other than being here as his apprentice. At this point, she was quite likely the most reliable resource he had.

"How well do you know the people here?"

She shrugged. "Well enough. I didn't live here long. Just for a few months after my mother died. Once I realized I wanted to be a physician, I only waited long enough to earn money for passage to Alapra. But they're nice people. To be honest, I can't imagine anyone here as a murderer."

"Well, someone is. What do you think of Mayor Shillia?"

"She's been mayor as long as I know of. I don't

think anyone has ever challenged her for the position. I don't think they'd dare. She's has a special connection with Duke Roydan."

"I heard Roydan is the father of her son," Brannon said.

"That's what they say."

"Do you believe it?"

Jessamine chuckled. "Morgin certainly believes it. He can be pretty full of himself sometimes. But yeah, it's been unofficially acknowledged."

Brannon considered it. "Does Shillia seem like the type to want more power than she has?"

"I . . . " She paused. "I wouldn't have said so. She's already the most powerful woman in town. Well, until now." She jerked her head toward the table where Lady Latricia sat quietly with her son Tomidan and Ambassador Ylani. "You think Shillia's involved?"

"She had unrestricted access to Kholi Gruul while he was in custody and she can't tell us if anyone else visited him before Draeson found him dead. We have to consider the possibilities."

Jessamine nodded slowly. "What would she gain from it?"

Brannon sighed. "That, I don't know."

He watched as Morgin Vere drifted away from the conversation, leaving his mother and Draeson to continue alone. Shillia laid her hand on the mage's arm and laughed at something he'd said. The mage was up to his tricks again. Brannon just hoped that his flirting wouldn't get in the way of the investigation. A moment later, Lady Latricia approached the pair and Draeson's attentions moved to the richer prospect.

Brannon shook his head. A grieving widow. Did the man have no boundaries?

Beside him, Jessamine shifted. "Do you think we'll actually solve this before the king's birthday celebrations?"

He felt himself slump further into the chair. "I hope so. For all our sakes."

She shivered. "You really think we'll go to war again?"

"If we can't find the truth, people will need a convenient villain." Brannon's eyes drifted across to Ylani. "It won't take much to fire them up against the Nilarians again. They stand to gain a lot from killing Kalan royals." He knew his king. Aldan wouldn't start a war, but if he believed the Nilarians were behind this attack, he'd consider one was already begun.

Jessamine touched his hand. "What will you do if it happens? I know you don't want to go back to war."

Brannon took a deep breath and let it out slowly. "The king has made it clear that my role will be to lead the army as before."

"He wouldn't allow you to be one of the army's physicians, perhaps? Put your new skills to use?"

Brannon shook his head. "I'm more use as a figurehead. He needs me fighting."

He ran his finger along the blunt edge of a table knife. It tilted to his touch, throwing reflected light across his arm. There was so much blood on his hands already. More than he was likely to ever balance out, no matter how many lives he saved as a physician. Another war would make Bloodhawk the Hooded One's most irredeemable contributor.

"You could leave." Jessamine's voice was barely above a whisper. "No one would blame you."

"Run away, you mean?" Could he? Could he really say no to his king and country, and walk away, knowing the horrors that would befall them?

"Not run as such but . . . stay out of it. Withdraw. Hide, even. You could go be a farmer somewhere. Or continue being a physician. You could do a lot of good from the sidelines. I'm sure Master Jordell would help you there. He'd keep you hidden in one of the hospitals. Nobody would have to know who you are."

"I would know." Brannon sighed. It was a pretty dream. As long as he didn't factor in disappointing his friend, a possible accusation of treason, and a required willingness to leave his country's defense in the hands of those less qualified than himself with no thought for the consequences.

"You're too honorable for your own good, you know."

He felt his lips twist in a wry smile. "Yes, I do know." He pushed the knife away. "Let's order dessert."

He lifted his hand to signal for a waiter, then lowered it again, suddenly aware that the tavern had gone quiet. Voices fell silent. Cutlery ceased to clatter. There was a soft thud as the open door bumped against the wall. He turned to see seven armed men taking positions inside the door. They wore chain mail and hardened leather breastplates with the Sandilar insignia of the wolf and pick-axe in yellow. "What are they doing here?"

He looked toward the window. Outside, the courtyard was lost to the night. Instinct and experience told him it was not empty.

"Captain." Brannon stood and moved quickly toward the ranking officer, the stripes on his shoulder were golden pins. "What brings you from the manor?"

"Sir Brannon." The man acknowledged him with a brisk nod. Brannon didn't recognize him, but the man obviously knew who he was. "Steward Fressin sent us to escort the duke's family."

Brannon flicked a glance toward Keldan's widow. She stood near Draeson, her son clutched close in her arms.

"You can get out," she said, her eyes fixed on the captain. "Go back where you came from. You're not taking my boy."

The man smiled and inclined his head ever so slightly in a mocking mini-bow. "Of course, My Lady. The steward is merely concerned for your safety. We heard you were attacked on the road."

Ambassador Ylani rose slowly from her seat. She caught Brannon's eye and mouthed the word "How?"

It was a good point. There had been only one attacker on the road, and only he and Draeson knew what had happened, as far as he was aware. These were Roydan's men and he couldn't imagine his friend doing anything to harm his family . . . but Roydan wasn't here, and it wouldn't be the first time an underling had done something foolish while his lord was away.

Brannon moved forward slowly, his hands spread. "She's safe now."

"She and the boy would be safer at the manor," the captain said.

Latricia shook her head. "I told Fressin, we'll stay

here with my guest, Ambassador Ylani. The King's Champion is here with his team. It's as safe as any place in town."

"Sounds like the lady has made her decision," Draeson said. The tiny dragon on his temple snarled.

The captain stepped back. He licked his lips, looking from side to side, then gathered himself. "In that case, our orders are to stay and guard Her Ladyship and Duke Roydan's heir."

Brannon jerked a thumb toward the door. "You can do that from outside, can't you? Set up a perimeter. There's no need to disturb the other patrons. We've got it covered in here."

The captain glanced at the men with him, then back to the door where, no doubt, many more waited. After a moment's hesitation, he made his decision. "Off you go then, men. You heard the Bloodhawk. Set up a perimeter around the inn. Nothing gets in or out without my say-so."

Brannon kept his face neutral and his body stiff as the militia oozed back out into the night, leaving behind muted anxiety like an oily residue throughout the room. When the door closed behind them, he approached Latricia.

"What was that about?"

The widow opened her mouth, then paused. Her eyes flicked to Ylani and then to Draeson. "Just what he told us," she said. Her fingers clenched on Tommy's shirt. "They're here to offer protection."

"Really?" He raised an eyebrow. "Somehow I think there's more to it than that."

Her face was a mask of sweetness. "I don't know

251

what to tell you."

"The truth would be nice," he muttered under his breath.

He felt a hand on his elbow and turned to see Ula beside him. Two of the Djin woman's dreadlocks were twisted around each other and hanging over her face, giving her a lopsided air. She held up a handful of the little mud and leather packets she'd spent the day making. "Soldiers not enough," she said. "We have our own protection."

When he turned back to Latricia, she and Tommy were gone.

CHAPTER THIRTY-TWO

The armed militiamen outside looked like muscular marionettes from the window of Brannon's upstairs room. They were strung along the side of the inn like a chain of festival decorations complete with lanterns, reminding him once again of the king's birthday celebration and the deadline for solving this case.

He sighed and set one of Ula's little pouches on the windowsill. As if the situation wasn't complicated enough already.

A soft and familiar voice addressed him from the open doorway. "Feels a little like being a prisoner of war, don't you think?"

Brannon turned as Ylani stepped into the room. The gentle light of the lamp was flattering, giving her an air of mystery and attraction.

"Something you're familiar with?" he said.

She gave a delicate shrug. "Once or twice."

Brannon felt his eyebrows rise. "What were you

doing in the war?" Somehow he couldn't imagine Ylani as a soldier.

"I did my part, just like everyone else." She trailed a delicate hand along the edge of the wooden bed end. "My family were traders before the war so I knew your country and its language. That was considered an asset."

Brannon folded his arms. "You were a spy."

"Sometimes," she said. "There are worse things to be."

He considered how many men and women had died at the end of his sword. "Perhaps. But how can you expect us to trust you now?"

"Because the war was a long time ago and because I'm being honest with you now. Which is more than we can say for the man whose soldiers are outside right now."

"Do you know something about that?" Brannon asked. "What's going on between Latricia and the manor? Why isn't she staying up there, really?"

Ylani nodded toward the window. "There are many more of those men at the manor. More . . . protection."

"And?"

"Have you noticed that, in this ring of guards they've made to surround the inn and protect us from whatever is out there, more than half of them are facing inward?"

Brannon couldn't help glancing out into the night. He had noticed. "Kalan soldiers are trained to be vigilant. We can't be sure that whoever is behind this isn't already inside the inn."

Ylani held up one of the little leather packets. "Isn't that what Ula's bags are for? How much do you trust

Duke Roydan? They're his men after all."

Brannon felt his hand clench. "Roydan and I served throughout the war together. I trust him with my life."

Ylani chewed her lip for a long moment. "Fair enough," she said at last. "Maybe he doesn't know what is happening in his town."

"What do you mean by that?" Brannon asked, but she had gone. "Really?" he said to the empty room. "Be all cryptic and then disappear. Brilliant."

He took the few steps to the door and looked out into the hallway, but Ylani was already out of sight. The ward-dog, curled up and snoozing while the door was open and he was inside the room, raised its head and sniffed at him.

"Fat lot of good you are," he said.

The trouble was, Ylani's words had stuck. How was it that Roydan didn't know what was happening at home? King Aldan had told them he'd intercepted the message from Sandilar's mayor, but there had to be other communications that had mentioned the murders. Even in his grief stricken state, Roydan must have expected and read reports from home—mining reports, household reports, yet more urgent requests for help from a town with a killer on the loose. How could he have missed them all without getting suspicious?

The answer was likely surrounding the inn at this very moment. Roydan had gotten suspicious. It would explain the strange behavior of his militia. What it didn't explain was their numbers. Even with so many here, surrounding the inn, there had to be many more back at the manor and guarding the prisoners in the mines – they wouldn't skimp on those posts. Exactly how many men did Roydan have?

And more importantly, why did he have them?

He shook his head and scooped up another few of Ula's pouches. Roydan was an old army man. Of course he would always have militia at the ready. It was a habit that was hard to break—not to mention a smart move for the Duke of Sandilar, protector of the gold mines Nilar had started the war over in the first place. It should take more than a few cryptic comments from a Nilarian woman he'd only just met to make him question his old friend. No matter what direction his men were facing.

He stepped out into the hallway and closed the door behind him. The ward-dogs on the other doors raised their heads to look at him, but remained silent.

There was one way to put his mind at rest. Whatever was going on with Roydan's militiamen, it had to do with Lady Latricia. She would be the best one to ask about it. And this time he would insist on answers. He'd had enough of people hiding things. This whole Hooded investigation had been rife with secrets, and what had it gotten them? Two more murder victims in just one day of having arrived in Sandilar. It was time to take off the gloves.

Mayor Shillia was in the hallway. She strode toward him with a face like a mountain wolf snarling over a fresh kill. "Those idiot men outside won't let anyone leave," she growled. "Do you have any idea how stupid that is? People can't get home to their families. How is that protecting anyone?"

Brannon sighed. "They're not my orders, Shillia. Try talking to the captain."

"I did. He says the orders are from the new steward

and that he has the authority of Duke Roydan."

"Well then." Brannon spread his hands helplessly. "Have you met the steward?"

"No. And you can be sure I'll be talking to Roydan about him when he gets back. Can't you use your authority as King's Champion to get them to back off?"

"For what reason, Shillia? Their orders are to protect us. I can hardly say that's unreasonable after what's been happening over the last twenty-four hours. I suggest you get a room and stay put until morning. We can address it then. In the meantime, be grateful you're in a place with an armed guard." He hefted Ula's pouches in his hand. "And other protections as well. This is probably the safest place in town. Unless you had somewhere else you need to be tonight?"

She scowled. "No. Nothing like that."

"Good." As she turned to leave, Brannon thought of something and called her back. "Shillia, you sent word to the capitol about what was going on here, didn't you? Asking for help?"

"Of course," she tilted her head to one side, flashing a glimmer of a gold earring. "That's why you're here, isn't it?"

Brannon nodded. "Part of it. Can I ask, how many messages did you send?"

Her head straightened up and the earring vanished beneath her hair. "Six. Why? How many were received?"

He shrugged and gave his most disarming smile. "I don't know. I was just curious. Take one of Ula's pouches. They're supposed to go in every room."

Shillia's eyes narrowed slightly, but she let it pass,

taking a pouch from his outstretched hand. "I'm surprised that woman has any spit left after the amount she dribbled into these," she muttered.

Brannon turned away before she could change her mind, searching for the room Keldan Sandilar's widow shared with their son.

Latricia's door had no wards on it. The bare wood was adorned only with a small bronze plaque stating the room number, which provided the base from which hung a knocker shaped like a leaf. Brannon reached for it, then hesitated. There was a sound inside the room.

He hissed for Shillia's attention and gestured her to come closer. They listened.

For a moment, all he could hear was the sound of his own breathing, then he heard it again: A yelp of pain and fear.

He put his shoulder to the door, turned the handle and burst inside.

Tomidan Sandilar sat on the bed. He looked up as Brannon entered, his eyes wet and his small lip trembling. Beside him and holding his hand, was his mother. Latricia's mouth made a perfect O shape.

On the other side of the boy was Draeson. The mage held Tomidan's arm steady with one hand and had laid his own arm over the top of it. The dragon tattoo clung to the underside of Draeson's wrist, the little dragon's head and neck bulging out of the skin. It had twisted like a serpent to bite Tommy's arm. The boy's blood ran along his arm and the dragon lapped at the wound.

"Blood and Hooded Tears!" Brannon said. "What are you doing?"

The dragon pulled back from Tomidan's arm and

hissed at him. Blood dripped from its tiny fangs. Shillia squealed.

"This is none of your business, Brannon," Draeson said. "Leave it alone."

"Really? None of my business? You're bleeding a six-year-old!"

"My Lady," Shillia said. "How can you let him do this to the Heir of Sandilar?"

Latricia looked away. "It's complicated."

Brannon laid a hand on his sword hilt. "Uncomplicate it."

Neither Latricia nor Draeson said a word. Tomidan moved closer to his mother. Discomfort poured out from the three of them, filling the room in a flood.

"You know what I think, Magus Draeson?" Shillia said at last. "We've had a spate of killings with strange rituals in this town. Now here you are with your magic and your bad attitude, conducting some kind of ritual with the grandson of our duke. How do we know it wasn't you this whole time?" She waved her hand over him and turned to Brannon. "Magic could be behind everything. Maybe he used it to lift Caidin and ram him onto the signpost deliberately to make it look like one of these Risen creatures had to be behind it."

Brannon felt his stomach tighten as he met Draeson's eyes. The mage was different from what he'd been in the war. More than just physically, he thought. Then, he'd been a grouchy old man but now . . . How well did he really know him? "You lifted me over the fence in the Sandilar house in Alapra," he said. "You could have done it. And you were the one to find Kholi Gruul. You could have killed him yourself."

Draeson stood up slowly. The tiny dragon on his forearm flicked out a tongue. Its lines seemed darker, more present somehow.

Brannon's hands clenched. Only an intense effort of will stopped him from drawing his sword. If it came to that, he knew, the weapon would do no good.

The mage took a long slow breath in, then let it out just as slowly. The muscles in his face were hard with barely contained tension. "Blood and Tears, you people frustrate me," he said. "No matter what I do for this country, there's always a point at which someone points to me and says, you're not like us." He lifted his hands and wiggled his fingers manically, his mouth twisted in scorn. "You withered the crops. You brought the bad weather and disease. You killed everyone when we weren't looking. The level of ignorance in the general population is astounding."

"And did you?" Brannon asked. "Do those things, I mean. Particularly the killing part. I can handle a little bad weather."

Draeson snorted. "Perhaps you can. You've grown up a bit since your youth."

"At least one of us has. How about you answer the question?" Brannon glanced across to where young Tommy sat, his face pale, his hand clamped over the bleeding wound in his arm. "All the questions."

A wave of heat blew out from Magus Draeson, burning across Brannon's skin, like the door had been opened into a furnace. The air in the room shifted and the drapes moved. It was followed by a blast of intense cold that made the women gasp and the hairs on Brannon's arm stand on end.

He held his ground. Then, slowly and deliberately, he took a step forward. "I'm not scared of you, Draeson."

A muscle in the corner of Draeson's eye twitched, just a bit, then he gave a resigned sort of half-chuckle. "Fine," he said, and sat down on the bed.

Brannon let go of the breath he'd been holding. He forced his hands to relax at his sides. No fists.

"You'll remember," Draeson said, "that when I lifted you over the fence, there wasn't a mark on you." He held up his hand. "No fingermarks."

"What's that got to do with anything?" Mayor Shillia said.

Brannon knew. "Caidin's body had bruises on it from where his killer had grabbed him and lifted him up. We could tell that he'd been gripped around the throat. That's how the killer held him and drove him onto the spike. It's why we were looking for someone with exceptional strength."

Draeson pointed to him with both hands. "Exactly. Yes, I could have lifted him up there with magic, but there would be no bruising. As for Gruul, he was dead when I found him, as I told you. Couldn't you make anything out about his time of death?"

Brannon shook his head. "It'd been within the last few hours. It was hard to get more than that."

"Rigor mortis?"

"He was starting to stiffen up when we left," Brannon admitted. "Which does make it more likely he was killed before you got there."

"There you go." Draeson leaned back, a smugly satisfied smile on his face.

"And the boy?" Brannon said, pointedly.

The smile vanished. "A private arrangement between myself and his mother."

Brannon raised an eyebrow. He looked from Draeson to Latricia and back again. "I don't think so. Spill it."

It was Latricia who finally spoke. "I approached the magus," she said. "My husband provided him a service when he was alive, as payment for a deal with the royal family. I offered him the same payment in return for protection for Tommy and myself."

"What payment?" Brannon's mouth seemed very dry. His stomach felt heavy. He needed to hear them say it.

Latricia's voice was barely a whisper. "Blood."

"It's not as bad as you think," Draeson said.

His eyes seemed somehow hollow as Brannon stared at him. He wondered how many more secrets the mage had beneath that flawless young man's face. How could trading in blood not be as bad as it seemed? "Is this how you became young again?"

"No, of course not. This deal is far older than that."

"Then explain."

Draeson sighed and hunched forward, resting his face in his hands and his elbows on his knees. "You remember I told you about my early life learning to become a mage?"

"You said it was a lot of study," Brannon said.

Draeson snorted. "An understatement, but yes. The first major task of a magus is to overcome the limited human lifespan. The study of power takes longer than any normal man can live. Mages guard the secret of their longevity very carefully. Each of us has come to it in his or her own way."

"I thought you had teachers. Didn't they teach you the secret?"

The mage shook his head. "No. They taught the tools and encouraged me in the ways of power, but I, like every other mage, had to find the answer for myself. Each of us does. It's a rite of passage. Proof that we are worthy of the power to follow."

Despite himself, Brannon found himself being drawn forward. "And your answer was a child's blood?"

"No. Not blood. A bloodline. My bloodline. The royal family. I managed to marry one of my great nephews to one of the princesses and bound myself to their line. I knew that of all the families in Kalanon, the royal line was most carefully guarded and most likely to endure. As long as they survive, so do I."

"But how?"

Draeson rolled his eyes. "It took me a lifetime to figure it out, Brannon. Do you really think you can grasp the secrets tonight? Suffice to say, the royal line and I are bound forever. All I need to keep living is for the descendants of Valdan to keep breeding and stay on the throne."

"All you need?" Brannon said. Tomidan was burrowed into his mother's side like a limpet. "Then why were you bleeding one of the royal line when we walked in here?"

"For this." Draeson held up his arm and the dragon tattoo shifted, twining itself around his wrist like a snake. "Part of my power comes from a creature from another dimension. We have a bond, it and I. But not quite enough." He lowered his arm again and traced the fingers of his other hand over the tattoo. A gentle smile played on his lips. "We share our power with each other, but for the dragon to keep its foothold in this world, it needs to access my bond to the royal bloodline. It needs royal blood."

Brannon felt the chill over his body again, but this time it was the mage's words that brought it, not his power. "You feed the dragon. You let it bite someone of royal blood so that it can live with you forever, the way you do."

Latricia, her chin resting on the crown of Tommy's head, spoke softly. "The royal family have had a deal with Magus Draeson for generations. Keldan kept him supplied with blood for the dragon. I read about it in his journals."

"The bite marks on Keldan's body," Brannon said. He pulled a chair from under the writing desk and sat down on it. "Of course."

"Don't you see?" Draeson said. "It's a good deal. The blood required for the dragon is only a little bit. It's not dangerous. And my loyalty is absolute, so the power it grants me is an asset for the kingdom. I will always act in the best interests of Kalanon because if the king and his family fall, so do I."

"Aldan knows?" Brannon closed his eyes. He could remember the king's voice the first day this nightmare of a case had begun. "You'll be paid what's owing," he'd told Draeson that day.

"Of course he knows."

The sad thing was, he couldn't even be surprised. His friend was a very practical king and Draeson was right about it being a good deal for the kingdom. Just, at this moment, it didn't seem like a good deal for the little boy who was the only member of the royal bloodline nearby.

"Tommy knows what he's doing," Latricia said, as though reading his mind. "I told him it would be okay."

The boy turned to look at Brannon. "The wizard will keep us safe from the bad man," he said.

"Mage," Draeson corrected, absently.

"I'm sure he will," Brannon told the boy. "He'll have to be very responsible, won't he?"

"Subtle," said Draeson.

"Don't push it. I take it you've done enough? Has the dragon got what it needed to get?"

"Yes."

"Then get out, Draeson. Leave them alone unless you're actually needed to keep them safe."

"Fine." The mage stood and moved toward the door.

Brannon, suddenly uncertain what he could say when left in a room with Latricia and her son, stood as well.

"Stay safe," breathed Mayor Shillia, her face a little paler than usual. She followed them out and shut the door behind them.

The hallway seemed dark and filled with shadow.

"Brannon," said Draeson, his voice pitched low. "There's something else."

Brannon swore under his breath and shut his eyes. When he opened them, the mage was still there. "What?"

"I make it a habit to keep track of members of the royal bloodline. Even the lesser ones. I've developed a spell for identifying anyone with even a little of it in them."

"And?" Even as he said it, Brannon remembered Draeson muttering over the corpse of Caidin Ray in the courtyard. Remembered the blood glowing with light as a result. "Blood and Tears."

"All but Kholi Gruul had royal blood in them. Roydan's family are known for throwing bastards. The stable boy was one. The seamstress was carrying one." He paused, as if weighing the value of his next words. "Brannon, I think someone is going after the royal family."

CHAPTER THIRTY-THREE

The change from deep sleep to wakefulness was sudden and sharp, like a knife thrust. Brannon's eyes opened and he felt the tension thrumming through him, his body charged like the air before a thunderstorm. He recognized it at once. This was waking in the battlefield. This was the warning from his deepest subconscious that something was not right. Something had happened while he was asleep—a sound or movement that ought not to be there. The part of him that stood guard even while sleeping, the soldier that could never feel safe enough to rest, had heard it and sounded the alarm.

He lay still, eyes and ears straining. Lamplight, oozing up from the armed men outside, turned the closed curtains into a shadow theater of tree branches and shifting shapes. None of them were a threat. The room around him was empty of people. The furniture, more ornate than he needed, stood in reserve, its prettiness lost in dark. Whatever it was that had woken him must have come from beyond.

He slipped silently from beneath the covers, pausing only to sling his sword belt around his waist over the loose, flowing pants he wore to bed. There was no clock in the room, but it had the feel of early hours of the morning—past midnight, but little more. Nothing stirred. He walked to the door, barefoot and bare chested, opened it slowly, and stepped out into the hall, moving as silently as a scout in enemy territory.

The air was chilled, raising a ripple of gooseflesh along his skin. The ward-dogs eyed him warily, their wolf-like eyes glowing with a soft, baleful light; in the empty hallway, with no lamps lit or guests awake, they took on an unnerving quality. The corridor seemed like a tunnel, leading the way through the realm of the Hooded One.

A low creaking noise came from the direction of the stairs and Brannon moved toward it. The glowing dog eyes followed his path.

As he came closer, the creak sounded again. One of the room doors was ajar. It shifted ever so slightly in a draft, pulling a low protest from the hinges, like an old horse made to plow.

He nudged it open.

The room inside was empty, but for a four-poster bed and dresser. It was smaller than his own room. Moonlight spilled in through the window that was also slightly ajar. The curtains were open and billowed in the breeze like languishing ghosts.

Brannon let out his breath and scratched at the scar on his cheek. He'd thought himself beyond waking in the middle of the night for a creaky door and an open window. Perhaps this case was getting to him even more than he thought.

He moved swiftly through the empty room and pulled down on the window. It closed with a satisfying thud. He rested his hands on the windowsill and peered out into the yard below. Roydan's militia still kept guard in both directions—toward and away from the inn. He was no closer to the meaning of that than before.

He ran his hand along the sill, the feel of something solid a kind of antidote to the ungraspable ideas and clues floating in his mind. Somewhere out there was likely a Risen, created by murder and for the intention of murder. Their main suspect was dead. His friend's soldiers were behaving oddly and his investigative partner spent more time looking for bedmates or blood for his dragon tattoo than solving the case. The Nilarians may or may not have been involved and either way the ambassador was a distraction. Keldan's widow was hiding something and Ula, who was his best source of information on the rituals used in the murders, was also a potential lightning rod for the fears of the townsfolk. And now it seemed the whole thing might be targeted at those related to the royal family. Add to that a king waiting in Alapra for conclusive proof of guilt and a reason not to go back to war, and it was small wonder Brannon found it difficult to sleep.

Still, there was little chance of it making sense in the morning if he didn't at least try to rest. He moved to turn away from the window, when a detail caught his attention.

The windowsill was bare.

"Ula's protection pouch." He checked the floor, it

wasn't there. There was no sign of one in any of the corners of the room and none near the window. Ula had been insistent—at least one pouch needed to be in every room and extras in strategic corners of the building to afford it the protection of her earth spirits against the kaluki inside a Risen. Where was it now?

"They're gone," a voice said from behind him. "Almost all of them are gone."

Brannon jumped, his sword in his hand and half out of the scabbard before he recognized the man in the doorway. "Taran! What are you doing?"

The young priest was fully dressed and had a slim bladed stiletto dagger in each hand. "Sorry, didn't mean to sneak up on you." He slipped the daggers into his sleeves and they disappeared. "I was running those tests you wanted on the blood samples and thought I heard something."

"You were running the tests in the middle of the night?"

Taran shrugged. "Fewer distractions."

Brannon let the sword slide back into place. "I suppose that's true. What did you hear?"

"I don't know. I thought maybe someone moving around but I didn't see anyone. Then I noticed Ula's spirit bags were missing so I went investigating. I think someone's taken them."

Brannon raised an eyebrow. "You don't behave like a normal priest."

"You don't need a normal priest." Taran spread his hands wide and innocent.

Brannon snorted. "Bring those daggers and help me search."

They crept along the dark corridor, senses straining for any sign of movement. The silence was eerie and broken only by the occasional creak of floorboards. Three more rooms on this level of the inn were unoccupied. One by one, they searched them. None of them had any spirit pouches. Brannon had to agree with Taran's assessment. Someone had deliberately removed them. But why?

"Is it true about Draeson?" Taran asked, his voice low.

The shadows seemed to darken as Brannon pulled the door of the last room closed behind them, despite the candle he had found and lit to guide them. "Yeah. He needs to feed his dragon tattoo with blood."

"They're saying he used the boy, Tommy, to do it. And his mother let him."

Brannon turned around, his eyes seeking out the priest's. "People do crazy things when they're scared. I've seen worse."

"Worse than doing that to a child?" The priest fell silent and glanced away. "Yeah, I suppose I have too. Doesn't make it right."

Brannon watched as the younger man moved away. There was nothing to say.

The carpet here, by the stairs, was more worn than the rest of the hallway and a darker patch of shadow showed where a rug had been laid over it. Brannon looked back the way they'd come. The rest of the rooms were locked, their occupants presumably asleep inside. He'd prefer to search the rest of the building before waking anyone else. Other than the missing pouches, there still wasn't any real reason to be concerned, but he couldn't shake the feeling of disquiet.

The stairwell was like an open maw and they descended down into the gullet, the candlelight barely touching the sides. In the main tavern room, the embers of the fire burned low and red. The tables with their chairs upturned upon them, looked like large, spiny beetles, hibernating in a den.

A cool brush of air trailed over Brannon's bare chest, raising the hairs on his arms. He edged forward, holding the candle high in his left hand, his right hovering near his sword. The door was open.

"Is anyone there?" he called.

There was no answer.

"Brannon." Brother Taran pointed to a patch of shadow on the floor beside the bar.

As he moved closer, the shadow seemed to spread, oozing outward. The light gleamed on it, and he realized it was liquid. Blood.

Brannon raised a finger to his lips, and motioned Taran to stay back. He slowly pulled the sword from its scabbard. The metal hiss sounded loud as a rockslide.

He could feel the cool night air being pulled into his lungs, tingling the inside of his throat. His heart beat faster as he followed the expanding river of blood along the side of the bar to the end.

A figure slumped against the wall, his legs sticking out like an abandoned doll. Brannon knelt and lifted the figure's head. A small gush of blood flowed from the slash in his neck, then dwindled to a trickle. Most of it was already on the floor. He was dead.

"Who is it?" Taran whispered.

"The captain of the guard." Brannon stood and

moved across to the door. The lock was broken. "I guess he was trying to do his job and someone got past him."

"Yeah," said Taran. "But were they trying to get in or trying to get out?"

CHAPTER THIRTY-FOUR

Latricia lay with her eyes open, listening to the sound of her son's slow breathing as he slept in the bed across the room. She found herself timing her own breaths, each rise and fall of her chest, to synchronize with his. Even as she noticed it, she couldn't make it stop.

Her mind circled endlessly around a single fear. Somehow, despite all her maneuvering, she could lose him. Just like she had lost Keldan, she could lose Tommy. Whether it was to the crazed killer that had taken his father, or whether it was to Duke Roydan's plan to take over the role of parent to his remaining heir, Latricia knew that her place in Tommy's life, and at Sandilar Manor, was something on which she had only the most tenuous of grips.

The bed felt hard and cold. She was still not used to sleeping a whole night alone. Even when he spent time with mistresses, Keldan would almost always return to their bed at some point during the night. Part of her still wanted to believe that he would appear. That he would regale her with his latest plot for outwitting his father and securing their little family trio in wealth and power.

"Ahpra's Tears, Keldan," she murmured to the shadows. "I'm no good at this without you. I need your help."

Only the sounds of the night responded. The occasional creak of floorboards, the slow, rhythmic tick of the clock, the gentle brush of breath. The oil lamp on the table was turned down to its lowest burn, barely an ember on the wick.

Latricia lifted herself up on her elbows and looked across at her boy. He'd been so brave today. He always was brave. More than she'd like at times. But today she had asked a lot of him and he had done it. When Sir Brannon and Mayor Shillia had burst in, she had been worried she'd gone too far, asked too much of him, but now she could see the peace on his face as he slept and knew that she had done the right thing. Whatever the cost, the deal she had made with the magus was worth it.

She let her head fall back to the pillow. Exposing the deal to the others had never been part of her plan. She knew they would judge her. That they wouldn't understand how a mother could offer up her son's blood. But then, they weren't in her position, were they? They hadn't lost a husband. Hadn't been attacked on the road in her own province—the province she had been set to govern. They didn't live in terror of losing the one remaining family member they had left. No, they might not understand her move, but neither did they know the game.

Ever since she'd read in Keldan's journal about

Draeson's arrangement with the royal family, she'd known she had an ace to play. The mage needed royal blood for his dragon-creature and Tommy needed protection. It was perfect. She knew the mage would not hurt her son—after all, her husband had donated the blood almost his whole life and she'd never even known about it, let alone seen any ill effects.

For a moment, she felt a flash of heat in her stomach at what he had kept from her all those years, but she pushed it down. That was Keldan. He had his secrets. Secrets, schemes, and women. Now, they were her secrets, her schemes. She knew he would say she'd blundered by letting this one be found out, but he'd admit the deal itself was masterful. Roydan himself would not stand against the magus head to head, and she and her son were under Draeson's protection. They would be safe. Surely there was nothing more she could do to keep them safe?

She rolled over, her eyes searching in the dark for the door. Was it locked?

She closed her eyes. Of course it was locked. She'd already checked it twice. The attack on the road had made her paranoid. She concentrated on her breathing again, slow and steady, mimicking restful sleep as though to trick the tension out of her muscles. The ticking clock sounded like a drum to her ears. She fancied that it was the Hooded One, tapping his foot.

A low scraping sound intruded into the room. Latricia's eyes opened. She waited. The clock ticked on. At last, she heard it again: a slow scrape of metal from the direction of the door, almost like a key turning in the lock.

She pushed back the covers and slipped her feet into the slippers beside the bed. Her fingers groped for the room key on the bedside table, its cold hard iron a comfort as she crept toward the door.

The sound came again. This time the scrape ended with a click. Cold iron fingers clenched around her chest as she watched the door handle slowly turn.

The door opened and a dark-haired, slim figure stepped into the room. The door clicked closed behind him.

Latricia backed up, feeling behind her for the lamp. Her hand closed around it and she lunged forward, swinging it like a weapon at the intruder's head.

His hand shot out and grabbed her wrist, quick as a wolf bite.

"Lady Latricia," the silky voice purred. "Is that any way to greet a guest?"

She dropped the room key and tried to pry his fingers from her arm but he held her firm. Light expanded from the lamp, like milk poured into black tea, exposing his face.

"Fressin! What are you doing?"

The steward pushed her arm up higher and stepped forward, forcing her back against the edge of the table. For such a slim man, he was remarkably strong. "That, my lady, is the question I have for you. What are you doing nosing around things that have nothing to do with you? And bringing the Nilarian Ambassador with you? Where's your loyalty, Latricia? Do you really think Duke Roydan wants that sort of influence around his heir?"

"That's hardly the business of a servant, is it?" Her

arm ached, but she kept her face a determined mask of outrage. "I'm the Lady of Sandilar. Take your hands off me at once."

"You don't give the orders here," Fressin said. "You're not the lady of *my* House."

Something about the quietness of his voice and the way he said it sent a chill to the core of her being. She could feel herself trembling. "House?" she said. Memories of history lessons in political intrigue broke the surface of her mind, bringing a kind of breathlessness with them. "Assassin House."

"You are well educated for a familyless orphan, aren't you?"

"I have a family," she said. "They died as heroes defending Kalanon."

"Well, perhaps you'll join them soon."

Latricia struggled, pulling her arm back as hard as she could. He twisted the grip on her wrist and she felt something warm and wet drizzle onto her head and over her shoulders. She looked up and the smelly liquid splashed onto her face. Fear burned up through her stomach into her throat. He was pouring oil from the lamp over her.

"No," she said, her voice a hoarse whisper. "Please, don't."

"You brought this on yourself," he said.

Latricia stared up at the lamp. The last of the oil dribbled out from under the wick cap, ran along the side of the tilted glass case and trickled down onto her. Now, only the remaining oil soaked into the wick kept the flame alive. She had been lucky beyond measure that it had not caught the leaking oil alight as it fell. If she dropped the lamp now and it broke, or if she came anywhere near an open flame, she would burn. There was nothing she could do.

"Mama?" Tommy's tousled head rose up from the pillow and looked across at them. "What's happening?"

His voice sparked a fire inside her that could rival any flame without. She would not die here at the hands of Roydan's assassin. And she would not let him take her son.

She flung herself forward, making full body contact with Fressin in the hope of getting some of the oil onto him as well. He gave a startled yelp and she drove her knee up into his groin. He let go.

She threw the lamp at him and ran to her son. "Help!" she screamed. "Magus! Help!"

Fressin swatted the lamp out of the air and it landed on the double bed she had been sleeping in. The still burning wick tumbled inside the glass like a trapped firefly. He shook his hand in pain and hunched over a little as he glared. "I thought there might be a bit of bitch in you," he said.

Latricia pulled the blankets back from Tomidan and he huddled in close to her. "Stay away from him, Tommy," she said. "He's the one who tried to get you back in Alapra."

Fressin sneered. "I wasn't trying to get anyone in Alapra. The boy got in the way is all."

"Really?" Latricia licked her lips. Where was Draeson? Surely the mage had heard her. He would protect them. That was their deal. She just had to delay things long enough for him to get here. "And what are you doing now then?"

Fressin went very still. "Now you're the one getting in the way."

The lamp wick had spilled out onto the bedspread and was burning a hole in the fabric, a seed of flame germinating in the spring.

Latricia pulled Tommy to his feet. "Get ready to run," she whispered in his ear. "Find Draeson."

"Come on, Latricia." Fressin stepped forward slowly. He had a dagger in his hand. She hadn't seen where it came from. "You and the Nilarian would be dead already if Sir Brannon hadn't interfered on the road this afternoon. You might as well give in and I'll make it painless. The boy won't be hurt."

She heard Tommy's breath catch in his throat and a little sob escaped him. Her awareness seemed to sharpen and the world around her shifted. Time slowed down and, despite the darkness in the room, she could see everything with razor-edged clarity: the broken lamp and tongue of flame eating up the pattern on the bedspread, the vase of fresh flowers that had been left on the writing desk, the small gap between the table and the wardrobe that was just big enough for her son to squeeze through. And the assassin advancing on them both, who blocked any other exit.

She pushed Tommy toward the gap. "Run!"

The boy bolted like a startled rabbit, darting under the rim of the table and wriggling toward the other side. Fressin lunged, reaching out for him. Latricia grabbed the flower vase and swung it with all her might at the back of Fressin's head. It connected hard and shattered. Shards of broken glass rained down like an ice storm, shining with orange light from the building fire on the bed.

Fressin stumbled and fell against the table. The knife dropped from his hand and skittered across the floor. "Hooded bitch!" He rubbed at the back of his head and his hand came away covered in blood.

Tomidan reached the door and paused. "Mama?"

"Go," she yelled. "Go!" She charged forward, shoving Fressin as hard as she could, hoping he was already off balance enough that she could force her way past. He lurched but kicked back with his foot, tripping her. She stumbled, almost fell, and caught herself. She kept her eyes fixed ahead, forcing her legs to propel her forward. Tommy opened the door and ran out into the corridor.

Fressin's hand caught the back of her nightdress and pulled her back. She screamed and flailed back at him. He caught her wrist again and this time bent it up behind her back painfully.

She struggled until it felt like her shoulder would wrench from its socket, but he was too strong. Her heart felt like a trapped animal in her chest. The smell of lamp oil filled her nostrils.

He pressed up against her, his breath hot in her ear. He held his bloody hand in front of her face. "I offered to make it painless. But for this, you can burn."

He gripped her shoulder hard and turned her around to face the bed. The flames were growing, their light casting a cabal of dancing shadows around the room. He pulled her twisted arm up higher, forcing her to bend at the waist. His pelvis pushed against her buttocks.

"Please," she said, stalling for time. "I'll do anything you want. You don't have to do this." The heat felt like waves against her face. She could hear the fabric of the bed crackling as it burned. Soon that would be her skin searing like pigmeat. Her hair, burning like a candlewick. "Please."

His laughter crackled like the fire. "No," he said, and pushed her forward, his grip like stone.

The flames burned hot against her face and she bent her knees, collapsing her weight downward to avoid them, ignoring the excruciating pain in her shoulder as she did so. She felt it pop and Fressin let go of her wrist. Her arm fell to her side, dangling uselessly. She knelt beside the burning bed, unable to move.

Fressin kicked her in the small of her back. "Get up."

Latricia took a deep breath. "No." Her son was safe. He would have reached the mage by now. Draeson might be too late to save her, but she could manage this small defiance. "No."

"Fine." He lifted a piece of paper from the writing desk and held it out to the building flames. Fire flickered around the edges.

She watched as the burning paper crept closer. Here it comes, she thought. A stray part of her brain wanted to close her eyes, as if not seeing it would stop it from happening, but she couldn't. Her vision shifted to Fressin's face. He smiled as he thrust painful death toward her.

The smile vanished. A hand clamped down on Fressin's shoulder and yanked him backward, away from her. She turned to see the assassin flung across the room with no more effort than a pillow. He crashed into the wall and collapsed to the floor like a broken marionette.

"Ahpra's Tears," she whispered, relief sagging

against her bones like weights in a vendor's scale. She was close to tears of her own. "Thank you." She crawled back from the bed, feeling the blessedly cool air from the open door take the place of the heat of the fire.

Her rescuer rolled her over and she got a good look at his face for the first time. "How did you get in here?" she said. Then shook her head. "Never mind. Thank you for saving me. I'll see that you get rewarded." She wasn't sure how, exactly, when her main source of income, Duke Roydan, had apparently hired the man who had just tried to kill her.

Her rescuer leaned in close enough that she could smell the meat on his breath. "Where's your son?"

For a moment she didn't understand. Then his hand gripped her around the throat, lifting her up.

"Where's Tomidan?"

Realization struck her. "No. It's you?"

The hand at her throat tightened, then abruptly released. Latricia blinked at the point of a blade protruding from the man's chest. Behind him, Fressin stood like a vengeful demon in the firelight.

"Payback," he said.

Latricia expected the stabbed man to fall. Instead, he smiled. He rose to his feet and turned to face Fressin, the long dagger still penetrating him all the way through. The handle jutted out from his back like the windup key of a clock.

Latricia ran. She stumbled into the hallway, screaming, as she hammered every door she passed. The ward-dogs growled and snarled and for the first time she began to truly believe that, even if he were to be woken in time, their master could not save her.

CHAPTER THIRTY-FIVE

There were five more bodies in the courtyard. Maybe more. The lanterns had gone dark and Brannon couldn't see very far beyond the doorsteps. The night hung like a blanket, smothering and still. Blood was an ink stain on the parchment of cobblestones. Limbs had been torn right off and lay separate to the men they belonged to.

"This had to have been the Risen," Brannon said. He pulled the door closed again and bolted it. "It's stronger and more vicious than before."

Taran was draping a tablecloth over the body of the captain of the guard. "Do you think it's inside?"

Brannon's gut felt tight. "Why else would someone remove Ula's spirit bags? We need to start waking people up."

Even as he said it, the sound of dogs barking burst from the floor above like hounds just scenting their prey. The sound bit into his stomach, savaging his nerves. Those were Draeson's wards against intruders.

He bolted for the stairs, Brother Taran barely a step behind. The wards would wake everyone, but they'd be lucky to react in time. Between what Ula had told him about Risen and what he'd seen of the guards' bodies outside, he wasn't sure if any reaction would be enough to save them.

At the top of the stairs, Tomidan Sandilar was screaming and beating his little fists against a door. Tears streamed down his face. "Help! Please, help my mama!"

The hallway was filled with smoke. It burned in Brannon's nostrils and made his eyes sting. An orange glow licked hungrily in the depths of the smoke. There'd been no sign of a fire when he'd been here just a few moments ago. How had it gotten so bad, so fast?

"Where's your mother, Tommy?" he asked, gripping the boy by the shoulders. "Where is she?"

"In the room with the bad man."

"Okay. Stay here." He turned to Taran. "Keep him safe."

"Shouldn't we evacuate the building?" Taran said.

"Not yet." Brannon stared into the smoke. "We don't know where the thing is yet. This could be a ruse to drive us out and separate us."

"Oh. That'd work."

"It has for me in the past."

Sword point low, Brannon moved forward. The flames were concentrated in Latricia's room, licking the corners of the door frame. It wouldn't be long now before the other guests came to investigate the noise, smelled the smoke, and began to panic. There would be very little chance of controlling the situation after that.

There were shapes moving in the smoke. He couldn't see for certain who they were.

Behind him, Tomidan Sandilar called out again.

"Tommy?" Latricia's voice came from up ahead. "Tommy, run! Blood and Tears, magus!"

A door across from Brannon banged open and a woman screamed. "Fire!"

"Latricia," Brannon called, moving toward the figures in the smoke. "Taran's got Tommy safe. Come this way. We need to get out of here." His mind raced over the question she had raised. Where was Draeson? Why wasn't he helping?

Another voice slithered out of the smoke, mocking and cruel. "Don't run, Tommy. If you want to see your mother again, you better come here and get her. I might have to kill her otherwise."

Brannon was closer now. The wards and screams had woken all of the inn's guests. Doors opened and people ran this way and that, like marbles on a tray. He could barely keep track of the figures of Latricia and the stranger in the chaos. Whoever was hiding in the smoke wanted Tomidan. Another member of the royal bloodline. Probably the next victim.

Jessamine appeared and grabbed his arm. "What's going on?"

"Find Ula and send her to me," he said. Then get yourself and everyone else out. Take your medical supplies. And be careful."

Her eyes were wide, but she pressed her lips tight and nodded. A moment later she was gone.

Latricia stumbled toward him, hugging the wall. Even through the smoke, he could see the fear in her eyes. Her arm dangled loosely at her side as though pulled from its socket. She looked into his face. "Help me."

Behind her was the saboteur from the boat, the man that had been in Latricia's garden in Alapra. Brannon's eyes widened and he felt a stab of hot guilt. He'd assured Latricia this man was dead, even when she'd told him she'd recognized him at the manor. He'd watched the man disappear beneath the water and Draeson's ice close over the top of him. He'd been sure he was gone. Yet here he was, a predator stalking his prey.

A mocking smile flicked onto the man's face. "Ah, Sir Brannon. Fancy meeting you again so soon."

Brannon tried to remember what Latricia had tried to tell him yesterday afternoon. The man's name was Fressin. He was Roydan's new steward at the manor. But why? Why would Roydan have hired such a man? Did he even know? Or had Fressin faked his documents entirely?

"Excuse us," Fressin said. He lunged forward and grabbed Latricia by the hair, pulling her backward into the smoke.

"No!" Brannon sprang after him, swinging the sword between them in the hope that Fressin would let go. Instead the man tugged Latricia closer, using her like a shield, forcing Brannon to pull the blow short.

"Drop the sword, Sir Brannon, or she gets my knife in her back."

Brannon lowered it. Fressin had her too close. He could kill her before Brannon had a chance to stop him. "What is it you want?"

"I said drop it," Fressin said. "Meaning out of your

hand and onto the floor."

Latricia whimpered.

Other guests were still emerging but they ignored what was happening in their rush toward the stairs to escape the flames. One of them bumped Brannon as he passed. Brannon didn't think he'd even seen him.

"Okay, take it easy." He let his sword clatter to the floor. "I'm sure we can work something out before things get too carried away. Why don't we follow everyone outside and talk about it there?"

Fressin wrinkled his nose and nodded his head toward the stairs. "You first."

There was a squeal from up the corridor and running footsteps. Tomidan had somehow slipped free of Brother Taran and ran toward his mother. Brannon cursed.

"Mama!"

Latricia gasped. "No, Tommy. Run!" The boy's steps faltered and he hesitated, uncertain.

"Trade," Fressin said and thrust Latricia toward Brannon. She stumbled a few steps and they collided. He caught her, turning to gently set her against the wall.

Fressin lunged forward to grasp Tomidan's arm, but the boy ducked to the side and ran to his mother.

Brannon put himself between them and Fressin. "Just leave," he said. "No one has to get hurt." The smoke was thick and choking now. It burned his lungs with every breath.

"Look out behind you," Fressin said, his voice light. He wiggled his fingers in a tiny wave.

"What?" Something hit Brannon from behind like a siege battering ram. He flew across the hallway and cracked his head against the doorjamb of an abandoned room. Pain speared into his brain and sparked down to his shoulder like hot metal chips from a blacksmith's anvil, as he slid to the floor. "Blood and Tears, what was that?"

Battle-honed instinct was the only thing that forced his eyes upward. The pain was incapacitating, shutting down his thoughts into one tense, silent scream, but his body knew better than to close down. If he let himself be stunned by an unexpected blow, the next one would kill him.

But the next blow didn't come. He took a deep breath, trying to focus, and coughed. The fire. He couldn't stay still. They had to get out of the building.

He pushed himself up, using the wall as a brace. The smoke made everything difficult to see. Fressin was to his right. Latricia and Tommy a little to the left. Latricia had picked up his sword and held it out in front of her like a yardstick, measuring the distance Fressin had to stay away.

The dog wards were still barking, the noise of them amplified in Brannon's skull.

Another figure materialized out of the thicker smoke. Latricia swung the sword to meet it but whoever it was casually batted the blade away. She hit at him with her fists but to no avail.

He grasped her chin in one hand and her shoulder in the other and tore off her head.

Blood sprayed across the corridor like warm rain on Brannon's skin. His insides were suddenly cold.

Latricia's head bounced when it hit the floor. It rolled, just a bit, then lay still.

Tommy was screaming.

The newcomer reached for the boy, but Fressin was there first. He thrust Tommy away from his mother's corpse, toward the stairs, and took position to defend him.

Brannon lurched forward. His head was still ringing but he knew what he'd seen. This was the Risen. The thing was after the boy. "Ula! Draeson! By all the Hooded Nameless things, help!"

Fressin threw a knife at the Risen. The blade sank into its stomach. The thing roared and broke into a run. It backhanded Fressin with a wide-armed blow and the assassin tumbled across the hallway, much as Brannon had done, landing in a crumpled heap.

Brannon kept his eyes on Tommy and ran toward him. The boy was frozen on the spot, blood dripping from his hair. The only chance to save him was to get to him before the Risen did, pick him up, and run. Latricia and Fressin had already shown that blades wouldn't stop the thing. If they could keep it trapped inside the building, perhaps the fire would destroy it.

His lungs strained against the smoke and every step jolted his aching head, but he ran as fast as he could.

It wasn't fast enough.

The Risen caught up and shoved him aside. It was like being nudged by a falling tree—solid and unstoppable. Brannon fell and slid across the floor, the carpet burning along his back.

He struggled to stand up, but fell back again, elbows hitting the floor hard. His body refused to obey him. The smoke was smothering him and the pain in his side and back was like being crushed beneath a boulder.

His eyes took in their first decent view of the Risen.

Smoke obscured the face but the shape of the body was distinctly male. Tall, not built like a soldier, but not like a scholar either. It was a naggingly familiar shape. All he could do was watch as it drew closer to Tomidan Sandilar.

Its hand was about to close on the back of the boy's neck when it jerked back its arm and screamed.

Brannon blinked. Ula was there. She raised her arm and threw one of the little spirit bags at the Risen. It struck the thing and it recoiled as if burned.

"Leave here, kaluki," Ula called. "Spirits no want you here."

She threw another one, then another. The Risen turned and fled back down the hall, toward the burning room.

Brannon let his head fall back. They'd done it. The thing was on the run. Tommy was safe. He let the smoke settle into his lungs like a fine cigar and felt himself drift. It was warm now. So warm. A good place to sleep.

Something cold and wet drifted over him, pushing through the drowsiness. He raised his hand to try to push it away but there was nothing there. He coughed, suddenly aware that the air was fresher than he'd been breathing, more pure.

He pulled his eyes open. The smoke was gone. The flames were gone.

Magus Draeson crouched beside him, wearing only a bed sheet draped around his waist. The dragon tattoo circled one of his nipples. Behind him, in the doorway to his room, Mayor Shillia was similarly wrapped in a bed sheet. The mayor refused to meet his eye.

Brannon sighed. "Really, Draeson?"

"The fire's out. Everything's safe now." The magus's voice was quiet. "I was late. I'm sorry."

"Latricia's dead. She trusted you to keep her safe."

"I know."

Brannon tried to lift himself up, tried to say more, but darkness was faster and he slept.

CHAPTER THIRTY-SIX

"So what do we do with him?" Brother Taran pointed to the captured man who was bound to a chair in the corner of the bedroom. Ula, Draeson, and Mayor Shillia looked to each other or the floor. Fressin, a bruise beginning to swell on his face, showed no expression at being discussed.

Brannon turned away. He wished he had a good answer. Instead he squinted against the morning sunlight spilling in through the window and studied the room. His head still felt like it was threaded with hot wires. He'd fortunately not felt ill or overly sleepy, so suspected any concussion he may have sustained was probably minor. Jessamine, who insisted on providing a second opinion, was not so sure. But given the urgency of the situation, he overrode her, made himself some willow bark tea laced with cinnamon, feverfew, and ginger, then put her to work looking after the other guests.

This was one of the rooms unaffected by the fire.

They had pushed the bed hard against the wall and brought in more chairs for the interrogation. A painting of a meadow hung above the writing desk. A coil of leftover rope, several knives, a razor-edged throwing star, and a garrote were piled in the corner, having been taken from Fressin before he was restrained.

It seemed strange to be carrying on with the investigation at the inn after the events of the night, but the flames had ultimately only destroyed Latricia's room and the ones to either side. Smoke and soot stained the walls of the hallway and many of the other rooms, but not as badly as Brannon had expected. Draeson's magic had pushed the smoke back like a blanket and stuffed it out the window in Latricia's room, smothering the flames completely as it passed.

Brannon, who had seen buildings destroyed by fire many times during the war, found it strangely unnerving to have the blackened hole, like a rotted cavity in a tooth, in an otherwise untouched inn.

Untouched, that was, but for the blood. Morning's light ripped the modest cloak of darkness from the red that stained the floor and walls of the hallway. The bloodstains were a harsh herald, screaming the news that Lady Latricia was dead and Tomidan Sandilar now an orphan. Her body was laid in one of the other bedrooms for now. It'd seemed wrong to leave her in the hall for people to step over.

"I could send for Morgin." Mayor Shillia was now fully clothed but still had trouble meeting Brannon's eye. "He can take away the, uh, the folks who didn't make it. Get them ready for burial."

"No," Brannon said. "We need to examine them

first. See if there are any clues about where the Risen is hiding." He'd rather dig latrines or lance boils.

"Of course," Shillia said. She glanced at Draeson, then looked away again, fidgeting.

Brannon sighed. "You could go and find him anyway, if you like. And let him know what's happened. I'm sure there's a lot he could get prepared ahead of time. Tools and coffins and so forth."

She nodded with such speed that it made Brannon's head hurt just to look at it, and made for the exit. "Good idea. I'll do that."

"Well, there's an awkward morning after, if ever there was one," Fressin said, as the door closed again. He let his head roll back as if to stare at the ceiling, watching his captors through the corner of his eyes. "I hope it wasn't a performance issue."

Draeson said nothing, but glanced toward Brannon.

"Ah," the spy said. "Different kind of performance issue. Someone was late to the party and didn't do his job. Oh dear."

"Shut up," Taran said. "Speak when you're spoken to."

Fressin lowered his chin and looked at Taran directly. "Uh-oh. Someone else didn't do as he was told. It's hard to keep hold of a child in a crisis, though, isn't it? What, with them being all small and weak and whatnot."

Taran's fists clenched at his sides. His eyes narrowed and he opened his mouth to speak again but Brannon interrupted him.

"Don't let him get to you, Taran. It's what he wants."

Fressin smiled. "Ah, the Bloodhawk joins the fray."

Brannon gave a small, mocking bow. "You're talking a lot. Have you decided to start your interrogation without us? How novel."

"I was getting bored," said Fressin. "Just trying to help."

"Really? You seem confident for a man tied to a chair. Why don't you tell us why?"

"Perhaps I have faith in your justice system."

"Good," said Brannon. "Because so far, the evidence is that I saw you attack Lady Latricia Sandilar, heard you threaten to kill her, and now she's dead. It doesn't look good for you."

The smug expression on Fressin's face faltered. "I didn't kill her. You know that."

Brannon shrugged. "Do I?"

"Of course you do. You were there."

"I was there fighting to protect Lady Latricia from you," Brannon said. "Then I got hit on the head and next thing I knew, she was dead. That looks pretty guilty to me, wouldn't you say?"

"Mmm," said Taran. "Very guilty."

"Rubbish," said Fressin. "You know full well that freak Risen killed her. I've got nothing to do with that."

Brannon laced his fingers together and stretched. "Maybe. Maybe not. You could be working with the Risen. By the Wolf, you could be a Risen yourself, for all I know." He paused. He didn't think for a moment that Fressin was a Risen, but he needed to have the man shaken. "Ula, do you think he could be one?"

The Djin woman scrunched up her face and leaned forward. Her dreadlocks fell from where she'd tucked them over her shoulders, to swing loosely, beads clacking. "Kaluki very strong to kill like that. Very strong. Maybe even in living body."

Brannon blinked. "I thought you said that was impossible?"

"Not impossible. Bad. Very bad thing for everyone." She spat onto the fingers of her right hand and reached out to rub it onto Fressin's forehead. He pulled back but her other hand snaked around and held him fast. She stared into his eyes for a long moment, muttering under her breath.

Finally she let him go and Fressin slumped down in the chair, breathing fast.

"Is not dead," Ula said, taking her seat once more. "Not know more than that."

Brannon frowned. "Well, then how would we know if he was a kaluki in a living body?"

"Strong," Ula said. "Hard to kill. Stab or hit and he not hurt. Kaluki in a living body bring much power into this world. Too much. Plenty to keep host body from harm."

Brannon scratched at his scar. The idea of a living Risen was enough to form a lump of ice in his gut. He'd seen the Risen that had killed Latricia take a knife to the chest and keep coming. And it'd had the strength to pull the widow's head right off her body with no difficulty at all. Whatever was in that body was very strong. If they were looking at a live person possessed by a kaluki then the suspect list could be very, very long.

"I'm not a kaluki or whatever she's saying," Fressin said. "If I was superhumanly strong, do you really think I'd still be tied up talking to you?"

"One way to test it," said Brother Taran. He stood, picked up the chair he'd been sitting on, and swung it at Fressin. The chair legs collided with the bound man's face and shoulder, the force of the blow rocking him in his own chair.

"Blood and Hooded Tears!" Fressin spat red from his bleeding lips and turned a dark scowl on the priest. "What did I ever do to you?"

Taran raised the chair again, and Brannon moved quickly to grasp it and take it from him.

"That's enough, Taran. Step back. He's bleeding. You've made your point."

The young priest nodded, his jaw set tight.

"Ula, would you say that's evidence enough that he's not a living Risen?"

Ula nodded, beads clacking like a miniature hailstorm. "Yes. He is not the one."

"By the Wolf," said Fressin. "I could have told you that. Do you people go around beating everyone you meet with furniture, just in case?"

"You're the reason a child saw his mother's head being torn off," Taran said, his voice very quiet. "Be grateful you didn't get what you truly deserve."

Brannon gave them both a stern look. Taran stared at the floor. Brannon glanced around to see if Draeson had anything to add, but the mage was silent. He too looked mainly at the carpet.

"So, Fressin, now we know you're not a Risen. But that still leaves us with a lot of questions. We don't know if you're involved with the Risen, but we do know you were involved in the murders in Alapra and the sabotage of our boat on the way here." Brannon paused.

"Everywhere something bad happens, there you are. Would you care to explain that?"

There was a long silence as everyone in the room waited. Brannon watched Fressin closely, noting the cut on his lip that could probably do with a stitch, and the way his breathing was swift and shallow as he wrestled with himself. His eyes flicked to the side, then back to meet Brannon's.

"I had nothing to do with the murders in Alapra," he said.

"You were there. We saw you in the garden at the Sandilar townhouse."

"Yes, but I didn't kill anyone."

Brannon spread his hands, palms up. "Then tell us."

Fressin sighed. "My employer is a man with singular needs. He is a tradesman who invests a lot of money in his deals. He likes to ensure that they go the way he wants them to go. And I am a man with a special skill set that is useful in these kinds of situations."

Brannon rubbed at his scar again. "Your employer is Duke Roydan Sandilar?"

Fressin shook his head. "No. One of his competitors. Don't ask me which one, I won't tell you. That's part of our deal."

"Then how did you manage to become the steward at the Sandilar manor?"

"Forged papers and stolen pigeons. It's easier than you think."

Brannon leaned back, shaking his head slowly. If it hadn't ached before, he was sure it would do by now. "Between that and getting on board the boat, it's pretty clear you've had training in infiltration. Ex military?"

Fressin tilted his head and gave him a flat stare. "You know I'm not."

Brannon nodded. In that, at least, the man was being honest. Only one kind of person carried throwing stars and garrotes. "You're a Child of Starlight. From one of the Assassin Houses."

"Correct."

"And you think this is something that will help you convince us that you weren't involved in the murders?" Brannon raised his eyebrow.

Fressin shrugged. "I'll kill someone if it's part of the job, but in this case, it wasn't. The assignment called for more subtlety than that."

"What was the assignment?"

Fressin licked his lips. "Can I get a drink? I'm a bit dry after that fire."

"You can have a drink after you tell us about your assignment." Brannon told him.

The assassin took a deep breath. "Fine. You already know from digging into Prince Keldan's death, that there's a bidding war going on with the Nilarian Ambassador. Well, the maneuverings for that particular deal have been going on for much longer than you might think. Cornering the market for Nilarian silk in Kalanon will make somebody a fortune."

Brannon nodded. "Keldan and Roydan were both front runners for the deal but there were others we don't know."

"Several others," Fressin agreed. "And many of them felt that the Sandilars are wealthy enough by virtue of managing the gold mines. They felt that someone else should have a chance at this new venture. One of these people employed me to even the playing field. They hired me to spy on the Sandilars and sabotage their efforts where I can."

"Killing Keldan Sandilar was a pretty effective sabotage," Draeson said quietly, looking up at last.

"It was," Fressin agreed. "But I didn't do it. I didn't even have eyes on him that night, so I can't give you any more clues about who did. I can tell you that if I'd killed him, I wouldn't have done it in such a flashy, obvious way. He'd have had an accident or been mugged in a bad part of town and no one would be any the wiser."

He shifted a little in his bonds, straining against the ropes in an effort to get comfortable. "What I did do," he continued, "was spy on your investigation. I knew it would lead you to the silk deal and so I needed to know what you were doing and how you might be messing it up for my employer. That's why I was in the garden at the Sandilar townhouse. That's why I was following you in Alapra. I needed to know how your investigation might affect my employer."

"And?" Brannon asked, leaning forward in his chair.

"And it wasn't good. Somehow Keldan's deal went to his widow and all the action was moving here, to Sandilar. I did what I could to slow you down by sinking the River Queen, then managed to get to the manor in time to disrupt Lady Latricia and Ambassador Ylani's visit. I hoped the rude welcome would break up their bond, but that didn't seem to work. So last night I broke in to threaten her. I figured, if I could scare her and her son enough, she'd run back to Alapra and forget about cementing the deal with Ylani. What I didn't count on was some crazed Djin shaman sending a Risen here to kill her."

"We don't think it was a Djin," Draeson said, with a glance at Ula. "Just someone who learned their secrets."

Fressin rolled his eyes. "Oh. So much better."

Brannon found himself scratching at his scar again. He pulled his hand away and laced his fingers. Something horrible was stirring in his mind. "What if one of the other traders hired someone as well? Your employer hired an assassin to spy and sabotage. Could one of the others have hired a Djin to use a Risen to eliminate the competition?"

"If they did . . . " Fressin paled and licked his lips. "You saw that thing," he said, his voice quiet. "However it got here, it's loose now. May the gods have mercy on us all."

Brannon felt as if a chill breeze traced over his skin. Behind him, Draeson shifted in his seat and coughed. Brannon touched his sword hilt. Somehow this closed room felt vulnerable and exposed.

"Okay," he said. "We need to take some action. We now know the pattern of victims. That gives us an advantage. They're going after Tommy Sandilar, but also anyone else with the same bloodline. We need to bring anyone who could be a target here so we can protect them. Who do we know of?"

"Morgin Vere," said Draeson. "The rumors are right about who his father is. No doubt Roydan has other bastards up at the manor as well. He's never been shy about dallying with parlor maids."

"Fine," Brannon said. "We need to round up as many of them as possible and get them here. Then we need to fortify the inn. Draeson, I want your wards at every entrance and exit and scattered throughout the inn. Set them to recognize a Risen if you can, otherwise set them to bark at anyone who isn't one of us, staff, or someone we specifically introduce to them. And when they bark, you take action. No more distractions. Deal?"

Draeson nodded. "Deal."

"Ula, your spirit pouches—they seemed to work but someone moved them. How do you keep them in place back in Djinan?"

"Not pouches in Djinan," Ula said. "Make spirit bricks and build them into the house. Hard to do here— building already made."

He couldn't argue with that. "What about if we hide them? Would they still be effective?"

"Of course."

"Great. Make lots more and get Jessamine to help you hide them throughout the inn. Double what we would normally need. I want this place impenetrable and this time I don't want anyone to be able to undo your good work. Somebody deliberately removed them last night to let that Risen in. Let's make it hard for them to do it again." He paused. "Do you have enough ingredients?"

Ula nodded. "Mostly made from here. Earth, spit, ash. Only need a little of the special dirt to make it work. Spirits of this place willing to fight kaluki hard, just like spirits in Djinan."

"Good. Taran, do you think you can restrain yourself enough to keep an eye on this guy?" Brannon gestured toward the captured assassin. "I don't want him going anywhere until we can verify his story."

Taran frowned. "How do you intend to do that?"

"I'm not sure yet. There are pigeons at the manor. Maybe we can get word to Roydan and see if he can shed any light on it. Meanwhile, keep Fressin hidden from the guards outside. They don't know he's here and I don't want them to."

He looked around at the three determined faces. Finally they had an edge; an understanding of what this murderer was up to—albeit a vague one. They still didn't know who or why, but they knew what. They knew who he was going to go for next and they knew how to prepare. They would be ready. "Okay, let's get busy."

He opened the door and found Ambassador Ylani pressed up against it. She straightened up and brushed at her skirts. "Good morning," she said.

Brannon frowned. "Were you just listening at the door?"

She tossed her hair back. "Actually, yes. I was."

"And?"

"And somebody in that room is lying. I can prove it."

CHAPTER THIRTY-SEVEN

The smithy was dark. No embers burned in the forge. The wide wooden doors, like folding sides of a barn, were stretched across the shopfront and locked, hiding rakes, hoes, and horseshoes from any potential customers outside. The usual smells of burning coal and hot iron had damped down to old ash and polishing oil, and the clang of hammer on anvil was long lost.

"Are you sure it's safe here?" he said.

"Of course. There's no reason for anyone to come here now that Kholi's dead. He didn't have an apprentice and it'll take weeks before the town gets a new blacksmith."

"What about Alena?"

"His wife? She never showed any interest in the place while he was alive. I don't see her hanging out here now. I doubt she even has a key. I wouldn't worry about it."

He took a deep breath and let it out, calming

himself. "Okay. You know them better than I do."

She chuckled, a wicked, musical sound. "Oh yes. I knew Kholi very well indeed. It really is surprising how much you can learn between the sheets."

He felt his cheeks flush.

She chuckled again and patted his shoulder. "Oh, lighten up. We're getting what we want, aren't we? No need to be embarrassed over a little nighttime fun." She took a few steps and lifted herself up onto a workbench, sitting on the edge of it like a church gargoyle on the eaves.

He rubbed at his forehead. "It's not that. It's just . . . it's getting stronger."

"What is?"

"The thing. The thing we put inside me." It was like little fingers scratching at his insides. "I can feel it trying to get control."

Her eyes narrowed. "We're getting very close to our goal now. You need to keep it together. The kaluki is a source of power and strength, that's all. You are in charge of how you use that strength. You choose who lives and who dies."

He gave a wry smile. "We choose, you mean."

She smiled back. "That's right. We choose."

He looked away. "That's just it though. I didn't mean to kill the Lady Latricia. I just did it. What if the thing . . . I think it got control of me, just for a moment."

"Or you just got carried away with your new strength in the heat of the moment. Blood and Tears, pull yourself together and stop imagining problems where there are none. Do you want to be the lord of Sandilar or not?"

That put a spark in his gut and steel in his spine. He stood up straight and strong. "Yes. Yes, I do."

She jumped down from the bench and strode over to him, clasping his shoulders in both hands. "That's my boy. You deserve it. That's what all this is about. We're taking what's yours. Are you ready?"

Morgin smiled and kissed her on the forehead. "I'm ready."

CHAPTER THIRTY-EIGHT

After the death of their commanding officer, the remaining guards surrounding the inn had sent word back to the manor for further instructions, presumably from Fressin. In the meantime, Brannon found they were receptive to his authority as King's Champion, particularly since he did little to alter their existing orders. He told them to remain in position, guard the inn, and allow himself and Ambassador Ylani clear passage to leave on horseback as they had a message to deliver to the manor. Eventually it would be discovered that Fressin was missing and orders would come back from whoever was next in charge, but for now this was enough.

The day was clear, but there was a brisk wind moving in off the mountains that brought a chill to the air. The ambassador wore one of her customary silk gowns, red and flowing with the shoulders cut out, but it was covered by a somber green cloak that occasionally flashed the brilliant colour beneath. The hood of the cloak was pushed back, letting her hair flow free in long waves, threaded with red and gold ribbons.

Brannon moved his horse closer. "You're not wearing a hat today," he commented.

Ylani reached up as if to adjust the missing accessory. "Scandalous, isn't it? I feel positively naked."

"Is there a reason?" Brannon asked. "It seems out of character for you."

She crinkled her nose. "Honestly? I'm trying to fit in and be more . . . appropriate. In Alapra, my position gives me a level of protection, but out here I don't want to highlight my difference too much. Your people don't like Nilarians. So, when in Kalanon, do as the Kalans do." She fingered the ribbons threaded through her curls. "I think this is as far as I'll go though. I might not have a hat, but at least I have some decoration for the gods. I don't feel like a total heretic."

Brannon smiled. "We all have a little heresy in us from time to time. How did you manage when you were a spy, though? You must have gone without any headgear during the war or you'd have been spotted immediately."

She dropped her hand back to the reins. "Yes," she said, "but that's not something I ever want to go back to."

Brannon's smile turned wry. "Well, that's something we have in common." They rode in silence for a while, the horses' hooves on the cobblestones a counterpoint for birdsong. News about the killings at the inn had spread. There were very few villagers out of their homes today. "So, how about you tell me what we're looking for and why I'm following you up to Sandilar Manor."

"Well, for starters, you were going there anyway to find anyone with the royal bloodline, if I'm not mistaken."

"True, but for that I could have taken Draeson, who can identify Roydan's bastards much more easily than I can, and instead I'm taking you. Why?"

Her lips quirked at the corner. "I suppose it's because Magus Draeson and I don't really get along."

Brannon gave her a look. "And?"

"Okay." Any hint of smile vanished. She chewed her bottom lip for a moment, then spoke again. "I need you to listen with an open mind. This may not be easy to hear, but what I'm going to show you should remove any doubts."

"I'm listening," Brannon said.

"When Latricia came to me, it wasn't about the silk deal. For her, trade negotiations have only ever been a cover story. She had found something that scared her and she didn't know who she could trust to tell."

"What do you mean?" Brannon said.

"I mean that the person who scared her was so well connected that she couldn't even be sure that you, the King's Champion, would believe what she had seen. So she came to me."

"But that's ridiculous." Brannon gripped the reins tightly, barely feeling the edges dig into his skin. "I've known her and Keldan for years. Why would she think that?"

"You agreed to listen with an open mind," Ylani reminded him.

"I am. Go on."

"She and I have been investigating on our own and

the trail led here." Ylani turned so that she could meet his eyes as they rode. "The man you have at the inn doesn't work for Roydan's rival. He works for Roydan. His mission wasn't to prevent a trade agreement. It was to prevent you or any of us from finding out that Roydan has already made an illegal trade agreement and is planning to overthrow your king."

Brannon's eyes bulged. "What?"

"Think about it," Ylani said, speaking quickly. "How does sabotaging your boat have any impact on a trade agreement between Latricia and me? Or Roydan and me? How could he get full control of the manor and its men so quickly without Roydan's help?"

"Forged documents," Brannon said weakly.

"And why are there so many armed men at Sandilar Manor in the first place? Latricia assured me the contingent there now is far in excess of what is usually held."

"That doesn't mean anything. Perhaps it was a cautionary measure. We can't judge without talking to Roydan first."

"Fine," she said. "I understand that. And without Latricia's testimony, the rest is circumstantial at best. But if I'm right, what I'm going to show you will be incontrovertible proof that a delivery has already taken place. And that, Sir Brannon, King's Champion, is something you're duty-bound to investigate."

Brannon's jaw was tight. "I know my duty, ambassador. And so does the duke. I don't think you realize that he and Aldan and I served side by side in the war since we were very young. Loyalty to each other is in our blood and bones. I can't see what you're telling me being true, but I will look and keep an open mind."

She nodded, almost a bow. "That's all I ask. And perhaps I'm wrong. All I know is what Latricia believed and what we found. But . . . people change, Brannon. Look at your own life. You were the Bloodhawk once, the terror of my people. Now you're a physician. I don't think you like killing anymore."

Brannon looked away. They'd left the town behind and there was only grassland, stone, and sheep beyond the cobbles of the road. "No one should like killing."

She gave a rueful smile. "I agree. But some of us come to the lesson later than others."

There was nothing to say to that. He concentrated on the road ahead and the fresh smells of the countryside. With the "bandit" who had attacked Ylani the last time she'd travelled this road in custody, they were relatively safe—except for the possibility of the Risen. It hadn't shown itself in daylight yet, but that could change.

He patted his pocket where one of Ula's spirit pouches was a comforting weight against his leg. She had warned him they were designed to protect a building and would be unlikely to work as personal protection, but he found he felt better having it with him. The manor would have its own pouches in place, but any extra safety they could get while on the road was invaluable.

He stole a glance at Ambassador Ylani. He probably should have suggested she carry one as well, but he had no idea where she would put it in that dress.

The thought he'd wanted to avoid forced its way into his head: what if she was right? Roydan had changed as he'd gotten older. He'd always been intelligent, but he'd become shrewd. As a businessman, it worked for him. But shrewd and loyal didn't always go together. Brannon still found it difficult to believe his friend would actually do something blatantly illegal, but he owed it to Latricia to check it out. If she hadn't been concerned about where his own loyalties lay, she probably wouldn't have been in Sandilar, let alone the Knox Inn last night and would still be alive.

"Brannon, can I ask you something?" Ylani's voice pulled him out of his thoughts.

"Sure."

"Why did you become a physician?"

Brannon shrugged. He was used to this question. "After so much killing in the war, I wanted to do something different. To kind of balance the scales. As a physician I get to save lives instead of taking them. That feels good."

She studied him for a long moment. Brannon met her gaze, fighting the urge to lick his lips or rub at his scar. "There's more to it than that, though, isn't there?" she said.

Brannon broke eye contact. "Yeah. Yeah, there is."

Ylani brought her horse to a stop and waited.

Brannon reined in and turned back to face her. "You really want to know?"

"Yes."

He pulled his sword partway out of the scabbard. "This is one of the few Nilarian swords in Kalanon. Do you know how I got it?"

She chewed her lip. "Rumors back home have you doing all sorts of things, Sir Bloodhawk. But I don't know the truth. Judging from the hilt, I'd say you took it from one of our generals."

Brannon nodded. "General Halaki. He'd been terrorizing farming communities up and down the Tilal but keeping just out of reach of our forces. So we split up and came at him from different directions. Once the battle was engaged, my squad and I made it through to the command tent. We knew that if we could kill Halaki, it would take time for his men to regroup."

"A sound strategy," Ylani admitted. Brannon admired her for not commenting on the slaughter of her countrymen.

"He was a good soldier and he fought hard. My sword broke in the battle, as our swords sometimes do against yours, but in the end I killed him. Unfortunately, he wasn't alone." Brannon swallowed, trying to block out the anguished cry ringing in his memory. *Papa!*

"He had his son with him. A boy of maybe fourteen. I guess Halaki figured they were far enough away from the main front that he'd be safe." Brannon shrugged. "The boy had seen me kill his father and he attacked. He cut my face before I managed to pick up the sword Halaki had dropped. He wouldn't stop. I tried, honestly, I tried to get him to stop but he wouldn't and more soldiers were coming. It was chaos."

Ylani covered her mouth with her hands. "You killed him."

A cloud rolled over the sun and the shadows were very cold.

"I killed him with his father's sword," Brannon said, shoving it back into the scabbard. "And I kept it to remind me. I have a lot to make up for, Ylani."

"Don't we all." She sighed. "You kept on killing after that?"

"My country needed me to." He turned away. "It still does."

"That's why you expect so much loyalty from your friend," she said. "You have so much of it yourself." She swung down from the saddle. "We should go the rest of the way on foot. We'll never get close to what I want to show you if we're seen."

They tied the horses to a tree and let them graze. A little further along, they left the road entirely and approached the manor from the side. "Too many people watch the front gate," Ylani said. She pulled up the hood of her cloak and the color blended like camouflage with the rolling fields they travelled through. At last they reached a rise that looked over the back of the manor house. There, they lay flat, just the top of their heads above the ridge of the hill as they viewed Sandilar Manor below.

From this angle, they faced the painted stone side of the manor and could still see the gardens at the front, though the front door itself was hidden from view. Toward the back of the building was a large wooden barn, which Brannon didn't remember from the last time he had been here. The timber was unpainted, but, from this distance at least, still looked to be in good condition.

"The barn's new," Brannon commented. "Hardly incriminating though."

"Wait 'til you see what's in it," Ylani said.

Brannon said nothing, watching instead the number of armed guards patrolling around the barn and along the side of the house where wagon tracks led from the new building to the main drive out front. There were many more guards than one would normally expect for a barn.

"It's going to be tricky getting inside without being seen."

Hoof beats pulled his attention back to the front of the house as a single rider approached from the road. "Another messenger from the guards at the inn?" he wondered aloud.

Ylani squinted. "I don't think so. I think it's the mayor's son, Morgin Vere."

Some of the guards patrolling the side of the house hurried to the front to meet him.

Brannon scowled. "He should be safely inside the inn by now. What's he doing here?"

"Creating a distraction for us, it seems," Ylani commented as several more guards vanished around the corner, presumably to cover the front door. "But not quite enough of one. Perhaps I can add to that." She stood up and unclasped her cloak. The green fabric fluttered to the ground, revealing the red dress beneath like a beacon. "I suggest you move quickly," she said, and glided down the slope like a brilliant butterfly.

Or perhaps, Brannon thought more cynically as he slipped past the distracted guards, some sort of honeytrap spider.

"Good morning, gentlemen," he heard her calling. "I seem to have gotten myself a little bit lost. Can you help me?"

He took out his dagger, then put it away again. He couldn't see himself using it on a fellow Kalan if he could avoid it.

The barn had a side door. He waited until all eyes were on Ylani, then strode toward it, keeping one eye on the nearest guard, and the other on the ground ahead of him—this was not the time to step on a twig. Moving swiftly but quietly, he reached the door handle and pulled.

The hinges squealed. Brannon held his breath and kept moving. The door had opened just enough to squeeze through.

The nearby guard started to turn.

Ambassador Ylani shrieked and stumbled, landing on her hands and knees in the grass. "Oh, my dress! Ahpra's Tears, I hate mud!"

The guard chuckled, his eyes glued to the spectacle.

Brannon slipped through the gap and out of sight.

The inside of the barn was dark and dusty. The smell of sawdust and straw filled his nostrils. Spikes of sunlight pierced the darkness from chinks in the wall beams, like javelins thrown by the gods. Long wooden crates were stacked three high, in orderly rows, turning the barn into a kind of warehouse. He could imagine shoppers wandering the aisles created by the rows of crates, rummaging for a bargain once the tops were popped open.

There were no markings on the outside of the crates to give any indication of their contents or origins. The wood they were made of was simple pine, sanded smooth and nailed tight.

Brannon pulled out his dagger again and used it to pry open one of the crate lids. Inside were bolts of brilliantly colored fabric. He reached out to touch it. Silk.

"So if the deal hasn't been finalized yet, what are you doing with crates and crates of silk?" he murmured.

"Exactly," Ylani said, making him jump. She moved

between the rows of crates with an effortless ease, as though she'd been there the whole time.

"How did you get in here? Past the guards?"

She grinned and wiggled her eyebrows. "I was a spy, remember?"

He rolled his eyes. "I assume this is what you wanted me to see."

"That's part of it," she said, her grin fading. "The only legal import of silk into Kalanon is through me and should have the ambassadorial seal on the box. This doesn't. But that's not the biggest thing. Help me unwrap one of the bolts."

The fabric unrolled easily, falling in ripples to pile on the ground like a many layered pastry confection. When at last the final piece fell away, Brannon felt his insides twist. Disappointment flashed through him in a hot flash, leaving sweat on his forehead and a foul taste in his mouth. At the center of the bolt of fabric, the pole the silk had been wrapped around was a sword.

Brannon set it down and stepped back. "They're all swords, aren't they?"

Ylani shrugged. "Unless you think somehow we picked up the only one."

He took a deep breath. This was bad. Very bad. He'd trusted Roydan his whole life. Aldan trusted him. What was he up to? "Maybe he's after a monopoly in Nilarian steel as well as silk. He'd make a fortune with that."

"He would," Ylani admitted. "But why import just swords? And anyway, it's illegal for Nilarians to sell our steel or the methods for making it. Our government knows exactly why we had the upper hand for most of the war. We're not stupid enough to give away the secret. Roydan and someone in Nilar are going against both governments, and I think your prisoner, Fressin, is the go-between."

Brannon nodded, steeling himself. "All right. You've convinced me there are definitely questions Roydan needs to answer. I'll talk more to Fressin when we get back. What does all this have to do with the murders I'm investigating?"

"Nothing, as far as I can tell," Ylani said. "It's all just a horrible coincidence. But Latricia died wanting you to know what was going on. I had to honor her wishes. Somebody needs to report Roydan to the king."

"Agreed. But for now, we need to get out of here without anyone knowing we've seen this, and bring anyone who might have illegitimate royal blood back to the inn for safekeeping." He bundled the silk and sword back into the crate and replaced the lid.

"Do you really think we need to?" Ylani gestured toward the outside. "They have plenty of militia standing guard and I gave them a huge supply of Ula's spirit pouches yesterday. They're probably just as safe here as anywhere."

"Maybe," he said, moving toward the door. "But we need to give them the option. People have the right to know who's being targeted."

He raised a finger to his lips and pressed up against the door opening, peering outside. The guards were gone. He gestured Ylani closer and looked again. There was no one. "Something's up," he whispered. "But this is probably our best chance to get out of here."

She nodded and Brannon wished they hadn't left her

muted green cloak behind. Ambassador Ylani was not the kind of woman who went unnoticed. Especially in that dress.

He nudged the door open a little further, then slipped part of the way out. Sure enough, the coast was clear. "Come on."

He made it a few steps before Ylani grabbed his collar and pulled him back. "Stop!" she hissed. "Get back!"

A second later, the body of a dead militiaman fell on the spot where he'd been standing.

"Blood and Tears!" Brannon looked around and up, trying to see where the man had come from. On the roof of the barn stood Morgin Vere. He had blood on his shirt and on his hands.

"Better call an undertaker," he said. "Whoops, that's me!" Then he dissolved into giggles.

Brannon exchanged a look with Ylani. "Um, Morgin? Are you okay?"

The young man cocked his head to one side as he looked down at them. He was standing right on the edge of the roof, the tips of his feet hanging over the edge. "Are you?"

"Morgin, be careful, okay?" Brannon called. "We don't want you to hurt yourself."

Morgin shook his head. "Nope, I can't." He stepped off the edge and plummeted to the ground. He landed easily, knees bent, and smiled. "All safe."

"Ahpra's Tears," Ylani swore. "It's him, isn't it? The live Risen."

Brannon gestured to her to stay behind him. "Morgin," he said. "What have you done? There's blood on your hands."

Morgin pointed a red finger at him. "Don't ask questions, Sir Brannon. You were nice to me. I like you and it's me who chooses who lives and dies now. Just me." He shook himself and pointed the finger at his own head. "In here."

Brannon fingered the spirit pouch in his pocket.

"Do you know what's in there?" Morgin said, suddenly. "In that barn, I mean?"

"No, Morgin," Brannon lied. "What?"

The young man leaned forward. His freckles stood out starkly against his very pale skin. "The deliveries," he whispered. "Mustn't mess up the deliveries. Mustn't!" He sighed and absently licked the blood off one of his fingers. "So many people telling me what to do. Not for much longer. I'm going to inherit Sandilar, you know. Finally get what I deserve. No more heirs. Just me."

Brannon felt himself go cold. "Have you been inside the manor, Morgin?"

He nodded. "Yes."

"But what about Ula's protections?" Ylani said. "I delivered them yesterday. How did you get in?"

"No little spirit packets," Morgin said, shaking his head. "They didn't use them. And I'm getting so much stronger now."

Brannon fought the urge to draw his sword or dagger. No doubt the manor guards had done so and it hadn't helped them one bit. His fingers closed on Ula's spirit pouch. It was the one thing he had that they hadn't used. "What did you do, Morgin? Who did you kill?"

Morgin blinked slowly. "Who I had to."

"You mean Roydan's other illegitimate children? So that you could be heir?"

Morgin frowned. "I shouldn't have told you that."

Brannon pulled the spirit pouch out of his pocket but Morgin had already lunged forward. The mayor's son backhanded Brannon and he flew back into the wall of the barn, slamming into the wood with enough force to crack the boards. The little packet dropped from his fingers.

Ylani screamed and Morgin turned his attention toward her. Her scream also caught the attention of a remaining guard, who rounded the side of the barn at a run. He had a crossbow in his hand, stopped, aimed and fired.

The bolt struck Morgin in the neck. He growled, a thick guttural sound, and ripped it out. He leaped, crossing the distance between him and the guard in a single bound, and plunged his hand into the man's chest, punching through his rib cage like it was spun sugar. A moment later, he pulled out the man's lung and a piece of bone. He flung it on the ground and turned back to Brannon and Ylani.

"People won't be so disrespectful when I'm the duke," he said.

Brannon scrambled toward the spirit pouch and snatched it up. His back and legs ached, and his shoulder, where the blow had caught him, felt pulverized, but he forced himself to stand next to Ylani, and held out the pouch like a shield. "Stay back."

Morgin walked steadily toward him. "I'm much stronger now." Fresh blood dribbled from his fingers like a tiny waterfall, leaving a thin trail of red on the grass.

Brannon shook the pouch. "Come on. Come on!" He was only a few steps away.

Ylani stepped forward, leaned over his hand and spat onto the spirit pouch. A big glob of saliva trailed down the side of the leather like a large, wet slug.

Brannon stared. "What was that?"

"I don't know," Ylani said. Her face was flushed. "It's to activate it. A sacrifice or spirit price? Something like that. Ask Ula."

Morgin's face had changed with Ylani's action. It was as if all the humanity was stripped away, his eyes dark and soulless. Then that inhuman face began to show fear.

The pouch in Brannon's hand began to vibrate—just a small thing, like a tuning fork or a plucked string on a bow. The ground beneath their feet trembled and the wind changed direction and blew past and through him, like an avenging spirit—like Ula's protecting earth spirits.

The wind touched Morgin and he hissed. "*Kaluk faa lek!*" he said. "*Shaa le khul.*" Then he turned and leaped, and in a couple of bounds he was gone.

CHAPTER THIRTY-NINE

Taran opened the door to Jessamine. Her blond hair was tied up in its usual ponytail, but a few wisps had come loose and dangled enticingly next to her face. Her blue eyes met his and she smiled like the sun sparkling on the water on a summer's day.

"Um," he said. "Hello."

Jessamine held up a glass of water. "Drink for the prisoner."

"Oh, yes, of course. Go right in."

"I could get one for you as well, if you like," she said, brushing past him.

"No, that's okay." He was about to follow her inside, when a movement caught his eye.

Tomidan Sandilar sat on the floor in the corridor. His small frame was hunched over, his knees pulled up to his chest and his arms wrapped around them in a hug. He rocked back and forth and stared at the carpet where his mother's blood had obliterated the pattern in a dark, sticky mess.

"Tommy?" Taran called. "What are you doing here? Where's your nanny?"

The boy said nothing for a long time and Taran began to wonder if he'd even heard, when he finally spoke. "Why did that happen to my mama?"

Taran swallowed. He looked back at Jessamine. She was holding the glass of water to the prisoner's lips. He looked up and down the hall. There was no one else to talk to the boy. This was the worst part of being a priest: having to interact with people.

He took a few steps and crouched down beside the boy, tentatively putting a hand on his shoulder. "I don't know, Tommy. We're trying to find out."

Tomidan looked up at him, his eyes big and wet. "Will the Hooded One look after her and Daddy now?"

Taran's chest contracted, his breath almost gone. "Yes."

"Who will look after me?"

Taran fought the urge to look away, and instead laid a hand on the boy's other shoulder. At this, Tommy flung himself forward, wrapping his arms around Taran and clinging tight.

"I don't know yet, Tommy," Taran choked. "But you have lots of people who love you. Your nanny, your grandfather, the king. You'll be okay." He held the boy for what seemed a very long time, until finally Tommy pulled away and looked him in the eye.

"Really?"

Taran nodded. "Yes, really. I know it hurts now, but you're going to be okay. I lost my parents when I was about your age and I turned out okay, didn't I?"

The beginnings of a smile tried to push through the tears on Tommy's face for just a moment. "Yes."

"Okay then. Now, why don't you go and find your nanny, because she'll be worried about you. And then maybe you could have a talk to Karia. Do you know who she is?"

Tommy nodded. "She brings me extra pudding at dinner."

Taran smiled. "She's nice like that. And she lost somebody she loves recently too. So maybe she'll understand what you're feeling."

Tommy wiped his eyes with his palms. "She might need a hug then."

"I'm sure she does." They both stood up and Taran watched as the little boy walked away toward the staircase. He hoped he and Karia could bring some comfort to each other for a while.

When he turned back to the room, Jessamine was standing in the doorway. "You're very sweet, you know."

Taran felt his face go red and shrugged. He moved to enter the room, expecting her to move, but she didn't.

"No, really. What you said to that little boy was really lovely. He needed that."

Taran blinked, not quite sure what to say.

Jessamine moved forward and before he realized what was happening, she kissed him. His eyes flew wide open, then slammed shut as her lips pressed against his, moving softly in slow gentle nibbles. His body froze as her hands slipped around his waist, sliding like fire to the small of his back. His own hands somehow found their way to her hips and hovered, like trembling moths.

Then it was over and she pulled away.

"I need to find Ula," she said, and gently pressed her nose against his before breaking their embrace.

"Oh."

She sauntered off, hips swaying, and disappeared after Tomidan down the stairwell.

Taran stared after her, his breath fast and his skin tingling.

"You think she likes you." The mocking voice trailed up his spine from inside the room.

Taran stepped inside and closed the door before turning around to face the man who was still bound to a chair, immobile. "Shut up, Fressin." He paced the room, his hand drifting to his lips. It was the strangest thing. He could still feel the warmth of her kiss as if it was still there, some disembodied entity with a life of its own, reminding him of the impossible. Jessamine Tral had kissed him!

As he turned around, he caught Fressin staring at him. The assassin's eyes were narrowed. "You've been away from the House too long," he said. "You've forgotten. People like us don't have love. There's no usefulness in it."

Taran felt his chest tighten. "So you do recognize me."

Fressin laughed. "Of course. I nearly shit myself when I saw you on that boat. I couldn't believe it. Everyone thinks you're dead."

"That's actually how I prefer it," Taran said.

"I get it," Fressin said. "You must be seriously deep undercover. I mean, after that thing with the contract on the Kalan king, nobody would ever have expected to see you again. I mean, there was no way to get out of that. How did you survive?"

Taran looked away. The clock ticked extra loud and he took a slow, deep breath and said nothing. He could almost hear Fressin's mind working it out.

"By the Wolf. You betrayed them." The assassin's voice was soft and breathless. "You warned the king and he's hidden you all these years. They killed your team! Other Children of Starlight died because you reneged on a contract. Doesn't that matter to you?"

Taran felt his hands press together like a pleading prayer. He wanted his old friend to understand. Wanted it so badly. But he knew he wouldn't. "It wasn't right, Fressin."

The assassin frowned. "What wasn't? Killing King Aldan?" He shrugged. "It was the job. You know that. Once the contract is taken, that's it. That's the deal."

"Not just Aldan. All of it." He gestured around him. "The Children of Starlight. Killing people, who don't deserve it, just because someone else wants them dead. Don't you see? It's wrong. I couldn't live that way anymore."

Fressin stared at him as if he were something new and dangerous. "You've bought into your own cover. You really think you're a priest."

Taran chuckled, the taste of it bitter in his mouth. "No. No, I'm nothing like a priest. Not really."

They watched each other for a long time. Taran wished there was something to say that would bring understanding, but every time he opened his mouth to speak, he knew Fressin would only laugh. There had never been any crisis of faith in Fressin, growing up; he had never questioned the ways of starlight. Not like Taran had.

"You know I'll tell the House you're alive when I get back," Fressin said at last. "They'll come after you."

"I know."

"I guess that means you'll have to kill me to keep your cover."

Taran swallowed. "Yes."

"You won't want your new friends finding out about you either, I suppose." Fressin took a deep breath. "So, when will you do it?"

Taran met his friend's eyes for the last time. "I already have."

Fressin glanced at the empty glass on the table. "Oh. The drink the girl brought. I didn't even see you near it." He coughed. "At least you haven't forgotten your skills."

Taran closed his eyes. "I'm sorry."

CHAPTER FORTY

T he common room at the Knox Inn and Tavern was crowded chaos. The story of what had happened the night before had spread, along with the fact that somehow there was a plan to protect the inn from another such attack. Villagers shouted over each other trying to book rooms, while others demanded to know the secrets to protect their own homes. Draeson's ward-dogs were on every door, many of them barking at the jostling villagers. The guards, still without new orders, as far as Brannon was aware, were now performing a filtering function to keep more customers out and try to calm down the more unruly ones. This brought them into conflict with Dargin Knox, who was fully aware that this chaos, while difficult, was good for business and his best chance to fund the repairs needed for the burned-out rooms upstairs.

Brannon made his way through the crowd, collecting his team and pulling them into a small side room to regroup and share what they had learned.

"What do you mean, Fressin's dead?" he exclaimed, after Taran spoke up. "How, in the name of the Hooded, did we lose another suspect in custody?"

"I don't know," Taran said. "I think he must have had a suicide pill. I could run some tests if you like."

"Blood and Tears." Brannon sighed and shook his head. "No. We've bigger problems right now. What about the tests you were running on the other victims?"

"Oh, they all had loredin in their systems. It's safe to say they were killed in the same manner as Prince Keldan."

Brannon swore again. What possible connection did Morgin, a small town undertaker, have to a murderer in Alapra, a place he'd never been? It seemed clear that Morgin was responsible for the killings here in Sandilar, but there was a missing piece that connected all the murders together. How had he known about the Djin rituals, and why had he decided to perform them? Was Fressin somehow involved? Aside from Brannon's own team, Lady Latricia, and Ambassador Ylani, the assassin was the only person who had been in Alapra at the time of Keldan's murder, then made his way here.

"First things first. Do we have enough spirit bags to keep this building safe?"

Ula nodded. "Your apprentice and I hide the last of them before you come back."

"Good. How effective will they be against this thing? We met it at the manor, and it claimed it was getting stronger. We managed to get the pouch I had to drive it off, but, it was a close thing."

Ula's eyes widened. "If you drove it off, the spirits

must like you very much."

"That's great," Brannon said, "but will they do it again?"

"Not you." Ula shook her head and pointed to the Nilarian ambassador. "The spirits like her."

Every face in the small room turned to look.

Ylani shrugged. "I'm sure the spirits liked us both," she said.

"Really?" Brannon said, with a raised eyebrow. "Thanks so much."

"The point is, can a pouch be used like that again?" Ylani said.

"No likely." Ula's dreadlocks swung side to side. "Spirit bricks are for protection of house. Djin houses made of mud—earth. Kalan houses are different. Pouches should work for a time, but not made to work outside."

"Great." Brannon's scar itched. "Anything else we should know?"

"Is definitely living Risen?" Ula asked.

Brannon nodded. "Oh yeah."

The Djin woman lowered her face. She clutched her arms, her fingernails scratched at her forearms and she cursed softly in her own language. Finally her words changed to Kalan. "A kaluki in a living body brings far too much power from the other realm. It will seek to bring others from their realm and destroy this place entirely. But first it must fight the other inhabitant of the body. Kaluki in a dead body is always kaluki. But a living Risen is sometimes kaluki, sometimes human. Until, at the end, human gone and it is always kaluki. Then it have full power. So far, humanity keep it weak.

Soon, it be truly strong."

"If that was weak," Ylani said. She didn't finish.

"Won't there still be someone controlling it?" Taran asked. "Like you did when you raised Prince Keldan."

Ula shook her head. "No one control a kaluki in a living body. A day, maybe two, then the kaluki have total control. Then it open the doorway."

"So how do we stop it?"

"We cannot. It would take the Priory of Gradinath to stop it. Here, there is only me." The Djin woman's skin was gray. "We be fools in our pride. This thing be our people's sacred duty to guard against. We never think it could happen anywhere but Djinan. All our people guard against it, but now I face it alone."

"Not alone," Draeson said.

"Okay," Brannon took a deep breath. "We need to act fast to protect ourselves and Tomidan. I don't think there's much humanity left in him now, but let's take advantage of it while it's there. Jessamine and Taran, I want you to start clearing all these extra people out of the inn. Unless they're related to Roydan in some way, they're safer in their own homes. Ula, double-check your protections and see if you can think of anything else that will help. If you can get a message to Gradinath, do it. Draeson, you and the mayor seem to have a . . . special bond. I'm going to need you to talk to her."

Draeson stood. "Talk to her about?"

"The fact that a kaluki is taking over her son."

The mage sat down again. "Morgin is the Risen? Morgin? The dorky undertaker? Wait, what could he have against the royal family?"

"He's not after the royal bloodline," Brannon said.

"He's specifically killing Roydan's bloodline. He's Roydan's bastard and he wants to be heir to Sandilar."

"But that's ridiculous," said a voice from the doorway. Brannon turned to see Mayor Shillia, her fingers still on the handle. "My son is already an heir to Sandilar. Roydan has acknowledged him. He's third in line after Keldan and . . . oh." Her eyes went very wide and she covered her mouth.

"After Keldan and Tomidan," Brannon finished for her. "Both of whom were targets of attacks."

Shillia shook her head. "My son wouldn't do that."

Brannon thought of how he'd last seen Morgin, hissing and covered in blood. "Have a seat and talk to Draeson," he said. "The rest of us will give you some space. If you can think of where he might be . . . well, the sooner we find him, the sooner we can clear this up."

Shillia walked slowly to the table. Brannon waited until she had taken a seat, then ushered the others out of the room. This was not a conversation he wanted to be part of. Let Draeson handle it. It would be the least of his penances for sleeping with the woman while Latricia died. He pulled the door closed behind him while Taran, Jessamine, and Ula spread out on their various tasks.

Ylani touched his shoulder. "You seemed very much the battle commander I've read about, just now," she said. "You're a good leader. You gave everyone a task, but I didn't hear how you're actually going to deal with the situation."

"Really, ambassador?" Brannon looked at her, the false confidence leaking away from his face. "Well, my nice little political murder case has turned into an invulnerable monster bent on destroying us all. You'll forgive me if I take a few moments to adjust my strategy." He turned to walk away.

"Brannon." She caught his arm. "I'm sorry, I didn't mean to sound like I'm on your back. I just want to help."

Brannon watched as the room began to clear. Taran and Jessamine, aided by a few of the armed guards, were herding people toward the door. Brannon hoped he was doing the right thing sending people away. If they kept Morgin's main targets here, this would be where he would come. And if he managed to get past their protections, Brannon wanted as few potential innocent victims as possible.

The room felt very warm. In the hearth, a fire crackled gently under a large cauldron of stew.

"If you really want to help," he said, "tell me about what you did back at the manor."

Ylani shifted. "What do you mean?"

He looked her in the eye. "Getting the spirit pouch to work—how did you know to do that?"

Ylani chewed her lip. "I . . . " She hesitated. He waited. Finally she spoke. "Sometimes I know things. I just do."

Brannon snorted. "Really? That's your answer? What does that even mean?"

"I . . . " She opened her mouth, then closed it again.

Brannon shook his head. He needed to keep his mind on the job. The Nilarian ambassador was a confusing distraction he did not need. "Fine. Whatever."

"Brannon," she began, but stopped.

Jessamine and one of the remaining manor guards had joined them. "Sir Brannon Kesh." The man rested his hand on his sword hilt and stood to attention. "We've had word from Sandilar Manor. We need to talk."

"I'm sure we do," Brannon said. "But now's not the time."

The guard's fingers wrapped around the hilt. "I'm afraid I must insist."

Jessamine frowned. "What's that smell?"

As soon as she said it, Brannon smelled it too. A scent like crushed almonds and burnt copper. He blinked. The air had taken on a greenish tinge.

The guard's eyes bulged and his breath came in gasps. "What have you done?" he said, then slowly slid to the floor.

Jessamine was swaying. The remaining people in the common room began to scream and point. "The fire!"

Brannon felt his body becoming heavy. So very heavy, like bundles of wet wool. He turned to look at the fireplace. Beneath the cauldron of stew, the flames were low, almost guttering, and from them poured a steady stream of green smoke.

Brannon had barely a moment to register that they were being poisoned and then the world went black.

CHAPTER FORTY-ONE

Sound trickled back first. The half-heard wuffing of a dog, the squeak of hinges, someone moaning, footsteps. Then it was feeling. The floor beneath him was hard and cold. His tongue felt gritty and tasted foul. Something touched his arm and he groaned, not wanting to wake up. Not wanting to move. His insides moved anyway. A moment later, his stomach heaved and he vomited.

"Ah, there it goes," said Taran's voice. "This is going to get very messy."

Brannon opened his eyes to see the priest crouching beside him. The smell of vomit was sharp and stinging. He rolled onto his hands and knees and wiped his mouth with his sleeve. "What happened?"

He looked around the room. Here and there, others were waking up as well. Many, as he had done, regurgitated the contents of their stomachs onto the floor. A smaller number stood or sat, looking drawn and dazed, but conscious and able to move. Clearly whatever they had been poisoned with was not lethal.

"Koroleen," Taran said. He had a damp smear down the front of his cowled priest's tunic where he too had vomited. "It was taken from my supplies."

Brannon pushed himself up into a sitting position, carefully monitoring his stomach. "What's koroleen?"

Taran blinked. "It's a poison when ingested and a strong sedative when burned. I use it as a reagent in some of my experiments . . . it's not good for the, ah . . . " He made a circling motion with his hand over his abdomen.

Brannon raised an eyebrow. "I noticed."

"It passes quickly."

Brannon glanced across to where Ylani lay, still unconscious. "Is there any danger from it?"

The priest shook his head. "The vomiting comes after waking. Everyone comes out of it in their own time. As long as no one chokes, they should be fine."

Brannon nodded. Choking would be a very real danger for anyone who vomited while unconscious. "We should check on everyone just to be sure."

He climbed to his feet. The dog he'd heard earlier was one of Draeson's wards. It was a white dog with black spots, standing with its head down and its tail between its legs. It guarded the front door of the tavern—a door now hanging crookedly on only one hinge.

He crouched beside Ylani and turned her onto her side, carefully moving her hair away from her face. "Find Jessamine. If she's awake, get her started on making sure anyone still unconscious is in a safe position. This could be good experience for her. I'll check on Draeson and Shillia."

Taran didn't move.

Brannon looked up. "What is it?"

"Jessamine was taken. So was Tomidan."

"Hooded Blood." He stood up and stared across at the broken door. "He came for them. Tommy because he's Roydan's last heir. Why Jessamine?"

Draeson's voice came from behind him. "Because he's sending you a message. That you can't protect your own."

Brannon sighed, looking around at the unconscious and semiconscious people, broken furniture, and vomit. His stomach felt hollow. "He's right. I'm used to enemies I can keep track of. Enemies I at least have a hope of matching physically and that face me head-on. Not some demon-enhanced, poison-throwing, superpowered freak with delusions of grandeur and a plan to take over the world. That, I'm out of my depth with. He's right."

Taran blinked at him. Draeson said nothing. At his feet, Ylani moaned, stirring at last.

The heat in the room was stifling, like fingers clawing at Brannon's throat. The acrid smell filled his nostrils. Memories flooded into his mind of broken, bleeding men and women. The smell of fear and feces and rotted meat. This was his legacy. His past and his future. War with Nilar, war with demons. It was all blood and death and horror.

He was Bloodhawk, the avatar of war. How was he supposed to stop it?

"Brannon?" Ylani's voice was weak.

His throat closed and he turned and walked away. A

hand reached out to get his attention. Words followed him, but there was a ringing in his ears and he blocked them out. His steps quickened and he hit the broken door at a run, bursting free of the building that had seen so much death.

He had trusted this inn to be a sanctuary—had built up its defenses as best he could—and still Morgin had reached in and taken what he wanted.

Fresh air hit him like a wave, crashing over him, pulling him down. Halfway across the courtyard he stopped, bent over, his hands braced on his knees as he drew in great gulps of air.

Footsteps sounded on the cobblestones behind him. They slowed as they came closer.

Brannon didn't look up. "Just leave me alone for a minute, okay?"

There was no reply.

"Hooded Blood, Wolf, Tears, Ahpra's bloody tits, Draeson, I didn't ask for this!"

"I know," the mage said quietly.

Brannon took another two slow, deep breaths and straightened up. "I didn't even want an apprentice, you know. I told Master Jordell it was a bad idea. Now that poor girl has been kidnapped because of me. I'm responsible for her and for my best friend's grandson and they're both in the hands of an enemy I don't know how to fight."

"Yes you do."

"What do you mean, I do?" Brannon turned to glare at the magus. He tugged at his sword. "You think this is going to make a bit of difference to that thing? That Risen? I saw what he did to the men at the manor. A sword isn't going to cut it anymore."

Draeson shook his head. "You might feel responsible for those two but what happened is not your fault. It's the fault of an idiot who chose the wrong path to power in order to take what wasn't his." He gripped Brannon's shoulder. "It happens. But you've been dealing with powerful people and putting them straight your whole life. The Nilarians, the king—me."

Brannon snorted. "Really? You're bringing that up now?"

Draeson shrugged. "You were right to tackle me about my behavior. I should have been more . . . professional. But the point is, what are you going to do about this one."

Brannon looked away. Someone had rehung the sign where Caidin Ray's body had been found, but the post still bore a dark stain. "I can't let him win. If Jessamine and Tommy are still alive, I need to get them back."

"And?"

"Ahpra's Tears, Draeson, do I have to do all the thinking around here?"

The mage laughed. "It's what you're good at. I never would have thought it in the old days, but that kaluki-possessed boy has underestimated you. You're not just the Bloodhawk anymore. You're the best of that and more. You'll find a way."

Brannon traced the line of his scar with his fingers, from his earlobe across his cheek. It was a reminder that even the weakest opponent can strike a blow if the circumstances are right. He had a team of some of the best experts in the country. Surely they could do better than a teenage boy trying to avenge his father.

Draeson gave his shoulder another squeeze and let go. "Are you ready to go back inside now?"

Brannon took a deep breath and blew it out again. "Yeah. Let's get this suicidal rescue mission on the road."

He turned his head and a movement caught his eye. Mayor Shillia slipped from the shadow along the side of the inn and hurried toward the road. She tugged her coat around her as she walked.

Brannon frowned. Why hadn't she walked out the front door? Why was she leaving at all?

"Draeson," he said quietly. "How good are you at following people without being seen?"

"Excellent," said the mage. "Why?"

He nodded toward the mayor. "Because I need to know where she's going."

Draeson frowned. "You think she knows where her son is?"

"I'm sure of it." Brannon watched Shillia's back. "Morgin must have had an accomplice to get rid of the first batch of spirit bags and slip the koroleen into the fire. She's been here both times."

Draeson went very still. "My . . . distraction on the night Latricia was killed. You think that was deliberate?"

"I don't know, but I hope to Ahpra and Valdan that it wasn't." He jerked his thumb toward the road. Shillia was out of sight. "There's one way to find out."

"All right," Draeson said. He sat down on the cobblestones and crossed his legs.

"Ah, she's getting away." Brannon tapped him on the shoulder and pointed.

"Ssh." The mage closed his eyes and held out his hands, cupped together. Light shone out from between his fingers, then faded. When he opened his hands, a small brown moth was sitting on his palm. He blew and the moth flew away.

"What does that do?"

"The moth tracks Shillia and I can track the moth. But I have to keep it focused on her."

Brannon watched the tiny creature flitter out into the street. "Can you track anyone that way?"

"Only someone I have a piece of." Draeson held up a long dark hair. "Now go away. I need to concentrate."

Brannon hovered for a moment, curious, but then Taran appeared at the tavern door. The priest gave several little half waves, trying to catch his attention, until Brannon walked over to him. "What is it?"

"Ula is asking for you," he said. "She has an idea."

CHAPTER FORTY-TWO

The abandoned stable that was Karia's secret hiding place had changed since Brannon had seen it last. The walls were painted with Djinian symbols, and a number of bowls and pots, each with flames burning in them, formed a wide circle around the room. Ula sat in the center of the circle, her hands buried in a large bowl of dirt and ash. A stack of empty leather pouches sat beside her.

Ylani stood to one side. She had changed into a silk gown of charcoal gray, threaded with silver. She showed no sign of the effects of koroleen poisoning.

"What's going on?" he asked her.

Ylani shrugged. "I don't know. She wanted us both here but she hasn't said a word since I arrived."

He took a few steps into the room. "Ula?" As he crossed into the circle, the flames in the bowls leaped higher.

The Djin woman's skin seemed to flicker with shifting shadows. Her tattoos took on a wild, organic quality in the firelight. She turned to look at him.

"Ah," she said, her voice strained. "You're here."

Brannon knelt beside her and took her hand. It was covered in mud. "What's going on? What is all this?"

"It is necessary," she said. "We need more power to defeat the kaluki in Morgin. I am not enough." She withdrew her hand from his and patted him on the wrist. "Perhaps with another we have enough. Wizard Draeson be host to a being from another place. Morgin be host to kaluki. Both get power from it. Perhaps this be what we must do also."

A shudder ran through her body. Her bare feet kicked out, heels digging into the dirt.

"Ula? What have you done?"

Ylani said something in Nilarian. "Is she okay?"

"I link myself to the Kaluk, the earth spirits. I be their voice—their host for a time. You must talk to them." Ula swallowed. "The two of you convinced them to help at the manor. Convince them to help us now."

Ylani came to sit beside them, her gown pooling elegantly around her. "These are your spirits, Ula. We don't know how to talk to them."

The Djin woman's breath came fast and shallow. Her eyes rolled back in her head and closed. Her limbs twitched and jerked like a seizure, but she remained upright. Her hands clenched in the bowl of mud, kneading it like dough.

The flames in the circle rose high, the burning bars of a cage. Wind blew through them, hot and dry.

At first it was gentle, a warming breeze. Then it grew stronger, hotter, fanning the flames. Ula's breathing changed to long, strained wheezing.

Brannon reached out to steady her but jerked back as the touch of her skin burned his hand.

The scalding wind swirled around them, whipping at their clothes and hair, tugging at the ribbons Ylani had threaded in her tresses. Dust from the dirt floor buffed against them like sandpaper.

"Is this supposed to happen?" Brannon shouted over the shriek of the wind.

Ylani cupped her hands around her mouth and leaned close. "Spit."

"What?" Brannon squinted, trying to keep the grit from his eyes.

She pointed around them. "Fire, wind, earth. We need water. Spit!" She leaned over Ula's bowl of dirt.

A moment later, the wind died and the flames cooled. The fires stayed burning high, though, keeping them effectively trapped within the circle.

Ula sat up straight. Her skin seemed clearer, brighter, than before. There was a glow about her. She looked around slowly, her lips relaxed and her expression serene. The beads in her dreadlocks shone, each with a different colored light, like a rainbow of fireflies in her hair.

"Ula?"

She looked at him. The whites had gone from her eyes, leaving only dark brown globes, shining like agate. "No," she said. The word spilled out to fill the room like the many voices of a choir. "Not Ula."

Brannon sat back on his heels. Despite the fires, his skin felt cold. That was definitely not Ula.

"Are you an earth spirit? One of the Kaluk?"

Ula's head tilted. "Yes."

Ylani leaned forward. "Are you aware of the situation here? One of your enemies has taken over a living body."

"We are aware. The Morgin-kaluki has sacrifices ready for his brethren. If you do not stop him, he will open a portal between realms and others will come to this place and destroy it."

Brannon's fingers clenched into fists. "Sacrifices? You mean Jessamine and Tomidan? They're still alive?"

"Yes. To murder a sibling is a powerful sacrifice. The other kaluki will come to be part of it."

"And after killing all the other potential heirs, Tommy is all he has left. So that's why he didn't kill him outright. The kaluki wanted him for the sacrifice." Brannon tapped his fist on the ground, thinking. They were still alive. There was still a chance. "Okay, so Ula said we have about a day before Morgin loses control completely. That's when he'll try to open the portal and kill his hostages. So we have that long to rescue them and come up with a plan to stop him."

Ylani nodded, chewing her lip. "If we can find where he's taken them and distract him long enough."

"Ssh," said the multilayered voice of the earth spirits. Ula's hand reached out and drew a line of mud down the center of Ylani's forehead, to the tip of her nose. She turned and drew the same line on Brannon. Her touch was cool and the mud tingled against his skin. "There is no time for that. The human has almost gone from his body. The kaluki will be in full control within an hour."

The unflappable serenity in Ula's face was at odds with the words formed by her lips.

Brannon stared. It was as if he couldn't feel his

body. "An hour? We have an hour before he kills his hostages and essentially starts the end of the world?"

"Yes."

He surged to his feet. "Help us! We need to stop this."

Ula's arms raised, hands palm up, elbows straight, encompassing them both. "You are two who will do this. It is the sacred duty we gave to you. The reason you have power over the kaluki."

"But we don't!" Ylani gripped one of Ula's hands. Brannon could see her knuckles whitening. "That's the Djin. We're a long way from Djinan."

The dark eyes looked at her and the brows closed in. "Not Djin, no. What are you?"

Ylani let go of Ula's hand.

"She's Nilarian," said Brannon. "And I'm Kalan. There are no Djin here but Ula and we don't know anything about your ways. If the kaluki are your enemies, you need to help us fight."

The agate eyes closed. "You have your friends to help. We cannot interfere directly at this time."

Brannon took a deep breath. "If you don't, we will fail. Ylani and I encountered Morgin earlier today. If you hadn't helped us then we would have died. He's stronger now."

The beads in Ula's dreadlocks pulsed brighter. Her dark eyes opened again and bore into his. "We can give you strength for the fight, but there will be a price."

Brannon held her gaze. "How much strength?"

"Brannon, be careful." Ylani's voice sounded far away.

"We will bind our strength to yours. You will not be his equal, but you will be like a Risen—strong and fast.

You will be our weapon."

"Will I be possessed?"

Ula's face twisted. "No. That is something only a kaluki could do. We will lend you our strength for a time only. But just as the Morgin-kaluki makes a sacrifice to bring his brethren through to this realm, so a sacrifice must be made to pay for our strength."

"Brannon, don't do it!"

He could feel Ylani tugging on his sleeve, but he ignored her. "What sacrifice?"

The agate eyes reflected the flames in the circle. They burned into his own retinas. "The weapon must be sacrificed."

"Ah." He looked away from those eyes. They seemed so out of place in the face of a woman he'd come to think of as a friend. Just as the words seemed out of place in her mouth. Sunlight sketched the edge of the door beyond the fire circle.

Ylani clutched at his elbow. "Brannon, she means you! You're the weapon. If you do this, you'll die!"

He looked down at the bowl of mud at Ula's feet.

It was a trade. The strength to stop a monster in exchange for . . . well, another monster. He'd known for a long time what being the Bloodhawk had made him. He'd caused so much death and mutilation. Even as a physician there was more death, more mutilation in the name of saving lives. He would never balance the scales that way. Here was the chance to make things right. If he did this, he would save everyone. Jessamine, Tommy, Ylani, Aldan—all of them. If the cost of that was his life, it was a bargain worth making.

He raised his head. "Do it."

Chapter Forty-three

The building that housed the morgue was large, sprawling, and run-down. A painted wooden sign by the door proclaimed "Undertaker" and directed visitors to turn right once inside. Ivy had taken over most of the walls outside, green leaves swallowing up the stone.

Draeson paused. The dragon tattoo was hidden somewhere under his clothes. "They're inside but somewhere below. The cellar or tunnels. I'll know more when we're closer."

"You're sure?" Brannon said.

"Shillia's been there for a while. I'd say this is the place."

"Okay. Let's go."

Brannon looked over the group as they followed Draeson into the building. It was small—the better to sneak up on Morgin and limit the potential casualties—and each with unique skills, but they didn't seem like much to rescue two people, destroy a demon, and save the world.

Taran had abandoned his priest's cowled tunic in favor of a gray, close-fitting one and wore a long knife on either side of his belt.

Ula's skin was still a paler shade of its usual dusky purple, but the whites had returned to her eyes and the glow was gone from the beads in her hair. Her body had an air of limpness about it. When the earth spirits had first left her, she'd been unable to stand on her own, but she had recovered quickly and assured them that she felt fine. Her pulse was normal and she didn't seem to have a fever, so Brannon took her word for it. She was, after all, the only one of them with the faintest idea of how to do what must be done.

Brannon touched the Djin woman's shoulder and fell into step beside her.

"I be okay," she said, automatically.

"I believe you." He held out his arms. Djin runic markings covered his skin, each drawn in the special mud by the earth spirits. "How do we know this will work? I don't feel any different."

She touched the marks with a kind of reverence. She had told him she remembered nothing of the time the earth spirits spent in her body and didn't recognize what they had done. "The spirits never lie. If they say they give you strength for the fight, they do it. But they not give more than what is needed." She gestured around them, taking in the hallway and the stairs leading down to the mortuary workroom. "No Morgin here. Not need strength yet. When you need, then it will come."

A whiff of formaldehyde and sawdust filled Brannon's nostrils as he took a deep breath. "And if

Morgin manages to kill me before the spirits decide I need help?"

Ula shrugged. "Then you will be safe from the terms of your bargain."

He looked to see if she was joking, but she had already moved away, following the mage and priest down the stairs.

Ylani, he noticed, had added a small hat to her outfit, perhaps having decided she had tempted fate with the gods enough for one day.

"Ambassador, you shouldn't be part of this. Take one of the horses and ride for Trallene. You can get a boat back to the capitol from there. You're not safe here." He was very conscious of the matching facial mud-marks the earth spirits had drawn on them both. Ylani wore hers like the latest fashion.

"Well, that's not going to happen, so let's skip ahead to the part where you've tried to convince me and now accept I'm coming with you, shall we?" She smiled, patted him on the shoulder and headed toward the staircase.

Brannon hurried after her. "At least promise me that you'll keep out of the main fighting. If you're killed, our chances of stopping another war with Nilar are pretty minimal."

Her smile disappeared. "I promise I'll try. But if this goes badly, a war will be the least of our problems."

They descended the stairs and entered a room with wide, high benches, and shelves piled with jars and folded sheets. The formaldehyde smell was stronger here, as was the unique smell of death, masked by small bunches of drooping flowers at intervals around the room. Several of the benches held shapes covered by sheets. The sheets were stuck down in places by blood.

Brannon made sure to notice each one. These were Morgin's victims. Only a portion of the people he had killed so far. There would be more if they could not stop him.

Ylani trailed a hand over the edge of one of the benches containing a corpse. "So many dead. I guess there really isn't any humanity left in him."

Brannon felt his gut twist and looked away. What must she think of him, the Bloodhawk? "He was killing long before his humanity left him."

Draeson gestured them forward. "Ssh, we're getting close now."

Beneath the morgue workroom was the cellar. Beyond that, passageways spread out like spokes on a wheel. The mage led the way into one of them and darkness closed in, hiding everything from sight.

Brannon laid one hand on Taran's shoulder in front of him and the other on the wall. The others did the same to form a chain and they moved slowly forward. As his eyes adjusted, he could see the first hint of light up ahead. They rounded a corner and heard voices as well.

"Wait here," Brannon whispered. He crept toward the light.

The corridor widened into a large round chamber. Lanterns hung at regular intervals around the walls, casting enough light to see by. The room had once been a crypt, but now the sarcophagi had been pushed up against the walls, stacked atop each other, and in some cases tipped over, spilling their skeletal contents onto the floor where the bones had been kicked into corners. The center of the room was cleared, a stage with its players set.

On the far side of the room, Jessamine and Tomidan were each bound with rope and lain across a sarcophagus. Even from this distance, Brannon could see the little boy was shaking. Jessamine had twisted her body so that she could see what was going on in the room. "Morgin," she was saying, "don't do this. I know you're still in there. Fight it!"

Brannon felt something inside him unclench. They were alive. There was still a chance.

Morgin and his mother were in the center of the room. They ignored Jessamine's pleas, engaged in a discussion of their own while Morgin drew a circle of runes on the floor in chalk.

"You've done enough, Morgin," Shillia said. "This is it. You're powerful and people recognize that. Karia will be impressed, I'm sure. You don't need any more."

Morgin sniggered. He finished the last curve on a rune, then leaped upward. His body twisted in the air, and he landed on the ceiling, clinging with his hands and feet like an insect. His head tilted to one side and he began drawing another circle of runes to match the one on the floor.

A gentle movement beside him let Brannon know Draeson had followed him. "She's lost control of him," the mage whispered. "And she doesn't even realize it yet."

Brannon nodded. "Has Ula started the banishing ritual?"

"Yes. But she needs line of sight to finish it."

"Morgin." Shillia's voice grew hard and

authoritative. "I said that's enough. You got what you wanted. You're important now, like you should be. Now get down!"

Brannon sucked his breath in through his teeth. Somehow he didn't think this new Morgin, wholly inhabited by a kaluki, would respond to parental bullying the way the old Morgin may have. From what he had seen of the boy since they arrived, Brannon suspected Mayor Shillia must have been the brains behind the plan, using her relationship with her son along with his dissatisfaction and ambition to easily win his cooperation. She was a politician and a mother—a master manipulator her son could never overthrow.

But Morgin was no longer her son.

He carried on drawing the runes. "Mother, mother, mother. Do shut up."

Shillia blinked. "Excuse me?"

"You heard me."

"Morgin Vere, I am your mother no matter how high you climb in this life and you will be respectful, is that clear?"

Still clinging to the ceiling, Morgin went very still.

Silence filled the space like cold cream, thick and greasy. The new circle of symbols was complete.

"Morgin?" Shillia sounded shrill. "I said, is that clear?"

The thing that was Morgin let go of the ceiling and fell, landing on his feet to face her. His fingernails had grown long and curved, like little grappling hooks. He held one hand out in front of him and the nails grew longer still.

"What's clear," he said, "is that I no longer need

you."

He lashed out and the hooked fingernails slashed across Shillia's throat. Her eyes bulged. Blood sprayed out and Jessamine screamed.

The mayor clutched at the gash as if to close it with her hands, but it was too late. She fell to her knees and then over onto her side, her eyes stared and her lips twitched as she died.

"He's killing people. Let's move." Brannon was halfway across the room almost before giving the order. Shillia's blood still pumped out of her throat in weak spurts, but he knew she was dead. Nothing he could do would repair that kind of damage to the jugular in time to save a life.

He hit Morgin at a run, using the force of his momentum and body weight to push him off balance. It was enough to easily knock a man over. Brannon raised his hand, ready to ride him down and bash the man's skull into the ground when they fell.

Morgin merely stumbled. He regained his balance immediately and slashed at Brannon's face with his sharp nails.

Brannon sprang back out of reach.

Morgin leaped upward, clinging to the ceiling once more. He scuttled a few steps over, then dropped just as Brannon drew his sword.

Brannon lunged forward, raising the blade so that it slid into Morgin's stomach like a knife into tender soft meat. It drove through his small intestines, probably nicked a kidney, and spiked out of his back like the beginning of an extra limb.

The physician part of his mind analyzed the impact.

Not an immediate kill, but likely to bleed out if not attended quickly. Very likely to die of infection later.

"That's not very polite," Morgin said. He turned, pulling the handle of the sword from Brannon's hand, then gripped the blade and drew it out of his body. Blood dripped from the end, adding to the slick of red that flowed from Shillia's throat.

He tossed the sword aside and fingered the gash where it had been. The wound knitted back together, skin smooth and unblemished. "You put a hole in my shirt."

"Really?" said Brannon. "Oh well." He feinted with his left fist, then aimed a kick at where the wound had been. His physician's brain refused to accept that it was completely gone. Perhaps there was some residual weakness.

Morgin stepped aside, moving like a flame in the breeze, fast and low. He dodged the kick and grasped Brannon's foot instead, twisting his leg roughly.

Brannon yelped.

Morgin shoved him backward by the leg and he fell. The stone floor slammed into his back like a dozen sledgehammers striking at once, winding him. A moment later, Morgin's boot struck his ribs.

Possible fractures, whispered the physician part of his mind.

Move! screamed the rest.

Brannon rolled, narrowly avoiding the next kick. He rolled again and again, but each time Morgin simply followed him.

Eventually something hard blocked his way. A sarcophagus. He pushed himself against it, using it to pull himself upright.

Another kick landed, this time cracking the stone of the sarcophagus where he had been a moment before.

"Whoops," said Morgin. "That was supposed to be your head." He pulled his foot back and chunks of stone fell to the floor.

"Draeson," Brannon called out. "Now would be good!"

The air chilled, turning hazy and thick around them both.

Morgin frowned, looking around for the source of the fog. "What's this?"

Brannon backed away. His chest felt like fiery pokers had been thrust between each rib and into his lung.

Morgin moved as if to follow him, but his feet had been trapped in a block of ice.

Brannon watched as more blocks formed out of the fog and merged with the first. They encased Morgin's legs, then his torso and his arms, growing like a snowdrift until the former undertaker was engulfed all the way to the neck in clear blue ice, literally frozen in place.

"That more or less what you had in mind?" Draeson said, stepping into the room with Ula and Taran.

Brannon gave a small chuckle, then flinched when it hurt his ribs. "Yeah. But quicker."

The mage rolled his eyes. "Some people are never satisfied."

Taran hurried over to Brannon, taking his elbow. "Are you okay?"

Brannon waved him off. "Yeah, I'm fine. Get

Jessamine and Tommy."

Morgin eyed the priest. "Stay away from them," he said. "They're mine."

"No, they're not," Brannon said. "And neither is that body you're wearing, so why don't you leave it voluntarily?"

Morgin raised his chin. "Make me."

Brannon sighed. "Ula, you're up."

The Djin woman stepped forward. She held out her hands, palms toward Morgin. They were gray to the wrists, as though she wore gloves of ash and mud. Her dreadlocks and face were smeared with dirt, her teeth sharp white against her blackened lips. She spoke in her own tongue first, and the air began to stir around them.

Brannon felt a burning tingle across his skin.

She was powerful, feral, a spirit-creature of the earth herself.

"Kaluki, I bind you," she said, switching to Kalan. The power stirring in the air became a swirling wind. "I bind you with the earth of this place and the earth of mine. I bind you with the fire that warms creatures of this realm. I bind you with the air we breathe. I bind you with the water of my body. You not belong here. Now go!"

The wind ceased swirling and whooshed toward Ula. Brannon felt it not on his skin but inside him, as if the current of power had set a hook into his core and tugged at it.

The kaluki in Morgin threw back his head and groaned between clenched teeth. The sound stretched into a shrill whistling wail.

Abruptly, it stopped. Morgin's head fell forward.

Brannon looked around the room. Taran had a knife in his hand, his face pale. He had obviously experienced the same tug that Brannon had felt—the edge of the force Ula had used to pull the kaluki out of Morgin.

Ula sagged, her breathing ragged.

Draeson caught her and eased her into a sitting position. "Did it work?"

For a moment, everything was silent. Brannon let himself breathe.

Then a low chuckle echoed around the room. Morgin lifted his head and the laughter transformed his face, vicious eyes and twisted mouth out of place among the freckles. "No," he said. "It didn't work. You're not nearly strong enough, Ula. You must have known it would take the full Priory of Gradinath to stop me now."

Brannon sighed and shuffled into the creature's line of sight. "She knew. But I asked her to try anyway."

Morgin's face twitched.

Taran reached Jessamine and began fumbling with the ropes holding her in place. She had a bruise over her eye.

"The Priory of Gradinath might be the only thing that can stop you, but we can trap you until they get here." Brannon stepped back. "Ice him, Draeson. Ice the whole Hooded room."

"With pleasure." Draeson raised his hand and the air thickened and chilled.

Frost formed on the stone walls. The column of ice already holding Morgin in place began to grow. Brannon watched as it closed over Morgin's head, sealing the young man and the kaluki possessing him inside.

He turned away.

Shillia's blood oozed toward the chalk runes on the floor. Directly toward them.

Brannon stared, watching as the blood moved closer, then flooded over the first of the markings. Rather than being hidden or washed away, the rune showed clearly, now marked in the blood, oily and black against the red. As he watched, the blood moved across the next rune and it too turned black. He swore.

"Something's going on here. Taran, hurry up."

"There's a lot of rope here," the priest called back. "And my fingers are cold."

Two more runes were swallowed and converted by the blood. The black ooze writhed like maggots, then put forth tiny tendrils of oily darkness, shiny and sleek. They reached toward the matching runes on the ceiling.

"Cut the rope," Brannon said. The chill he felt had little to do with Draeson's spell.

"I *am* cutting it."

"Ula, what is this?" He pointed to the rune circle as the blood closed over the last symbol. The tentacles rose higher.

The Djin woman's face was pale. She murmured in her own language before taking a deep breath. Her eyes were very wide. "Portal to kaluki realm."

A loud crack pulled their attention.

The ice column had shattered. Morgin stepped free and smiled, sharp teeth bared. He picked up a chunk of ice and threw it across the room. It struck Taran in the side of the head and the priest fell to the floor. "I told you to leave my guests alone."

Brannon ran to check on Taran but Morgin threw another chunk of ice, striking him in the shoulder with enough force to knock him off his feet. He hit the cold ground and slipped in the blood. The black tentacles twitched for a moment as his ankle came close, then stretched toward the ceiling once more.

"That's enough of that," Draeson muttered. The dragon tattoo crawled out of his sleeve, down to his elbow, and hissed. He raised his hand and sparks sprayed from the fingers, as a bolt of lightning shot out, striking Morgin square in the chest.

A wide patch of the young man's shirt burned away and his skin was charred, raw and blistered.

He laughed and tore off the rest of the shirt, dropping it to the ground. "You still think you can hurt me?" He peeled back the burnt pieces of flesh, showing the ribs beneath. "Watch."

He let go and the skin pulled itself back into place. Charred pieces fell like black snowflakes and fresh, new skin grew, binding the old together. The redness faded and blisters disappeared. He was healthy and unharmed.

Brannon looked from Morgin to the writhing black tentacles of the runes. His body ached and every breath brought a sharp pain in his chest. A churning sick feeling rose in the pit of his stomach. The portal was opening already and Morgin was proving immune to Draeson's magic—their most powerful weapon. Years of battle strategy was deserting him. Worse, it was telling him all was lost.

He scraped his fingers over the useless mud runes on his arm. "Do something, dammit!"

"You see the portal, prioress?" Morgin gloated as he watched Ula. The Djin woman trembled and he smiled. "The prophecy is coming true and you're the only one of your kind in the right place. My kaluki brethren will feast, then we will bring forth our makers. We will shred your flesh, but before you die you will see the final failure of your kind."

Tears ran down Ula's cheeks, but she remained silent. She held her hands loosely by her sides then brought them up in a rush, clenched into fists.

The supernatural wind rushed through the room once more, tugging at the core of each of them.

This time, Morgin only laughed.

The first of the black tentacles reached the ceiling and the rune it touched burned white. The white spilled down, caressing the black, filling the gaps between it and the tendrils surrounding it. The next one struck the ceiling and did the same. The remaining black tentacles seemed to gain speed from their fellows and shot upward. The rush of white flowed down like a fountain, mixing with the oily blackness and merging the entire mass together into a writhing, undulating column of shining silver, like some twisted mirror in a carnival.

"Here they come," said Morgin, his eyes alight as he watched the silvery surface bulge.

Behind him, Ylani slipped into the room.

Brannon's eyes bulged. "No," he mouthed to her.

She lifted a finger to her lips and crept along the wall toward Jessamine and Tomidan.

Brannon struggled to push himself upright. She would be killed along with the rest of them. He had to do something.

A jab of pain shot through his chest. The tiny part of his mind that was still functioning as an impartial physician diagnosed it. A broken rib puncturing his lung.

Another blow to the chest could be fatal.

He could hear Master Jordell's voice in his head. "Bind it up tight. No lifting of any kind. No running. Rest for a good month."

He ignored it. A kind of peace came over him. He met Ylani's eyes again. This time, he mouthed a different message. "Get them out of here." He could buy her time for that.

Morgin didn't see his charge until it was almost too late. Brannon pulled a dagger from his belt as he ran, thinking he could at least try to do enough damage to slow him down. It'd taken a moment to heal from Draeson's lightning attack. Perhaps that moment's delay would be enough for Ylani to get Jessamine and Tomidan to safety.

Whatever safety meant in a world about to be overrun by free kaluki.

Brannon raised the knife to strike, just as Morgin turned his head.

"Pathetic," the kaluki said, and backhanded him.

Brannon flew backward. His body slammed into the wall and he slid to the ground. Something hard and cold was underneath him. He'd landed on his sword. His chest quivered as he fought to breathe, every shallow intake bringing pain.

Morgin took a slow step toward him.

Brannon closed his eyes.

The sounds of the room filled him: Footsteps as Morgin drew closer. Draeson's voice calling out his name. Animalistic grunts and squeals of the kaluki beyond the portal coming closer. The faint hissing scrape of a knife cutting rope.

He smiled. Ylani would get them free.

A tingling sensation began on the back of his hand. Brannon ignored it. He'd done what he could. His body could do no more. It was broken.

The feeling intensified, rivulets of heat spreading up his arm.

Morgin's footsteps stopped. "What is that? What are you doing?"

Brannon opened his eyes. The mud runes Ula had painted on his skin while she had been an avatar for the earth spirits had changed. The mud was gone and they now burned with fire. As he watched, the flame spread along each rune, burning hot and brief, leaving a trail of pink scar tissue behind it.

Warmth filled him and suddenly he could breathe easily. The pain in his chest was gone, the aches and bruises vanished. He could feel his body filling with strength.

"Really?" he muttered to the invisible earth spirits. "Now is when you decide to help?"

"Who are you talking to?" Morgin's brows drew close and he took a step back. "What just happened?"

Brannon felt the hilt of his sword beneath his palm and closed his fingers around it. He surged to his feet and closed the gap between him and Morgin in one swift movement. "This," he said, and slammed the pommel of the sword up into Morgin's face.

The kaluki stumbled back, blood flowing from his nose for just a moment before it stopped like a tap turned off.

Brannon had a moment to bask in his new strength before the young man recovered.

"You've had help," Morgin said. He gestured toward the portal. "It won't matter now. The others are coming and you can't fight us all."

The silver column hummed with energy. The surface of it bulged and a black scaled hand pierced through. Its fingers clutched at the empty air.

"Draeson." Brannon searched for his friend. The mage was locked in urgent conversation with Ula. "You need to close that portal!"

"We don't know how!"

Morgin smirked. Another clawed hand broke the surface of the portal. Then a tentacle.

Brannon stepped over and lopped off the tip of the tentacle with his sword. "Then stop whatever tries to come through it!"

Morgin's hand on his shoulder pulled him back. "We're not done yet, Bloodhawk."

Brannon reversed his grip on his sword and thrust it behind him. "No, we're not."

A grunt from behind him let him know the blade had found its mark, but he knew there would be no sustained damage. He pulled the sword free again and spun, aiming at Morgin's neck.

The kaluki leaped back, hissing in fury. "*Kaluk fuulah!*" It spat.

"*Kaluk fuulah yrl,*" Ula responded. The wind roared through the room once more, tugging and whipping in a frenzy, but still Morgin was untouched.

There was a flash of light and a crackle as Draeson threw lightning at whatever was coming through the portal. The stench of sizzling offal filled the air.

Brannon swung his sword again, feeling the power

of the earth spirits fueling his muscles. He felt invincible. Was this how Morgin felt all the time? It was amazing.

His enemy stepped back once more, driven back by Brannon's blade. Another step, and another. Then he surged forward, catapulting over Brannon's head to land behind him.

Long, sharp claws scraped across Brannon's back, slashing his shirt and his flesh. He screamed and spun, bringing up his blade to meet the next attack.

The sword slashed a river of red across Morgin's forearm, but the limb stayed strong. The gash healed almost instantly.

Brannon shifted, testing the muscles in his back. His own wounds had also healed.

"Your earth spirits may have made you stronger, but that won't save you now."

Brannon risked a glance back at the portal. The entire column buckled. Something huge was pushing its way through.

Draeson was surrounded by a swarm of smaller creatures, mostly black and scaly. Some the size of dogs or cats, with many legs, some with three legs each ending in a humanoid hand rather than a foot. Others were winged and lunged at him from above.

Fire poured from the mage's hands, searing the kaluki creatures that came too close. The dragon tattoo rode his cheek, puffed up large and roaring.

Ula stood rooted to the spot where he'd seen her last. Her eyes were closed and her fists at her sides. She again summoned the wind that tried to pull the kaluki from Morgin's body.

"By the Wolf, woman," Draeson yelled at her. "Try something else!"

She stayed where she was. Her lips barely moved. "Nothing else will work."

Ylani yelled a warning. "Look out!"

Brannon turned just in time to see the lid of a sarcophagus flying toward his head. He raised an arm to protect himself and the stone shattered against it. He felt the bones in his arm break, then mend themselves.

"Bitch," said Morgin. He pulled the lid from a second sarcophagus, this time hurling it at Ylani.

She threw herself to the ground, next to Taran's unconscious body.

Jessamine, free but for one arm, screamed, pulling at the remaining bonds.

Brannon saw the motion of the throw and leaped forward, faster than he'd thought possible, to fling himself in the stone panel's path. He dropped his sword, thrust his arms out, palms forward, and braced.

The carved lid hit him with the force of an avalanche and shattered into rubble. Dust and pebbles showered them all like a hailstorm.

Brannon glared. "Really, Morgin? Hurting women and a child to get to me? You've killed your family. You've killed people I care about. You've unleashed monsters on our world. And all because you wanted more attention. You're a sick piece of shit and I'm just the physician you need."

He lunged at Morgin. His hand closed around the younger man's throat and he leaped upward, thrusting Morgin above him like a trophy held aloft. Morgin's head bashed against the stone ceiling and caved in like a dropped watermelon. He gave a little squeak and went limp.

As they fell back to the floor, Brannon shoved the still body away from him. The eyes opened and the crushed skull began to fill out again even before it hit the ground.

Ylani had picked up the knife again and was sawing through the last of Jessamine's ropes.

"You all okay?" Brannon dropped to his knee and checked Taran's pulse. It was strong and the priest was breathing. He stirred at Brannon's touch. It was a good sign.

Morgin stood and shook his head. "You're learning," he said.

Brannon scooped up his sword. "I try."

Ula's wind flowed uselessly around the room once more. The Djin woman seemed trapped in a pointless loop of recasting the same spell over and over.

"Nothing else will work," she had said. The words played over and over in Brannon's mind. Ula could return any Risen to the ground and banish any kaluki with her powers. She was a shaman and a prioress of Gradinath. The spell didn't work because this was a powerful kaluki in a living body.

The last hollow in Morgin's staved in skull had repaired. How long had it taken?

"Ula," he called. "How long does it usually take to banish a kaluki?"

"Moments only. But this one too strong."

"I know. Be ready."

There was a boom and a flash of heat. Brannon caught his breath and shot a glance at Draeson.

Smoke and ash drifted around the mage and scorch marks formed a kind of star spreading out from where he stood. He held his hands in front of him with the palms facing each other and a small sphere of light hung between them, increasing in brightness.

More of the smaller kaluki creatures poured through the portal, flowing across the floor like an oily tide or filling the air with membranous wings and spikes. Flailing amongst them were long thin tentacles that all reached out from the portal.

The portal itself throbbed. Brannon was sure it had grown.

Long fingers of lightning twitched out from Draeson's light globe, burning and slicing through kaluki wherever they touched.

Morgin lunged, slashing at Brannon with his sharp fingernails.

Brannon leaped back, then jabbed with his sword.

Morgin grabbed the blade in his hands and held tight. "You heard the shaman," he said. His face twisted into a smirk. "I'm too strong for you now."

"Maybe. Maybe not." Brannon yanked the sword free.

Morgin held up his cut hands. They had healed already. "You still think you can beat me?"

Superficial cuts were almost instantly deal with, Brannon realized. But more significant injuries took time. He feinted to the left, danced right, and hacked into Morgin's side. Neither Morgin nor the kaluki inside him were skilled in swordplay. The blade bit deep.

Morgin hissed at him. The wound healed—again quickly—but not as quickly as the smaller cuts.

This time Brannon was sure. If Ula could remove a kaluki from a dead body, then doing enough damage to this living one could, for a moment, provide a window of opportunity when the host would be technically dead, before the kaluki's power could heal it. It was a plan that required perfect timing, but it was a plan.

Morgin's fist lashed out.

Brannon dodged, but the other fist connected with his jaw. He fell, landing on his back.

Morgin followed him down, pinning Brannon's legs with his body weight and began stabbing into his stomach with his claws. The jabs came fast and furious, shredding Brannon's intestines.

Blood sprayed. Brannon screamed as each blow ripped his insides with burning hooks.

"Let's see just how much your precious earth spirits can heal," Morgin sneered.

The physician part of Brannon's mind was screaming. Blood loss. Infection. Disembowelment. He pushed it aside and battered at Morgin's arms with his fist.

The pain was excruciating, but he forced himself to think. He stopped fighting, pulled his sword up, lifting the point to aim at Morgin's chest. With both hands on the hilt, he thrust forward.

Morgin twisted and the blade sank into his side, well short of his heart, the intended target. He jabbed his fingers into Brannon's stomach and twisted.

Brannon bit down on a scream and blood filled his mouth. He needed a better weapon. Needed to do more damage. "Draeson!" He voice came out as a croak. "Draeson, blast him!"

"I'm a little busy!" called the mage.

Brannon turned his head to see the black creatures filling the room, spilling past Draeson and his light globe. A long tentacle wrapped itself around the mage's ankles and pulled tight. Draeson fell and disappeared beneath the black tide.

The winged creatures swirled overhead and blacked out the ceiling. Brannon felt his vision blurring. He diagnosed blood loss. Even his earth spirit enhanced body couldn't keep up with the constant slashing of Morgin's claws.

Suddenly Morgin screeched and the stabbing stopped. He fell backward, freeing Brannon's legs.

Brannon's inner organs immediately began knitting back together in a wriggling mass of pain. He scrambled back, away from the kaluki, blinking furiously as his vision cleared.

Morgin was clutching at his face where three sharp-edged throwing stars jutted from his eyes and cheek.

"Not so fun when people throw things at you, is it?" Taran said. The young man was leaning against a sarcophagus, half held up by Jessamine. He had a fourth throwing star in his hand. He threw it and it embedded itself in Morgin's shoulder.

Brannon stared. A priest proficient in Child of Starlight weaponry? Taran's words to him the night Latricia had died played back in his mind. "You don't need an average priest."

Morgin pulled the star from his eye and dropped it to the ground. Blood and ichor dribbled down his cheek. "You think your little tricks can hurt me?" His punctured eye closed over, color spilling back into the iris. "My

372

brothers and sisters will take care of you."

The swirling, winged kaluki began to swoop downward. Taran drew a dagger and began to slash at the air above him, trying to keep them away.

Brannon struggled to his feet, one hand still clutching his belly. The deepest gouges were now shallow cuts but the echo of the pain still clung to his insides.

Ylani stepped forward. She had a glass jar in her hand. "I can't hurt you, Morgin, but I can slow you down." She threw the contents of the jar into his face.

The caustic smell of formaldehyde filled the air. Morgin screamed and lashed out, catching her in the shoulder and sending her flying. "You bitch!" He rubbed at his eyes, stumbling.

Brannon felt the rush of battle fill him. "Now!" he yelled. "Draeson! Strike now!"

There was an explosion. Black chunks of kaluki rained down over them. A massive bolt of lightning blasted from the direction of the mage and slammed into Morgin from behind. The stench of burning flesh was everywhere.

Morgin howled. "Fools!"

Brannon ran forward, his sword raised.

Jessamine beat him there. The blond girl had the knife used to free her in her fist. She slashed it across Morgin's throat and blood spilled down his chest.

"Ula!" Brannon shouted. "Now! Do it now!"

He brought the sword up under Morgin's ribcage. He could see the edges of the gash already beginning to close.

"Not this time," he murmured to the kaluki. "We

have enough monsters here already." He shoved the sword deep, piercing Morgin's heart. "Heal this."

A gurgle sounded from the ruined throat, even as the cut vocal cords knitted back together.

Brannon held the kaluki close, keeping his sword in place while Ula's wind rose at last. When it happened, he felt the tug at his own core, and the corresponding one that shook the kaluki free of Morgin's body.

A dark, glittering mist was pulled out on the wind.

The remaining kaluki creatures paused. All eyes turned to Ula.

The Djin woman held her hands out in fists. "Kaluki," she said in a voice that boomed. "I banish you now!"

The mist swirled like a miniature tornado and dragged toward the portal. It touched the silvery surface and melted into it.

The surface of the portal darkened as though the touch of its creator had somehow tainted it.

The smaller creatures screamed and, en masse, ran for the portal, retreating back to their realm. Only some of them made it through before, with an enormous boom, the column collapsed, and dark ooze splattered all over the floor.

The portal was closed.

CHAPTER FORTY-FOUR

The world was somehow quiet. The screeches of kaluki, shouting of allies, and Draeson's explosions were gone and the regular sounds of life, even Brannon's own panting as he caught his breath, seemed nothing by comparison.

Brannon searched the room for signs of movement, but there were none. They had slaughtered the last of the small kaluki creatures and the collapsing portal had severed the tentacles of the larger one before the thing itself had managed to come through. Brannon would be eternally grateful that whatever creature they had belonged to was no longer at risk of coming into this realm.

"Everyone okay?" he asked.

"I be fine," Ula said, the words sounding thicker than usual in her mouth, as though the battle had strengthened her accent. "It surprise we be alive. Good surprise."

"Very good!" Brannon laughed. "Taran? Head

injury?"

The priest shrugged. "I've had worse. I'm okay."

Draeson looked at the now pale tattoo on his arm, then at Tomidan Sandilar. Ylani cut the last of the ropes holding the boy in place and he ran to Taran and wrapped his arms around the young man's legs.

"Don't even think about it," Brannon said. "There's no way that child is ready to bleed for your dragon right now. Or ever."

The mage nodded. "I'll be fine for now, but the fight took a lot out of me. Let's just not do that again, okay?"

"Agreed." Brannon took a deep breath. The room was a mess. Kaluki body parts were scattered everywhere, blood covered much of the floor and there were Morgin and Shillia's corpses to deal with. He wondered vaguely who would deal to that, given that Morgin had been the town's undertaker. Probably a town physician. Possibly even himself and Jessamine.

He glanced across at his apprentice. The fact that she was even alive and in one piece was something he'd barely been able to hope for an hour ago. Not only had she survived the ordeal, but she had contributed to Morgin's downfall. He couldn't be more proud.

Jessamine herself, however, looked pale. The bloody knife dropped from her fingers and clattered onto the stone floor, sounding very loud in the silence.

"Jessamine? Are you all right?" Fool that he was, he'd forgotten the girl wasn't a soldier.

"Yeah. Yeah, I, um . . . " Her lip quivered as she wiped her hand on her skirt. She took a deep breath and straightened her spine. "I guess it's just as well I didn't take that physician's oath yet after all."

Brannon smiled and squeezed her arm. "You did well," he said.

She turned in to his shoulder, clinging like a child. "He was so strong," she said, her body shaking against his. "I tried fighting him but . . . Then I just kept trying to reach the real Morgin, trying to get him to stop. I was so sure he would kill us both."

Brannon awkwardly patted her back while she sobbed. "It's okay. You're okay."

He looked around the room for assistance.

Ylani caught his eye and barely concealed a smirk.

"Help!" he mouthed.

She pointed to herself with big, innocent eyes. "Me?"

He glared, which only made her chuckle.

After a moment, Jessamine pulled back. Brannon gripped her shoulders and looked her in the eye. "You were amazing today. Now I want you to go back to the inn and get some rest. Ambassador Ylani will go with you and take Tomidan as well. Check him out and make sure he's not hurt, okay?"

She took a deep breath and nodded. "Okay." She retied her ponytail, seemingly unaware that she smeared a streak of red in the blond by doing so. "Come on, Tommy. Let's get out of here."

Ylani, still with a hint of a smile, took Tomidan's hand and peeled him away from a grateful Brother Taran. "Come on. Let's go somewhere safe."

She was heading for Jessamine and the exit when her face paled.

"Brannon!" She pointed.

Ula's eyes had lost the whites. Her face was

unnaturally still. The beads in her hair began to glow.

"Take them. They shouldn't be here for what happens next."

Ylani looked from the Djin woman to Brannon. Her lower lip caught in her teeth. "Brannon . . ."

"Go," he said. "This is what I agreed to. It's all right. Some battles can only be won by sacrificing troops. I'm just glad it wasn't any of you."

Ylani hesitated, her eyes on his for a long time.

"It's all right," he said again.

She nodded. "I know. But it isn't." She leaned in and kissed him on the lips, gentle and slow. The feel of her was warm and good and breathless. "You're a good man, Sir Brannon Kesh," she said, breaking away. "I'll never forget that."

He watched her leave, taking his best friend's grandson and his apprentice to safety. He smiled. She was a remarkable woman, the Nilarian ambassador. And right now, those three were the closest he'd get to a family. They were his responsibility to keep safe, and he'd done it.

"Not a bad last memory," he murmured to himself.

He approached Ula—or rather, the entity in Ula's body. "You're here to settle our debt. At least you're prompt."

Ula's head tilted to the side. "You have succeeded," the multilayered voice said. "Was our assistance beneficial to the outcome?"

Taran and Draeson drew close, staring. "What's going on?" Draeson said.

Brannon held out a hand. "It's fine. Yes, your assistance was very beneficial."

Ula's hand reached forward and wiped the line of clay from his forehead.

He felt the enhanced strength leave his body. He was just Brannon again. King's Champion, physician, war hero, Bloodhawk. It was enough. It was too much. He would never be able to wash himself clean of what he was, what he had been. Now, perhaps, he wouldn't have to.

"Take your sacrifice."

"Brannon?" Draeson's voice had a sharp edge.

He closed his eyes and waited.

For a long time, nothing happened. The world remained dark behind his eyelids. Nothing made a noise. The air was warm and slightly damp from the exertions of the battle. None of this changed. Death did not come.

"Hold out your weapon," the spirits said.

Brannon opened his eyes. "What?"

He could have imagined it, but there seemed to be a tiny crinkle in the corner of Ula's eyes. "Your sword, Sir Brannon. The weapon that struck the final blow. It is our chosen sacrifice."

"But, I thought . . . " Brannon stumbled over the words.

Ula's mouth twitched at him. "We are not kaluki, Brannon Kesh, to be demanding death. Our requirements are . . . different."

"You want my sword?"

"We do."

Brannon put his hand on the hilt and hesitated, somehow reluctant to give up the blade. He flicked his gaze to the floor, where blood was still wet, to Draeson and Taran's concerned faces, to Ula's impassive stone eyes.

"It is more than a sword, is it not?"

He sighed. "Yes, I suppose it is."

Ula leaned forward. "You have carried it too long. The sword and the guilt. Give them to us."

His heart felt suddenly too big and beating too fast. His hand was shaking as he drew the blade slowly out of his scabbard and held it out in front of him, a horizontal line. The face of the boy he had killed with it rose in his mind, the boy who had only tried to avenge his father. Who had been too young for battle.

"I'm sorry," he said, a tear rolling down his cheek. "I'm so sorry."

Ula held out her hands. "Let it go."

His fingers released the hilt and the sword dropped into her outstretched palms.

At the touch of her skin, the strong Nilarian steel shattered to pieces.

Brannon jerked back in shock. That sword had kept him safe for years. But it had kept him tied to the past.

"You're a good man, Sir Brannon Kesh," the spirits said, echoing Ylani's words from moments before. "Never forget that."

Then the stone color cleared from her eyes, and it was Ula again. She blinked and looked around. "Deal done?"

"Yes."

"Blood and Tears, Brannon, what was that?" Draeson said.

Brannon didn't answer. He wiped his face with his palm. "We need to get on with clearing up here. I want as much evidence collected as possible before we move the bodies. We have a lot to explain when we get back to Alapra. Ula, would you mind grabbing some of the sheets from the morgue?"

"Poor woman," Draeson said, looking down at the mayor's body. "She just wanted the best for him."

"Really?" Brannon said. "How do you get from wanting the best for your child to summoning monsters and murdering people?"

The mage shrugged. "I didn't say it was sane. But she did a lot for him and this is how he repaid her."

The mayor's eyes stared blankly. Her freckled face was like an island in an ocean of her own blood.

"I suppose it's nice to see you have some feelings for the people you've been sleeping with," Brannon said.

The mage shot him a dirty look.

"I wonder how she got past the ward on my door," Taran mused.

"What do you mean?"

"Well, she had to have gone into my room to take the koroleen from my supplies, but the ward never went off. I wonder how she did it."

"Don't look at me," Draeson said. "I gave her access to my room, and my room only."

Brannon went cold. "She was never in Taran's room." He clapped his hands over his face. "Blood and Tears! She was never in Alapra either. People remember her being here in town the whole time. Morgin too."

Draeson sat back, leaning against a sarcophagus. "Hooded Wolf. We've missed an accomplice."

Brannon nodded. "One that can get past your wards." His bones felt as shattered as his sword. "It's one of us."

CHAPTER FORTY-FIVE

The fresh air as they exited the building was a blessed relief for Ylani. She could only imagine how Jessamine and Tomidan, kept prisoner in that underground room for hours, must feel. The cool dusk light made shapes with the shadows and brought goosebumps out across her forearms. She squeezed the little boy's hand in hers as they stepped out into the street.

"Are you warm enough, Tommy?" She stopped and crouched down beside him, tugging his jacket better into place. "That better?"

He shrugged.

Jessamine flanked her other side, holding tightly to a fallen tree branch she had picked up just outside the door. The young woman seemed to gain some comfort from having it. She gripped the end like a club. Ylani noticed that her eyes watched their surroundings carefully, despite her calm exterior.

"You know you're safe now, right?" she said,

aiming the question at Tommy but intending the message for them both. "Morgin's gone. He's not coming back."

"Yes, ma'am." The little boy looked from her, to Jessamine, then back again. "He killed my parents, didn't he?"

"Yes, Tommy, he did." Even as she said it, the instinct twinged inside her. Some part of what she'd spoken was a lie. Her breath caught in her throat and she stumbled, swallowing quickly to recover. "That's why Sir Brannon went after him. That, and so we could get you back."

The instinct's message made little sense, but then they often didn't make sense at first. She stood up and took his hand again. "Come on. Let's go back to the inn. We will . . . send word to your grandfather that you're okay."

That one she knew was a lie. Duke Roydan was the last man she wanted to send a message to. With all that had happened, she'd be lucky to prove what he was up to until it was too late. And without Brannon as a corroborating witness . . .

She pushed her disturbing thoughts aside and concentrated on placing one foot in front of the other, a cheerful and comforting look on her face. There had been enough pain and misery for one day. Any more could wait.

"You must be looking forward to getting back to Alapra," she said to Jessamine. "This isn't quite the trip home you might have hoped for."

Jessamine shook her head. "This was never my home."

"Oh. I thought you lived here for a while."

"I did."

The light had fled in earnest now. The streets were completely deserted. Ylani couldn't blame the townsfolk. After this, she wondered if many of them would pack up their homes and leave. Despite Jessamine's words, most of the people here called Sandilar home. From what she knew, they may find it hard to live anywhere else in Kalanon after here. The prosperity that came with the gold mines was hard to come by without them.

A few crickets started their nightly chorus and an owl swooped by, searching for mice.

Tomidan jumped.

Ylani ruffled his hair. "Not scared of birds, are you?" she teased.

"No." He pulled a face. "Did you know you have mud on your forehead?"

She laughed. "Nice distraction, kid. You'll be a good politician yet."

"Brannon had the same mark," Jessamine said. "How'd you get it?"

"Ula's earth spirits. It's how Brannon got strong enough to fight Morgin."

"What?" Jessamine grabbed her arm. "How?"

At Jessamine's touch, a stab of pain shot through Ylani's forehead, as if the clay mark had burst into flame. The instinct flared inside her, vivid and bright enough to hurt her eyes. She swayed in its grasp, her hand clenching on Tommy's small fingers until he squealed.

The image burned into her mind: Morgin, Tomidan,

Jessamine. Together. The same.

She gasped and pulled away from them both. "Ahpra's Tears!"

"What is it?" Jessamine said. "Are you all right?"

Ylani struggled to bring her body back under control. The pain was fading but her breathing was still ragged. "The spirits," she said. "They said a sibling sacrifice would be powerful. We thought they meant Tomidan because he was the only heir left. But no." She looked up into Jessamine's face. "They meant a real sibling. They meant you."

The blond girl's concern melted away. The gentle lines of her face hardened and her eyes went flat. "Ah," she said. "It would have been better if you hadn't known that."

She raised her club.

CHAPTER FORTY-SIX

Brannon entered the smithy with slow, careful steps. The shaded lantern he carried let out a soft light, barely illuminating what was inside. A lantern designed for thieves and Children of Starlight, Taran had told him when handing it over. It gave enough light to see by but not enough to be noticed from the outside.

The door clicked closed behind him. The sound was very loud in the dim light. He felt very alone.

He increased the light from the lantern just a notch and looked around.

The smithy was essentially divided into two rooms: the outer shop, which contained the forge, workspace, and the finished products, and the storeroom in the back for raw materials and records. The outer shop was spacious and cluttered. In the darkness, racks of hoes and scythes made shapes that reminded him of the tentacled creature from Morgin's portal.

He moved forward slowly, turning his head this way

and that, searching for anything that didn't belong, anything that moved.

A muffled shout came from somewhere ahead.

Brannon hurried toward it. His foot connected with something thin, stretched across the floor.

There was a twang and a sudden, sharp pain in his neck.

He reached up to find a small dart, little bigger than a toothpick, penetrating his skin just below his right ear. He pulled it out quickly and dropped it on the ground.

Several lanterns flared up at once, highlighting the far side of the room, beyond the forge. Ambassador Ylani and Tomidan were gagged and bound to chairs. Ylani had a trickle of blood dried and crusted down the side of her face. She strained against her bonds and made muffled noises into the gag. Jessamine held a dagger up to her throat and she quieted.

"I'm impressed, Brannon," Jessamine said. "You found me pretty quickly."

Brannon shrugged. "People go to places they're familiar with. Morgin went to the tunnels under his workplace. Once I realized it was you who'd had the affair with Kholi Gruul, it was pretty simple to figure out where you'd be." He gestured to her wrist. "The burn scar from a forge."

"Ah. I see. It seems there are a few things you can still teach me. It's a pity my apprenticeship is ending."

"It doesn't have to," Brannon said. "Put down the knife and we can call this a youthful indiscretion due to stress."

"Brannon," she chided. "Come on. I appreciate you coming alone though. Didn't want to raise suspicions with the others until you were sure, huh? Figured you could handle me on your own."

He gave a half shrug. "It was worth a try." He began moving forward. "I'm curious, was Mayor Shillia in on it at all? Or was she just collateral damage?"

Jessamine pressed the knife against Ylani's neck.

The ambassador lifted her chin, trying to pull away, her eyes wide.

"Collateral damage," Jessamine said. "Another step and there'll be more."

"Okay, okay." Brannon stopped. He kept his arms out from his sides, one hand open, the other holding a sword. He'd borrowed it before coming and had no intention of giving it up. "I was sure Shillia was the mastermind."

She laughed. The sound was incongruously innocent. "No, that would be me. Morgin was the perfect ally. Brother and sister, both wanting something from dear old Dad. Different somethings, of course." She shrugged. "His mother had no idea who I was or how many other women her precious Roydan had impregnated."

Brannon felt a tingling in his neck. His breath quickened. The dart had been dipped in something. Of course. It was the killer's modus operandi. Jessamine's modus operandi. She would have planned for this.

"I always knew you were a clever one. I think maybe you deserved a better mentor than me."

"But I asked for you, Brannon."

"So you could do all this? Kill people and then watch us try to solve it?"

She shook her head. "So I could learn things.

Remember, I told you the rituals were done by an apprentice." She gestured to herself with her free hand. "I've been an apprentice to all of you. Four experts in various forms of power. I learned so much."

Brannon swayed, suddenly unsteady on his feet.

"For example, there was loredin on that dart. Not as effective as ingesting it, but it should be weakening you pretty good by now. I learned that trick from talking to Taran."

"And you learned how to use a kaluki to make Morgin stronger from Kholi and from Ula—then you stole some of her supplies to make it happen."

She took a little bow. "Exactly. Poor little innocent Jessamine saw the big bad burglar get away. No one could possibly suspect her."

"You slipped up stealing the koroleen from Taran though. He figured out that you lifted his room key when you kissed him." Brannon's legs began to tremble. He clutched his borrowed sword tightly but the tip was drooping.

"Really?" Jessamine's eyebrows raised. "I was sure I had him lovesick enough to miss that. I guess this is all quite timely then." She gestured to her captives.

Brannon forced his knees to lock. There would be no point attacking in a weakened, drugged state. Once the drug had full effect, Jessamine could do what she wanted. Until then, he needed to keep her talking. To find out the truth behind all of it. He had trusted her. He had brought her into the center of the investigation. And she had manipulated the whole thing.

"Is Jessamine Tral even your real name?"

The expression left her face. "Yes. Yes it is."

His sword wavered, dipping even lower.

"Don't fight it," Jessamine said. "We both know how loredin works. Such a wonderful paralytic. Your legs really won't be able to hold you up much longer."

As if to prove her right, his legs gave way beneath him and Brannon fell to his knees. The sword clattered to the floor as he braced himself with his hands.

"Oops," she said, in a little singsong voice. "Need a physician?"

Brannon glared. "Not one who commits murder. I assume it was you who killed Keldan and that woman back in Alapra."

"Oh yes." She stepped back a little from Ylani, fiddling with the knife in her hand. Still too close for Brannon's comfort. "Actually, I feel bad for the woman. She wasn't in the original plan."

"Then why did you kill her?"

"You were intent on finding the woman you'd seen Keldan with before he died. I couldn't risk you figuring out it was me. So I went to the docks, found a whore that could pass and killed her. After a while, I started worrying that the connection wouldn't be made, so I stashed the body in your cupboard."

"But what about her friends? Her family? What if someone had reported her missing?"

Jessamine snorted. "I made sure she had no children. And nobody else ever cares about street whores, Brannon. No one knows that better than me."

Brannon slumped back, half sitting, half lying on the floor. His mind whirled. He didn't have much time left before loredin would render him completely immobile and speechless.

"You killed Kholi because he could reveal that it was you he had told about the ritual. You must have planned this all before you even came to Alapra. Maybe even before you came to Sandilar. You slept with Kholi to learn what you could and then you used Morgin's insecurity to manipulate him into joining you. Why?"

Jessamine smiled. It was a tight, hard smile below dead eyes. "Vengeance."

"For what?"

She licked her lips and stared off into the distance. "You remember what I told you about my mother?"

He watched her carefully. The knuckles on her hand were white as she gripped the dagger. "You said she died because her employer wouldn't send for a physician."

She sneered and shook her head. "My mother didn't have an employer. Or rather, she had many—sometimes several a night." She turned and looked directly into Brannon's eyes. "Do you have any idea what it's like to grow up watching your mother be a whore because it's the only way to put food in your stomach? That your father is the richest man in the kingdom but won't spare a single coin to save her?"

Brannon swallowed. Memories of his own childhood were sometimes tough—that of a younger son, considered irrelevant until he made a name for himself in the army—but nothing like this. "No. I don't." Surely Roydan hadn't known the girl was his. The man was generous with his seed but he wouldn't leave even a bastard child and her mother so uncared for. That wasn't the friend he knew. Was it? "What happened?"

"Like I said, my mother got sick. We couldn't afford

a physician and we couldn't afford food. But I knew who my father was and I knew he wouldn't let us down. So I borrowed a horse and I rode as fast as I could to Sandilar Manor to beg my father, the legendary Duke Roydan, for his physician to save my mother, the woman he had given a child to. He had his men run me out of town without my horse. I was eleven years old."

"He . . . " The words stumbled on Brannon's tongue. "Are you sure? I mean, did he see you himself?"

"Oh yes." Jessamine lashed out a hand at a stand of wooden-handled rakes and the whole thing crashed to the ground. She stood over it, breathing hard.

Brannon twitched. She was distracted. But still close to the captives. The tingling in his neck where the dart had struck faded and he let his head roll to the side, his eyes still on her.

"Yes," Jessamine continued. "He and his precious wife granted me audience but that ended as soon as I spoke. When I finally made it back to Trallene on foot, my mother was dead. I swore then that I would destroy him for what he'd done."

"Ahpra's Tears, girl, you very nearly destroyed us all!" Brannon thought it over. The elaborateness of the plan. The years that had gone into designing it. This girl was not satisfied with simply killing Roydan for revenge. She wanted him to suffer. In Alapra, she had been the one close when Roydan had been grieving. She'd wanted to be there to see her handiwork as he wept for the loss of his son. Then he was tormented further when that son was raised by Ula and put down again. And that had been just the beginning of the killings. She was wiping out Roydan's entire line so that when she finally came to him, he would know nothing of him would survive her vengeance. She was twisting the knife all the time and he didn't even know it.

"Blood and Tears. He requested you as his physician. He has no idea who you are, does he?"

"No, he doesn't. And every time his sleazy gaze comes near me I think about slitting his throat and it makes me smile. He loves my smile, he told me." Her laughter ran sharp, serrated chills across Brannon's skin.

He swallowed. "You have more planned for him?"

"I do." The smile Roydan had commented on graced her lips. "But now, of course, the plan must change. It's always important to have a contingency."

She reached up with both hands, one still gripping the knife. The other she used to pull her ponytail taut before cutting it off. The remaining hair fell forward, framing her eyes and hanging to just below her jawline. She threw the severed ponytail on the floor. "That, with a bit of my blood to react to Draeson's spell, ought to convince people I died with the rest of you. We'll all be in pieces, after all. A few symbols on the walls, and we're the latest victims of the murderer on the rampage."

"What murderer? Morgin's dead. He can't be your scapegoat anymore."

"True," she said. "But once I kill Taran, the only ones saying that will be a Djin and a wizard. People don't trust Djin or wizards."

She pointed the dagger at Ylani. "Her death might start that war you're so worried about, but at least you won't be here to see it. More likely both countries will attack Djinan. That should be interesting. Either way, there'll be confusion and I'll be starting my life over somewhere else."

She moved over to Tomidan, tracing a finger over his shoulder. The little boy flinched. "The question is, do I kill this one outright or maim him beyond repair? Which do you think would hurt Roydan most? I could cut off his tongue, hands, and balls. That'd make him pretty useless as an heir. He might die of infection anyway, of course—maybe even in Roydan's arms. That'd be such a poignant way to go, don't you think?"

"Please," Brannon croaked, his body at last giving out on him completely. "Please."

"Oh, Brannon. Begging for me to spare you all? That's no way to go. The mighty Bloodhawk, begging for his life. Tragic."

"No," he said, struggling to form the words. "Kill me first. Please."

"Ah. That's more like it. Noble to the end. Buying the innocents a few seconds reprieve." She walked out from behind Tommy's chair, the dagger held loosely now, casual. "You'll forgive the mutilation that comes after. All part of setting the scene."

She leaned forward and took a handful of his hair, pulling his head up to face her. "Physicians know how to kill," she reminded him. "Thanks for being a good teacher."

She pulled back the blade to strike.

Brannon launched himself upward, and drove his fist into her stomach.

Jessamine grunted in surprise and let go of his hair, stumbling back, doubled over in pain. "No! That's impossible!" She slashed at him with the knife.

Brannon grabbed her wrist and twisted her arm

behind her.

She pulled away but he went with her, pushing forward and using his weight and momentum to slam them into a workbench. He pinned her down.

"Let it go."

She struggled and he pulled her arm up higher. Her fingers opened and the dagger fell to the floor.

"That's better." He looked up to see Taran already cutting Ylani and Tomidan free. "Nice work."

"You cut it a little fine there," Taran said. "I thought I might have to step in."

"Nah, I had it covered. I needed to hear everything."

"Where did he come from?" Jessamine spluttered. "How are you moving? I saw you get dosed. The dart!"

Brannon chuckled and pulled her other arm into place, ready to be tied.

Taran joined him with some rope.

"Our Brother Taran has quite a knack for sneaking into places and picked the lock on the back door. He also realized you'd taken some of the loredin from his supplies along with the koroleen and he dosed us both with the antidotes before we came." He pulled her up off the workbench and turned her around. "You're not the only one who can plan ahead."

Ylani picked up Tommy and held him close. He buried his head in her shoulder. "Do your contingencies include a way to avoid the death sentence?" she hissed at Jessamine. "Because that's what you'll be getting when we get back to Alapra."

Jessamine licked her lips. "Actually," she said, "They do. I can give you Roydan's plans. All of them."

CHAPTER FORTY-SEVEN

The palace balcony overlooked the whole of Alapra. The city was awash with lights and music, festooned with streamers and banners, a riot of color and celebration. Fireworks sprinkled the night sky with bursts of crimson and green and gold, like fantastic flowers in the garden of the gods.

The crowd that was gathered in the palace grounds below cheered and clapped with each new colorful display. They themselves were decked with many-hued splendor, all dressed in their best for the king's celebrations.

Brannon clapped the king on the shoulder as they watched the fireworks display in his honor. "Happy birthday."

"Thanks." Aldan smiled. The light from the lanterns inside gleamed on his hair, making it seem as golden as the crown he wore. "This celebration wouldn't be happening if it wasn't for you. You've done well."

"It was a group effort, Your Majesty."

"So you said." Another burst of red sparks highlighted the king's face. His lips were tight.

"You still don't trust Ambassador Ylani."

Aldan sighed. "She's Nilarian. It's difficult to see past that."

"Yet you trust a Child of Starlight."

The fireworks changed to brilliant green, lighting the sky like a handful of spilled emeralds on black silk.

"Taran earned my trust when he warned me about the assassination attempt years ago. He saved my life."

"And now Ylani has as well. We'd have never found out what we did without her."

"Perhaps." Aldan stared down at the gathered Kalans below. The jovial atmosphere no longer reached the balcony. "Ahpra's Tears, Brannon, I know you told me what you found, but I just hope you're wrong."

Brannon scratched at his earlobe where his scar began. "So do I."

They continued to watch in silence as the hail of colored sparks entertained the crowd. As the last firework faded, the band began to play. King Aldan waved to the crowd below and the people cheered, a sound that lifted almost as high as the fireworks had done. The king smiled for his people, though Brannon knew the concern that was in his heart.

A valet stepped forward and cleared his throat, a gesture more than sound given the ongoing cheers.

"They do love a celebration, don't they?" Aldan said.

"They love you, Your Majesty," the valet said quickly.

Aldan chuckled. "That too, perhaps."

Brannon jerked his head toward the crowd. "Really? Only perhaps?"

Aldan laughed properly this time. It was a sight and sound Brannon had gone too long without. "Well, it's good to be loved! And Ahpra knows they deserve a celebration. It's been a hard few decades."

"Blood and Tears, that's the truth," Brannon said. "But you do know how to throw a party."

"Your Majesty," the valet said, clutching his hands together. "You're due at the gala performance. We need to leave now."

Aldan gave one final wave to the crowd. "Yes, well, they'll hardly start without me. Don't fret."

"It's my job to fret, Your Majesty," the young man said. He led the way inside and Brannon, Aldan, and a few other attendants followed.

The room off the balcony was a broad entertainment hall lined with portraits of previous monarchs of Kalanon and a polished wooden floor that shone like a mirror. Reflected in its surface was an array of armed men.

Twenty or so men in visored helmets and the livery of the palace guard were stretched across the room, blocking the path to the door.

Roydan led them. At his gesture, they drew their swords.

"What's going on here?" Aldan asked, his voice firm.

"I've decided," Roydan said quietly, "that it's time for a leadership change in Kalanon. I'm taking the Crown."

Brannon stepped in front of his king. "Roydan, don't

do this!"

The duke held out a hand. "Stand down, Brannon. You're a friend. There's room for you in my court."

Brannon felt as though his guts had been pulled out with a hot hook. He'd not truly dared to hope that they'd been wrong about Roydan, but some part of him had refused to believe. That part was now crushed. He drew his own sword. "No, Roydan. There's no room for me in a traitor's court."

Roydan shrugged. "Have it your way. It's your funeral. As you can see, I've recruited most of the palace guard. There's no way out of this room alive. I've also brought my own men in from Sandilar and they're capturing strategic locations around the city as we speak." He nodded toward Aldan. "Your fireworks were the signal to attack."

The king stroked his beard and frowned. "But why? I don't understand why you would do this, Roydan. You're already my heir. You're my cousin!"

"Fat lot of good it does me," Roydan spat. "We're the same age. No, it's time I took the power for myself. I own Sandilar, which means I control the economy. Why shouldn't I rule the kingdom as well?"

Brannon turned to look at the king.

Aldan nodded. "That's enough. It's what I needed to hear."

Brannon put his sword away. "All right then. Arrest him."

The palace guardsmen moved in, grasping Roydan by the arms and holding him tight.

Roydan looked around, his eyes wide. He tried to shake them off, but could not. "What? You work for me!

What are you doing? Stop this!"

The sound of feminine laughter filled the room and two more palace guards brought in Jessamine, shackled hands and feet, to face her father.

"You!"

"I told them everything, old man," she said. Her face was radiant with glee. "Your men never made it to Alapra. Brannon intercepted them along the way. And your precious Nilarian swords? Confiscated and replaced with fakes. You never had a chance. And I brought you down!" She laughed again, her body shaking with it so that the guards had to hold her up.

Roydan fought as his own shackles were put on. "But this whole thing was her idea," he said. "She came to me! She told me how to do it!"

"We know," said King Aldan. "But it was you who did it." He turned away. "Get them out of my sight."

One of the guards pulled off his helmet. It was Darnec Raldene, the young man Brannon had wounded in trial by combat before all this had begun.

"Darnec." Brannon gestured him to come forward.

"The compromised guards are already locked up, Sir Brannon. He claimed to have most of us but I'd say it's more like a third. We've made sure that no one is on duty alone, just in case there's someone we missed."

Brannon nodded thoughtfully. "Good work. You did an impressive job identifying the traitors."

Darnec made a rueful face. "I'm new and have a reputation for being easily corrupted. Mostly they came to me."

Brannon chuckled. "Well, I'm glad to say your reputation will probably change."

The young man blushed and pulled himself to attention. "That's because of you, sir. You got me this post and I'm grateful. I'm indebted to you, Sir Brannon, and from now on I pay my debts."

Brannon smiled, pride warming the wound in his heart left by Roydan. "Good man. Now see to the prisoners."

Aldan settled into a plush, brocade sofa, his hands over his face. The valet came close but the king waved him away.

Brannon crept closer. "Aldan? Are you okay?"

The king took off his crown and turned it over in his hands, inspecting it. "Part of me just didn't believe this would be enough to turn him. I really thought he was my friend."

Brannon sighed and sat down beside him. "So did I. To be fair, Jessamine spent her entire life planning how to bring him down. She's a master manipulator."

"But she couldn't make him do it if he'd only said no," Aldan said.

Brannon stared at the ground. A rough reflection of himself stared back from the polished wood. It was older than he remembered.

"I'll need a new heir," said the king after a long silence.

"Tomidan."

"Yeah. It'll be strange to have a child around."

"If I had to deal with having an apprentice, you can deal with having a child."

"And look how that turned out."

They both laughed. It was nice to just be friends again. Not king and subject. Not champion and lord. Just friends, talking about the ordinary madness that was their world.

"This physician thing," Aldan said. "It's not really a phase, is it?"

"No," said Brannon. "It's not."

"And you don't like killing anymore. Fighting, I mean."

"No."

They sat quietly for a while. Thoughtful. Brannon stared at his friend's reflection in the polished wood. He looked older as well. Wiser.

"I think I need to make better use of your talents," Aldan said at last, shaking himself and sitting up straight. "You're good with a sword, but this business has shown me you're an asset in other ways and I've been neglecting that." He stood up.

Brannon lifted his head to look up at his king. "What do you mean?"

Aldan paced a few steps then turned back. "There are all sorts of things that go on in this kingdom. Crimes and mysteries that might never be understood. I want to set up a position—a team, actually—to look into such things for me. I think you should be the head of that team. But it would require you to delegate some of your responsibilities as King's Champion."

Brannon felt his breath stop.

The king's gaze was steady. "You probably wouldn't have time for trials by combat, for example. So it'd be up to you. Will you accept this new position as Master of Investigations?"

Brannon closed his eyes and took a deep breath. "I'd like that very much."

KEEP READING FOR AN EXCERPT FROM

AGENTS OF KALANON: BOOK TWO
STARLIGHT'S CHILDREN

AUTHOR'S NOTE

Thank you for taking the time to read my book. I hope you enjoyed reading it as much as I enjoyed creating it.

Please post a review online and tell your friends about this book. Word of mouth makes a huge difference to an author and is greatly appreciated.

If you'd like to read some of my other work or keep up to date with future books, you can check out my website, join my e-mail list, or follow me on Facebook or Twitter.

Website: www.darian-smith.com

Facebook: DarianSmithAuthor

Twitter: @DarianWordSmith

ABOUT THE AUTHOR

Darian Smith lives in Auckland, New Zealand with his wife (who also writes) and their Siamese cat (who doesn't).

By day, he works with people who have neuromuscular conditions such as muscular dystrophy or charcot marie tooth disease. He is also a qualified counsellor/family therapist and can be seen – by those very swift with the pause button – on television shows such as Legend of the Seeker and Spartacus.

For more information about Darian and his upcoming work, please check out his website at www.darian-smith.com.

SHIFTING WORLDS

A collection of short stories by Darian Smith
Foreword by Jennifer Fallon

Drag queens fight zombies.
An immigrant artist hopes love conquers all.
Deep space explorers wrestle with an alien artifact.
A superhero is locked in an insane asylum.
These 16 stories span the worlds of fantasy, sci-fi, and literary fiction, and cause the characters' worlds to fundamentally change. Includes several prize winning stories as well as some that are seen for the first time in this collection.

"Never fails to entertain and surprise…this collection has it all" – Jennifer Fallon

Excerpt:

There's a moment, just before waking, when I forget it's gone. I feel the ghost of it on my shoulders, the warmth inside. It boosts my confidence and makes me stronger. I am more myself. I am ready to rule the islands and mould the day to my bidding.

Opening my eyes is a disappointment. My old bones ache with craving. It's been missing from me for almost three decades, but I feel it just the same. I'm simply an old man with his memories and regrets. I had my chance. I was not worthy.

Get your copy at Amazon.com & selected bookstores.

CURRENTS OF CHANGE
by Darian Smith

A suspenseful novel about magic, secrets, a haunted house, and a touch of romance.

Haunted house. Haunted heart.
When Sara O'Neill goes on the run, she believes the tiny New Zealand town of Kowhiowhio is just the sanctuary she needs. But a dangerous presence haunts her new home, threatening Sara's chance at peace. Can she create a new life while dealing with ghosts from the old?
For local electrician, Nate Adams, parenting his young daughter alone has not been easy. Even with his help, can the house – or Sara's heart – be repaired?
Someone doesn't want an O'Neill in Kowhiowhio.
Sara's return is awakening generations of secrets.
Why has the house never had electricity?
What was the fate of Sara's ancestors?
Can she discover the ghost's story before it's too late?
The truth will set…something…free.

"Well-paced paranormal romance. . . would appeal to readers who like a good ghost story, with a little bit of history and a dash of romance in the mix."
- SQ Mag International Speculative Fiction eZine

"I really enjoyed this book - a light, but interesting read that I didn't want to put down." - The Happy Homemaker

Get your copy at Amazon.com or selected bookstores.

AN EXCERPT FROM

AGENTS OF KALANON: BOOK TWO
STARLIGHT'S CHILDREN

Taran leaned over and studied the gravel path. The alley smelled of old urine, rotted scraps, and horse dung. Garbage was piled against the walls. In a more affluent part of the city, it would have been cleared and sanitised. Here, it merely collected, growing like moss over the brick. Foot traffic in the time since the killing had churned the stones, making the evidence difficult to see. Even taking that into account, there was less blood than there should have been. It speckled the gravel but there was no sign of pooling where the body had lain. "Hmmm. Are you sure this is where he was actually killed?"

"Yes, yes, of course. We have a witness, remember?" Magistrate Gawrick hugged himself and glanced up the alleyway for what seemed like the hundredth time. "I do wish you'd waited for my guards to attend the scene with us."

Taran picked up a stone with a splash of red on it. He wrapped it in a handkerchief and put it in his pocket. "It's best to see the scene as quickly as possible. Before things get disturbed too much."

"This is a less than savoury part of the city," the magistrate said, louder.

Taran nodded, keeping his expression mild. "Mmm. Many poor people live here." He gestured to the other end of the alley. "My monastery brings food to an orphanage just down there. A lot of children lost parents in the war. Not everyone is paid to pass judgements, Magistrate."

Gawrick's eyes narrowed. "You've been spending too much time with your boss."

Taran widened his eyes and spread his hands innocently. "The goddess, Ahpra?"

"Sir Brannon."

Taran turned away to hide his smile. "Perhaps."

"One should always be careful who one's mentors are."

The smile vanished. Taran swallowed. "That's true."

A few steps on, the blood had sprayed up the wall, drops splashing on the collected refuse, dark red. Still less than he'd expect from a sword strike to the heart, but a better indicator of where the man whose blood it was had been attacked.

It had sprayed in an arc, like water from a wet umbrella as it lowered, but thicker, congealing as it dried, almost like a paint.

Taran heard the memory of a past mentor in his mind.

"That's what a shallow wound looks like," Fressin had told him the first time he'd seen such a spray of blood. The older boy had just two years on Taran in age, but his training was much further along. "You could clean it up quickly, but it won't kill your target."

The pig they'd cut wriggled and squealed beneath Taran's hand, but the ropes binding its feet held strong. They were in one of the storerooms on the far edge of the compound, away from the rest of the livestock and where they were unlikely to be disturbed. "Are you sure we should be doing this? It seems cruel."

"We're supposed to be Children of Starlight, Taran. Harden up. Besides, I brought this pig down here especially so you can get a head start on the others this time." Fressin pointed to the creature's belly. "Stab it there. Deep, but don't kill it yet. We need the heart pumping for the next examples."

The pig squealed again and Taran, still just a boy, hesitated. The knife in his hand dripped blood down onto the hilt and over his fingers.

"Come on. You need to see how the blood pools. Don't want to fail another class, do you?" Fressin folded his arms. "If you're giving up, then I don't know why I bother teaching you out of class. You can end up like your friend or worse if you want. I don't think the Master likes you anyway."

Taran sliced the knife downward and the pig screamed.

Magistrate Gawrick's voice intruded on the memory, pulling Taran back to the present as the black robed man leaned down to pick up a child's discarded shoe from beside the bloodstained refuse. "One shoe. There's a frustrated parent somewhere." He dropped it onto the pile and wiped his hand on his robes. "Ah, the carelessness of children. Not a worry in the world.

410

Wouldn't you love to go back to those days?"

Taran considered his childhood training. He pulled a flask from his pocket and took a long swig, draining it. "I can't think of anything worse."

"Fine." Gawrick's jaw tightened and he gestured to the entrance of the alley. "Well, the guards have arrived so my job here is done. Tell Sir Brannon he can interview the witness whenever he likes but that I expect this case to be finished up quickly and with a minimum of fuss since we've pretty much already solved it for him. You can also tell him that if he's this desperate to find something for your team to work on, perhaps he can report to King Aldan that there's little need for it in the first place. Good day." He strode away, barking orders at the guards as he passed.

Taran blinked at the magistrate's back, then shrugged. The man had done as he was asked so Taran put him out of his head and focussed on retrieving samples. Given that the blood was spread out, he thought it best to collect from multiple sources. There was always the chance that more than one person had bled here. If that were the case, test results on different samples would give different results.

He scraped flecks of dried blood from the wall and collected another of the stones from the gravel path. He looked more closely at the pile of garbage, looking for any blood that broke the spray pattern or seemed out of place.

The shoe Magistrate Gawrick had dropped lay on its side in the pile. Blood coated the sole.

"Blood and Tears," Taran swore under his breath. Blood there meant the shoe had been in the blood while it was fresh. Either dropped or, more likely, the child who'd worn it had stepped in blood. "We might have another witness."

Leaving the guards to keep the scene secure til Brannon was able to inspect it, he took the shoe and hurried to the end of the alley. The last door on the left was a wooden panel covered in faded red paint in a stone frame with cracked mortar. Above it was a sign that read "Lady Magda's Orphanage" and a roughly drawn image of a child.

Taran rapped on the door.

A few moments later, it opened to reveal a tall woman with grey hair pulled back into a messy bun. She wore a green dress with colourful paint splotches around the lower part of the skirt where children had grabbed at it for her attention during a crafts session. She wore a crown of paper flowers. Behind her, the sounds of children playing spilled out into the street.

She smiled. "Brother Taran. It's been a long time. Come in."

Taran followed her into the house. He had no idea if Magda had ever actually held the title of Lady or whether it was an affectation of the orphanage, but the building had once been quite a grand home. Years and lack of maintenance had given it a rather worn air now, and the many children who lived or spent time here had hastened that wear even more. Still, it had a feeling of warmth to it. Magda did the best she could with her resources and the Alapran Third Monastery supported her with donations and food brought in by their congregation.

"There wasn't a service this morning, so I assume you're not here with a delivery," Magda said.

Taran nodded. "Um...I need your help. I'm helping

Sir Brannon with an investigation and I'm hoping you might have some information for me."

She frowned. "Sir Brannon? Bloodhawk? The King's Champion?"

"Yes." Taran held up the shoe. "Do you know who this belongs to?"

She looked at it closely. "That looks like Shalyn's shoe. Her father usually leaves her here during the day while he works at the cobbler's four streets over. Her mother died in the war. You can see he made them especially for her with her initial in the stitching." She reached closer to touch the spot, then pulled her hand back all the way to her shoulder. "Ahpra's Tears. That's blood, isn't it?"

"Yes." Taran tucked the shoe into his knapsack. "Do you know where Shalyn is now?"

Magda let her hand settle on her chest. "No. I haven't seen her or her father for two days. Do you think...has something happened?"

Taran looked away, staring instead at the threadbare pattern on the mat they stood on. Nothing in his training had covered comforting those left behind after a death. "If...um...if Sir Brannon could ask you some questions about them..." He took a breath and raised his gaze. "Do you think you could identify the father's body if you had to?"

Magda closed her eyes. The muscles in her throat moved as she swallowed. When she spoke it was in a very small voice. "Yes. Yes, I could do that. When? I'll need to arrange for someone to take care of the children while I'm gone."

"In the next day or so. I'll send word for Sir

Brannon to get in touch with you."

She nodded. Children were laughing in the next room, the sound strangely incongruous for the seriousness of the moment.

"I'll see you later then," Taran said. He turned and reached for the door but Magda put a hand on his shoulder.

"Bishop Naran was here last week," she said. "He was asking questions about our guest."

Taran's stomach twisted as if he'd been punched in the gut. "How did he find out about her?"

"I don't know." Magda shrugged. "He didn't say."

Taran scratched at his arm and turned to look at her. "What did you tell him?"

"Nothing. But he seemed oddly interested. I thought you would want to know."

He nodded, swallowing. "Thank you."

"Since you're here," she said. "Do you want to see her?"

He took a slow breath before answering. "I suppose I should."

"I think she misses you."

He shook his head. "I doubt she even remembers me."

"Shall we go and see?"

She led him up two flights of stairs and down a corridor. While old and worn, the house was clean and tidy but for the children's toys scattered here and there. More than once Taran heard a door slam and giggling behind him as if he and Magda were unwitting participants in some giant game of hide and seek.

As they approached the end of the corridor,

however, the signs of children vanished. The last part of the hallway was separated from the rest by a wooden fence that came up to his waist. Magda opened a gate in it and ushered him through.

"The older children know to stay away but we had this installed to keep the younger ones away."

A few steps past the gate, the corridor ended with a single locked door. A heavy wheel, like that for steering a ship, was set into the wall and thick chains ran from the barrel behind it and threaded through an aperture in the wall into the room beyond. Magda took hold of the wheel and turned it, winding the chains around the barrel and pulling. A woman's wild voice screamed behind the door as the chains pulled through.

Taran peered through the aperture. The gap was very small – space for the chains but little else. He could see little of the room beyond.

Magda watched him, continuing to turn the wheel until finally the chains would move no more. "I don't like doing this but..."

Taran nodded, his face a grimace. "It's the only way to be safe."

Magda clamped the wheel in place and then unlocked the door. Taran hesitated, then stripped the daggers from the sheathes hidden in his sleeves and left them in the corridor before stepping through the doorway.

The room inside was sparsely furnished with a bed, small table, and a chamber pot in the corner. The table had remnants of a meal but much of the food was on the floor. The chamber pot had been tipped over and the contents smeared on the carpet. Star-shaped symbols were etched into the walls as well as drawn in food and faeces. The smell hit them like a solid thing, crawling up Taran's nostrils to burrow down into his throat.

"I have one of the older children clean up in here once a day," Magda said quietly. She moved aside, letting Taran go ahead of her into the room. "But it doesn't last."

On the bed was a thin woman in a nightgown that billowed around her like a ghost. Her hair was dishevelled and her hands filthy. Manacles on her wrists were attached to the heavy chains which where, in turn, guided through pulleys and back through the hole in the wall to the wheel outside. Magda's turning of the wheel had shortened the length of play on the chains, forcing the woman back onto the bed whereas before she'd had the run of the room. A red circle painted on the floor around the bed indicated a safe distance.

"Marbella," Magda called gently. "Look who has come to see you."

Taran edged forward. "Marbella?"

The woman on the bed had stopped screaming when they'd entered and now sang softly to herself. The words were a garbled version of a child's nursery rhyme. Taran wondered if she'd heard it from the other inhabitants of the house – the free inhabitants.

As he came closer, she stopped singing and looked up. Her lips pulled back into a smile, showing teeth yellowed with grime. "Ah, the Lord of Stars has come to see me. All hail the Lord of Stars." She fell into a fit of giggles, her body convulsing on the bed like a seizure.

Taran reached forward to touch her foot. "Marbella? Are you…okay?" His voice trailed off. It was a stupid question.

It was Magda who answered. "The madness grips her hard most days, but we do our best to keep her in good spirits. The sedatives do help but she seems to have figured out that it's in her food so she doesn't always eat. It's rare for her to injure herself these days and as long as no one gets too close, she can't hurt anyone else."

Taran nodded. "Thank you. Has she said anything about her life before?"

"Nothing that makes a lick of sense, I'm afraid." Magda clucked her tongue like a worried mother hen. "The poor dear. She's lucky you brought her here when you did."

Taran forced himself to give an appreciative smile. "I suppose she is. Do you think I could have a few moments alone with her?"

"Of course, dear. Take as long as you like. I'll have one of the girls come and clean up when you're done. It upsets her to be pulled back to the bed so there's no point doing it more often than we need to." She scurried out and Taran waited until he heard the click of the wooden gate in the corridor before he stepped forward again and sat on the edge of the bed next to the mad woman. There was more grey in her hair than he remembered.

"Marbella?"

She lay facing away from him, trembling but silent.

"What we were doing was wrong. You gave me no choice. You know that, right?" He closed his eyes against the burning guilt. "Somewhere inside, you must understand my decision. You have to."

Marbella's weight on the bed shifted. Taran opened his eyes just in time to see her arm swinging at his head. The metal shackle struck his forehead before he could get his arm up to block it and a burst of pain shot through his skull.

"Blood and Tears!" He'd let down his guard. He knew better than that. "Marbella, stop! Stop!"

She was on top of him, stretched to the maximum length of chain remaining to her, but determined. She pulled at his clothes, not to hurt him but searching with a feral desperation to get what she wanted. He batted her hands away, fighting past the ache in his head, but it was too late. She'd found the flask.

She sat back and quickly raised it to her lips. Her tongue hung out like a panting dog, eager to catch the smallest drop. Nothing came out. Her brow crinkled and she shook it vigorously but still the flask was dry.

"It's empty, Marbella." Taran held out his hand to take it from her. "It's empty."

A wail burst from her throat, raw and despairing. It was the sound he imagined Ahpra made when she discovered her husband and brother had fought to the death and she was alone in the world. The sound a parent might make at the death of a child. The sound of lost hope and horror. And it was aimed at him.

She hurled the empty flask across the room and screamed at him, spittle flying from her filthy teeth. "You did this! You did this! May the Hooded One feed you to his wolves! Get out! Get out!"

Taran stumbled back, his face hot and his hands trembling. "Marbella, I'm sorry. I'm so sorry."

And then he fled.

www.ingramcontent.com/pod-product-compliance
Lightning Source LLC
Chambersburg PA
CBHW030618250626
47154CB00006B/1833